HIS NOBLE RUIN

HEIR OF CAMBRIA
BOOK ONE

LISA CAMPBELL

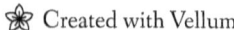 Created with Vellum

CHAPTER
ONE

My father never asked me to risk my life and freedom. He never wanted me to take on countless lies and a false identity. And he certainly never planned on letting his own daughter take down the tyrants of Cambria.

So, naturally, I volunteered.

Neither of us spoke as we walked across the grass, our boots scattering dewdrops with each determined step. The silence between us was typical, but I hoped my father would have a little more to say on a day like this.

When he cleared his throat, I stopped and looked at him.

He glanced at the sky. "Weather's nice."

I shrugged. The cool spring air was hardly worth commenting on.

"Did you sharpen your knives?" he asked.

That question again. I took back my desire for conversation. "Don't worry. I know what I'm doing."

His frown bore through me until I turned away, unwilling to meet his eye in case it revealed my apprehension. My gaze landed on the stone wall that towered over us, dividing the sky, and our world, in two. On our side, seagulls circled between the clouds, their wings catching the red glint of the approaching sun. I wasn't afraid for the reasons I should've been. It was the inevitable awkward goodbye that made my hands sweat.

I looked back at my father. His frown was directed at the wall now. I suspected the part of the plan requiring me to climb it weighed on his mind.

"The Brennins won't make this easy," he said.

"Yeah, you've said that. Several times." I stopped and rested my hand on the stone, letting the damp cold soak into my fingertips. The scent of nighttime rain lingered on its rough surface.

"I'd stop saying it if you believed me." His voice was even more gruff than usual.

I sighed. *And I'd listen if you believed in me.*

His eyes intensified. "Are you really capable of deceiving the entire city?"

I smiled, attempting to lift his mood the way only I could. "I've been lying since I could talk, haven't I?"

His lips tightened like they always did when he held back a smile, forming the expression I knew I'd envision while we were apart. I'd inherited a lot from him: above-average height, a strong build, unstoppable determination, and a fierce pride. But his seriousness was his alone.

"This isn't the only way," he said in a rush.

"It's the only way no one dies." I gripped the strap of the sharkskin bag on my shoulder. The rising seagulls' cries reminded me that the island was awakening. A distant bell tolled deep inside the city, the crisp ring shattering the morning's stillness. "I should go."

He nodded abruptly and pulled a book from his coat. "Then take this. Make sure Cael gets it before he sets sail. And *please* don't try to ditch him. You know we can't do this without his help."

"I wouldn't dream of it." I didn't try to hide my irritation that Cael would be tracking my every move—to keep me safe, at my father's insistence. As if I couldn't handle myself.

"I'm serious," he said, handing over the book.

I grasped it, examining the well-worn cover of my father's journal. It would be nice having it with me, as long as it stayed hidden. The thought of my rebellion sent energy coursing through my body, my excitement rising with the sun. But I hung back, waiting for something I couldn't name.

"Will you manage without me?" I asked, keeping my tone casual.

"I'll be fine. As long as you get the heir out of the city before the king's sleeping with the fishes, you won't be missed." He took a breath as if to say more, then paused and shut his mouth.

I stood there stupidly, hoping to hear what he wouldn't say. I never expected him to express feelings that bordered on sentimentality, but there was a chance this could be the last time we saw each other.

Only the sound of the ringing bell met my ears.

I reluctantly turned to go.

"One more thing," my father said.

I looked back, the corners of my mouth lifting.

"Keep your knives sharp from now on."

My smile fell, but I shook off the disappointment. I didn't need to hear him say it; they were only words. Besides, once I showed him what I was capable of, he'd be too proud to hold it back. The one thing I was sure of was my father's love for me.

No, that was a lie. I was pretty sure of myself too.

He reached out and patted my arm. "If you fail—"

"I won't." I hitched my bag higher on my shoulder, put my hand on the stone wall, and took a deep breath.

WHEN THE SUN SHONE HIGH BEHIND THE CLOUDS, I focused on calming my rapid heart as I slipped through the gray streets of Cambria, the wall far behind me.

I was glad to see it go. I'd spent too much time in its shadow.

My feet slowed as I passed a pair of gates with a sign that read *Quarter B*. Two guards in suits and ties greeted me with glares that would've successfully kept anyone away, even without the spiked iron fence and padlock between them.

I instinctively ducked my head as if looking a little shorter might make me invisible. Luckily, my destination was humbler, a place with family willing to bend the rules, but it would take hours to walk that far. I tried to watch the cobblestones pass by, but I couldn't resist the urge to look up at every new face.

Some looked back at me, but their composed expressions hardly offered a glimpse of the truth behind the top hats and stifling corsets. Whatever went on behind the carefully chosen words and calm propriety wasn't mine to know.

I hoped I could remain as mysterious.

With my simple, gray dress and light brown hair, I imagined myself blending into the scene. Under the soaring columns and high roofs on each side of the street, I almost felt small. I kept my stride purposeful and my face serious enough to make even my father proud. Looking too happy around here might earn more disapproval than wearing a sign labeling myself an outlaw.

Well, not *quite*. The Cambrians reserved a special hatred for the banished rebels outside the wall.

When I turned another corner, the cobbled path widened into a market. Citizens crowded the scene, along with men and women in black suits, white shirts, and overly large badges even a blind man couldn't miss. The Academy Law Enforcers lurked in the crowd like sharks waiting for a kill.

If I'd been wiser, and less hungry, I wouldn't have stopped, but my stomach twisted and I couldn't help myself. Giant pink and silver tuna, black mussels and clams, and multi-colored crabs filled the stalls. I took a breath and tried to imagine I was on a boat again. Nothing brought me to life like the ocean breeze, but the city wall kept it from me, and the piles of dead fish couldn't compare.

But it was the words, not the smells, that made my nose wrinkle. Posters spewing propaganda lined the market. *Support schooling from infancy. Protect Cambria from destructive grammar. Abolish our dependence on outlaws. Long live Imperator Brennin.*

I shook my head. We were the last civilization on earth and *these* were their priorities.

I moved on, my mouth watering as I left behind the seafood and found myself in front of a cart of speckled green pears. I reached into my bag and slid my fingers between some clinking cowry shells, tempted to spend them all on a few pieces of fruit. But then I noticed the letters stamped below *Pears* on the wooden sign: A and B.

My stomach rumbled in protest. Only the elite were allowed to let that delicacy touch their perfect tongues.

"Rank card, please," said a man behind the stall, raising an eyebrow at my bland clothing.

I checked to make sure no Enforcers stood within earshot before I allowed myself to speak. "I'm just looking."

He frowned and crossed his arms as if I'd wasted his time.

"Then go look at something you can afford." He gestured to the seafood stalls.

I shot him a withering glare, but when he dropped his eyes, I pitied him. He was a simple merchant who probably wasn't ranked highly enough to eat the fruit he sold.

"Excuse me, miss." Another man gestured toward me, his coarse gray hair sprouting out from under his hat. He stood behind an apple cart the next stall over.

I cautiously obeyed, wondering what I'd done to catch his notice.

"You're in the mood for some fruit, aren't ya?"

I shook my head. "Not unless you can make me a noble."

He gestured for me to come even closer, then lowered his voice. "Show me your card."

"But I'm not—"

"Just let me see it."

I hesitated. The rank requirements on his stall were too high, but the pile of shiny red and green fruit beckoned to me. I reached into my bag and pulled out a small leather rectangle and handed it to him. I held my breath as the forged rank card left my fingers.

"I thought so," he said. "Brand new card. Just turned seventeen, eh?"

"Yes. I wish I'd ranked higher than Class C, but the grammar tests . . . well, you know."

The merchant dropped his voice to a whisper. "I'll tell you what, uh"—he squinted at my card—"Bryn. I'm in a good mood today. If you've got the money, I might be willing to make an exception for a pretty young lady like yourself."

"No, thanks. I'll just find another . . ." My words trailed away when two young faces peered around the cart. Their eyes were wide and hopeful, but their ragged clothing revealed scrawny arms and legs.

I bit my lip and glanced back at the street. Before I could stop and think what my father would say, I pushed a handful of cowry shells into the merchant's hand. "What will this get me?"

His smile widened as he swept up an armful of apples.

I fidgeted with my bag's strap, anxious to take my purchase and leave. But just before he handed over the fruit, an angry voice barked from behind me.

I dropped my bag to the ground and kicked it under the fruit cart, then lifted my head high before turning around.

"I sincerely hope you are both respecting the law with this transaction." An Enforcer brushed a hand across his prominent badge and glared at me before looking at the merchant.

"Of course, sir. As always." The merchant gulped, his eyes flitting to his children as he flashed a smile.

"Is that so? She doesn't *look* like a noble." He put his hand out toward me. "Reveal your card."

I stood up straighter, preparing my tongue for a noble accent. "Please, Enforcer. I do hope you will accept my sincerest apologies for this unfortunate misunderstanding."

The Enforcer's eyebrows lowered and he fixed a skeptical eye on my clothing, his distrust as obvious as the badge on his chest.

I pushed my shoulders back and lifted my chin. Underneath my pride, my heart pounded. "As I arrived, I came to the startling realization that I had misplaced my clutch—one of those new designs that every woman in my quarter covets. Such exquisite pearl detail! Of course, my rank card was lost with it. So, you see, I am not able to present it at this moment, but this respectable merchant agreed to the purchase since he knows perfectly well who I am."

Both the merchant and the Enforcer gaped.

The Enforcer eyed my dress, clearly wanting an explanation for my poor taste but apparently afraid to insult me in case

I was telling the truth. "Carry on, then," he finally said. "Excuse me, milady." The Enforcer nodded his head in a slight bow.

My breath released, but before he took two steps, a voice called out.

"That's not fair!" shouted the pear merchant. "She came to my cart first! If I'd been willing to break the law, those shells would be mine!"

The Enforcer stopped and turned back to me, his face reddening. "I'm afraid he is correct. Whether or not you are a noble, protocol dictates—"

"Leave her alone, sir." The apple merchant shot a worried look at the ground, where his children cowered behind the cart. "We didn't do nothing wrong."

The Enforcer shut his eyes and groaned. "That is the most intolerable grammar I've heard in weeks." He reached a hand inside his suit coat and pulled out a metal contraption, stepping around the stall toward the man. "Let me prevent you from damaging more ears."

The merchant held up his hands and backed away. "No, no, please! I've worn branks before. I still have the scars. Please!"

"Resistance will only increase the punishment," said the Enforcer as he forced the silver bridle over the merchant's head. "I had already intended to revoke your market privileges for at least a week, but I can certainly make it longer."

"No! My family—"

This was my chance to run. But when I reached down to retrieve my bag from under the cart, a glimpse of a small, trembling hand stopped me. I froze, crouched on the ground with my hand on the strap. I felt stares on my back; the whole street was likely watching the drama unfold.

The merchant let out a gagged scream from the other side

of the cart. The bridle would soon be in place, pinning his tongue in an excruciating position that would make it impossible to speak until the Enforcers decided his punishment was complete. That is, if they didn't forget and let him starve to death first.

The war between what I should do and what I wanted to do raged inside my heart. I knew what my father would say. He wouldn't want me to risk the mission on one family when so many lives were at stake. Besides, the man was beyond my help.

But maybe his children weren't.

I fumbled with my bag, taking out a handful of shiny white shells before pulling the strap back over my shoulder. Reaching under the cart, I searched for the tiny hands. As the merchant's screams turned into suppressed whimpers, a child reached for the shells and I let them go.

I jumped to my feet, pushing past the gathered crowd and darting through an alleyway. Once I made it to the next street, I ran. As my side ached and my stomach growled, I reminded myself to stick to the plan from now on. There was only one way to save this city. The Brennins had to fall.

CHAPTER

TWO

I WAS FAMISHED AND ACHING WHEN I ARRIVED AT Quarter C. A uniformed woman guarded the gates. My hands shook when I showed her my rank card.

She moved to unlock the gate, scrutinizing my face. "Are you new here?"

"Yes, madam."

"I see," she said. "Did you class up or down?"

I had no desire to stand there and answer her nosy questions, but I didn't want to cause any more trouble. "Down," I lied.

"How unfortunate." Her tone was emotionless. She finished unlocking the gate and pushed it open. "Remember, no visits to your old quarter, and when—or if—your family comes to see you, make sure they leave before the ten o'clock curfew."

I nodded and stepped inside.

The guard slammed and locked the gates behind me. Narrow gray brick row homes lined both sides of the street. I walked slower, checking the numbers on each door. When I saw my target on my right, I smiled and picked up the pace, excited to fill my stomach, experience a bit of home, and give my blistered toes a rest.

Before I could knock, the door swung open and a voice called from inside, warm and familiar. "Is it really you, my dear?"

An old woman with the kindest face I'd ever known stepped out.

I exhaled, relieved to finally be here. "Hi, Etna."

She rushed down the steps and grasped me in a hug as tight as the ones she used to give. "Has it been so long? Look how tall you've grown."

The top of her gray head came to my shoulder. I'd definitely grown a few inches since the last time I saw her. She backed away and glanced around, still holding my hands in her dark brown wrinkled ones. "Let's get you out of the street."

I followed her up the steps and through the door into a cramped entryway with a narrow staircase on one side. The scents of mint tea and freshly baked bread filled the house.

Etna peered out the door once more before shutting it and turning the lock. "I've thought of you constantly since your father's message arrived the other day. I can hardly believe you're standing in front of me. I've missed you so much." Her almond brown eyes welled with sadness, but her cheeks were round, framing the smile I remembered.

"I'm sorry, Etna. I wish I could've visited."

"I understand, dear, and I promise your identity will be protected while you're in my home. But please, call me Grandma."

She led me down the hall to the kitchen. Planters full of herbs lined the sill of the one window in the room, giving off sweet and sharp aromas. Few citizens had any land of their own or a place to grow food. For someone in Quarter C, this miniature garden was close to luxury.

I sat on one of the two chairs by the small table and tried to let my stress fade away. "Thank you for all your help, Et—Grandma."

"Oh, don't be silly. Marcus and I would always help. Your father is like a son to us, and anyway, where else would you stay?"

She was right. Other than its prisons, Cambria didn't exactly have a place for those who needed a temporary home. There was no point in a city where no one traveled in or out. She and her husband were taking risks for me that I never would've expected of anyone.

"Are you hungry?" asked Etna, reaching for a knife and loaf of bread on the counter.

"Yes!" I blurted out. "I mean, yes, thank you."

Etna's cheeks rounded from her warm smile. "Don't worry too much about politeness with me. We're family." She set a slice of warm bread slathered with herbed butter on the table. My stomach gave a final desperate rumble as I took my first bite.

We may not have shared the same blood, but Etna and Marcus Lenox had once given my father a new life. Now they were helping me create a new one, along with a new world.

I TOOK OFF MY BOOTS AND STRETCHED OUT ON THE RUG, AS comfortable as I would've been in my own home. The hour hand on the clock above the mantle had almost reached four. Its ticking might've normally made me antsy, but in this home, it felt lazy and relaxing. Raindrops pattered on the windows behind the heavy curtains, making me feel safe and hidden. Tomorrow, the real work would begin. According to rumor, Graham Brennin would be making his first public appearance to speak to journalists about his upcoming reign—that is, if an elitist Academy club counted as public.

As my mind wandered toward sleep, the front doorknob rattled. I shot up, my heart on high alert.

"It's just Marcus," Etna said calmly from her armchair.

Moments later, her husband walked into the room, dressed in his damp laborer clothing, his black hair slick with rain. He smiled at me as if he weren't completely exhausted. "So! Here's our young revolutionary."

I relaxed, leaning back onto the floor.

"Look at you!" Marcus continued. "I can't say I would've recognized you if I'd seen you on the street."

I laughed. "That's probably a good thing."

"I wish your father could be here. It's been too long since we've had a visit from Orrin," said Marcus.

Three sharp knocks on the door jarred my tired head. Etna and Marcus both jumped at the aggressive hammering.

I leaped to my feet, my fear returning in full force.

Etna stood and pulled back the curtain. She gasped quietly and let go, stepping away from the window. "It's an Enforcer," she whispered.

I froze, internally debating whether to hide upstairs or flee out the back door.

The three of us stood there, paralyzed with indecision.

The pounding returned, more urgent than before.

"Hide," said Marcus. "We'll do the talking."

I didn't want them to take this risk. I wished I hadn't involved them at all. Before I knew where to hide, a voice shouted from the other side of the door.

"Open up before I drown out here."

I knew that voice. "It's just Cael," I said, my panic calming.

Etna put a hand over her heart, sighing with relief, while Marcus pulled her into his arms.

I hurried into the entry and opened the door to a scowling man with an aristocratic blonde mustache and close-cropped hair. My gaze immediately landed on the badge on his black uniform.

"Invite him in, dear," Etna called from the living room.

I opened the door wider and gestured for him to enter. He pushed his way in, slamming the door behind him. Rain dripped from his uniform onto the floor and my bare feet.

"Why are you wearing that?" I asked, pointing at the badge.

He shrugged. "It'll be useful, won't it? Gets me everywhere I want to go. No class restrictions."

"We talked about this and agreed it wasn't a good idea." I tried to keep the fury from my voice but couldn't when I didn't even know how he'd gotten his hands on that thing. Theft—or worse—came to mind.

"Relax," said Cael. "It was very . . . skillfully acquired. It won't be a problem."

"You didn't hurt anyone, I hope. You *know* the plan."

"Me?" he asked. "I'm more worried about what you might do with those knives you carry the moment your temper flares up."

I stepped away from the puddle forming on the floor. "Well, the look suits you. Now you can tell *everybody* what to do."

Marcus and Etna joined us in the entryway.

"Would you like to sit down and have some tea?" Etna asked.

"I don't like tea," said Cael.

I rolled my eyes and mouthed an apology to Etna, but her smile never faltered.

Cael's eyes met mine, his brows low. "Plans have changed. The heir will be at The Wordsmith at five o'clock."

I nodded, careful to hide the anxiety that threatened to

swallow me at the thought of trying to win the heir's trust. Making friends wasn't my forte. I'd rather climb ten stone walls.

Then I realized what Cael had just said.

"Wait. Five o'clock tomorrow?"

A smirk appeared on his lips, his version of a smile. "Tonight."

My words abandoned me, along with the air in my lungs. The blisters on my feet ached at the thought of walking again so soon. "In an hour?" My voice came out weak. "There's no way. If I don't have time to change, I won't pass for a journalist."

He glowered from the doorway. "This is your only chance to get to him before he becomes king."

He was right, but I shook my head. "I can't walk that far in an hour."

Cael stepped forward, his mustache too close to my face. "Then *run*. I'll meet you there." Without another word, he opened the door and took the steps into the rainy street. I closed it after him, swearing when my foot landed in the cold puddle.

Marcus raised his eyebrows and whistled. "He makes your father look like a perfect gentleman."

I smiled, but inside I bristled with anger. I could deal with Cael's rudeness, but this was too much. With that uniform, he was overstepping, treating the plan like his own. Any deviations from the plan could have serious consequences, but he didn't even seem to care. What did my father see in him anyway?

I sighed. "Better get my boots."

THREE

Running over cobblestones was twice as painful as walking on them. I pushed myself forward with all the energy I could muster, but it didn't help that the path to the scholars' club was entirely uphill and slippery with the falling rain. My boots pounded over the streets toward the hill that dominated the center of Cambria. My raincoat kept my dress partially dry, but my hair was soaked before I'd even left Quarter C. I didn't stand a chance of blending in at a scholars' club if I looked as bedraggled as I felt.

Everything passed by in a rain-soaked blur: horse-drawn carriages, sharp-pressed suits, tall hats, elaborate braids, fine gowns, and umbrellas trimmed in lace. I clearly didn't belong here.

Finally, when the stitch in my side threatened to take me down, I turned a corner and The Wordsmith came into view. The clock below its dome revealed it was ten minutes to five and I mentally congratulated myself for my speed.

I marched up to the palatial building, keeping my back

straight and my head high to compensate for my less than impressive appearance.

Cael prowled nearby in the street, his blonde hair and uniform slick with rain, but he didn't seem winded. He must've used his uniform to catch a carriage, which my Class C rank card wouldn't allow. My envy sparked over the stolen uniform that gave him an advantage over me.

I approached him. "Has the heir arrived?"

He rolled his eyes. "I don't know. They wouldn't let me in."

"Well, it looks like your uniform won't get you *everywhere*, will it?"

"Journalists only." He gestured toward the entrance with raised eyebrows. "Go on, then. Give it a try."

I nodded once and headed toward the white-gloved doorman.

"Only journalists are permitted tonight, miss," he said the moment I arrived at the front doors. "Special orders."

I pulled out my rank card from beneath my raincoat, hoping the words stamped under *Employer* would be enough, and handed it to him.

He frowned as he read the card. "You work for the Cambrian Tribune? What is your role there? Brewing tea?"

I kept my expression neutral and my accent crisp. "I am a journalist, sir."

He looked back at my card. "A Class C journalist, however, which does not obligate me to grant you entry."

"But you said journalists only. And I *am* a journalist."

"Yes, but"—he eyed my dripping wet hair—"we have certain standards to uphold."

I set my jaw, determined to get inside. I had a question to ask the heir and I wasn't leaving until he heard it.

Time for a new tactic. I reached for the handful of cowry shells remaining in the bottom of my bag, careful to leave a few for later. Thanks to my rash generosity earlier today, I didn't have as many as I wanted, but I discreetly held them out, giving the doorman a meaningful look.

His eyes widened at the sight of my money. His gloved hand crept forward, then pulled back before touching the shells, a guilty expression souring his face. He sighed. "I cannot."

"I'll stay in the back." I tried to keep my voice low since a line was forming behind me, but my formality was slipping as my desperation rose. "No one will even notice I'm there."

He paused, eyeing the shells with a gleam in his eye before shaking his head. "My apologies, miss. Please step aside."

I bristled, furious with my lack of control.

But then he leaned in, grabbed the shells from my hand, and whispered, "You'll find a servants' door in the back."

I smiled and nodded before stepping out of line and hurrying past Cael, who watched me with suspicion as I rounded the corner of the building and crept into the narrow alleyway.

Cael followed at my heels. "Where are you going?"

"The servants' door."

"You can't be serious."

I spotted the single door at the back and headed toward it.

"If only you looked decent, this wouldn't have happened," said Cael.

"You don't happen to be hiding a gown under your uniform, do you?" I asked.

He stared at me without a hint of a smile.

"Oh, I forgot. No reason to be civil when my father's not around."

He shrugged. "I'm just not amused."

I groaned and turned away from the soulless man before I acted on the urge to punch him in the mustache. I tested the handle of the back door. It shifted under my grip and my hope soared.

"You can't just waltz in there," said Cael.

"Do you have any other ideas?"

He folded his arms. "I have one, but you've already shot it down."

Not this again. Cael couldn't seem to get it through his head that I wasn't willing to murder people. "Yeah, we're not killing him. I'm going in."

His eyes narrowed. "They'll catch you."

"Not if I'm lucky." I shed my raincoat, took a folded paper from my bag, then tossed my things to Cael. "Keep these safe." I tucked the paper into my boot, then turned the knob and slipped into the building, shutting the door to cut off his protests.

I found myself in a dark hall. Before stepping forward, I watched and waited, listening for the sounds to tell me I was captured and that Cael had been right.

But for the moment, I was alone.

I slowly ventured away from the door. The buzz of a crowd and heavy footsteps rumbled through the ceiling. I needed to find my way up there. I continued down the hall. An archway opened up on my left, revealing an enormous well-stocked wine cellar. At the opposite end of the room was a staircase.

I hurried toward it, the sounds of the crowd growing louder, then halted as a row of white clothing on the wall caught my eye. If I didn't look like a journalist, maybe I could at least pass for a server. I darted over, tying on an apron and tucking my wet hair under a cap. Lastly, I turned to the wine rack and grabbed one of the oldest bottles. Not only would it complete my look, but since I left my money with Cael, I liked the idea of carrying something valuable.

"Okay," I whispered to myself to calm my nerves before

taking the steps. "I can do this." This was a significant deviation from my plan and uncertainty dominated my mind.

I emerged from the stairs to see a grand—and crowded—room.

Marble pillars extended to the high ceiling. Thick, patterned rugs cushioned the well-shined shoes of the room's many inhabitants. Dark wood bookshelves lined the walls, and chairs dotted the perimeter of the room, all occupied by overeager men and women. I didn't think there were this many journalists in Cambria. For the moment, I didn't have to worry about anyone looking at me. Their attention was riveted on the main entrance.

A tall man with hollow cheekbones and lifeless eyes stood there: Sir Cardiff Pearce. He wore a black tailcoat, the lapels embroidered with shimmering green laurel leaves. He was the First Immortal, the most powerful person in Cambria besides the king.

The room of journalists bowed to him and I forced my back to bend to maintain appearances, as much as my body rebelled against it.

Pearce stood with his nose in the air and swept his haughty gaze over the room as if its fine carpets and carved mahogany weren't good enough for him. Then he stepped through the crowd, climbed a raised stage, and took a seat in a tall-backed spindle chair.

I turned back to the main doors, watching for the reason I'd come.

I knew him as soon as he stepped through the entryway.

His neatly parted black hair matched his crisp ironed suit. The knot of his white silk tie was perfectly symmetrical, and his back seemed incapable of anything but its current rigid posture. He should've looked flawless, or at least respectable, but his furrowed eyebrows accented hesitant blue eyes that lent him a lonely expression. With those eyes, even the best tailors in the city couldn't make him look powerful.

His name was Graham Brennin, heir of the Second House and first in line to rule the entire nation.

The crowd bowed again, but this time more heads remained up, out of lack of respect or curiosity, I wasn't sure.

Beside the heir was a young dark-skinned man with a proud expression. A footman stepped up and took his coat, then the heir's, before they went toward the stage. The heir joined the First Immortal on the platform while the other man stayed in the front row facing the stage expectantly.

The crowd watched with rapt attention, eyes gleaming with ambition and quills grasped tight.

"Good evening," said Pearce, his voice dry. His eyes were sunken like tide pools in his wrinkled face. He'd held the most coveted position in the Academy since Imperator Brennin had appointed him twenty years ago. The other twenty-five Immortals were elected by the nobility, but this man was the sole member hand-selected by the reigning king or queen. As for the others, only death could remove them from their positions. It always struck me as funny that they were only called Immortals until they were dead.

Only now did I notice the royal guards lining the room. The one nearest to me turned his scowling face my way as if he'd felt my stare. I tugged my cap down lower and moved deeper into the crowd.

"Let us commence," said Pearce from the stage. "By a raise of hands, please indicate your desire to propose a question to Sir Brennin."

Almost every hand in the room shot up. Mine almost did until I remembered that I looked like a server, not a journalist. I'd have to find someone else willing to ask my question.

Pearce scanned the crowd. "Since it would veritably

exhaust our dear heir were we to permit every question, I will select ten hands from the audience."

The crowd buzzed.

"Only ten?" A man near me complained. "That's nothing!"

"One." Pearce pointed to someone in the crowd. "Two, three, four . . ." He continued selecting journalists slowly until he'd counted to ten. I stood tall, watching carefully to try to keep track of who he selected, but I was only sure of the fourth and the eighth.

"Question number one, please," said Pearce.

I inched my way toward number four as the first journalist began to speak. Eager quills scribbled across their scrolls.

"In consideration of your youth and lack of experience, how do you expect to have the maturity and intellect to rule with the moral and intellectual fortitude your parents possess?" the journalist asked.

Graham Brennin's face paled at the leading question that seemed aimed to tear him down more than anything. "Indeed, at eighteen, I . . . I have not yet had the opportunity to acquire all the knowledge I desire, but I assure you that my parents have schooled me from birth and employed the best scholars in my education." He paused. "It is also my deepest hope that my father may yet recover and allow me ample time to prepare."

His voice wasn't what I'd expected for the son of a tyrant. Something in the sound made me pity him until I remembered who he'd become. With parents like his schooling him from birth, as he put it, he didn't stand a chance of becoming a decent king, let alone a decent person.

"Thank you for the insightful question," said Pearce. "Second question, please."

A woman spoke up. "Do you intend to respect familial alliances and ensure a smooth transition by retaining Sir Pearce as First Immortal?"

I frowned. This question was even more biased than the last. I was beginning to suspect Pearce's selections had been anything but random. I pushed through the crowd until I stood behind journalist number four. Reaching down, I pulled the paper from my boot.

"I will certainly respect alliances to ensure a smooth transition." The heir paused, glancing briefly between Pearce and Brennin's eager friend in the front row. "Sir Pearce is the most experienced candidate, naturally."

The young man in the front row stiffened at the heir's response.

"Indeed. Thank you, Sir Brennin," said Pearce, an ingratiating smile on his wrinkled face. "Question number three."

"Excuse me." I tapped the woman in front of me on the shoulder. "You're asking a question, aren't you?" I whispered.

"Yes. Why?" she asked, raising an eyebrow at my apron.

I tried to summon a friendly but convincing smile. "I'll give you this bottle of wine if you ask this instead." I held the folded paper toward her.

She looked down, shaking her head. "They already assigned me a question."

"What? Who did?"

She shook her head and turned away.

I tapped her again. "Please. This is, uh, your new assignment."

She hissed back at me. "Leave me alone, maid. It's almost my turn."

I looked back at the stage, realizing I'd missed the previous question.

"Question number four," the First Immortal announced.

I ducked and slipped through the crowd, away from the woman, desperate not to be seen when everyone looked her way. I stopped by a marble pillar, reorienting myself while I peered across the room at journalist number eight. If I couldn't get him to ask my question—which admittedly was just as manipulative as all the others I'd heard so far—I didn't stand a chance of getting the heir where I needed him.

"Your mother, our dear queen, has unsurpassed experience and grace," said the woman I'd unsuccessfully approached. "Have you considered delegating your reign to Imperatrix Brennin after you inherit the throne in order to keep Cambria stable?"

My jaw dropped at the brazen question. It created no doubt in my mind that someone was pulling strings. I'd come here expecting to make Graham Brennin my pawn, but I was beginning to see that he was already being knocked around a chessboard far bigger than my own making.

The heir looked at the woman who'd spoken, his brow furrowing as if he might've been making the same connections I was. "I will do everything in my power to keep Cambria stable." For a moment, his posture faltered. He sighed and pushed his fingers through his hair, messing up the perfect line of his part before speaking so softly I could hardly hear him. "If that requires delegation, I will strive for the wisdom to make such a decision."

I pulled my gaze away and squeezed through the crowd, heading for journalist number eight. When I got to his side, he scrutinized the bottle in my arms before looking up at me.

"Number eight," I addressed him, my voice confident.

"Yes?" he asked.

"There's been a mistake," I said, handing him my paper. "They sent me to update your assignment."

He unfolded the paper. "It's a bit of an inconvenience to change it on such late notice," he said under his breath.

"Of course. That's why they sent this as well." I held up the expensive wine so he could see its value, trying to steady my trembling hands.

He smiled and took it without hesitation. "I hoped you might say that."

I gave him a small bow, then crept to the back of the room and waited while the next few questions were asked.

"Number seven," the First Immortal called out.

"If you die without an heir of your own, the inheritance will pass to the Third House, which would be a great tragedy. When do you plan to marry and produce an heir so the Brennins may rule long into the future?"

I scoffed before I could stop myself. If this didn't confirm that the queen had a hand in these questions, I don't know what did.

"Well . . . soon, I suppose," said Graham.

The crowd laughed.

Graham's face flushed up to his hairline and he sat taller in his chair. "I can assure you the last thing I want is a reclusive Stroud on the throne," he said, his expression somber. "It is clear by Lady Mara Stroud's lack of involvement that she has no concern for the welfare of Cambria. I will do everything in my ability to keep the Third House from gaining the power they would most certainly abuse."

"Hear, hear!" Someone shouted. Clearly that question had ignited some actual passion in the heir. The audience clapped heartily for the first time tonight.

I didn't join in.

"Question number eight," said Pearce, his voice rising to cut through the din of the crowd.

I crossed my fingers.

The man I'd intercepted spoke up, reading the question just as I'd written it. "Imperator Brennin followed in the footsteps of the rulers before him by studying dutifully in the historic Irvine Library before his reign to connect with the intellect of our dear founder in the place he most cherished. Will you vow to uphold this tradition by studying in the Irvine Library daily leading up to your coronation?"

I took note of the confusion on Pearce's face before looking at the heir's reaction.

Graham straightened and nodded. "I admit I wasn't aware of the . . . depth of this tradition, but I'd be honored to make that promise."

I clapped hard, the rest of the crowd joining me. As I'd intended, the question left no room to say no without practically insulting the revered first king, Imperator Irvine. It didn't matter that I'd invented the whole thing. Even the king wouldn't want to deny the story when it ended up in the papers. And now everyone would hold the heir accountable to fulfill this made-up "tradition."

And I'd be able to get close to him.

I was done here. I didn't care to hear the other pre-selected questions. I took one last look at the stage.

"I fear we have run out of time," said Pearce, who was glowering at the man who'd asked the question. He nodded to a couple of guards near the stage, then flicked a finger toward the journalist.

I muttered a word that could earn me a set of branks and froze, my eyes darting between the unlucky man and the stairway. I hadn't imagined he'd be punished for something so small, but I should've seen it coming. This was what happened when you manipulated somebody else's pawn.

The guards approached the man, wrenched the wine bottle from his grip, then grabbed him by the arms and pulled him from the crowd.

The rest of the journalists didn't seem to notice or care.

With raised hands and voices, they pushed closer to the stage, shouting the questions they hadn't been able to ask.

Journalist number eight was dragged toward the doors, his mouth moving in desperate objection. I couldn't hear him over the noise in the room, but he pointed an accusatory finger toward me, his eyes flashing with anger.

The guards holding his arms looked right at me.

I ran.

I reached the stairs and leaped most of the way down, then pivoted and jumped down the next flight into the wine cellar. I collided with a butler at the bottom of the stairs before I could even see his face. He fell to the ground with a shout. A glass bottle shattered, wine exploding everywhere. And I ran.

CHAPTER

FOUR

I BURST THROUGH THE DOOR INTO THE ALLEYWAY WHERE I'd left Cael. I didn't see him, but I didn't care. I tore off my cap and apron, leaving them abandoned in the street behind me, and kept on running.

I sped downhill, darting through alleyways. Not only did I need to get far from this place, but I had to go to the Irvine Library before it closed for the night. I ran hard, my lungs burning and my blisters breaking. The narrow alleys became a maze before me. Water still pooled among the cobblestones, though the rain had passed. The sun approached the city wall, draping the streets in washed-out gold.

I kept up the pace until my side ached and I tasted blood. Finally, when I didn't know if I could keep it up any longer, a shout came from behind.

"I knew you'd get caught!"

My feet pounded to a stop and I turned to face Cael, clutching my ribs. "What do you mean?" I panted. "I'm as free as ever."

"That doesn't mean you weren't seen." He tossed my bag and coat into my hands, panting as hard I was.

"I wasn't seen by anyone important." *Hopefully.*

He shook his head. "I saw the man they dragged out of there. He was shouting that it was *her* question, not his own, so don't pretend like it all went as smoothly as you'd planned."

I studied the surrounding streets. Every direction looked the same in the waning light. "Which way to the library?" I asked.

Cael pointed to a street on my left.

As soon as I caught my breath, I continued my run.

THE IRVINE LIBRARY WAS RIGHT AT THE BORDERS OF THE inner city, beyond the streets where the overdressed nobles swarmed like a hive of queen bees. Its stately pillars must have looked magnificent back when Cambria had built its first library. But now, amid larger and more prestigious libraries, it was hardly given a glance from the citizens shuffling past its wide stone steps.

I was sore and panting when I made my way up to the tall wooden doors. I looked back into the street. Cael was doubled over with his hands on his thighs and face flushed, breathing heavily. I smiled, glad he'd been forced to join me in my sprint across the city this time.

I pulled open the heavy door, letting it close behind me as I stepped into the warm glow of candlelight. Inside, it seemed as if a heavy layer of dust muffled all sound.

The cavernous room was filled with enough books to rival the population of the entire city, and judging by the musty smell, each one must have absorbed a bit of the salty sea air over the past hundred years. The shelves reached up to a high ceiling painted with a faded sky and clouds that might've once been white but had become an accurate depiction of Cambria's typical gloomy gray.

Only a few people meandered around. A teenage girl scanned the titles of books on the nearest shelf. She was probably here to study for the ranking test she'd take at age seventeen. The results would define her life: where she'd live, how she'd eat, who she could marry, and what her occupation would be. But that was the fate of every Cambrian—well, everyone except the chosen Immovable families. They'd never have to take a test in their lives unless they wanted a position within the Academy.

When she looked my way, I gave her a sympathetic smile. My own mission was probably more complicated than what she was facing, but I still felt a sense of relief that I wasn't in her shoes.

I dragged my fingers along the brittle book spines until my hands were coated in powder. At the end of the aisle, a woman with gray hair in a severe bun walked briskly out of a wide arched corridor carrying a stack of books. She set them on the librarians' desk in the center of the main room, then took a seat next to a large man who held a copy of the Cambrian Tribune.

I headed toward the desk, smiling as warmly as I knew how. Once tomorrow's papers came out, this library might not be so quiet. Lower classes could even be restricted from entry as long as the heir was studying here. I had to do whatever I could to make sure I'd be allowed inside.

"The library is closing in ten minutes," said the gray-haired woman as I arrived beside the desk.

"Thank you, madam," I replied, trying to withstand her disdainful glare. "Actually, I am hoping to work here. I've always adored this library and it seems as if you could use the help."

Her wrinkled mouth tightened. "Are you educated in librarianship or archival studies?"

"Well, no, but I have experience working for the Cambrian Tribune." I gestured to the man's paper, glad that was his newspaper of choice.

He gave me a weak smile.

The librarian shook her head. "Journalists are not librarians."

"Please, madam. I could help with cleaning or sorting books."

The woman shook her head condescendingly. "I clean this library myself."

I wiped a finger through the layer of dust on the edge of the desk, holding it up for her to see. "You're certain you couldn't use just a little more help?"

She stood up, folding her arms. "What is your rank, young lady?"

I fumbled with my bag before handing her my card.

"Class C? It's better than your manners would suggest, Miss Yarrow, but your grammar isn't sophisticated enough to work alongside me." She handed back the leather card. "To be quite honest, even if we could use the help, we don't have the budget. The Irvine Library, as historic as it may be, is no longer a *priority* to the Academy." She sniffed as if she highly resented this fact.

I caught myself frowning, but I forced a smile in its place, determined to win this battle. "You don't have to pay me. I'll volunteer."

She crossed her arms higher, pursed her lips, and narrowed her eyes until the wrinkles overtook them.

I took a step back. I wasn't getting anywhere with this shrew.

The man sitting at the other end of the desk cleared his throat. "Perhaps a little help with cleaning would be nice."

The librarian turned her glare on him. "Isn't that what I keep telling *you*?"

The man withered in his chair and returned to his newspaper.

I covered my mouth to hide my smirk.

The woman peered back at me and tapped the tip of her chin. "Why you're willing to work for free is a mystery. People of your rank certainly can't survive on taxes as the nobles can."

My smile became genuine as optimism rose in my chest.

She sighed. "I suppose I'll give you a chance. You'll report to me, Mrs. Whitting. And this is my husband." She waved a dismissive hand at him. "Arrive early tomorrow or I'll change my mind."

I thanked them both, promising to come back the next day, before walking away with a spring in my step, blisters and all. One day closer to saving the world.

THAT NIGHT, BACK AT MARCUS AND ETNA'S HOUSE, I washed off the day's sweat and carried a candle upstairs to a small bedroom. A single bed and a dresser filled most of the space. One rain-streaked window faced the dark street. It was nothing like my own home, but I found it peaceful and comfortable, a welcome contrast to the worries brewing in my mind.

My bag sat on the floor by the bed. I opened it and took out four silver knives with leather sheaths over the blades. Weapons were forbidden in the city for everyone except Law Enforcers, so it would be best to leave them hidden here. I was unlikely to be in serious danger in a dusty old library anyway. I slid open the dresser drawer and placed them inside. Cael was here for my protection, as my father had required, and I should try to trust him.

I shut the drawer, but the moment the knives were out of sight, I wanted them back in my hands. What was the point of all that training if I didn't even carry the weapon I'd mastered? All that time spent listening to my father and Cael drone on about correct knife-throwing techniques would be wasted.

Besides, could I really depend on someone else to protect me?

I hastily pulled the drawer open and took back all four knives, returning them to my bag, next to my father's journal. A small part of me protested, aware that carrying them could be a risk to my mission, but leaving them could be even worse.

Just as I lay down, I heard a soft tap on the door.

I sat up. "Come in."

Etna opened the door timidly. "I hope I didn't wake you."

"You didn't." I wasn't in the mood for conversation, but I gestured for her to come in anyway.

She crossed the room on quiet feet and sat on the edge of my bed. I leaned against the headboard, too tired to sit up any longer.

"Did you get a chance to read today's news?" she asked.

"Not yet. Why?"

"The king announced a public address in three days. According to rumor, this is likely to be his farewell speech."

I shrugged. "Well, I just hope he stays alive long enough for me to get the job done."

Etna's smile weakened as she searched my tired face. "Is this really what you want? Or what your father wants?"

I shook my head, surprised by the underlying accusation. "What do you mean? It was my idea. And my father would never support something that wasn't right."

Her forehead remained creased. "That could be true, but I

can't help but wonder if he's making decisions to respect your mother's memory instead of considering the living."

"All we want is for everyone to be safe, and I'm one of the few people with family on both sides to protect. The islanders won't put up with the Brennins any longer. If we don't deliver the heir to Tramore by the next new moon, war will break out. Thousands will die! You and Marcus could be—"

Etna nodded and patted my knee. "I know, dear. I just can't stop worrying myself sick thinking of the trouble you could get into."

"It's okay. All I have to do is get the heir outside the wall. Then Cael will do the rest." I leaned forward, resting my head on her shoulder the way I used to do with my mother, so long ago. "Thank you for worrying about me."

"Oh, my sweet girl. That's what we do when we love."

I stayed there and let her stroke my hair down my back as if I were a child. The closeness of touch had become so foreign that I'd almost forgotten the way it could melt away fears and make the world seem promising again.

"I'll let you rest," said Etna. "Goodnight, love."

I whispered goodnight and fell asleep almost content.

CHAPTER
FIVE

Before the sun broke over the top of the wall the next morning, I climbed the stone steps of the library, hoping that Graham Brennin would keep his promise.

I tugged the door handle, sighing in irritation when it didn't budge. I yawned and sat on a stair, the tug of sleep still pulling at my eyelids. If I'd known the Whittings wouldn't even be here yet, I could've slept a few minutes longer.

A few people trudged by on the street below, making their way to jobs their test scores had chosen for them. None of them looked up the stairs at me. In fact, none looked up at all.

"You're actually here," said Mrs. Whitting when she arrived.

Her round, smiling husband escorted her by the arm, though it looked more like she was the one tugging him up the steps.

"I must say, I would have greatly preferred to see you in a different dress," she said. "That shade of gray is terribly unfashionable, even for a girl of your rank."

I took note of her severely tight gray bun and the high-collared, long-sleeved, ankle-length dress that would do nicely as mourning garb and tried to envision it as fashionable. My imagination failed me.

"Well!" She clapped her hands with an enthusiasm that wiped away my smile. "Time to get to work!"

Being a volunteer didn't seem to lighten the workload Mrs. Whitting demanded of me. She followed me every step of the way, hands on her hips, scrutinizing my work while I climbed rickety ladders to reach the dust on the highest shelves.

I watched the doors constantly for any sign of the heir's arrival while I dusted shelf by shelf, book by book. As the morning went on with no sign of him, I was beginning to believe I'd made a huge mistake—no, I was one hundred percent sure.

Not only was the heir not making an appearance, but the library remained as quiet as it had been yesterday. I needed to get my hands on the day's news, but when the delivery finally came, Mr. Whitting buried his nose in the paper, never giving me a moment to sneak a glimpse at the articles.

Finally, at noon, Mrs. Whitting beckoned me down from a ladder. "We're going to lunch. You have one hour until you're expected back."

I showed her my cleaning bucket, hoping for at least a little praise or acknowledgment for my work. "Look at all this dust," I said. "You could knit a blanket from it."

"Ugh." She wrinkled her nose and walked away. "I don't knit."

I sagged, setting the bucket on the floor. Clearly, she wasn't the grateful type.

Her husband joined her at the end of the long aisle, keeping his newspaper clasped firmly in his hands as they exited the library together.

I glanced around to make sure I was alone in the aisle

before sinking to the floor in exhaustion, my back aching. I was a grimy, sweaty mess, and if I had enough vanity, I would've walked out the doors and given up on trying to get to the heir today.

My stomach growled, reminding me I only had an hour to eat, but just before I stood up to leave, a familiar voice spoke on the opposite side of the bookshelf behind me.

"It's not only that, Patrick. This feels bigger than Sir Pearce trying to maintain his position. I'm almost certain my mother is behind this."

My breath caught. The heir had arrived.

"Do you think she's the one who planted the questions?" Patrick replied.

"At least some of them, yes," Graham said. "The question about studying here was the only one that didn't seem intended to belittle and control me. And then, coincidentally enough, it was the only one excluded from the papers. Of course, the Academy has to edit and screen the news—it would be irresponsible not to—but doesn't this seem a bit . . . suspicious?"

"More than a bit," said Patrick. "But what I don't understand is why you're coming here to study now that the city won't even hear about your promise. Do you really want to spend your days surrounded by the stench of commoners?"

"The city might not know, but the journalists do. And, in all honesty, I somewhat like the idea. My parents never mentioned the tradition, but sometimes I suspect there's a lot they didn't bother to tell me."

"Perhaps your mother intends to keep you ignorant," said Patrick. "That way, you might feel more inclined to delegate your rule to her, as she would obviously prefer."

Graham let out a long sigh. "Maybe I *should* delegate to her. I've never felt like king material."

"Don't say that," said Patrick. "Imperator Irvine made no

mistakes when creating the inheritance order. You *are* meant to be king."

There was a long pause before Graham responded softly. "My brother was meant to be king."

I held my breath, hoping he'd say more. How his older brother died was one of Cambria's best kept secrets.

"Well . . . circumstances being what they are, it's your turn," said Patrick. "The people are depending on you."

"I suppose, but sometimes it feels as if they really don't like me."

"Why wouldn't they like you? You're Graham Brennin."

"Are you being sarcastic?"

"No. You *are* Graham Brennin."

Graham laughed softly. "I can always depend on you for such astute observations."

"Yes, you can," said Patrick. "You can always depend on me, period. So, keep thinking about my idea. I assure you I'd be your most loyal option."

"My mother won't allow me much room to make my own choices," said Graham, "but I am certainly considering the possibility."

"Wonderful. Well, it's time for me to clear out of these musty ruins. I'm not the one who vowed to be here, after all."

"Fair enough," said Graham. "Goodbye, then. Tell my guards to wait on the steps. I'd rather keep them at a distance and remain anonymous while I'm here."

"It will be done," said Patrick. "I'll come back for you this afternoon."

"Thank you."

I moved to the end of the aisle, curious to see the man Graham Brennin had been speaking with.

A young, dark-skinned noble crossed the room, going toward the main doors—the same man who'd entered The

Wordsmith with the heir yesterday. He seemed to be a friend, but his last words made me highly suspect that he was yet another player eager to make Graham his pawn.

I turned around, hurrying the opposite way to find the heir. Before leaving the safety of the bookshelves, I paused, standing in the shadows.

He emerged from the aisle beside mine but didn't look my way. He carried a heavy book and was dressed in nondescript gray clothing that made him look more like a commoner than a noble. Hurrying away, he entered an arched corridor at the back of the library where the private study rooms were.

I followed at a distance, watching as he disappeared into the farthest door on the left.

Once he was out of sight, I swallowed, solidifying my plan. I went to the librarians' desk, my eye on the stack of books that needed to be returned to their shelves. I reached under the desk where I'd carefully stashed my bag, then took my father's journal out of it and set it on top of the pile. Its rough pages were bound with leather ties and it had no spine, unlike the other books in this library, so I knew it would catch Graham's eye and pique his curiosity. Cambrians were forbidden to read anything written by an outlaw, or even those in a class lower than their own, but I suspected—or hoped—that his curiosity would be stronger than his fear.

But first, to pass for a library book, it needed a title. I picked up a quill from the desk and dipped it in a black inkpot before carefully writing a title across the leather cover. *An Explorer's Guide to the Cambrian Islands.* I fanned the ink, waiting until it was completely dry before picking up the stack of books and heading down the corridor.

I passed the other study rooms before arriving at the last one on the left with a lump in my throat. This was it, the moment I'd worked toward for so long; fear of failure made my heart pound against my stack of books.

Well, here goes.

My nervous hand slipped on the knob as I twisted it. I shifted the books to one arm and pushed the door open.

The heir sat alone on a sofa inside, his head turned down over a book. The small room was lit by a multi-paned window that was too dirty to see through.

"Oh! Please excuse me, sir," I said.

He flinched and jumped to his feet. His posture stiffened and surprised blue eyes met mine.

"I'm so sorry," I said, "I thought this room was unoccupied!" I took a step back and bumped into the doorframe, intentionally releasing my grip on the books. They fell to the floor in a messy heap. I dropped to the ground, hastily grasping at them. I noticed, with satisfaction, that the journal had landed face up.

"Let me help." The heir knelt and reached for a book.

I stared, taken aback that he'd help someone who he must've seen as far beneath him, but I figured it was an act to disguise his identity.

"There's no need," I said. "This is my job, not yours."

"No, milady. I'm the one who surprised you."

"Milady?" I laughed. "I'm only a library worker." His voice had taken me off guard again. Quiet and kind—or perhaps just weak. There was a fine line between the two.

He turned his gaze back to the floor, picking up another book, before looking at me with a quizzical raise of his eyebrows. "Have I seen you before?"

I stared for a moment too long, hoping he didn't recognize me from The Wordsmith—or anywhere else for that matter. "No, not that I recall."

"Oh." He frowned. "Sorry."

40

"For what?"

He shrugged. "I have an awful habit of saying the wrong thing."

"I've got that problem, too. Not the best quality in a Cambrian."

One corner of his mouth lifted, revealing the closest thing I'd seen to a smile.

I added another book to my stack. Only one remained on the floor. He picked up my father's journal, his eyes widening.

"Is something wrong?" I asked innocently.

He turned the book over in his hands, studying its odd binding. "Where did you find this?"

I smiled, pleased with his curiosity. "It belongs to this library."

He opened it up, flipping through the handwritten pages and maps. "But it's an explorer's guide. It almost looks like it was written by"—he lowered his voice to a whisper—"but I suppose that's not possible, is it?"

"I'm sure it's an old book," I assured him. "It must've been written back when exploration wasn't yet forbidden. Either way, it's one-of-a-kind. Part of our special collection. We don't permit it to leave the library."

He studied its pages for a long moment before closing it and looking up at me. A new spark lit his eyes and they seemed a little less lonely than before. "If it's that old and belongs to the library, it can't be illicit then, I suppose. It's just that . . . the ink on the cover looks fresh."

I shook my head. "I assure you we don't keep illicit material in our library, sir. However, if you're concerned, we could turn it into the Academy for review." I reached my hand toward the book.

He tightened his grip on it. "Oh, that's not necessary. I believe you."

"Well, since you seem interested, I'll leave it with you for now. Please make sure to turn it in to me before you go so I can put it back where it belongs."

I held my stack of books tight and stood up.

The heir stood, too, his eyes at the same level as mine. "Thank you, milady."

I turned to go, then stopped and added one last thing. "You've chosen a good study room, by the way. My favorite. It's where I like to read."

He nodded and his mouth turned up again.

I smiled back, feeling strangely uncomfortable. As my face warmed, I left the room before he could say another word.

I walked down the corridor, glad the heir was inching toward my grasp. As he read my father's journal, I hoped his view of outlaws would change, making it safer for me to tell him I was one of them. Even his perception of the city might shift, which was what I needed. He had to realize his precious Cambria wasn't perfect before I could possibly get him to leave it.

CHAPTER
SIX

Cleaning hundred-year-old dust and grime occupied my hands for the next few hours. Graham stayed in his study room, never once making an appearance. When closing time approached, Mr. Whitting finally left his desk, leaving his newspaper alone for the first time that day.

I hurried over and picked it up, glancing around to make sure Mrs. Whitting wasn't watching. I took a seat, ducking low over the paper in the candlelight, scanning the front page for anything I might need to know.

As expected, the heir's question and answer session had been whitewashed, but it was accurate other than the exclusion of my question. I saw no mention of the journalist's arrest, but when I turned the page, I found something worse.

I had made the *Wanted* list. Twice. They didn't have a name or drawing attached to me, but my stomach twisted at the realization that I'd already gotten myself on the Academy's watch.

The first profile described a young woman who'd impersonated a maid at The Wordsmith during the journalist event. Her crimes: injury to a butler, property damage, theft, and other suspicious behavior.

The next profile was an "alleged noblewoman" who'd made a purchase in the market without proof of rank. A brief description followed: brown hair, tall, between sixteen and twenty years of age.

I stared at the page until the meaning of the words got lost among the tiny symbols.

"Excuse me," said a man's voice.

I jumped, closing the newspaper and dropping it on the desk.

The heir stood in front of me, his expression as guilty as my own. He frowned at the front page of the paper before looking up at me.

I almost laughed at the ridiculousness of the situation. Both of us were featured in this paper and neither wanted the other one to know.

He smiled. "I'm sorry for startling you. I was just returning this book." He held out my father's journal.

"I thought you might've fallen asleep in there." I took the book from him, glad to feel its familiar weight again.

He shook his head. "How could I? That book is . . . compelling."

I nodded enthusiastically.

His dark brows furrowed. "You've read it, then?"

"Oh, um, a little," I said.

His eyes gleamed. "I've never seen drawings of the other islands like that—and the detail is amazing. I had no idea the outlaws built such organized towns or that they educated their children. I'd imagined it all so differently."

"I know what you mean," I said.

"I'd like to retrieve the book from the special collection again if you don't mind. Will you be here tomorrow?"

"Every day." I smiled.

"Cousin!" A man called from behind Graham. "I've been waiting for you."

I grabbed the paper and held it up in front of my face, pretending to suddenly be absorbed in the news. I couldn't afford to let him see me.

"Patrick," said Graham. "I'm on my way. Please excuse me, milady."

I kept the paper in front of me, speaking to him through it. "Yes. Goodbye."

"Goodbye," he said, his voice uncertain. He must've been puzzled by my sudden need to read the paper.

I waited until they were long gone before I set it down.

Mrs. Whitting stood at the desk facing me, her hands on her hips. "No dawdling, Miss Yarrow. You still have ten minutes." She handed me a pile of books to put away.

I sighed and headed toward the tall shelves. As I returned the books to their places, I caught sight of a mustached face coming my way. Cael strutted down the aisle with all the arrogance of a genuine Law Enforcer, like he was meant to wear that uniform.

"Looks like you made the wanted list," he said with quiet disapproval once he was close.

I didn't look at him. "It's fine. They won't know it's me. I won't make any more mistakes."

"You better not," he said. "Your mistakes will cost me as much as they'll cost you."

"I know," I said.

"Well?" he asked. "Any progress with the heir?"

"He's reading the journal."

"Good," said Cael. "Maybe it will make up for your lack of charm."

I rolled my eyes. "Says the expert on charm."

"I'm not the one risking the world's welfare on the off chance of making someone fall in love with me."

I breathed deeply and gripped the books in my hands to keep from throwing them at his face. "I never planned to make him *fall in love* with me." My voice strained to break through my whisper. "He only needs to *believe me*. That's it!"

"It's a shame you're too soft to use your knives on him," he muttered, facing me with smug anger in his face. "Because your personality won't get you anywhere."

"I'm not *soft*. I'm cautious." I shoved the rest of my books onto the shelf and met his gaze with equal anger. "If he gets murdered, all of Cambria will be looking for someone to blame. You know that."

Mrs. Whitting appeared at the end of the aisle.

I backed away from Cael.

"Oh, good evening, Enforcer," she said, her voice dripping with so much politeness that she almost didn't sound like herself. "Is there a problem?"

"Not at all," said Cael, his tone taking on the same transformation. "I was merely inquiring about a book."

"Oh, please allow me to help you! My new employee is not nearly as familiar with this library as I am, but I am honored to help you. Come this way, please." She smiled, beckoning Cael over.

"Wonderful," he said, his brow twitching.

I tried to keep the smile off my face.

Mrs. Whitting turned back to me. "You're dismissed, Miss Yarrow, but make sure to arrive promptly tomorrow morning."

I gave Cael one last amused look before grabbing my things and heading through the doors into the colorless evening light. I took the stairs and went into the street, glad I'd soon be safe and secure in the Lenoxes' home.

Citizens pushed through the busy streets, making their way

home. The bustling crowd disrupted my desire for peace and solitude, but at least I was less likely to stand out. Windows lit up with firelight one by one. The last rays of sunlight peeked from behind the clouds. If only I could reach it and be free from the bricks, the stones, the dust, and the stifling blanket between me and the sky. Getting out of this lifeless city would be freedom itself.

As I passed a church, I heard footsteps behind me. I sighed. Probably just Cael.

I continued forward, my ears telling me something wasn't right. The steps were quick and eager, not at all like the saunter I'd become used to. I gathered my courage and peeked over my shoulder.

As expected, the man behind me wore an Enforcer's uniform. But he wasn't Cael. He was short, with shaggy brown hair and a boyish face.

"Stop!" he shouted.

That was my cue to run.

I took off, confident that my long stride would help me outrun this man. I darted into an alley, determined to lose him. Not only was prison unappealing, but I didn't dare lead this Enforcer to the Lenoxes' home. I'd have to take a circuitous route. I ran through the streets, turning at random intervals until I'd lost myself as well as I'd lost him.

I stopped to catch my breath when I came to a brick wall covered in ivy. I wasn't certain, but judging by the crumbling brick and overgrown vines, this seemed to be the border of Quarter D. I started along the wall, the shadows growing longer. The direction of the setting sun was the only hint of which direction to go.

As the light faded, something tugged on my bag. I spun around, my hand darting toward the knives inside.

A small figure stood in the dark. A child.

My heart slowed and I let my hand fall to my side.

A boy no taller than my waist stepped forward. His eyes were pained and pleading, and his wrists looked as skinny as a rope. He took another cautious step and the light reflected off something metallic on his face.

Branks.

The silver bridle extended from both sides of his mouth and wrapped around his head. His chin was crusted with old blood. A surge of pity flowed through me at the same time my stomach sickened. I didn't think a child could be punished like this, not even in Cambria.

This was the world the Brennins ruled. *This* was the reason I was here.

My teeth clenched. It was safer for me to just move along; I'd be an idiot to interfere. But how could I possibly walk away?

I knelt on the ground and spoke softly. "Come here."

His eyes were afraid but tinged with exhaustion as he dragged his feet forward. I carefully touched his bony shoulder and turned him around. At the back of the branks was a keyhole.

"Don't be afraid." I pulled out a knife and raised it to the lock.

When my blade touched the metal, he flinched, letting out a muffled cry.

"I'm sorry." I twisted the razor-sharp tip of the knife until something released. "This will hurt."

He gripped his hands and whimpered while I lifted the bridle off his tongue and over his head.

"There." I threw the branks into the shadows, where they landed with a clatter.

He turned to me, his round eyes welling with tears. He opened his mouth to say something, but it came out as a mumble.

"Do you have a home?" I asked.

He nodded.

"Take this to your family." I reached into my bag and pulled out the very last of my cowry shells, placing them in his shaking hands.

His mouth lifted just a little before he turned and scurried along the brick wall.

I had only taken two steps when a nasal voice spoke behind me and I heard the unmistakable click of a pistol. "Stop. You are under arrest."

CHAPTER
SEVEN

I TURNED AROUND, SLOWLY RAISING MY ARMS IN THE AIR.

The Enforcer had followed me after all. He came toward me with his pistol extended. He nearly walked on his toes, but it did little to hide the fact that he was at least six inches shorter than me. "You have bypassed justice and deprived that child's family of the opportunity to earn an honest income."

I should've stayed quiet, but the state of the child had made my blood boil. And this pint-sized Enforcer didn't intimidate me, not even with his weapon pointed my way. "That was not justice." My voice burned with fury. "It was torture."

"How dare you speak with such disrespect to an Academy Law Enforcer!" His face twitched beneath the redness. "Rank card, now!"

I glanced at his pistol, trying to decide if he'd dare to use it. The hint of fear in his eyes made me bolder.

"Yes, of course, sir." I reached into my bag and gripped a knife, not even bothering to remove the sheath. In one rapid movement, I launched it toward the man's pistol.

The knife collided with the barrel and both weapons clattered to the ground.

The Enforcer's eyes widened in shock.

We both dove, scrambling for the pistol. He reached it first, but I pinned him down, wrestling the gun from his hands. Then I grabbed the fallen knife and stood up, pointing both weapons at him.

He raised his arms and slowly got to his feet, panting hard. "Mercy, please."

"Mercy?" I asked. "Just a minute ago, you were going on about justice." I cocked the pistol.

He choked on his words as he begged.

I smiled. "Don't be afraid. I'm sure it will go right over your head."

He ducked.

I breathed hard, gripping the two weapons tighter to keep myself from actually using them. I'd promised myself no one would die because of my plan. That included this pathetic Enforcer. "If you follow me again, you won't get a second chance. Now leave me alone."

With a final whimper, he turned on his heels and ran into the closest alleyway.

I tucked the knife and pistol into my bag and took off before Cael could show up to tell me what a terrible mistake I'd just made.

When I left the Lenoxes' house the next morning, the streets gleamed silver from the night's rain. I pulled my coat tighter around my shoulders to keep out the chill. My hair was braided and I wore a dusty lavender dress I'd found in the closet of my temporary bedroom. It was out of fashion by several years, but it was better than wearing the gray one I'd been seen too many times in.

I had to be more careful today, even if that meant taking a longer route to get to the library. I couldn't risk running into any Enforcers, particularly the one who'd followed me last night. When the Irvine Library came into sight, I heard loud footsteps falling on wet stone behind me. I ducked into an alleyway, keeping to the shadows.

A moment later, Cael—accompanied by his judgmental frown—joined me.

"There's an interesting story in today's paper." His tone conveyed even more irritation than usual. "About a Law Enforcer who was attacked by a woman with a knife. The victim even had his pistol stolen. Sound familiar?"

I blew out the air between my lips. "I haven't seen the news, but I'm sure the so-called attacker had a perfectly good reason."

"The whole city's going to be talking about this." Cael spoke through gritted teeth. "You're not being careful enough."

"Well, where were *you* last night? When you might've actually been useful, I was on my own."

He glared. "Don't blame me for your mistakes. By the time I got away from that librarian, you were gone. If you'd waited for me, none of this would've happened."

"But there was a child in branks," I whispered, remembering the boy's bloody face. By freeing him, I'd made everything worse for myself, but at the same time, I knew I'd make that decision again if I had to.

"And?" asked Cael.

I shook my head. There was no use explaining when Cael clearly didn't have the capacity for compassion.

"Do you still have the pistol?" he asked.

I nodded. I didn't dare leave anything in the Lenoxes'

house that would get them into trouble, but I didn't want to leave it on the street, either.

Cael stepped closer. "Give it to me."

I met his gray eyes, a tinge of unexpected fear sinking into my chest. I wasn't sure what made me afraid, but the weight in my bag begged to be lightened. I didn't want him to have it, but I didn't want to carry it either, so I took out the pistol and placed it in his hand.

He slid it under his coat, his cold glare never softening. "You're running out of time. If you don't get the heir out of the city *very* soon, our chance is over."

"Thank you for your concern." I smiled, well aware that he was right, but unwilling to acknowledge it. "Have a nice day."

His sour expression was the only goodbye he gave me.

"You're late," said Mrs. Whitting when I came in. She eagerly updated me on the sensationalized "attack" in the news, but never connected it to me, thankfully, before giving me the day's assignments. "We have a lot to do today. *And* we have a nobleman in study room five, so please be on your best behavior."

It seems she'd found out about Graham—sort of.

"Do you know who he is?" I asked casually.

"I didn't get a look at him, but if he has his own guards, he must be someone important. Possibly even from one of the Immovable Houses."

I glanced down the corridor and saw two guards flanking his door. I suspected the news of the attack had put him on edge and made him afraid. Graham was only accessible as long as everyone believed in the perfect safety of the city. And I'd ruined that. A disappointed sigh escaped my lips.

"Don't even think about it, young lady," said Mrs. Whitting.

"What do you mean? I—"

"I heard that sigh. You're practically going weak in the knees over the idea of a nobleman in the library, aren't you?" She pursed her lips, looking very pleased with herself.

If she wanted to think I was fawning over a nobleman, I'd let her. Better than the truth.

"I'm delighted to see you wearing a different dress today, Miss Yarrow. The color is so meek and delicate. I must say it's a big improvement."

I forced myself to smile. "Why, thank you, Mrs. Whitting."

She clapped her hands. "Well, time to get to work." She led me to the corner of the library, where miniature drawers filled the shelves instead of books. "This catalog is in desperate need of reorganization. Some patrons can be so careless."

I looked at the drawers hanging out, cards spilled on the ground, and shelves that rose to the ceiling. "This looks like an important job," I said. "Out of my abilities, in fact. Wouldn't you say this falls more under the responsibility of an *actual* librarian?" A *paid* one, I thought but didn't say aloud.

"It is indeed arduous," Mrs. Whitting said gravely, "which is why I will remain beside you to supervise the task."

"Oh no, no, no," I said. "That won't be necessary." As unpleasant as the job looked, spending the day with Mrs. Whitting would be far worse. And I might never get a chance to give Graham my book, even if he didn't have guards at his door.

But, to my misfortune, she stayed.

BALANCING ON A CREAKY LADDER WHILE SORTING through thousands of cards in a musty library was my worst task so far. Dusting was almost fun in comparison. My hands were full of paper cuts and my mouth full of curse words, at least when Mrs. Whitting wasn't listening. At midday, she finally left for lunch, giving me my desperately needed hour of freedom.

I was climbing down the wooden ladder when I saw Graham coming my way. His two guards trailed him, turning my relief into anxiety.

When my feet hit the ground, he stopped in front of me and bowed, his expression brightening as he met my eye.

I put my hands up. "Please. You don't have to bow!" I couldn't decide if he was enjoying my discomfort or just unaware, but either way, I couldn't take it.

"Sorry, milady. I suppose it's a habit."

"Would you mind losing the 'milady' habit as well?" I asked.

He frowned. "Then what shall I call you?"

"My name is Bryn Yarrow."

He extended his hand. "I'm pleased to meet you, Miss Yarrow."

I stood and faced him, waiting to see if he'd offer his name, or maybe a false one. But he didn't. I was beginning to realize he was the hopelessly honest type who hadn't yet learned that the truth would give him nothing in return. When the silence grew awkward, I abruptly reached out and shook his hand, feeling an unexpected heat in the touch.

I pulled back my hand and nodded toward the guards watching us from about twenty feet away. "I see you brought friends with you today."

He laughed. "Well . . . it was my mother's idea. She's afraid for my safety so she insisted that these guards not let me out of their sight."

"So you're a nobleman," I said, my voice tinged with a hint

of accusation. "That explains the bowing. And the milady. And the general"—I gestured toward him—"you know."

He bit his lip. "Does that bother you?"

I hesitated. "It confuses me. I wouldn't have expected a nobleman to enjoy a book about outlaws."

He glanced back at his guards before lowering his voice. "Do you have any idea how it came to be here? Or who wrote it?"

"I told you. It belongs to the library."

He shook his head. "I don't think so. I searched the entire catalog this morning and I swear there's nothing—"

"That was you?" I interrupted.

He cringed under my glare. "I'm sorry, but I had to know. I nearly asked the other librarians to find the book for me, but I was ashamed to even mention the title. I have a growing suspicion that it's not an Academy-approved book." He ended his sentence in a whisper.

I wasn't sure what to say. I wanted his curiosity, but I didn't want to reveal too much. "Would you still read it if you found out it wasn't?"

He frowned. "I shouldn't."

"Why not?"

His eyes widened, surprised at my rebellious words. "What if it's written by an outlaw? Their philosophies are corrupt. Their very *words* are corrupt. No Cambrian should read anything but the purest language."

I smiled. "I'm sure a respectable nobleman such as yourself could not be so easily corrupted."

He stared at me. "Do you really believe that?"

"I've read the book. Do I seem corrupt?"

"No! Of course not," said Graham, his face reddening. "Wait . . . have you read all of it?"

"Yes," I confessed. "But then again, I'm not like you, so

perhaps I never had much nobility to corrupt in the first place."

Graham was quiet for a moment. "Regardless of your rank, I see nobility in you, Miss Yarrow."

My smile fell. It was an odd thing to say and I didn't know what he meant by it. "Uh, thank you," I muttered, trying to hide my discomfort.

"Well, in that case," said Graham, "may I borrow the book again?"

I nodded. "Yes. Of course." I crossed the main room to retrieve the book from my bag under the librarians' desk, then brought it back to him.

He took it with a smile. A real, full one this time, instead of his previous half-smiles, before leaving for his study room, his guards following dutifully behind him.

Graham may not have trusted me enough to tell me who he was yet, but his smile told me he was getting there. For some reason, that simple turn of his mouth filled me with a strange pride. Maybe I wasn't quite as unlikable as Cael said I was. But then again, I hadn't come here to make the heir like me. And I certainly didn't intend to make him happy.

WHEN EVENING ARRIVED, MY FINGERS STUNG WITH A dozen paper cuts, unsettled dust tickled at my nose, and my stomach growled. At least Mrs. Whitting had forgotten to supervise me for the rest of the day. Before the library closed, Graham found me at the catalog drawers and returned the book, his expression clouded. His guards kept their eyes fixed on us, but they remained out of earshot.

"So? Are you corrupted?" I asked.

"I don't *feel* corrupted," he said, "but I am confused. I would love to hear your perspective if I could, but these two wouldn't stand for it." He tilted his head toward the guards. "If they don't accompany me home before sunset, my mother will be worried."

I laughed. "Aw, that's sweet."

"No." He shook his head emphatically. "If you knew my mother, you'd know it's not even a little bit sweet. She allows me no choices of my own whatsoever."

"Well, what would you do, if you could choose?" I asked.

"If I could choose?" He looked up. "Well . . . I'd run out of here with you, catch a carriage, eat—definitely—and leave my guards to figure out where I've gone."

I leaned toward him. "Sounds like a plan."

He laughed. "If only."

"I'm serious. I mean, it might need some tweaking, but it's a start."

"You honestly think we should abandon my guards and take off into the streets?" He raised his eyebrows.

I shrugged. "What's the worst that could happen?"

He paused as if he were honestly considering the question. "I don't know. But I do know that if this book doesn't corrupt me, *you* certainly will."

I smiled. "There's a window in the study room."

"I can't," he said, running both hands through his hair. He breathed deeply through his nose. "What would I tell the guards?"

"Tell them you want a few more minutes of study time. The library isn't quite closed yet, after all. Then, when they shut the door, open the window and jump. It's not far. They won't check the room until you're long gone."

Graham stared in shock. "Do you truly want to do this?"

"Yes. And so do you."

He nodded slightly, his face a bit green.

"Go on, then," I said. "I'll meet you outside."

EIGHT

Graham and I rushed through the darkening streets. Suppressed laughter lingered in my throat from the euphoria of our escape. Thanks to the crowds pushing their way home for the night, we didn't stand out. Graham's simple clothing would keep most people from paying him notice or recognizing him, but it was no guarantee. As we went, the crowds thinned, and rain began to drizzle from the sky.

Through senses heightened by nerves, I heard the rhythm of determined footfalls several paces behind me. Cael's boots had their own timbre—one that filled me with aggravation.

We left the center of the city, skirting the place where quarters D and C met, and spotted a pub without rank requirements. It would be best if Graham didn't have to show his gold Immovable rank card. I was sure he didn't want me to see it.

He pulled open the plain wooden pub door and peered inside. "Well, it's certainly nothing fancy."

"What do you expect?" I laughed. "It will probably be the humblest place you've ever stepped foot in."

He smiled. "As long as it has food, it's good enough."

"Agreed." I smiled.

He opened the door wider and waited for me to enter. I glanced back and briefly met eyes with Cael through the drizzling rain. He stood under the eaves across the street.

I stepped through the doorway and was greeted with a room as dim as the twilight outside. A low fire burned in a hearth, giving off the only light in the room. Just one occupant sat at a table. I chose a table for two in the corner, glad there weren't any windows for a certain guard to spy through.

I nodded, inwardly approving. Quiet, cozy, and with an air of mystery, this pub was the perfect place to tell a secret, or to persuade someone to reveal his.

A server brought out pewter mugs and plates of seafood. Graham held his utensils regally, eating slowly and carefully. I ate heartily, with little concern for manners.

When I looked up from my plate, Graham was watching me with a raised eyebrow and a half-smile.

"If you knew how hungry I am, you wouldn't judge my manners," I said.

"I'm not judging them. I was attempting to figure you out, I suppose."

I stopped stuffing shrimp in my mouth long enough to ask, "Have you come to a conclusion?"

He shook his head. "Hardly. Your accent and manners are casual, but you carry yourself like a queen." He lifted his hand to his chin and narrowed his eyes. "You work in the library and look like a humble citizen, but still, something doesn't fit."

"I can't say I'm often referred to as humble."

"I didn't intend to insult you. I meant that you simply look ordinary."

"Humble *and* ordinary? Your compliments get better with each attempt."

Graham's face reddened. "Forgive me. I never know what to say."

I didn't mind. I didn't need to look beautiful. I only needed to blend in.

"You're equally confusing—a mysterious nobleman who prefers to remain nameless, apparently, eats dinner with commoners, and reads books written by outlaws."

His mouth fell open. "So, the book *was* written by an outlaw?"

"Did I say that?" I speared some shrimp with my fork.

He frowned. "You know more than you're telling me. I understand if you're reluctant to tell me the truth, but your secrets are safe with me."

"Are they?" I leaned over the table, looking him directly in the eye. "If you want to know my secrets, you have to be willing to share some of your own."

"Like what?" he asked.

"Your name, for a start."

He stared at his plate, the space between his eyebrows returning to its typical furrow. I pitied him for the way he didn't seem capable of hiding his emotions.

"That's what I thought," I said, taking another bite of my dinner.

He stayed quiet for a long moment before looking back up at me. "My name is Graham," he whispered.

I studied him, unsure of what to say. Without his last name, I didn't know whether to react to him as Graham Brennin or just some guy named Graham. The nervousness in his eyes told me he hoped I wouldn't know who he was, so I decided to let him keep up the pretense.

"Graham?" I asked. "I was expecting something *much* worse—like Wulfric. You didn't need to be so ashamed. Not terribly, anyway."

He laughed, his face reddening. "Uh, thank you."

"Really. I met a Wulfric once. And yes, he was as dull as he sounds."

"Well," Graham began, "now that you know my name, will you answer a question?"

"It depends on what you want to know."

He fixed his eyes on me, a flicker of fear passing through them. "Is the book yours?"

My mouth fell open, my composure forgotten. "What?"

"You were carrying it yesterday, though there's no record of it in the library. You've read it and know more than you dare admit. And"—he paused, glancing at my bag on the floor—"I saw you put it in your bag. I could be mistaken, but it looks as if it's still in there."

I kept my expression neutral, inwardly hiding my pleasure that he'd come to this conclusion and was still choosing to talk to me. "Maybe nobles really are as clever as they say."

His mouth lifted in a smile, a dimple forming on one side of his mouth. "Why do you have it? I assure you I'm not making any accusations. I suspect it's for purely academic purposes."

"Yes," I said, my tone flat with sarcasm. "One hundred percent academic."

He squinted, taking a drink from his mug. "You wouldn't . . . use it, would you?"

"Why are you so interested?" I said. "Planning to go somewhere?"

He laughed and shook his head. "No. I'm certain to stay inside these walls for the rest of my life."

I pushed my empty plate away. "What a shame. I was hoping I'd met an adventurer."

His smile faded and his eyes turned serious. "But"—he swallowed and looked away, toward the blank brick wall—"that's not an option."

I lowered my voice. "There are people who have left Cambria."

"Yes, as banished criminals," he said in a whisper.

"Not only them. Haven't you heard about those who disappear in the night and are never seen again?" I asked.

"It's all hearsay. The Academy would never allow them to leave."

"You don't have a very vivid imagination," I said.

He fidgeted with his fork. "I suppose not. My parents have made sure of that."

"You're not a child. Why do you let your parents control the way you think?"

He avoided my eyes. "They have a lot of influence . . . over me."

I thought of my own father. Maybe Graham and I weren't that different, except for the fact that his parents were the king and queen. And horrible. "Well, when you decide to stop caring about their opinion so much, let me know."

"Why? You couldn't possibly be planning to *leave*."

"No, of course not." I wiped my face with my napkin, then set it on the table between us. "But that could change if I had someone to join me."

The fork fell from his hand, clattering on the stone floor.

I watched him with my breath in my throat. His eyes became distant and glazed. He studied the door of the restaurant as if he were considering walking right out of here and escaping this gray city. Then he turned back to me, his face lit with the fire's glow.

I started to squirm under his gaze. "Well, now that I told you something, are you ready to tell me your last name?"

He ran a hand through his hair. "I don't know. It's . . . nothing personal, but—"

"If you won't, I'll have to start calling you Graham the Nobleman." There was always the option of calling him out and getting past this nonsense, but only one thing held me back: how he might react when he discovered I'd been pretending not to know who he was. It might make him wonder what else I'd been hiding.

He shrugged. "I've been called worse."

The server returned to our table. "Pub's closin.' That'll be four cowries."

I reached into my bag. My hand brushed past the book and knives in their sheaths, scraping the bottom of the sharkskin. *Ugh.* I'd forgotten I'd given the last of my cowries away. Before I could explain, Graham placed five shells on the table.

Unwelcome guilt settled in my stomach at his kindness. He obviously had plenty of money—thanks to citizens' taxes—so I knew it hardly mattered, but I hadn't wanted him to do me any favors. However, since I had no money of my own and no room to refuse, there was only one thing I could say.

"Thank you," I muttered.

We left the pub, stepping into the misty drizzle.

"I . . . guess I'll see you at the library tomorrow," I said, starting down the street toward Quarter C.

He stayed by my side. "Wait. Let me escort you."

I glanced over to the last place I saw Cael, but he wasn't there. Still, he always managed to follow me. "Don't you have somewhere to go? A house full of servants ready to give you a bubble bath?"

"I wouldn't be a gentleman if I didn't see you safely home, especially after yesterday's attack in these very streets," he said. "Anyhow, my bubble bath can wait."

I didn't want Graham to know where I was staying, but I figured it couldn't hurt to let him walk me to the gates. Light rain sprinkled the stone and brick as we walked in the darkening night.

When the entrance to Quarter C came into view, I stopped. "Well, it's nearly curfew. Time for you to catch a carriage." I turned away.

"Wait!" said Graham.

I faced him. "Yes?"

"I know I should mind my own business and I doubt you'll want to tell me, but . . . where *did* you get that book?"

I shielded my eyes against the rain and looked him in the eye. I still couldn't tell him too much unless the book had lessened his prejudice, at least a little. "Would you be afraid if you found out there was an outlaw in the city?"

He hesitated. "Is there?"

"Just answer the question."

"Well . . . yes, I suppose. Maybe." He gritted his teeth, then sighed. "It depends. I must admit they might not be as threatening as I've always been told—and they're sometimes even mistreated if the book is accurate—but still, they don't belong in Cambria. They're uncivilized criminals, after all."

His parents' influence was still strong. I folded my arms and let a hint of steel into my voice. "Uncivilized isn't a very nice way to put it."

"But it's the truth, isn't it?"

"That depends on who you ask. Or *whom*, if I'm trying to sound more *civilized*." As soon as I said the word, I bit my tongue. In my anger, I'd let my caution slide. As much as I wanted to say more, he wasn't ready to hear it.

He tilted his head. "What do you mean by that?"

"Nothing," I said, forcing a laugh. "It was a joke."

"Oh." He frowned. "Look, I understand if you're afraid to tell me the truth, but you already admitted you wanted to leave the city, and yet, here I am, speaking with you instead of reporting you. Your hesitation is reasonable, given the fact that

I am a nobleman, but I hope you've begun to see that you can trust me."

I looked around. Citizens passed by in the rain, hurrying to get home before curfew. Too close for comfort.

"Can I?" I asked. "I don't even know your last name. How can I trust you when you're still half a stranger?"

"It's just that I—my family . . ." he trailed off pathetically.

"Is it because I'm a commoner and you're afraid I'll tell people we're friends?" I asked, prodding him to admit who he was so I could move forward with my plans.

His wet hair clung to his forehead, and he was beginning to look like he'd drown, but he still smiled. "We are friends, then?"

My frustration wasn't enough to keep me from smiling back. "I think so, unless my less than impressive rank is a deal-breaker. Who knows, maybe the only reason you're still talking to me is because of my book."

He shook his head. "That's not true. Your rank makes no difference to me."

I narrowed my eyes, unable to hide my skepticism. I'd thought he was the honest type, but this couldn't possibly be true. "How? How could it make no difference? You can't deny that nothing matters more to a Cambrian. Especially"—I stepped closer, staring him straight in the eye—"to the heir."

He stepped back and his eyebrows drew together, dark and serious.

My heart beat faster and I wished I could take back my words. Why couldn't I control my tongue?

"When did you realize?" he asked solemnly.

"Well, it doesn't take a Class A rank to put Graham and Brennin together."

We stood facing each other, with only the sound of fast and persistent raindrops surrounding us. I couldn't recall when the rain had picked up, but water ran down Graham's hair into his face. I must've looked the same.

I put my hand out toward him, my anxiety retreating as I realized he didn't seem angry. "It's nice to officially meet you, Graham Brennin."

He reached out and shook my hand, the rain running between our fingers.

"You don't mind?" he asked.

I smiled. "Your rank makes no difference to me."

He smiled back with a new boldness, a happier one than all his previous smiles, triggering a surge of guilt inside me.

"It's almost ten o'clock," he said, "and I'm sure you'd like to get out of the rain."

"Maybe not. If I stay out a few minutes longer, I won't have to bathe tonight."

He laughed freely as if something in him had been unlocked with the reveal of his secret.

I wiped the water from my eyes. "Your parents will be furious you escaped from your guards."

"Most definitely. I'm sure they'll never forgive me."

I shivered and rubbed my arms, my skin finally registering the cold. "Well, then. I'm sorry for evoking the eternal wrath of the king and queen."

He gave me a funny look. "It was worth it."

I wished he hadn't said that. And yet, the corners of my mouth turned up in rebellion as if my mind no longer controlled my actions.

"Will you be all right from here?" he asked, looking at the Quarter C gates.

"Yes." I laughed. "Honestly, I'm more worried about you making it home on your own."

"I'll survive, I'm sure. Goodnight, Miss Yarrow." Graham

bowed as if I were a queen. The motion sent a stream of water down his hair.

"Goodnight." I was soaked through, but somehow my voice still managed to feel as dry as sand. I watched him leave, unwilling to force my feet to step away. Moving forward seemed impossible, but I couldn't stay in the storm.

A figure emerged from the rain after Graham disappeared. Cael sauntered over, his smug smile contradicting the anger in his eyes. "No kiss?"

I clenched my hands into fists and turned toward the gates. I could always count on Cael to ruin my good mood.

I entered the quarter and took a path around the back of the houses toward the Lenoxes' kitchen door. An awning sheltered the back porch, keeping off most of the rain, and a tall picket fence bordered each side. Cael stopped and nodded, seemingly satisfied with escorting me back without incident. He grunted something much less nice than "good night" and disappeared into the rain.

Before going inside, I hesitated. Being cooped up in a small room with this much pent-up energy wouldn't do me any favors. I took a knife from my bag and removed the leather sheath, my fingers itching to throw it.

My plan was for the good of everyone I loved, so why was I beginning to question it? Leaving power in the hands of the Brennins and war in the hands of the outlaws wasn't an option. I gripped my knife tighter and nodded. This was what I wanted. More importantly, it was what my father wanted. I'd make him prouder than ever if I could manage to keep my emotions out of this.

Thunk. My blade landed in the fence bordering the porch. It let out some frustration, but not nearly enough.

I longed to talk to my father. I pictured him all alone,

waiting for my return. He claimed to enjoy solitude, but he must've been secretly missing me as much as I missed him.

I crossed the porch and yanked my knife from the fence, remembering how I used to see him as intimidating and short-tempered when I was younger. But when I was twelve, and my mother was dying, I spent days crying at her bedside with my father, clinging to him with a trust I'd never lose. Our tears broke the boundary that used to stand between us, and from that time on, I understood him.

Small, insignificant details remained in my memory from that time, like the smell of lavender in the room and the pattern on my mother's quilt. But the things I longed to grasp, like the sound of her laugh or the feeling of her kiss on my cheek, had become hazy and distant. I did remember her copper brown eyes, mostly because mine were the same color, but they lacked her warmth.

For the first time, I realized I had no idea what she'd think of the person I'd become. I had memories of her, but I didn't *know* her. What would she think of my mission? All the time I'd spent preparing? Would she have done the same in my place?

I studied my blade in the darkness, searching for a reflection that wouldn't reveal itself. Whatever she might have chosen, it was too late to consider alternatives. I spun my knife at the fence one last time, lodging it in the crack I'd already made.

CHAPTER
NINE

Graham didn't show up at the library the next morning.

My eyes constantly lingered on the front doors, but I was disappointed every time they opened. Maybe his parents had locked him in his room to punish him for yesterday's rebellion. Or maybe I'd just scared him away.

At least my mind was back to its original resolve. I trusted my father and knew he'd never support a plan that wasn't for the good of all Cambria. *Just not for Graham's good.* The unwanted thought nagged in the weaker part of my mind. I pushed it away before the guilt set in again. No more doubts.

Mrs. Whitting seemed dead set on making my day as unbearable as possible. She followed me around, prattling on non-stop while I cleaned.

"Our children are exceptionally intelligent. My daughter even ranked in Class A. I wouldn't be surprised if she becomes an Immortal someday. Just imagine how rich and respected she would be."

I groaned and willed my ears to stop working.

"You missed a spot—yes, right there. One day, she could have a seat upon the balcony of the Academy beside the king and queen. My neighbor fears Imperator Brennin will be too ill to deliver his address tonight, but I assured her that he wouldn't disappoint us. Oh, and the queen! Isn't she the epitome of grace and intelligence? You could learn a lot from her, I must say. Did you see the gown she wore at the last address?"

I climbed higher up the ladder to get away from the sound, but Mrs. Whitting's voice grew louder and shriller. The last thing I wanted was to hear about the queen's wardrobe and all the ways she was better than me. Only the reminder of the king's speech did me any good. I wondered if that was why Graham hadn't shown up.

"I do hope the young heir marries soon," she said.

I glanced back for the hundredth time when I heard the main doors shut, but it still wasn't Graham.

"The sooner he has children, the better. Heaven knows the Strouds would be dreadful leaders. I hear they have no taste at all—not like our dear queen . . ."

I clenched my jaw and turned back to my dusty shelf, with no choice but to be assaulted by Mrs. Whitting's gossip. I considered abandoning the library for good, but I couldn't bring myself to go anywhere else in case Graham still managed to come.

"Work quickly, Miss Yarrow! We'll be closing early to make it to the Academy on time."

That was the first good news I'd heard all day.

Hours later, in a lonely study room, I half-heartedly scraped books off the chairs and sofas. It was nearly time to leave for the king's address and Graham was probably already there. With my arms full, I stepped out the door into the hallway, the late afternoon sun landing in patches on the worn stone tiles.

"Miss Yarrow."

I almost dropped my books at the sight of Graham. He hurried down the hall toward me wearing his finest suit. His face was flushed, and his black tie was crooked.

In that clothing, he wouldn't be overlooked. Mrs. Whitting would fawn all over him if she saw that suit and our privacy would cease to exist. I pulled him back into the study room I'd just left and shut the door. "What happened? Were you punished?"

"Well, my mother spent all morning scolding me . . . but it wasn't that." His eyes turned serious. "My father needed help."

"Is he okay?" I couldn't hide my fear. The king would ruin everything if he died too soon.

Graham bit his lip. "More or less. He's still insistent about giving his speech."

"Shouldn't you be at the Academy then?" I asked.

He glanced at his gold pocket watch before sitting on a faded blue sofa. "I have time."

I smiled and set my books on a table, taking a seat beside him. "If your mother was so angry, why did she let you leave—and without guards?"

"Well, I didn't exactly ask permission. I convinced my coachman I needed to stop for important business on the way to the Academy. It helps that my cousin is driving the carriage and listens to me over my mother."

"So, what's the important business?"

He shrugged. "I wanted to see you."

My stomach twisted.

"I wish I could stay longer, but if I arrive late for the

speech, I wouldn't be surprised if the Academy disqualifies me from inheriting."

"We wouldn't want that." I laughed. What he said was a joke, on the surface, but I had a feeling it revealed his genuine fears. I reached out and straightened his crooked tie. "The Third House doesn't dress as well as yours, according to Mrs. Whitting."

He blushed. "If only that were the Strouds' worst flaw."

"Why does everyone hate the Strouds so much?"

"They're arrogant and exclusive—even for nobles. Evander Stroud refuses to keep servants because he can't bear to mingle with lower-ranked citizens. And his daughter always claims to be too tired or ill to attend a single event, no matter how important. You would think she'd be more concerned with appearances, considering she's second in line for the throne."

"Maybe she doesn't want the throne," I said.

Graham raised an eyebrow. "I doubt it. I met her when I was younger, back when she occasionally made an appearance, and all I remember is an obnoxious blonde bully who wanted nothing more than to boss all the other kids around. She would be horrible for Cambria."

Better than the Brennins, I thought, biting my tongue.

"Anyhow, I didn't come here to bore you with noble gossip."

"Good," I said. "I get plenty of that from Mrs. Whitting."

"My apologies." He laughed and glanced at his pocket watch again.

"The Academy couldn't *really* disqualify you for being late, could they?" I asked.

He shook his head. "Only a majority vote by the Immortals could override the laws of traditional inheritance—but that's never happened. Besides, Sir Pearce may not like me, but he'd lose his title if the Third House inherited. No one really knows who Mara Stroud would choose as First Immortal, but it's guaranteed not to be him."

I slouched into the sofa. "But you would choose Sir Pearce, wouldn't you? He's been loyal to your family for twenty years."

He bit his lip. "Honestly, I'm not sure."

"Does he know that?"

"No." Graham shook his head. "I haven't told anyone I'm even considering choosing someone else, except my cousin, Patrick—and now you know. But I can tell Sir Pearce has his suspicions."

"And that's why he wants you to delegate to your mother," I said, revealing I knew more about politics than I'd let on. "She would keep him in his position."

He nodded. "Yes . . . exactly."

"That makes sense. But why does your mother want you to delegate to her so much?"

Graham's eyes widened. "Why do you say that? Have you . . . heard something?"

"I read the news. I saw the questions the journalists asked you. It wasn't hard to see the queen's hand in them."

He sighed. "I know she wants what's best for Cambria. I haven't always been the most responsible person and she knows that better than anyone. For a while, I've been considering delegating the throne to her . . . but after reading your book, I'm starting to believe change would be a good thing. In fact"—his eyes took on a sheen of pride—"this morning, in my anger, I stood up to her for the first time and told her I'd never give her power."

I sat up straighter. It seemed my book had made an impact. A dangerous response was traveling to the tip of my tongue, but I wasn't sure I could say it just yet. "Maybe it's time to prove you're responsible."

"How?" asked Graham. "Besides being on time tonight?"

My pulse quickened. "Can I trust you to keep a secret?"

"Of course. I haven't told anyone about your book, so I'm getting used to keeping your secrets."

"Promise me you won't tell a soul."

He looked at me with solemn blue eyes. "I promise."

I took a breath. "Rumors say that the outlaws are planning an attack."

Before he had a chance to respond, the door to the study room burst open and a dramatic gasp sucked all the air from the room. Mrs. Whitting stepped inside, her hands covering her gaping mouth. "Miss Yarrow, this is highly inappropriate! You're alone in a room with a man and you're sitting *this close*" —she took a better look at Graham and gasped again—"Sir Brennin! I am so terribly sorry this disrespectful girl is bothering you. I assure you this behavior will not be tolerated." She looked back at me, her eyes blazing. "You are promptly and permanently dismissed."

I stared back at her in shock, then looked at Graham to see his mouth hanging open. He looked as speechless as I was.

"Get up, Miss Yarrow" Mrs. Whitting shouted, "and get out."

"Please, milady," said Graham. "She was assisting me. I just . . . had a question."

She turned to him, her anger dissolving into a sickly sweet smile. "It is so very gentlemanly of you to try to defend her, but I'm afraid this is indefensible." She looked back at me, the smile instantly vanishing.

"Very well." I stood up and left the room with heat in my veins. I followed the corridor, crossing the main room, then went through the door to the front steps, where I planned to wait for Graham. A carriage bearing the Brennin insignia—a blue horse on a white shield—waited at the base of the steps.

I swore and darted back inside the library, pressing my back against the solid wood door. I'd forgotten Patrick was out there. Things had already taken a turn for the worse and being seen by him would only make me sink lower. I only needed to know where I'd find Graham next. Then I'd leave.

"Miss Yarrow!" Mrs. Whitting's furious voice echoed through the library. She had left the corridor and was headed toward me.

I huddled against the door, trying to decide whether I'd rather face Mrs. Whitting or let Patrick get suspicious about me.

Just then, the door beside me opened and a familiar man in a pressed suit pushed inside. Patrick looked at me and frowned.

If I stayed, I'd have to deal with them both.

I pulled the door open and ran down the steps, but before I passed the carriage and entered the street, Graham called to me.

I stopped, hesitating. I really, *really* didn't want Patrick to get a better look at me than he already had, but I didn't want to walk away from Graham, not now, when I was so close to getting what I needed.

"Miss Yarrow, wait!" he shouted.

I turned around.

He ran down the steps toward me.

"I'm so sorry. I can't believe she dismissed you for that. I'm to blame."

"It doesn't matter," I said. "She didn't pay me well enough anyway."

"We need to leave." Patrick joined us at the bottom of the steps beside the carriage, raising a judgmental eyebrow at me. "Who's this?"

Graham looked nervous. "Patrick, this is Miss Yarrow. Miss Yarrow, this is my cousin, Patrick Donovan."

I knew that name. The Donovans were Immovables from

the Eighth House. I didn't put out my hand. And neither did he.

Patrick looked me up and down, then turned to Graham. "Why do you associate with people who are so far beneath you?"

"Watch your manners, Patrick," Graham muttered.

"But you aren't *so* far beneath the Brennins," I said in a gentle tone, watching Patrick's pride turn to confusion. "Only, what, six Houses?"

His eyes narrowed and he stepped toward me.

"Time to go," said Graham, grabbing Patrick's arm and pulling him toward the carriage. Then he jumped inside and shut the door.

Patrick climbed into the driver's seat, his face red with fury.

I moved out of the way before he could run me over with the carriage, as I'm sure he would've happily done. I watched them go, then headed up the curving path toward the center of the city. I didn't dare miss the king's address.

TEN

CHAOTIC URGENCY FILLED THE STREETS. HORSE-DRAWN carriages passed me, their windows full of feathered hats and shimmering fabric. Mid-ranked citizens were also permitted to attend, but no one from Class D was allowed into the Academy's grounds, where Immortals spent their lives debating Cambrian grammar and writing verbal constraints into binding laws.

I looked down reflexively whenever I caught a glimpse of a black and white uniform. Law Enforcers were everywhere this evening, quieting citizens' conversations as they passed.

I flinched when Cael stepped next to me, his clothing blending in with the rest of the Enforcers.

"I'd hate for you to think I wasn't enjoying my time alone," I said, "but where have you been?"

He kept his gaze ahead. "Around."

I pushed ahead. It wasn't worth trying to get a solid answer, not if it slowed me down.

A cloudy slate blue enveloped the sky as it began to rain. I took my raincoat from my bag and pulled it on. If the rain fell any harder, it could drown out the king's words, even if I made it in time. I wrapped the coat around my shoulders and picked up my pace.

A LONG WALK LATER, I ARRIVED AT THE ENORMOUS Academy Square, where Enforcers checked citizens' rank cards as they filed through the gates. I showed mine and went in, pushing my way up, as close as I could get to the center of the Academy. The majestic building curved around both sides of the crowd, its tall Corinthian pillars propped between the lower and upper balconies. Enforcers lined the perimeter of the building, their pistols drawn.

Graham wasn't on the upper balcony yet. Neither were the king and queen.

Most of the nobles' seats were occupied, other than a few empty ones here and there. I took note of the Immovable Houses represented: the Byrnes from the Fourth House, the Eiders from the Fifth, the Shannons from the Sixth, and so on. Two of the ten surviving Houses weren't here. The Strouds' seats were empty, as well as the Ruskins,' the unlucky Eleventh House at the tail end of the line of inheritance.

On the left and right balconies were the Immortals, with their embroidered laurel leaves and stuffy high-collared tail-coats. Most upper-ranked citizens saw them as heroes, protectors of the language, defenders of purity. Not enough saw them for what they really were: a pompous bunch of zealots with no grasp of the reality around them.

The crowd waited with their eyes fixed on the balcony. Umbrellas nearly blocked my view, but I stood on my toes and peered around them.

All at once, a hush fell over the square.

The queen, escorted by Graham, emerged from the doors and walked toward the center of the balcony, her arm raised in a flourishing wave. After the tiniest delay, the onlookers greeted them with applause.

Where was the king?

The applause continued until the queen took her seat in a throne-like chair. Graham sat beside her, his mouth set in a line as straight as his eyebrows. He didn't smile or wave. His mood had changed dramatically in the past hour and I was afraid to know why.

The crowd quieted when the First Immortal appeared at the podium. The austere creases in his face weren't as obvious from here, but his frown was as distinguished as ever. He raised a hand to quiet an already silent crowd.

Even the rain seemed to pause for him.

"Loyal citizens of Cambria," he spoke in his dry, though surprisingly loud, voice. "Indeed, you have been anticipating Imperator Brennin's address with great excitement. However" —he paused and glanced over his shoulder—"due to the sudden gravity of the king's illness, that will no longer be possible."

My vision pulsed with the pressure from my beating heart. The crowd reacted with a buzz of surprise until the First Immortal held up his hand again.

"We will instead be honored to hear from our most gracious queen. I present to you Imperatrix Maeve Brennin." He gestured grandly toward the queen and bowed before taking his seat.

The noise of the crowd heightened into a roar. As much as she pretended to be, Imperatrix Brennin wasn't a true ruler of Cambria. Her influence may have been strong, but she didn't technically wield political power. It was her husband who was the descendant of the Second House. Because of the laws of genetic inheritance, she was only queen for now. She'd lose her title the moment the king was dead.

Maeve Brennin stood and walked to the podium. She smoothed her violet dress and adjusted her sharp gold crown over the black and silver strands weaving through her elaborate braided hairstyle. She looked down, her cheeks stretched in a tight grin. "My beloved citizens." Her voice was high and condescending as if she were addressing a disobedient toddler. "I am despondent to stand here this evening with unfortunate news, but my dear husband, and your beloved Imperator, Desmond Brennin"—she sniffed and dabbed a handkerchief at her eyes—"has fallen into a truly lamentable state."

A sigh breathed through the audience. Her attempts to garner sympathy must have worked since the king was well-liked by the nobles. The oppressed majority knew him as a tyrant, but unfortunately, most of them weren't here to express themselves.

"He has been a most exceptional leader over this blessed city. There has never been a ruler, excepting Imperator Irvine, who has possessed such intellect, such morality . . ."

I rolled my eyes while she listed his virtues. The high-pitched adulation went on for so long that I wished the rain would start up again to drown it out.

"While reluctantly accepting the grim reality of his imminent departure, I have grown concerned for our future and have been compelled to reconsider what is optimal for our kingdom." Her smile grew wider until it was nearly a grimace. "Citizens, do not fear! I value the sanctity of tradition above all else and I am extremely disinclined to induce even a modicum of change within these walls." She swept her eyes through the crowd, but there was no sign of disagreement so far.

Graham hadn't lifted his eyes from the balcony floor since

the queen started her speech. His emotions were on full display in front of thousands.

"However," the queen said, "a very inexperienced young man is next in line to rule." Her voice suddenly lost its sweetness and seemed to drop an octave. "While he has attempted to learn the statutes of the Academy, he lacks the understanding and responsibility necessary to be an effective leader. His character issues, no doubt stemming from the tragic loss of his older brother at a tender age, require remedial improvements. I am unable, in good conscience, to allow his shortcomings to affect you all, dear citizens. My loyalty to Cambria comes first, always."

Graham's face flushed, and I wondered what kept him from making a run for it.

The queen continued. "Only in dire circumstances would I suggest a departure from tradition."

Dread filled me as I realized what the queen was about to say. I remembered Graham's argument and how he'd told her he would never delegate to her. My heartbeat quickened and my fingernails dug into my palms.

"One day, perhaps, my son will be sufficiently prepared, but for the time being, we need someone who truly knows how to rule. I may not have been born into the Second House, but Imperator Brennin and I are aligned in purpose. Every decision of the past twenty years has been influenced by my opinion. Both my heart and mind are firmly embedded with the desire to protect our city, our culture, our values, and our most virtuous language. No one could be more qualified."

I couldn't begin to imagine how she could betray her own son. Family was sacred—the one thing I'd never risk. And she did it all with a smile on her face. Didn't she feel some pity? Some sense of loyalty?

She's no more power-hungry than you are. The thought crept into my mind along with a heavy dose of self-loathing.

I shook my head to push it away. I wasn't like her.

The queen's voice returned to its false sweetness. "I am not suggesting a long-standing shift in tradition, merely a temporary solution to the problems at hand. I am hopeful that my son will one day be worthy of the throne. Until then, let us sustain a leader who will carry on the virtues of our beloved Imperator Irvine."

She paused. "I believe that if our dear founder were alive today, he himself wouldn't hesitate to alter our current policy of genetic inheritance, given the circumstances. After all, I was born a Donovan. Imperator Irvine selected my own family to one day rule Cambria. This remains entirely within his will."

The swell of applause made me sick to my stomach.

"It is now that I must ask for your support, my dear citizens and glorious Immortals. Please write to the Academy, share your desire for stability, and petition them to support my proposal to remain Queen of Cambria. Use the power of your words to persuade and I assure you, we cannot fail!"

With a false smile and self-congratulatory waves, Imperatrix Maeve Brennin turned and glided the length of the balcony before disappearing into the building.

CHAPTER
ELEVEN

THE APPLAUSE ERUPTED INTO A CLAMOR. AFTER A moment, the crowd began to flow back toward the gates on the other side of the square, but my legs had lost their mobility.

I couldn't tear my eyes from Graham. While the nobles and Immortals socialized on the balcony, he made a quick retreat through one of the Academy's doors. The urge to run and find him nudged at me, but there was no point. He'd be gone before I came close, assuming I didn't get caught by an Enforcer's pistol first.

The crowd shoved me along, so I finally forced my feet to act. I crossed the expanse of Academy Square, where the citizens exited through the gates. The noise around me sliced apart the fragments of my thoughts, preventing them from coming together into something that made sense.

The sky darkened into a swirl of gray and black. The rain returned in large, angry drops and the world pushed in on me from every side. My chest constricted and I forgot how to breathe. The sounds faded away, except for the rush of blood through my veins.

I was alone inside my head, but without the peace of solitude.

There was no escaping this crippling pressure if I stayed in the streets. The noisy crowds would continue for hours, gossiping about the unprecedented news. I longed to find a quiet place, free from the masses.

Just before I was swept through the gates, I acted on impulse and cut through the human current, back inside the darkening square. I ran along the iron fence, toward one edge of the U-shaped Academy. The rain partially blocked my view, but at least it would help me remain unnoticed.

The need to be alone drove me. When I reached the building, I didn't stop. I took hold of a column on the ground level and pulled myself up to the second-story balcony, gripping the seams in the stone with shaking fingers.

The long, covered walkway was deserted. Doors were set into the exterior wall, but I didn't intend to go inside. I only wanted to go up.

Up above the rest of the world was where I'd find peace.

I climbed another pillar and pulled myself onto the wet roof. The firelights in the windows below were smudged and indistinct as if my eyes refused to focus. I collapsed onto the shingles, dropping my head into my hands. Breathing deeply, I tried to lighten the pressure threatening to force its way through my skin.

This can't happen.

In the dim light of the full moon glowing behind the clouds on the eastern horizon, the expanse of the city appeared to stretch on endlessly, without the entrapment of the wall. The rain fell hard, drowning out all other sounds.

This changes everything.

I raised the hood on my coat, wishing it could shut out the world completely. The rain pelted my back until my skin grew numb in defense, but it was nothing compared to the torrent of thoughts smashing through my mind.

This is my fault.

Because of me and my father's journal, Graham had found a reason to want the throne. He'd stood up to his mother and refused to give her what she wanted.

This was her retaliation.

Images of Graham flashed between my fears. Sad blue eyes. His defeated posture. We must have been vastly different in character or he would've strangled his mother by now. Maybe it would be a good thing if he were more like me.

What would my father say? How could I succeed if this power-hungry monster wrapped her tentacles around everything?

My plan required me to remove the future king, not some rejected nobleman. The attack would still happen if Maeve got her way, no matter where I took Graham. As long as the Brennins remained in power, the islanders would launch from Tramore the morning after the next new moon. In only sixteen days.

Thousands would die.

Graham would die.

I needed to send a message to my father. Cael would have to make himself useful.

As the rain quieted and faded away, my mind cleared with it and I began to panic for a new reason.

I shouldn't have come up here.

I held onto the edge of the roof and lowered myself down to one of the pillars. My boots slipped on the wet stone, but my fingers gripped the grooves. I dropped onto the balcony and swung my leg over the railing.

"Halt!" shouted a voice from behind.

I froze with one leg on each side of the railing and peered out from under my hood, trying to keep my face hidden.

A tall figure in a green and black tailcoat stood on the balcony watching my every move. The familiar creases in his face stood out even in the shadows.

I would've dropped to the ground, but without the crowd to hide me, the guards would catch me before I took ten steps. If there had been a convincing enough lie, I would have told it, but the First Immortal wasn't likely to believe a word I said. And one glimpse of my face would make things a whole lot harder.

My eyes darted to the door behind him and I slowly brought my leg back over the railing, still keeping my face down. I bowed as if I intended to apologize and surrender. Instead, I lunged and sprinted past him, yanking open the door. I slipped inside a dim room and locked the bolt.

The Immortal pounded at the door and shouted for the guards, but I was already running through a candlelit study. I dashed past a desk, between chairs and bookshelves, and through a door in the opposite corner. I found myself in a long hallway with doors lining both sides and sconces flickering against the dark walls.

I crept forward. Any one of the twenty-six Immortals could be waiting behind each door.

The maze-like building was enormous. I had little chance of finding my way to a stairway before guards showed up to haul me off to prison. All I knew was that the doors on my right would lead to rooms facing the outer grounds. And those rooms might have windows.

I listened by a door. When I heard nothing, I turned the knob and peeked inside. A woman's wide eyes stared back at me. I slammed the door and ran. Even through the heavy wood, her shouts echoed down the corridor.

Footsteps pounded up ahead.

I had no choice but to try another door. I opened one a crack. It was empty. I darted in and locked it behind me. A desk dominated the space, and there were two windows on the opposite wall. The workspace was covered in books, quills, and piles of paper. I dove under the desk and waited for the rush of footsteps to pass, willing my body to be strong and my heart to slow. When it was quiet outside the door, I jumped to my feet.

The two windows had levers. I tried the first, but it wouldn't budge. Rust caked the handle, flaking away as I pulled, but it held on stubbornly.

I tried the second window's lever. It too was rusted. I finally felt it move as it broke off in my hands. I wanted to throw my fist into the window, but I forced myself to slow down and think.

A door slammed nearby. Then another, louder. I had no time to decide. I could only act. I grabbed a book off the desk and smashed it into the window, sending a cascade of glass to the ground below. I scraped the book along the lower edge of the window to break off the rest of the jagged shards.

Someone shouted right outside the door.

I climbed onto the windowsill, my breath catching in my throat. The distance to the ground was farther than I'd expected.

The doorknob rattled. Then came furious pounding that shook the whole room.

I dropped my legs off the ledge and gripped the sill, slivers of glass digging into my palms. The door crashed open behind me. I didn't look back.

My only choice was to let go and fall into the open air.

CHAPTER
TWELVE

My feet slammed into the ground and I fell flat onto my back, gritting my teeth to keep from screaming in pain. I sat up, surprised to see that the book I used to break the glass had fallen to the gravel beside me.

Guards leaned out the window, shouting to others below. Dark figures swooped in on me from both sides.

I reached for the book, then leaped to my feet, wincing as the pain in my left heel paralyzed me. I tried to run, but all I could manage was to limp toward the outer gates, trying to withstand the pain shooting through my foot.

The fence loomed ahead. I was almost there.

But as I came to it, I ran straight into the arms of a Law Enforcer.

He caught me by one arm and I smashed the book into his head. He grunted, then spun me around and grabbed my other arm, pulling them both tight behind me until my shoulders burned. Then he jerked the book from my grasp. I struggled and kicked, but he deflected my blows as if he knew exactly what I'd do next.

"Stop fighting me or I'll hand you over to the real guards," he hissed.

I froze out of shock rather than trust. The darkness had hidden his face, but nothing could disguise Cael's irritated voice.

The guards still ran toward us.

"I have her, men! There's no need to exert yourselves," said Cael.

They slowed and stopped several feet away.

He forced my head down until my neck felt like it would break, then led me away, scolding me loudly enough for all the guards to hear. I was sure he was enjoying every moment of it.

He shoved me toward a gate. "Open up!" he ordered the guards on the outside. "This trespasser will be behind bars tonight."

The anger and authority in his command almost convinced me he meant it, though I knew better. I wasn't stupid enough to think he cared about me, but he'd lose his promised reward if I ended up in prison.

The gate opened without delay and Cael pushed me forward into the street. I had nowhere to look but the ground as I limped along with my arms twisted hard behind my back.

Cael kept up the appearance until we were well away from Academy Square. He didn't release my hands until he led me into a dark alleyway.

I turned to face him, rubbing my neck and shoulders. "Did you have to be so rough?"

"What was the point of *that*?" he hissed.

Heat filled my chest, and I hoped it wouldn't make its way to my face. "I don't know! I wasn't thinking—"

"Then that's your problem right there," he said.

I crossed my arms and turned away from his insufferable frown, but he was right. That was what made me so ashamed. I had put my plan and the people I cared for in jeopardy. All for reasons I couldn't understand.

He grabbed my shoulder. "Are you taking this seriously? Or are you just some entitled—"

"Please! I would've preferred jail." I wrenched away from his grip and took a step, but pain stabbed through my foot. My sharp inhale gave me away before I could hide it.

"I'll keep that in mind next time," said Cael. "And if there is a next time, I'll tell your father to get a new man for the job."

"You'd give up your reward that easily?" I asked.

"I was referring to *your* job."

I rolled my eyes. "If only. I wouldn't be doing this myself if there were anyone else I trusted. But there's not, is there?" I didn't even trust Cael, but dragging more people into this conspiracy wasn't an option. So here we were. Stuck with each other.

"Here." He pulled the stolen book from his belt and tossed it to me. "Keep your prize. I don't want this thing."

I stared at it for a moment before tucking it into my bag. I didn't want him to know I hadn't intended to steal it. It would only make me look more incompetent. I turned and stepped away, more delicately this time. Just then, bells rang throughout the city. I closed my eyes and counted the tolls. Nine. The gates to Quarter C would lock in an hour.

I didn't stand a chance.

With my injured heel, I couldn't possibly run—or even walk at a normal speed. Getting caught in the streets after curfew would take me to the very place I'd just managed to avoid. Citizens and carriages still passed by at the end of the alleyway, but they'd become far less frequent than before.

"Time to find somewhere to hide for the night," said Cael.

I bristled at the satisfaction in his voice. With his uniform, he wouldn't have to worry about being out after curfew. "Or you could use your costume to get me a carriage."

"Won't work. If we get caught, we'll both go to jail."

I left the alleyway and started down the main street, with no idea of where to go. I couldn't focus on anything but the throbbing in my heel.

A carriage came barreling down the road.

I jumped to the side, barely getting out of the way in time. Bolts of pain shot through my foot and I lost my balance and fell. The wheels flicked off a stream of muddy water, splashing my hair and clothes when they'd just begun to dry.

A nobleman stepped around me, disdain on his face as he passed by without a word.

I braced myself for the pain and managed to stand as another horse-drawn carriage lumbered toward me.

The nobleman lifted his arm to wave it down. The horses halted and the man showed his rank card to the driver before climbing inside. I shook my head and sighed, wishing I'd forged myself a high enough rank card to hire a carriage.

The horses' hooves clicked rhythmically on the cobblestones as they trotted away. Just before the carriage disappeared, my eye caught the platform on the back where a footman would stand.

My breath quickened and I turned around, a new excitement kicking in. There would be more carriages. And though none of the passengers would be going to Quarter C, the drivers might. Wherever it took me, it was guaranteed to be farther from the Academy and its Enforcers.

It was worth a try.

Cael stopped a few feet away, watching with a raised eyebrow.

The clatter of more hooves alerted me to my next chance. I stepped to the right side of the street, as close as I could get without being trampled. The carriage wasn't stopping, but I crouched, getting ready to spring.

Just as it passed, I grabbed hold of the footman's handle and jumped, my feet landing on the edge of the platform. The carriage bounced under my weight and I tried to ignore the shock that coursed through my feet and into my bones.

"What in Irvine's name was that?" a woman's frightened voice asked from inside.

I ducked low behind the back and held on tight.

"Just a missing cobblestone," called the driver. "Do not fear, milady. I'll have you home in no time."

I gripped the handle with one hand and waved goodbye to Cael with the other.

The buildings and streets passed by in shadow as the carriage took me downhill. I couldn't tell where it was headed. I hung on with both hands and tried to keep the weight off my heel, but each bump and turn made it impossible. The Lenoxes would worry themselves to death if I didn't come home tonight. Maybe I should've had Cael tell them. But it was too late now.

The carriage turned onto a wide road before veering toward another street on the right. It came to an abrupt stop at a pair of gates that led to nice-looking homes that looked like they belonged in Quarter B.

The platform shifted as the woman climbed out.

"Welcome back, milady," said a voice.

I peered around the carriage. Two guards stood at the gates and the street was bright with lamplight. If I stayed on the platform, they'd see me the moment the horses started moving. Waiting to go where the driver went next was too risky.

I stepped down to the ground carefully to keep the carriage

from bouncing. The south side of the street was bordered by the fence that surrounded the Quarter B homes. The north side was a row of connected buildings without any alleyways or a good place to hide.

The quarter's gates creaked open at the same time the horses' hooves began to click on the cobblestones.

The end of the street wasn't far. I hurried toward it as fast as my heel would allow. Quarter D was on the other side of this wide avenue. I paused, considering heading that way. My rank card could normally get me in, but not this close to curfew.

"You!" a voice behind me yelled.

I froze, afraid that all my stupid decisions had come down to this moment.

"The curfew is in ten minutes. Return to your quarter immediately!"

I nodded and limped away, turning right when I reached the corner of the street. The city wall and its enormous gates loomed ahead. The fence to Quarter D was on my left, on the other side of the nearly deserted avenue. Only Enforcers and the occasional passerby lingered.

There was nowhere to go in time.

A few Enforcers headed down the street in my direction, so I took a chance and hurried toward the wall, staying in the shadows. I was beginning to grow numb to the pain in my foot when the city bells tolled.

Ten. My time was up.

I took a corner to my right and leaned into a fence. My heart pounded in my chest, trapped between my ribs and the bars. On the opposite side of the street was another fence.

In the shadows behind it stood the abandoned First House.

A smile lifted the corners of my mouth. I peered down the lamp-lit street, searching for the guards that prowled this area. It was the Avenue of the Immovables, the street that curved around the border of the city in one gigantic circle. Nestled between the avenue and the city wall were the eleven Immovable mansions and their grounds. Each had its own set of guards at the gates.

Except for this one.

I crept closer. The deserted house rose up in the center of the grounds, dark and forbidding, behind a rusted iron fence overtaken by vines. Farther up ahead were the gates, wrapped in a heavy chain and padlock.

I lifted the bag higher on my shoulder and gripped the bars. The rusted iron was rough on my hands as I pulled myself up. I held onto the spear-like finials at the top and stepped onto the rail, which shook and creaked under my weight.

Raised voices and the patter of feet echoed down the street in response to the noise I'd made.

Not again. Please, not again.

A tangled hedge filled the space between the fence and the overgrown lawn, giving me no option but to jump. Again. My feet ached in apprehension. I was at least ten feet up, and it would be impossible to land without bringing back all of tonight's pain.

". . . you hear that?" a distant voice called.

I took a breath and leaped. As I cleared the hedge, the strap from my bag was ripped from my shoulder. My feet hit the ground and I collapsed, groaning as I clutched my heel through my boot.

Voices came from the other side of the fence. I hadn't been quiet enough.

I got to my knees, frantically searching the damp ground for my bag. When I didn't see it, I peered upward. There it was, hanging high above me on an iron finial, separated from me by a seven-foot-tall prickly hedge.

I swore just to keep from crying.

If I didn't have my knives in there, I could've left it. But no, my book was there too. And the book I'd stolen. Every single thing in there would send all the Enforcers in Cambria into these grounds to capture the criminal who dared to break so many laws.

I had to get it.

I reached into the hedge, but the brambles caught my sleeves and hands, piercing and scratching my skin.

I backed away, furious with the stupid bag at the top of the fence. My foot hit something, and I tripped and fell for what seemed like the hundredth time that night. My hands landed on a broken branch. I picked it up and climbed onto shaky feet.

I stepped back to the hedge and reached the branch up. It wasn't quite long enough, so I pushed against the brambles, the twigs snapping with the pressure as thorns tore into my skin.

There.

The branch caught the strap and I lifted it up over the finial. Twigs crunched under my weight as I pushed into the thorny hedge, so loud in the night that they seemed to echo off the nearby stone wall. I pulled the bag to me just as Enforcers' boots slapped against the cobblestones on the other side.

"I don't see anyone," a man said.

"That's because it's dark, idiot," said a woman.

"What should we do?"

"*You* should search the grounds," the woman replied.

"Me? How? I don't have the key."

"Then find another way in."

I hurried deeper into the grounds, weaving between trees and bushes. My surroundings darkened to black as the lamplight from the street faded, but desperation enhanced my senses and my ears caught every rustle.

I made it to the side of the mansion, searching for a way in, but boards covered all the doors and windows. I went around the back, but it was the same. Every entry was blocked.

The rattle of gates traveled through the dark to my ears.

Time ticked by without mercy.

I looked back at the boarded-up house and took a knife from my bag. Wedging it between one of the wide boards and a door frame, I carefully pried, popping a nail out into my hand. With the first nail gone, I moved on to the second.

Twigs broke somewhere on the grounds, accompanied by the sound of footfalls on the grass.

I hurried to the third nail, prying it out slowly to keep the rotted wood from breaking. One nail was all that remained. With the rest of the board now loose, I pivoted it down to reveal a doorknob.

The glow of torchlight shone on the ground beside me.

I checked the knob. Locked.

But there *was* a tiny gap beside the knob where the door met the frame. I slid my knife into it. A click later, the latch released.

The footsteps came closer. I pushed the door inward and dropped my bag inside before diving headfirst between the boards. At the last second, I reached for the loose board and lifted it over the empty space.

"Hello?" a man's voice called from the other side of the door.

I shut my mouth, cutting off my ragged breathing.

His torch shone brightly through the cracks, so close that its heat warmed my face.

I still held the board, begging my shaking hand not to reveal my hiding place. The torchlight lingered until I couldn't hold my breath anymore, but eventually, the orange glow shifted away and left me alone in the dark.

CHAPTER

THIRTEEN

I OPENED MY EYES, BLINKING AWAY A HUNDRED nightmares only to remember I was still in one. The ghostly shapes of furniture draped in white cloth greeted me. I sat up on a sofa with a chipped gilded frame and pushed off a dusty grayed sheet.

The room lay in shadow, but a bit of light streamed in from between the boards that covered the windows. Each faint ray of sunlight was alive with dancing specks of dust. I stretched my aching body and lowered my feet to the faded rug on the floor, wincing when I put weight on my heel, but the pain had diminished compared to the night before.

A life-sized portrait of a crowned woman hung on the wall above an empty hearth. The dignified eyes of Imperatrix Lena Irvine gazed back through crackled paint. She had ruled for forty long years, but since she had no children, the title moved on to the Second House and the surviving members of her family lost their rank. It didn't matter now that their ancestor had been the founder and first king of Cambria. Immovable was as empty a promise as Immortal.

I reached down and retrieved my bag from where I'd dropped it the night before. The heavier weight reminded me of the stolen book inside. I pulled it out, intending to leave it here, abandoned like the house itself, but curiosity overtook me.

It had no title. I flipped it open. Handwritten pages alternated between drawings and text, but the drawings, in particular, caught my eye. Most of them seemed to be strange machines and tools I'd never seen before. I wasn't sure if they were fictional or something from the distant past. I flipped back to the first page. A circular seal was stamped there, above some text:

Property of the Cambrian Academy

This reference is intended only for the use of the Immortals of the Cambrian Academy. Any use outside the Academy is prohibited and the perpetrator will be punished for treason.

For the first time in too long, my spirits lifted. Maybe my break-in hadn't been completely pointless. I turned the page, eager to see what I'd discovered, when a crash broke the silence.

I dropped the book and scrambled to my feet to find a place to hide.

A muffled voice called through the door. "Time to wake up."

"Cael? You followed me?"

"That's my job, isn't it?"

I opened the door and moved the loose board. "Any word from my father?"

He leaned over and peered through the gap. "You fit through that?"

"You know," I said, "no matter how much time I spend without you, it's never enough. Have you gotten a message or not?"

"Look," he said, pushing a newspaper between the boards and into my hands.

I unrolled the paper slowly, terrified to see it. The upper half of the Cambrian Tribune's front page was a transcript of Imperatrix Brennin's address. My eyes traveled down, and I caught the second headline: *Break-in at the Academy.*

But it was the picture that made my stomach drop. I stared unblinking at the detailed sketch of a girl wearing a raincoat, a simple dress, and a bag across her shoulder. A hood covered most of the face, but a braid hung out of one side.

I'd become the most wanted criminal in the city.

"Shouldn't have been an idiot," said Cael.

I wouldn't admit just how much I agreed with him.

I searched the article, desperate to discover how much they knew. It mentioned *assault, stolen property, considerable damage, a threat to Cambria,* and *on the loose.* I wondered how one broken window could be called "considerable damage" or how assault had come into the picture. I *had* hit Cael with the book, but I didn't think anyone had seen that.

I looked back at the drawing. Even if it didn't show my face, my clothing would be enough to give me away. Graham would recognize me the moment he opened the paper.

"I need to find some clothes," I said, more to myself than to Cael, who still waited on the other side of the boards.

"You need to get out of here," he said.

I had to do both. I turned and left the room, hoping to find something wearable in this place.

WHEN I GOT BACK TO THE SITTING ROOM, CAEL WAS lounging on a threadbare sofa.

He held the Academy's book in his hand. "This looks interesting, I admit, but hardly worth it."

I pulled it out of his grasp and put it back where it belonged —with me. The promise of forbidden information was too tempting.

He appraised my new twenty-year-old faded brown dress. "I thought you'd find something nicer than a sack in a queen's house."

"The upstairs closets were completely stripped. But I'd rather wear servant's clothing than an outdated frilly gown anyway."

"And your bag?" he asked.

I began pulling my hair into a bun. "I'll cover it up. No one will notice." I was okay with leaving my raincoat and other clothing behind, but my bag, and especially its contents, had to stay with me. Besides, I hadn't found any other options in this house.

"Still overconfident," said Cael.

I picked up my bag and draped it with a scrap of fabric I'd found. "Always."

I climbed between the boards, Cael squeezing through after me. The early morning was cool and quiet. It was Sunday, so the streets would soon be filled with citizens on their way to church to listen to hours of poetry. The library wouldn't be open, but then again, I couldn't go back there anyway.

I headed toward the back of the grounds, my boots wet with

dew from the overgrown grass. I stopped at the corner where the end of the iron fence met the soaring stone wall and separated the grounds from the street.

Cael left me on my own and went the other way, to the front gates. I wished I could get my hands on a uniform of my own. If I had the humility—and if I thought it would work—I would've asked Cael to steal another for me.

I craned my neck and looked up the wall, my eyes barely able to find the top. Fortunately, I wouldn't have to climb the entire thing—not today, anyway. I only needed to get up high enough to clear the brambles and the fence. If I'd had the chance to run to this point last night, I would've been able to save myself from the battle of a thousand thorns.

I gripped a knife in each hand and began to climb, wedging my blades between the stones.

THE WALK ACROSS THE CITY TOOK MUCH LONGER THAN IT should have. My heel, though improved, kept me from my normal pace. My empty stomach and lack of energy slowed me down even further. I tried to avoid the main avenues and Law Enforcers as much as possible, which meant I ended up winding through dozens of small back streets and alleyways on my way back to the Lenoxes' house.

Was it safe to go back? I asked myself for the tenth time. Or would I endanger the Lenoxes? I knew they'd be sick with worry if I didn't return to tell them I was okay. And my job wasn't done here. In the end, I decided to go, but I'd be careful.

I went to a different set of gates this time. The usual Quarter C guard could've recognized me and connected me to the drawing in the paper, though I suspected she'd hardly paid any attention to me at all. At the entry, I took out my rank card, holding my breath when the guard looked it over. Thankfully, he handed it back without a word.

My hesitation grew as I walked through the quarter, making my way to the Lenoxes' street by a different route. At their door, my shaky hand hovered above the knob. Going in could endanger them. I couldn't deny it. I never should have involved them in my plan.

The door swung open. "You're back!" Etna beamed. "Marcus, she's back! Come in, quickly." She grabbed my wrist and pulled me in before I could argue.

Etna shut the door and locked it behind me.

I collapsed on the bottom stair.

"Are you hurt?" Marcus asked.

I buried my hands in my hair and shook my head. "I'm so sorry I've put you in danger."

"We were terrified when we saw the news," said Etna, "but not for our own sake. What made you go inside the Academy? And what will you do if the queen gets her way?"

I shook my head again. How could I possibly explain when I didn't know the answers?

Etna sat beside me on the steps and put her arm around my shoulder. "We can talk about it later, my sweet girl. For now, come eat dinner."

CHAPTER

FOURTEEN

I AWOKE EARLY THE NEXT DAY AND PUT ON THE SAME musty dress as the day before, then twisted my hair and pinned it up on the back of my head. My heel felt almost normal. I didn't expect it to slow me down anymore.

"You look lovely," said Etna when I came down for breakfast. "That dress matches your eyes."

I looked down at the old-fashioned cut and dull brown of my dress. "Uh, thanks."

"Although . . . I hope it doesn't hurt your feelings if I say I miss the way you used to look."

"Not at all. I kind of do, too." I smiled and picked up one of Etna's biscuits and a bowl of seaweed soup.

"Has your father ever told you about the first time we met?" asked Marcus.

"I don't think so." I knew he was trying to cheer me up, so I was happy to let him.

"Our son had been hiding Orrin in the house for a week without us noticing. Then one day, we walked in and found him raiding the cupboards. We were about to turn him in. We thought Orrin was some kind of savage," he said.

I laughed. "Well, he was."

"I suppose so. But he grew on us once we realized what a good friend he was to our son."

"It takes time to see his virtues," I said, "but they do exist."

"Of course, dear," said Etna. "We just mean that he had different manners and such, being raised on Tramore."

"I'm glad he met you. And your son," I said. If he hadn't, he wouldn't have married my mother.

"I'm sure your father talks about him all the time," said Marcus.

"Yeah," I said, "all the time." But the truth was, my father almost never mentioned his old best friend. It was the same with my mother. He hated to relive his past pain, but I knew he still did, every day, whether he talked about it or not.

"Well," said Marcus, planting a kiss on Etna's cheek before standing up from the table. "I have to go. My team's behind schedule on the new testing center." He picked up his hat and left the room.

"Another testing center, really?" I asked. "Crazy Academy."

"I hope you don't talk like that in public, dear," said Etna, "especially *now*."

My face reddened. For the most part, Marcus and Etna had dropped any discussion of my blunder, but it was obviously as much on their minds as it was mine.

"I better go too," I said. "And don't worry. I've got it under control."

We said goodbye and I went out the front door, about to take the stairs into the street.

It didn't take long to realize something was off.

I stopped in my tracks. A crowd gathered near the gates up

ahead. And instead of the usual guard, the street swam with Enforcers. One by one, the citizens presented their cards before leaving the quarter.

I darted back inside and shut the door behind me, my hands trembling on the doorknob. They'd never made us show our cards to get *out* of the quarter before. There was only one explanation—they knew I was here.

"Is everything okay?" Etna asked from the kitchen as if she could sense my fear even with a wall between us.

"Yes, Grandma." I hoped she wouldn't notice the tremble in my voice. "I just forgot something."

It was only a matter of time before the entire quarter would be searched. I'd have to make a run for it somehow, before they found me here. Before I could decide what to do, Marcus came back inside through the front door, bolting it behind him.

"It looks like you're stuck," he said.

"What?" asked Etna, joining us at the bottom of the stairs.

"They've started searching the quarter. Someone must've recognized the sketch."

Someone like Graham. My heart sank as I reached for the door. "I have to leave."

Marcus moved to block it.

Etna stepped forward and touched my arm. "You can't."

I buried my face in my hands. "I can't stay! What if they search your home?"

"We'll take our chances," said Etna.

I shook my head. I wouldn't let them hide me.

Someone banged on the front door.

"Go upstairs," Marcus whispered.

I was about to run to the back of the house and escape when Cael spoke from the other side of the door. "Me again."

Marcus and Etna opened it.

Cael stepped in and shut the door. "Judging by the look on

your face, you've figured out what's going on. Looks like the librarian reported you."

Mrs. Whitting. *Of course.* Not Graham. I almost smiled.

"There's more," he continued. "They're starting to say your break-in was an assassination attempt."

"What?" I shook my head in denial. As my brain searched for a solution, my gaze landed on Cael's clothing. "Give me your uniform."

"Excuse me?"

"I need to get out of here."

He shook his head fiercely. "No. I can't afford that."

"*You* can't afford that?"

"The other Enforcers know me by now. They'll notice if I'm suddenly not wearing it, trust me."

"But I have to find Graham. He has to know I'm not an assassin. I have to—"

"The game's up," said Cael. "Haven't you realized? He won't trust you anymore."

I squeezed my eyes shut. He was probably right, but part of me doubted him. I had to see for myself.

"Even your father agrees," Cael said, pulling a torn envelope from his pocket.

I ripped it from his hands and opened the letter, my eyes landing on the untidy scrawl.

I wish I could tell you what you want to hear, but I'm afraid your mission has come to an end. The Immortals are sure to vote for the queen's proposal, and your Academy incident has compromised your safety. Forget about the war. Come home. You'll get your chance another day.

AND JUST LIKE THAT, MY HOPE WAS GONE. IF I WENT BACK home, war was inevitable. My thoughts landed on Graham. He would be one of the first targets in the attack, not to mention all the other lives at risk. I would *not* be forgetting about the war.

Marcus took the letter from my hand, reading it over. "We need to get you home," he said. "That's our priority now."

"But how?" I asked, too spiritless to fight.

Etna spoke up softly, her voice hesitant. "I might know a way."

"What?" Cael and I asked at the same time.

She cleared her throat. "Well, Orrin used to take the aqueducts."

I frowned. "He did?"

My father had never talked about that. According to what I knew about the city, the aqueducts had underground grates at the perimeters of every quarter.

"He and our son removed a few grates from the tunnels," said Etna. "Although, that *was* over twenty years ago."

"Show me where to go," I said.

"Not so fast," said Marcus. "They carry rainwater downhill from the center of the city. If the grate has been replaced, there might be no way to get back up."

"I'm a good climber," I said.

"I don't know," said Etna. "Perhaps I shouldn't have suggested it."

"Please," I said. "I have to get out of here."

She and Marcus looked at each other sadly.

"Fine," said Marcus.

I followed them through the kitchen and out the back door. There, by the fence that separated their porch from the one next door, was a square grate set into the ground. I stepped closer and heard the sound of flowing water. With all the recent rain, it would be deep.

I opened my bag and took out the rank card. It served no purpose except to give me away at this point, so I dropped it between the bars of the grate, letting the water bury it. Then I took out the books, wanting to keep them safe, and handed them to Cael. "Take these."

He tucked the books under his coat, shaking his head. "The two most incriminating books in the city. They'll think *I'm* the Academy assassin."

"The *assassin*." I clenched my fists, looking down at the grate. "Who do they think I was trying to kill anyway?"

"Who knows?" said Cael. "The First Immortal. The queen. The heir. All of them were at the Academy that night."

I looked up, an idea brewing in my mind. "The heir."

If I survived the aqueducts, I might have one last chance to make my plan work—as long as Graham believed I wasn't trying to kill him, of course.

I faced Cael. "I'm not going home. Send a message to my father. Tell him we can feed the rumors. Do whatever it takes to make them think the queen hired Bryn Yarrow to kill her son." I felt a smile creep back onto my face. "She'll lose a few votes, don't you think?"

He didn't look impressed. "There's no point. Like I said, Brennin won't trust you."

I crossed my arms and lowered my voice. "Send the message. Now. Or I swear you will lose your reward."

He glared back but didn't protest.

I lifted the grate and peered down at the rushing water.

"I know it's not my place to tell you what to do," said Etna, "but I do wish you'd listen to your father."

Marcus nodded fervently.

I hugged them both. "Thank you, but I won't give up."

They looked at me with sadness etched into the lines of their faces.

"Then be safe, dear," said Etna.

I dropped my feet through the opening. "I will." I gripped the rim and lowered myself into the water. The cold shocked my skin, but I didn't let it show.

"Get moving, Cael," I called through the opening. "I'm going to the library." Once my father got that message, he might finally see what I was capable of. *If I survive.*

I held my breath and let go, falling into the swirling darkness.

CHAPTER

FIFTEEN

THE WATER SWEPT ME THROUGH THE SLIPPERY TUNNELS. Now I understood what Marcus meant when he said I'd only be able to go downhill.

A sharp drop sent my stomach to my throat. Occasional grates in the ceiling offered a glimpse of sunlight, but it was gone in a flash. I had no way of knowing when I passed the boundaries of the quarter, and I was going too fast to stop. I'd just have to hope I could survive what my father had twenty years ago.

I was sure I'd gone too far when the tunnel plummeted downward. Just as the ground leveled out, I slammed into something hard. The water flowed over my head and into my lungs. My hands gripped for a hold, landing on rusted metal bars. I pulled myself up to standing, but the water rushed against my legs, threatening to knock me back under the torrent. I held on, coughing and gasping for air. Dim sunlight shone through a ceiling grate like the one I'd entered, but it was on the other side of the bars.

Clearly, things had changed in the past twenty years.

I shivered in the waist-high flow. The bars of the grate were vertical, wide enough for most debris to get through but too narrow for me. I looked back up the tunnel, but it was close to a sheer drop and the walls were slick with algae.

I groped under the water and all around the bars, searching for something useful. My hands landed on a pile of rocks. I picked up the largest one, hoping I could use it to loosen the bars.

When I pulled it into the light, I screamed.

It wasn't a rock. It was a skull.

I gasped and dropped it, my lungs tightening until I could hardly pull in a breath. Someone had died here, who knows how long ago.

The same thing would happen to me.

I tried to rein in my panic before my world closed in.

Think.

My back rested against the bars. I closed my eyes and tried to pretend the sound of water was nothing but waves in the ocean, but the dank mildew was nothing like the salty sea breeze.

My bag tugged against my shoulder, dragged by the rushing flow. Although the sharkskin was waterproof, my fall under the water had filled it and soaked my belongings. All I had were a few slippery knives and the bag itself.

But that was something.

I took out a knife and set to work, wrapping my bag's sturdy strap several times around two of the rusty bars. With shivering hands, I twisted it and pulled hard, but the bars held strong.

I took out a knife and wedged the handle into the twisted strap. But that gave me nothing to hold but the blade. I thought of my father, blaming him for insisting that I keep them so well sharpened. I threw the knife back into the bag. It wouldn't do any good.

My feet shifted, rolling over something in the water. I backed into the tunnel wall, shuddering. I couldn't pretend they were rocks when I knew otherwise. All I could think of was the person who'd gotten trapped here and died a terrible and lonely death.

Wait.

Bones. Before I could change my mind, I crouched down and reached into the water. My hand searched the debris on the floor of the tunnel. I tried not to think about what I touched. I had to be strong if I didn't want to end up as a pile of bones while a war above ground destroyed everyone I cared about.

My fingers wrapped around something long and thin. I pulled it out of its place where it was trapped against the bars. It was white and as long as my thigh. I twisted the bone into the strap and began to rotate it. The bars started to creak and bend.

A laugh escaped my throat until I remembered I was holding someone's femur.

I twisted the bone harder and harder, squeezing the bars together with each turn. When they wouldn't go any farther, I unwrapped the strap and moved it to the next pair of bars. I strained and twisted as the rush of water tried to sweep my legs out from under me. My arms grew weak and my hands slipped, but I wouldn't give up. Only a little bit more.

The strap tightened, compressing the bars inward. Water swirled through the wide opening. It could be enough.

Before dropping the bone, I whispered a thank you to the poor dead soul who saved my life so I didn't have to suffer the same fate. I unwrapped the strap of the bag and put it over my head and shoulder. Then I squeezed between the narrow bars.

The grate in the ceiling was only a few steps away. The ground of the tunnel leveled out, but the water still flowed with enough strength to sweep me downward. I held tight to the bars with one hand and reached up with the other. One finger managed to wrap around the ceiling grate and I lunged for it with both hands, gripping tight.

I shoved the grate up and slid it out of place. The cloudy sky above was calm as an ordinary day. I braced my boots against the tunnel and lifted myself out of the deadly aqueduct.

I gasped and dropped to my knees, trying to still my trembling body. The grate had led me to the quiet Avenue of the Immovables, near the noble mansions on the east side of the city. I ducked as a carriage drove past on the opposite end of the wide street. Then I returned the grate to its place and hurried uphill before anyone noticed the soaking wet girl who'd just materialized out of the ground.

My clothes had dried by the time I stopped at the edge of a brick-lined alleyway near the Irvine library. My fabric scrap had been washed away in the aqueduct, so my bag was on display, making me feel particularly vulnerable. I rested a hand over it, trying to cover the one thing that tied me to the sketch. My hair and clothing were different enough, but I had no idea how much Mrs. Whitting had told them.

With her as the whistleblower, Law Enforcers would be searching for me around here, too. But, if Graham was a man of his word, he'd be returning to study today—unless his mother forbade him, which was perfectly likely. I truly had no idea if he'd be here or if I'd be able to get to him, but I was willing to try just about anything.

If I didn't, I'd be at a dead end.

I stayed in the alley and peeked around a corner.

A couple dozen men and women crowded the library steps, their voices talking over the other. An Enforcer went through the doors and another came out. Who knew how many were in there hoping I'd make an appearance?

I could do nothing but wait in the alley, watching while citizens passed, the sun moving higher in the cloudy sky. I sat on the ground, trying to think up some other plan. Eventually, the clicking of hooves and the creak of a carriage made my ears perk up. I jumped to my feet again and checked around the corner.

A black carriage stopped down the street, a good distance from the library. After a moment, the door swung open. A man stepped out, dressed in commoner's clothing and holding a book under his arm. A pair of guards followed.

A weight lifted off my heart at the sight of that lonely figure. I smiled through my surprise until I realized Graham could be part of a ploy to draw me out from hiding.

But it didn't matter. I'd made up my mind.

He came closer, then slowed as the crowd on the steps quieted and turned toward him with hungry eyes. I noticed the notebooks and quills in their hands.

Journalists.

Of course. They'd come hoping to witness my capture and now they'd get a bonus: the disgraced heir of Cambria.

They rushed down the steps like a wave and enveloped Graham before he could take a step back. They swarmed in, pushing closer and closer. A flurry of questions assaulted him, and he disappeared from view. He must've still been trying to walk toward the library steps because the crowd shifted in that direction.

He reappeared, moving up the steps with his head down and an arm held out to keep the crowd at bay, but the journalists maintained their tight circle, following him up the stairs and into the library.

When the doors closed with a thud, I could only stare at

the forbidden building. I leaned against the rough wall beside me. It could be hours before Graham came back out, and when he did, he was sure to be surrounded.

I had to find a way to get to him.

I lifted my head and looked around the corner again. Graham's carriage remained where the coachman had parked it. I couldn't go into the library to get Graham out. There was no question about that.

But someone else could.

I smiled and got to my feet, a new energy lifting my hope. Cael hadn't come back yet, but I couldn't have stomached the idea of asking him for help anyway. Still, there was one other person on this street who didn't want to wait all day either.

I turned the corner and headed toward the carriage, my hands covering my bag. An Enforcer squinted at me from the bottom of the steps. My breath caught until his eyes moved lazily away.

The carriage was only a few paces down the street. It wasn't marked with the Brennin's insignia. I suspected Graham did not get his mother's permission to take the family carriage and had been forced to hire one for the day. I hadn't decided what to say yet, but I knew the coachman wouldn't believe me if I tried to tell him Graham was my friend.

I stopped and cleared my throat when I came to the side of the carriage. My overeager journalist act would have to be obnoxious enough to be convincing. "Excuse me, sir. Excuse me! An interview, please?"

The coachman leaned back in his seat and stammered out a reply. "What? With me? Are you sure you're speaking to the right person?"

"Well, an interview with his driver isn't *ideal* . . ."

The man's eyes widened. Graham had likely paid him not to reveal this information.

". . . but every other journalist in Cambria has Graham Brennin cornered inside the Irvine Library, so you're better than nothing," I said.

He tilted his head back and muttered to himself, "I shouldn't have agreed to this."

I stepped closer, grinning widely. "Thank you! So, my first question is—"

"No, no, *no*." The driver held up a hand. "I'm not saying anything, so don't waste your time."

"He must be paying you well, then," I said.

He shrugged.

"So, it could be better?"

"I didn't say that! Just leave me alone, will you?" He pulled on the reins impatiently and the horses stomped their hooves.

"Fine, I'll go." I turned around. "But if I were you, I'd do something to make Sir Brennin grateful." I pursed my lips. "Several cowries more grateful."

He furrowed his brow but was quiet.

I stepped over to his horses and stroked one on its velvety nose. "I hear the heir's a bit of a pushover. Without some help, he'll be in there all day. I hope you're prepared to wait that long to get paid."

"It's really none of your business."

"True. I'm simply telling you what I would do."

I moved my hand up to the horse's forelock, my fingers twisting through the coarse strands. Its ears angled back, and it yanked its head away. Apparently, even the animals in this city didn't care for me.

"Leave my horses alone." The man picked up the reins and clicked his tongue.

The horses jolted forward.

I backed away to avoid the hooves and wheels. The streets cleared for the carriage, revealing a familiar uniformed figure under the eaves. Cael looked back at me, his eyes carrying a hint of surprise. He was back sooner than expected. I wondered if he'd sent my message.

I kept up, following on the opposite side of the carriage from the library, and passing Cael on the way. He watched with a wary question on his face.

The horses stopped in front of the library and the driver climbed down from his seat. He rushed up the steps and through the doors.

I stepped up to the empty carriage, my pace casual but every nerve on the alert. The horses rotated their ears my way and whinnied as if they could tell I was up to something. I unlatched the carriage door and stepped inside, shutting it and drawing the thin curtains.

There was a door on each side. Between them, two bench seats faced each other. There wouldn't be much to hide behind when the door opened. I peered out a slit in the curtain and waited.

Within a minute or two, the library doors burst open and the driver rushed out with Graham close behind.

The journalists surrounded them, shouting and pushing to get closer to the heir.

The driver stood in their path, trying to hold them back while Graham made his escape down the steps.

I let go of the curtain and pulled my knees to my chest, pushing myself as far back into the seat as possible.

A few pounding heartbeats later, the door opened.

Graham stopped in the doorway, his eyes widening when he saw me.

"Please. Just get in and I'll explain," I said in a rush. I held my breath. This was the moment I'd find out what he thought of me.

"You?" The driver's ruddy face appeared behind Graham's. He pulled the door open all the way. "Get out of my carriage!"

I looked at Graham, my eyes pleading with the words I couldn't say.

"Move, you common girl!" the driver shouted.

"Let her stay," said Graham. "Let's go."

I smiled, relieved that I hadn't lost his trust. Somehow.

"She obviously doesn't have the rank to—"

"Do as I say," said Graham, forcing authority into his voice, "and I'll pay you double."

The smile slipped from my lips when my gaze landed between Graham and the driver and I met eyes with Mrs. Whitting. She glared fiercely from the top of the steps, her chin lifting in satisfaction. Then she nodded to someone out of my view and pointed at the carriage. At me.

Graham climbed in, taking a seat on the bench across from me. "Take us away from here. Fast."

The driver nodded curtly and slammed the door. Seconds later, the carriage jerked forward. Angry shouts followed as we drove away, but they fell behind us as the driver brought the horses to a trot.

Graham sighed and sank into his seat. "Thank you."

I looked at him curiously, wondering why he hadn't brought up my crimes. He couldn't be *that* polite.

"Did you happen to, uh, read the papers today?" I asked. "Or yesterday?"

He raised an eyebrow. "Let me guess. They're all talking about how useless I am, aren't they?"

I stared at him in disbelief. "So, you haven't been following the news?"

He shook his head. "Why would I? I was there for my mother's dreadful speech. I'm not interested in reading about it."

"And has she said . . . anything?"

"She told me I couldn't leave the house and that the city's not safe right now, but otherwise, I've been keeping my distance. She's particularly paranoid at the moment, which makes her especially controlling."

I nodded, glad I wouldn't have to deal with his questions— yet. But my trouble was far from over. Mrs. Whitting had most likely sent every Enforcer at the library after me. I gripped the side of the carriage as we took a sharp turn.

"We need to get out," I said.

"What do you mean?" asked Graham. "We just got in."

"We're being followed."

"Are you sure?"

In reply, I pulled on a cord that hung from the ceiling. A bell jingled and the carriage came to an abrupt halt. I moved the curtain aside. We had stopped in front of a church with a tall steeple and a laurel wreath engraved above the doors. The street was just busy enough for me to have a shot at blending in.

"Pay the driver and meet me inside." I opened the door and jumped out, making my way toward the church.

When I reached the black arched doors, I turned an aged brass knob and pushed them open, slipping into a deserted chapel. Soft light floated through faded stained-glass windows, casting a misty glow on the empty pews. A portrait of Kendrick Irvine hung in front of a row of altars. The eerie silence fell heavily on my ears, but the stone floor hummed with a faint vibration from the rushing world outside.

I stepped into the aisle hesitantly, feeling more like an intruder than ever.

CHAPTER
SIXTEEN

A WARM HAND TOUCHED MY SHOULDER AND I PULLED back. I hadn't noticed Graham enter the church.

"Sorry." He pulled his hand back to his side. "I'm indebted to you. I don't know how to express it."

He wouldn't have been grateful had he known my true motives, but I could almost fool myself into believing I did it for him. Now that the fear from minutes ago seemed so far away, my mood began to lift.

"Don't thank me yet," I said. "Now you're stuck hiding out with me until those parasites find something else to do."

He smiled fully, revealing the elusive dimple on his cheek. "That doesn't sound so terrible."

I glanced over my shoulder. "Let's find somewhere we—you—can be safe."

"This chapel seems quite safe," he said. "I don't think journalists will be bold enough to charge through its doors."

"Let's not take our chances."

"I'd rather not go back outside just yet," he said.

"I'm not suggesting we go out. Let's go up."

"Up?" he asked, his eyebrows furrowing.

I pointed to the opposite end of the chapel. An inconspicuous door was set in the wall beside the tall brass pipes of an organ that rose to the vaulted ceiling. "To the belfry."

"Are you sure?" Graham whispered. "The chapel seems fine to me."

"Then stay. But I'm going."

He reluctantly followed me past the pews and through the door. The tall narrow space was empty except for a spiral staircase. I started up it.

The iron steps creaked and shuddered as I climbed. I glanced down to see Graham holding tightly to the railing, his knuckles whitening as he slowly made his way up. Eventually, we emerged onto a circular platform. A rope hung in the center of the steeple and a wooden ladder rested against the stone wall, leading to another platform above. I grasped a rung and pulled myself up.

"I'm not climbing that flimsy thing," said Graham, his face as pale as his hands.

I continued up the ladder. "What? Don't tell me you're afraid of heights."

He bit his lip.

"You'll have to get over that if you intend to spend much time with me."

"Can't we stay down here?" he asked in a quiet voice. "It's secluded enough."

"See that rope? If someone comes to ring the bell, we'll lose our hiding place."

I reached the top of the ladder and pulled myself onto the upper platform. A bell hung from the ceiling, green with patina and bigger than my head. Two windows were set into the stone. From up here, nothing obstructed the view all the way to the city wall, even with hundreds of rooftops in between.

I looked down through the hole in the platform. Graham was only halfway up the ladder. He climbed with his teeth clenched and his jaw tight. When he got to the top, I offered my hand. He took it and stepped onto the platform, breathing a pinched sigh.

We sat down and leaned against the cool curved walls, quiet other than our breathing. I wished it could stay that way —peaceful, quiet, without lies. I longed for honest, unrestrained conversation instead of these calculated ones. What would I give to have nothing to hide?

Graham stared at the city through the arched window. His gaze pointed toward the distant Brennin House. If we weren't so far away, we'd see the white flag waving on its roof, emblazoned with a blue horse.

"Maybe it's better if I don't become king," he said, breaking the silence.

"I wouldn't want all that attention either," I said.

"It's not just that." He paused and looked at me, his eyes reflecting the solemn gray of the sky, before looking back out the window. "My brother should have been in my place."

I fidgeted, suddenly unsure of what to do with my fingers. "I know. I'm sorry."

"Ewan would have done this so much better than I could." He sighed and clasped his hands over his knees.

"I'm sure you'd be better than your mother," I blurted out. "No offense."

He smiled, despite my disrespect. "I don't know. She's more capable than I am."

"Do you really believe that?"

"I don't know." He looked down and rested his hand on the rough wood platform. "Before reading your book, I believed my parents ruled Cambria with perfect wisdom and justice. Certainly, they had to make difficult decisions, but now I'm starting to wonder if banishing people is . . . cruel." He lowered his voice to a whisper as if he could barely handle hearing his own words. "And wrong."

I nodded, urging him on.

He swallowed. "No one can know I said that."

"It's fine," I said. "I agree completely."

He leaned into the wall behind him. "But then again, if the outlaws really are planning an attack, perhaps they *should* be feared."

I held my breath. What I said next could change the course of the future. "Look. Your father has banished more people in his reign than the Irvines did in the eighty years before him. Every time he creates an outlaw, he adds another soldier to their army. These people don't *want* violence. The king has ripped them from their homes and torn families apart. Can you blame them for wanting their lives back?"

"I don't know." Graham buried his face in his hands. "I don't know anything anymore."

"Graham—"

He looked up at me with surprise and I realized I'd called him by his first name. I was about to apologize, but by the look on his face, he didn't seem to mind. He leaned toward me, listening intently.

"Graham," I repeated, "there's a reason I'm telling you all this."

"Why? What could I do about it?"

"You could speak to them."

"To the outlaws?" Graham said, his tone flat. "How?"

"You've read my book. It tells you how to get there. How to sail. How to navigate. You have everything you need to get to them."

His brows furrowed and he shook his head. "I couldn't *go* anywhere. It feels treasonous to even consider."

"Why?"

"I have duties to fulfill. Countless expectations are resting on me—from my father, my mother, the citizens, my ancestors—"

"Your ancestors are dead," I said. "But your citizens are very much alive. What higher duty do you have than to protect them?"

Graham stared hard at me. "How do you know all this? If it's true, I'll have to tell—"

"No!" I sat up straight. "If you tell anyone, the Academy will gather every Enforcer in Cambria and wipe out the outlaws without even giving them a chance. But if you go—if you offer them an alliance—you'll save thousands of lives, you'll gain the gratitude of the citizens, and you'll have something your mother won't."

Graham pulled back, the shock clear on his face. "You think I should compete with my mother for the throne?"

"I think you should do what's right."

"I want to help. I truly do, but . . ." his voice trailed off into confused silence.

"Then do it."

"You think it's that simple? That I should just do what I *want*?"

I nodded firmly. "Yes."

He looked out the window, his gaze landing on the distant wall. "Even if I went, why would they listen to me? If they hate my family so much, they'd kill me."

"That's why you won't be alone."

He turned back to me. "You—"

A deafening ring from the bell above our heads cut off his words.

I slammed my hands over my ears, but it hardly made a difference. Graham did the same, gritting his teeth with every peal. Finally, after an unbearably long time, the bell came to a stop.

"Why did it have to be twelve?" Graham's voice came to me muffled and distorted.

"I should've waited an hour to rescue you." I rubbed my ears and braced myself against the start of a splitting headache.

His laugh echoed in my ringing ears.

"What soul doth dare invade this solemn church?" a deep voice called from below.

I held a finger to my lips. Graham covered his mouth, stifling the laugh, but it was too late.

"Come down! Descend at once and show your face!" the man shouted. We'd been caught by the Poet Laureate at the head of this chapel, judging by his fondness for iambic pentameter.

Graham pointed to himself, then down at the opening in the platform. I opened my mouth to argue, but I didn't trust myself to speak.

"I'll take this crime to the Academy!" the poet called.

"Meet me outside," Graham whispered in my ringing ear. Then he cautiously took hold of the ladder and went down.

There was a brief delay, then the sound of his feet landing on the lower platform.

"Sir Brennin?" The man's smooth rhythm fell away, leaving his voice tinged with nervousness.

"Please, Laureate," said Graham. I imagined him bowing, though I couldn't see him. "I humbly apologize for the disturbance. I simply needed a quiet, peaceful place, and your church provided me that."

"Oh!" said the Laureate. "Forgive me, sir!" He cleared his throat and regained his composure. "You are most welcome here at any time."

I rolled my eyes. No other citizen would get off that easily.

The Poet Laureate must have been too polite to ask if Graham was alone, or maybe he just hadn't thought of a way to put it into poetic phrasing. But he had to wonder why the heir was laughing at the top of a tower.

"Thank you. I'd love to see more of your chapel if you wouldn't mind giving me a tour."

"I would be very much obliged, good sir."

Their footsteps triggered metallic vibrations through the iron staircase, and the door to the chapel clicked shut as they left. This was my cue. Graham would have to keep him occupied long enough for me to sneak out. I wouldn't get away with trespassing like he had.

I climbed to the ground and pulled open the chapel door in time to see Graham disappear through a curtained alcove. The robed Laureate followed after him, gesturing dramatically with his wide sleeves and bowing his tasseled hat.

The chapel was empty. I crept past the pews to the front doors, taking a deep breath before pulling them open and stepping into the busy street. I leaned against the stone exterior of the church, waiting for Graham to come out.

Maybe I'd finally get him out of this city.

I noticed a little too late that the street was filled with too many black and white uniforms. Enforcers seemed to peer from each corner and scrutinize every citizen. I held my bag behind me. As I watched the church doors with rising anxiety, an Enforcer looked my way, staring me straight in the face.

Shifting along the chapel wall, I rounded the corner of the building. I slid into the alleyway, preparing to run, when two Enforcers closed off the opposite end. I shot back the way I'd come, only to find myself face to face with the first Enforcer who'd spotted me.

I swore under my breath and kept my face neutral.

"Hand over your bag," said the tall bearded man in front of me. He put his hand on the pistol in his belt.

I reached for my bag, but I doubted I could get past all three of them. Even if I did, they'd send more Enforcers after me.

"Your little knife won't help you this time," said a nasal voice behind me.

CHAPTER
SEVENTEEN

A FAMILIAR AND VERY SHORT ENFORCER WALKED INTO view.

My spirits sank so low at the sight of him that I lost the enthusiasm to respond with the insult on the tip of my tongue.

The Enforcers ripped the bag from my shoulder, but not before I grabbed a knife. I held it to my side, hidden under my wrist.

They opened the bag and took out my remaining weapons.

"Three knives," said the bearded Enforcer. He dug through the bag again but came up empty-handed. "And no rank card."

I tightened my grip on the knife in my hand, ready to use it if they came even one step closer.

"Well, well." The tall man looked me up and down. "It seems the old librarian sent us after the right girl."

I clenched my jaw. Mrs. Whitting was my new least favorite person.

"She's definitely our suspect," said the short Enforcer.

His partner spoke up. "She doesn't have the book."

"No matter." He examined the knife in his hand. "She has the tools of an assassin. Arrest her, men."

The first Enforcer unlucky enough to get close was the short one. I grabbed him by the hair and pressed my knife to his throat, backing away from the others. I tried not to falter when I felt him swallow against the blade.

"Pistols down or he's dead!" I shouted.

One Enforcer dropped his weapon, but the bearded one lifted his and pointed it at me.

The man in my grip whimpered. I looked down the end of the barrel, but I didn't let go of my knife. I couldn't. Even if I didn't stand a chance, I'd fight for my freedom.

"Gentlemen," said a calm voice behind me, "is this our criminal?"

"Without a doubt," said the bearded man, still aiming his gun at me.

"And what exactly—" Cael stepped forward and saw my knife against the man's throat. "Oh. I see."

Come on, help me! I screamed inside my head.

"It's best not to shoot, sir. The Academy will want to interrogate her. I'm sure she'll come peacefully if we ask." He shot me a warning glare.

"Ask?" The bearded man laughed. "She's unhinged. She won't listen—"

"She will," said Cael, talking over the man. He turned to me, his voice low and threatening. "Won't you?"

I hesitated, wondering if his strategy would actually help me. His mouth was set in a smug line as usual and his voice sent a chill through me, but I wanted to trust my father. If he chose Cael for his loyalty, I'd try to do the same.

I lowered the knife. Cael wrenched it from my hand.

The other men grabbed my arms, slapping handcuffs on my wrists. The short man backed away from me with fear and fury in his eyes. He rubbed his throat, then checked his fingers for blood. He suddenly looked so young that I had to bite my tongue to keep from apologizing.

"Slap some branks on her," he said.

I narrowed my eyes, losing my pity.

"Good idea," said Cael.

My blood grew hot under my skin.

The bearded Enforcer pulled out the contraption, the metal clinking together menacingly. The others held my arms, but I didn't dare fight as they slipped the spiked piece over my tongue and attached it around my head. It would only hurt more if I did. It took just one swallow for my eyes to squeeze shut in pain.

"That's better," said the short Enforcer. "You don't seem so high and mighty now, do you?"

The sharp metal on my tongue kept me from even thinking up a retort. When they pushed me forward, it took all my strength not to whimper.

Cael walked with the bearded man, speaking with him as the other two pushed me through the streets. His voice sounded uncharacteristically friendly, a tone I'd never heard directed at me, and it made me like him less than ever. Maybe I should've trusted my instincts and fought. I kept my head down as they marched me through the streets. In case this wasn't over, I couldn't let my face be known to the whole city.

But the taste of blood and metal told me I'd been beaten.

The Enforcers dragged me down the prison steps. The afternoon light faded and the stench of mildew, sweat, and rotten fish assaulted my nose. I breathed through my mouth on instinct, but the branks dug into my tongue again.

At the bottom of the stairs was a stone hallway. I squinted into the darkness. The men pushed me through an aisle of cells with faces watching from behind bars on both sides. My gaze locked on a woman's dejected brown eyes peering out from a mess of auburn tangles before they shoved me past her.

The Enforcers roughly unlatched my handcuffs and led me to an empty cell, slamming the barred door behind me.

The bearded man spoke to a prison guard. "Keep those branks on until tomorrow at the very least." Then he turned to Cael and handed him my bag. "Deliver this to the Academy and take the prison report with you. I intend to get credit for her capture."

"Yes, sir." Cael smiled and bowed. "As do I." He walked away without so much as a glance.

Desperation, fury, and blood rose in my throat. I sank to the filthy floor and shook silently, breathing in the rotten air. My stupidity had caught up to me, and whatever strength or pride I'd had was gone with my freedom.

I pushed the foul air out of my lungs, wishing I'd never have to breathe it in again, but my body wouldn't cooperate. Another breath came in, and another went out. In, out. In, out. I lacked the will to do anything but breathe, and even that was almost too painful. I was as powerless as the dead and just as alone. I tried to push the darkness away, but it settled on me instead, finding its way under my skin. It swirled inside my mind and heart, familiar, as if it had always belonged there.

A voice broke through my solitude. I lifted my head and leaned toward the bars. Across the aisle was a scrawny man with a shaggy beard and graying hair. He watched me with a friendly smile.

"Evenin' lass." He spoke in a humble style I hadn't heard in too long.

I stared at him through the bars, unwilling to attempt the slightest sound.

"You're not the usual type. Whatcha in for? Splittin' an infinitive?" His wheezing laughter burst out so enthusiastically that I wasn't sure we were experiencing the same reality.

I shivered in the chill of the dank prison and tightened my arms around my knees. The rows of bars and moldy stones separating the cells seemed to close in on me in the dim torchlight.

"Eh, it ain't so bad," the man said. "The company's better than what they got above ground."

If I didn't have spikes in my mouth, I might've cared.

"The name's Aldric. Most folks call me Al. Don't you worry. I'm used to bein' the talker. Even when the other guys don't have branks, plenty of 'em's scared into silence." Al licked his chapped lips and went on. "That's a whole 'nother perk 'bout down here. You can talk how you damn well please!" His laugh echoed on the stone and bars. "Once you get yer branks off, anyhow. Is this your first time wearin' that trap?"

I nodded.

"The first time's the worst. Come to think of it, every time's the worst. I'm dyin' to know what you did." He tilted his head and winked. "Wanna hear what I did?"

I shrugged.

"I take it that's a yes." Al's beard lifted around his mouth and his eyes sparkled. "I was caught with a woman and she weren't my wife, if ya know what I mean." He ended his sentence with another wink. "'Course, that's just this time. I been here before, I'll get free again. Hell, I'll likely be here a dozen times before I'm dead."

I was glad I didn't have to respond. Even if I could have, I wasn't in the mood to add my noise to the world. Vanishing from it would've been preferable.

"Sometimes I wish they'd kick me outta this city," said Al, "but I s'pose my crimes aren't enough to get me banished. Yet. No outright rebellion, anyhow."

Mine were. There was only one punishment harsher than banishment, and if they found out who I was and what I'd been plotting, I'd earned it.

I pointed at myself and nodded.

"Nah, you?" He wheezed out another laugh. "You don't look the rebel type."

I nodded again.

"Can't wait to hear about what you did then. I hope it was good."

I shook my head.

"No? Not even a tiny bit good?"

One thumb down.

"Just plain stupid?"

Two thumbs up.

"That's okay. We're all stupid!" He tapped his head. "But the stupidest ones think they're smarter 'n the rest of us, so you're doin' all right."

I tried to keep the corners of my mouth from lifting, but I couldn't stop them in time. The spikes drew blood and I let out a pathetic whimper.

"Sorry. Smiling's no good. I shoulda warned ya."

My head sank, weakened by the weight on my heart. Would my father find out I was here? When the Immortals came to question me, they'd soon discover my secrets. The entire city would know. And so would Graham.

Graham. How long did he wait outside the church before giving up on me? And when would he finally read the news? I wondered if he'd care about my fate, or just hate me for my lies. The image of his shy smile and questioning eyes remained in my mind, tormenting me. I needed a distraction or I'd end up like one of those psychotic prisoners, repeating the same two words and banging my head against the wall.

To make things worse, Al started whistling an upbeat tune that didn't belong in prison, or even Cambria. When he looked back at me, I made a slicing gesture across my neck. The shrill irritation wasn't exactly the distraction I was hoping for.

His whistle died abruptly. "Aw, that was a beau'iful tune."

I opened my hands in the shape of a book, then pointed at him.

He frowned. "You wanna know if I can read?"

I shook my head and did the gestures again, pointing to myself afterward.

"You want me to tell you a story?"

I nodded at the same time groans issued from the nearby cells.

He clapped his hands together. "Then you've come to the right place!"

Al's story began at once, his animated voice keeping my thoughts within the borders of sanity. Eventually, I closed my eyes and fell asleep on the cold floor.

EIGHTEEN

"GET UP!"

The shout startled me to my feet. The branks cut into my swollen tongue, drawing fresh blood. A guard paced the aisle, yelling at the prisoners. Al yawned lazily and stretched before he stood up as if this were any other gentle morning.

The guard lifted a key to the lock on my cell.

I wondered how long I'd slept, and if someone from the Academy had come to question me. My body ached from sleeping in an awkward position, and my neck was so stiff I could hardly turn my head. But neither compared to the fire in my mouth.

The guards led us out of the cells and down the aisle with the rest of the captives in line behind me. I searched every dark corner and barred window as we walked.

"Some new prisoners try to run," said the guard behind me. "But that won't get you anything but a good beating."

Even with the branks on, I kept my chin high. I didn't want them to think they'd taken anything from me. The act made me feel more like myself, and I felt my resolve rising.

We came to a room filled with tables and benches. One table held an enormous copper pot full of something that vaguely resembled food. The prisoners lifted a ladle to their bowls, pouring in a chunky brown liquid.

I thought I'd adjusted to the prison smells, but the odor of rancid seafood made my stomach churn.

A guard grabbed me by the arm and pulled me out of line. He took a tiny key from his pocket and put it up to the back of my head, releasing the brank's spiky grip from my tongue. "Eat. You'll need the energy for your interrogation."

I swallowed and touched the tip of my tongue. It was swollen and raw, but not as damaged as I'd expected.

He pushed me back into the line of prisoners and walked away. I obediently followed the others and poured myself a bowl. A fish head floated to the surface, the cavities of its eyes hollow.

I gagged and looked away, clutching my stomach.

I was greeted with the same face I'd seen while being dragged to my cell. The young wild-haired woman stood behind me in line. She smiled, her brown eyes warm with sympathy. "I can tell you're not hungry enough for this yet."

"I won't be tomorrow either," I said, every word stinging my tongue.

"Nobody *wants* to eat scraps," she said, "but you'll be surprised at what you can handle."

I looked down at my bowl.

Nope. Couldn't handle it.

Al waved from a table on the other side of the room. I went over and sat next to him on the bench. He gave me a wide grin, revealing a black flake stuck between his front teeth. I smiled back. He'd gotten me through my first awful night and I'd always remember him for that.

"You got yer branks off. Congrats!" said Al. "Nice to see your smile."

The red-haired woman from the line brought over her bowl and sat across the table from us. She picked up her spoon and took a bite of the vile stew. So did everybody except me.

"Mornin', Cait," said Al.

"I should've known you'd be the first to make friends with the pretty new inmate," she said.

I liked Cait already. "I'm Bryn." I held out my hand to her over the table.

She shook it warmly with both hands. Not many people compelled me to offer personal information, but something about her made me think I'd tell her everything if she asked. Luckily, she didn't.

"Bryn, eh?" said Al. "I hope you'll tell *me* some stories now that you can talk."

"I guess I owe you," I said.

Cait finished her bowl and eyed mine hungrily. I slid it across the table. She thanked me and dug in immediately.

"You'll go hungry real soon if you're too fancy for this stew," said Al. "It's all we ever get and there's only two meals a day."

"Is it stew or sewage?" I asked, still feeling a bit queasy.

"Call it stewage!" He slapped his thigh and wheezed out a laugh.

I was still hoping I might get out of here before I got hungry enough. If not, I'd have to swallow my pride, along with the prison stewage.

Breakfast ended and the guards escorted us back to the cells. I ended up across from Cait this time, with Al in the

138

cell beside me. I couldn't see him on the other side of the wall, but his voice carried as loudly as before.

"Since ya like good stories an' all," said Al, "guess what Cait did to land herself in here."

Cait smoothed back her curly mess of hair, revealing her delicate features. "Al loves to volunteer other people's secrets."

"Only the best ones," he said.

I hoped she'd tell me, but I didn't want to be nosy. I felt at ease with her, but maybe she only saw me as the stranger that I was.

She held onto the bars of the cell, then closed her eyes, taking in a slow breath. "It's been a long time since I talked about it."

"It's okay," I said. "You don't have to." I wanted to spare her from the pain, though I longed to know her story.

But she continued. "It was three years ago. I had just turned seventeen. I took my first exam and ranked in Class A. I wanted my friend, Lachlan, to rank as highly as I had. He studied hard, but I knew he wouldn't perform well enough. He was never really the scholarly type."

She pursed her lips and looked at the ceiling, her eyes glistening in the dim light. "I couldn't bear to see him rank lower than he deserved. And if his rank wasn't the same as mine, we obviously couldn't live in the same quarter or marry—" she cut herself off. "You get the point. He needed a high rank.

"The night before his test, I stole his rank card and some clothes from his bedroom. I chopped off all my hair—he had red hair like mine—so the description on his card wouldn't be a problem. It worked. I passed for a boy just fine."

Al snickered, and I understood why. It was hard to imagine her features as anything but feminine.

"I got into the testing center before Lachlan arrived. When he did, they turned him away because he'd lost his card. I took the test and left, confident that everything was working out perfectly."

Her chin trembled, but she set her jaw and continued. "When I saw Lachlan next, I kept my secret. He was unfailingly honest, and I knew he wouldn't like what I'd done. I returned his clothing and card without him noticing. I couldn't take back the haircut, but he didn't suspect anything." Her mouth turned up slightly as if she were amused by something unsaid.

"He went back the next day with his card, but they told him he'd already ranked in Class A, so he was forced to leave without taking the test. But he couldn't stop obsessing over it. He refused to be content with a rank he hadn't earned. He was convinced he'd done something wrong and would be punished.

"His anxiety was eating away at us both, so I had to tell him. I thought it would ease his fear, but it did the opposite. He was furious and determined to take responsibility for my cheating. He made up his mind to go back and confess to a crime he hadn't committed.

"But I got there first."

Cait rested her head against the bars and sighed. The rest of her story was clear enough, but I wondered what had become of Lachlan. Was he going about his life with the guilt constantly beside him? I pressed my hands against my heart, feeling the pain of Cait's story as if it were my own.

"Ready to tell us why you're here, Bryn?" Al said from the other side of the wall.

Cait, who had a view of both of us from her cell, shook her head. "Not everyone's as willing to confess as you are."

I never liked to reveal my secrets, but after hearing Cait's story, I felt like mine was almost entirely impersonal, and I didn't have to tell them *everything*. "I broke into the Academy and stole a forbidden book."

I watched her expectantly, but it was Al who reacted first. "Away with ya! We're friends, ain't we? Tell us the truth!"

Cait kept her round brown eyes locked on mine. "I think she *is* telling the truth." She had a satisfied smile on her face, but I didn't know if it was because she was right or because of what I'd done.

"Blimey," said Al.

"Impressive," said Cait.

"Impressive? It was the most idiotic thing I've ever done." I felt my shame and frustration return. My motives had been much less admirable than Cait's.

"You took a bit of power from those useless Immortals, so I'd consider that a success," she said.

If that had been my goal, I might've agreed with her. I pushed my hands to my forehead. "I let my emotion override logic, and nothing's worse than that." I still didn't understand the feelings that had overtaken me that night, but I couldn't seem to separate them from the name pacing through my mind.

"I know that's what you've been taught," Cait said softly. "It's what we've all been taught, that logic and intelligence are everything. But look at what that belief has created."

I wasn't ready to believe her. If I let emotion propel me, who knew what other life-destroying decisions I'd make. I put my head on my knees, wondering why someone from the Academy hadn't shown up to question me yet. It was bound to happen soon, and when it did, it would all be over for me, my mission dashed to an irreparable defeat.

CHAPTER

NINETEEN

Breakfast the next morning was no different than the previous day, except that I found a fish tail in my bowl instead of a head. A small improvement. I scooped it out and dropped it on the table.

"Nice one!" Al picked up the tail, admiring its size. "Best I ever found was a crab claw. I stuck it in my pocket and entertained everyone for a whole day by pullin' on its little claw strings."

"Well, *he* was entertained," said Cait, "but the rest of us wished the 'singing claw' could've been a little less tone-deaf."

The others at the table nodded vigorously, but Al laughed, snorting stew out his nose. "Ha! The singin' claw was brilliant."

I laughed with him, unable to resist his enthusiastic wheeze. A part of me, albeit a tiny, almost nonexistent part, wished I could stay here. These people made me feel new, like I could become a different person. It didn't make sense to feel happy and free while in prison, but there was something strangely liberating about having nothing to control. For once, I could sit back and let fate take the reins.

I looked down at the sludge in my bowl. I was afraid I'd become too hungry to turn it down any longer. I hesitantly lifted a spoonful to my mouth. Al and Cait watched me, waiting for a reaction.

I fought the urge to gag. "It's actually . . . not bad, for stewage."

Al patted me on the back. "That's my girl."

When breakfast ended and they returned me to my prison cell, I sat on the floor absent-mindedly weaving my hair into braids. Maybe I was already losing my mind.

"How much longer do you have in here?" I asked Cait.

She was in the cell across from me again. She lay on her back, tossing a clamshell from her stew up at the ceiling and catching it with the opposite hand. "Most likely a whole lot longer."

"But you just cheated," I said. "It's not like you murdered a noble."

"*Just* cheated? What I did undermined the Cambrian ranking system and challenged the Academy."

"Then why didn't they banish you?" I knew of people who'd been outlawed for less.

"I don't know." She threw the clamshell and caught it again. "I'm sure I'll be here until I die."

"No, you won't."

"What?" she asked as she tossed the shell. "Why do you say that?"

"Because I'll get you out," I said, surprised at my bold statement.

She stared at me, forgetting the shell and letting it clatter to the floor. Her brown eyes turned intense. "What makes you say that?"

"I broke into the Academy, didn't I?" I tried to put the conviction into my words.

"I'll tell you what," she said, smiling in spite of her cynical tone. "If you can get yourself out, maybe I'll believe you."

I leaned against the brick wall of my cell. I wasn't sure why I'd regained enough hope to make extreme promises, but somehow, I meant what I said.

A jangle of keys echoed down the hall. Two guards stopped in front of my cell.

I stood to face them.

"This is her?" one guard asked, looking me up and down.

"She matches his description," said the other.

One pulled out his keys and unlocked the gate to my cell. The metal hinges swung open with a screech.

Cait stared open-mouthed. I didn't want her to worry for me, so I winked at her as I imagined Al would've done.

The guards pulled my arms behind my back and locked handcuffs onto my wrists before taking me down the hall. Al gave me a thumbs-up as I passed. I didn't know who was here for me, but I hoped whoever it was might banish rather than execute me.

They took me down the hall, up the stairs, and through a door into a room that seemed enormous compared to the cell I'd been in. A blast of fresh air wafted through an open window, almost as shocking as the initial stench from when I'd first arrived at the prison. I breathed it in deeply, feeling like I hadn't taken a proper breath in days. My eyes squinted against the bright light, but I opened them wide when I realized who stood in front of me.

"Sir Brennin," said the short Law Enforcer who I'd threatened with my knife. Twice. "Are you *completely* certain this is the prisoner the king requested?"

I pulled against the guards' hold and bent into a grateful bow—the first one I'd ever given the heir of Cambria.

When I lifted my head and met his eyes, he blinked a few times, then nodded. "Yes. She is."

I could only smile at him, though I realized how awful I must have looked and smelled in my filthy sack of a dress. Graham, on the other hand, was practically regal with his jet-black suit and neatly combed dark hair. Something seemed different compared to the first time I'd seen him dressed this way. I didn't know what, but it almost made me want to bow again.

"The king's orders." Graham gave the Law Enforcer a scroll.

The man unraveled it, revealing an elaborate black signature next to the Brennin seal. He studied it carefully, frowning. "I feel compelled to warn you that this woman has been proven dangerous. Is Imperator Brennin aware of the details, sir?"

"Yes," said Graham. "That's why he insisted on questioning her himself."

I realized, with impressed surprise, that he was lying. The king was in no condition to meet with criminals.

"But she's a suspected assassin, sir! She was carrying knives!"

Graham nodded solemnly. "He's read the news."

"Does he know she attempted to use her weapons on a Law Enforcer—on more than one occasion?" The short man glared at me and brushed his hand over his throat.

Graham kept his eyes on the Enforcer. He hesitated before nodding.

"Sir, you should also know that we have found no evidence of a Bryn Yarrow in Cambria. No records of birth, schooling, or rank."

Graham's eyes flitted to mine briefly, betraying a trace of surprise before his face returned to neutral.

Please, I thought. *Please don't give up on me.*

He looked back at the Enforcer and cleared his throat. "That's even more reason for him to question her."

I tried to suppress my smile.

"Very well, Sir Brennin," said the Enforcer, though his frown suggested the opposite. "We will accompany you to the Brennin grounds."

"That won't be necessary, thank you. My own guards are waiting outside. If you could please remove her handcuffs, we'll take her to the king now."

"I'm sorry, sir, but we cannot," he said. "She must be returned with the cuffs in place."

"Yes, of course," said Graham, smiling. "I understand."

The guards released me, and I stumbled forward.

Graham gave me a knowing look. I couldn't help but feel a little shame as he walked me out into the street. The bright afternoon sun seared my eyes, but I squinted at the surrounding buildings, memorizing the place so I'd be able to return one day to help the friends who remained there.

Unless my eyes hadn't fully adjusted, the street was vacant.

"Where are your guards?" I asked.

"Well," said Graham, "that wasn't quite true, so we should hurry before they notice." He placed a hand on the small of my back above my cuffed wrists.

My breath caught at his unexpected touch and I turned away to hide my flushed face.

He took me down the street and around a corner into an alleyway, where I stopped and faced him. "The king didn't ask to question me, did he?" I asked.

"Not exactly."

I smiled through my confusion, studying his eyes questioningly. "I know you don't owe me anything after all you've done, but I'd love an explanation."

He raised an eyebrow. "So would I. Although I'm beginning to put it together. We'll talk when we get somewhere safe. For now, let's enjoy one last hour of ignorance."

I smiled. "Ignorance sounds good."

We left the alleyway together, sticking to the quieter streets as much as possible. If it hadn't been for the guilt that had reawakened inside me, and the handcuffs digging into my wrists, I would've felt almost happy. Every citizen we passed stopped and stared, their mouths falling open at the sight of the heir walking beside a dingy-looking handcuffed girl.

"We'll have to get you something to wear," he said, "or I won't have much luck sneaking you into my house."

I snorted out an awkward laugh. "Your house? You said we were going somewhere safe!"

"Trust me," he said. "The Brennin grounds are the least likely place a criminal would hide."

His use of the word *criminal* prickled. I knew I was one, but what did it make me in his eyes? "Wait, no! I'd have to dress like a noble to get in."

"Exactly. We'll stop at the nearest dress shop."

I held back, shaking my head. "What about a rank card? And my hands are cuffed behind my back, remember?"

"You don't have a very vivid imagination." Graham smiled, repeating the words I'd used on him a few days earlier.

A tingle flowed over my skin. I couldn't help but feel secretly glad that he remembered our conversations as well as I did.

"So you have a plan?" I asked.

He nodded. "It will take a few lies, but I think I can manage."

Graham visited a nearby dress shop while I hid alone in an alley. I fiddled with my handcuffs, but they obviously weren't going anywhere.

A change of clothing wouldn't be enough. My hair was matted and tangled, and my smell was sure to alert any Law Enforcer within a twenty-foot radius that there was a fugitive on the loose. I rested a shoulder on the brick wall beside me and tried to step over my handcuffs, struggling to bend my long legs enough to get them through.

I had one foot over the cuffs and my dress lifted up to my thighs when Graham returned with a long puffy gown, a feathered hat, and a purse.

"This might be hard to believe," I huffed, "but this is the most disgraceful moment of my life."

He covered his mouth and looked down, but the laugh made it through. "No, I believe it. Here, let me help."

"I got it." My voice was strained as I leaned against the wall and forced my other leg through, finally bringing my hands in front of me.

"I'm sorry this won't have a custom fit, but at least your handcuffs shouldn't be a problem." Graham glanced back at the street. Fortunately, this alleyway was in a quiet part of the city with few pedestrians. He smiled and held up a dark blue strapless dress.

"I'll be happy if I can pull it on at all," I said. "Although, I've never seen a noblewoman with bare shoulders."

"That's why I brought this." He pulled out a long shawl from inside the ridiculous hat.

"Well done," I said. "But that feathered disaster? Would anyone under the age of fifty wear that?"

"You know a lot about noble fashion for a girl who has no record of being a Cambrian."

"I'm observant. Now, would you mind helping me into that

dress before we have company and this gets a whole lot more awkward?"

Graham pulled open the top of the gown. I stepped into it, holding up my cuffed hands. He lifted it up, over my filthy dress, and buttoned the back. My cheeks burned while he tucked my long, grimy strands into the hat and wiped smudges off my face with the shawl.

He stepped back and frowned. "Your sleeves."

The dirty brown sleeves of my original dress wouldn't be hidden by the shawl.

"Rip them off."

He furrowed his brows.

"Come on, just do it." I raised my arms and waited.

He grabbed the fabric and tore it at the seams until the sleeves were in shreds on the ground.

"I believe this will do." I spoke with the dramatic accent of an elderly noblewoman as he adjusted the shawl over my shoulders. "However, I fear that the horrid stench has not been eradicated."

"I thought of that, too." Graham laughed and took a rounded glass bottle out of his pocket.

"Do you think dipping a rotten fish in perfume would make it smell fresh?" I asked.

"Not fresh," he said, "but perhaps a tiny bit better?"

Sometime between lifting my arms to be doused with perfume and watching Graham position the straps of the satin purse over my wrists to hide my handcuffs, my dignity sank to a new low.

CHAPTER

TWENTY

IT MIGHT'VE BEEN THE FADING LIGHT, BUT AS WE approached the Brennin gates, I was sure Graham's face grew more and more pale. I looked longingly down the Avenue of the Immovables and fought the urge to run and save myself. The house and its grounds were draped in the wall's shadow. The golden light of the sun only lit the eastern half of the city now.

We'd received plenty of curious looks on the avenue between the A and B quarters, mostly from nobles eager for gossip. It gave me satisfaction to think they'd never know who I was. Now that we were at the home of the king, I gripped the purse awkwardly in front of my wrists to keep it from slipping and revealing my handcuffs.

Two guards flanked the gates. One was young with close-cropped black hair. The other had two massive sideburns dominating his face. They bowed when we were close.

Graham wrung his hands and took a breath. "Good afternoon." He looked up and realized the sun was out of sight. "Er, evening, that is. We'd like to, well, I'm just . . . . returning. Home. As usual."

The guards glanced at each other, then at me. I wanted to bury my head.

"Is something distressing you, Sir Brennin?" asked the young guard.

"Not at all, not at all." He stammered. "Not . . . no."

It seemed his ability to lie had evaporated. What happened at the prison must've been a fluke.

"Who might your guest be, sir?" the sideburned man asked.

"This is . . . my friend, Lady—"

"Lady Ruskin," I said, holding my head high and putting on a noble accent.

Graham nodded for a little too long. "Yes, Lady Ruskin. Eleventh House. Obviously. She's joining me for . . . tea."

The young guard stared. "Sir Brennin, forgive me for asking, but are you feeling well?"

He opened his mouth, but I didn't trust him to speak again.

"Unfortunately, he is not," I said. "He's in a terrible state and has been ever since discovering he may have been the target of the Academy assassin. Naturally, he's horrified."

Graham looked at me, nodding absently. "It's true. Lady Ruskin accompanied me home because I'm so . . . very afraid . . . of assassins."

I clenched my teeth, then tried to pass it off as a smile.

"I was under the impression that Imperatrix Brennin had assigned guards to remain with you at all times," said the young guard. "Have they abandoned their duty, sir?"

Graham started to shake his head.

"Yes," I said in a rush. "It seems they have. Now, please open the gates so we may get him to safety."

The guard with sideburns looked back at me. "Indeed, Lady Ruskin, but may we please see your rank card?"

I pushed out my lips in an exaggerated pout. "Really?

Everywhere I go! No one ever cares to remember the Eleventh House. We're Immovables too!"

"Excuse me, milady, but we meant no disrespect. We're required to ask, no matter how well-ranked our visitors may appear."

"No. I won't put up with this. I shouldn't have to show my card like an ordinary citizen!"

Graham straightened and addressed the men. "Lady Ruskin has shown me great kindness today. She's my honorable guest, and I expect her to be treated as such. Now, will you *please* let us into my own home?"

I looked away haughtily.

The sideburned guard spoke in a low voice. "As you wish, sir."

"Thank you," said Graham.

The guards finally put the key in the lock and opened the gates.

I tried to keep my distance as I passed them, but I thought I saw one of the men put a hand over his nose.

We crossed the grounds, skirting around the edge of the mansion to a back door into the servant's kitchen. We went through it, up the stairs, down a corridor to another flight of stairs, and past dozens of doors until we stopped at the end of a hall.

Graham opened the hall's final door and I went in ahead of him.

He peered back before coming in and closing the door. The gigantic bed between two windows was the first thing I noticed. The pile of newspapers on his desk was the second.

"I'm sorry to take you in here," he said. "I know it's terribly inappropriate."

"You lied for me, broke me out of prison, bought me a

gown, and now you expect me to be offended because I'm in your bedroom?"

He stood awkwardly in the middle of the room, glancing between the chairs and the door. "Here," he said. "I have something for you." He opened a nightstand drawer and pulled out a familiar gray bag.

My heart leaped at the sight. "I can't believe it!" I ran over and took it from his hands, opening it the best I could with my hands still cuffed together. I saw the four knives with their sheaths, plus the two books I'd last seen in Cael's hands. "You've broken so many laws for me today. I can't thank you enough."

He shrugged. "I didn't break as many laws as you think."

I studied his face, trying to figure out what was different about him. I thought maybe his eyes looked bolder, his jaw sharper. Or maybe it was just my perception that had changed. All I knew was that weak and lonely didn't describe him anymore.

I pulled my gaze away. "How'd you get my bag?"

"As strange as it sounds, a Law Enforcer brought it to the gates yesterday and asked the guards to give it to me. I don't know why. It should have gone to the Academy, but through some mistake, it ended up here, along with the prison report."

"Thank you," I said, still wondering why Graham had decided to help a lying criminal. I knew I also owed Cael my gratitude, but it was much easier to direct it at Graham. Still, Cael had proven he was a good man for the job. I just wasn't convinced he was a good man. And I wondered why he'd chosen to give my belongings to Graham instead of keeping them safe for me. I could never understand that man.

"You can imagine my shock when I realized this was you." He picked up a newspaper from the desk. "I should've been paying attention to the news, but after my mother's speech—well, you understand. I wish you'd told me the truth, not only about the break-in, but"—he gestured toward me—"who you are."

"How could I? 'Hello, my name is Bryn Yarrow and I'm an outlaw.' Is that what I should've said?"

He stepped back. "So it's true," he muttered, more to himself than to me.

"Yes." I bit my lip and nodded. "But I'm not an assassin! They were wrong about that."

He dropped into an armchair. "I never thought you were, or I *definitely* wouldn't have released you from prison. But . . . how'd you get past the wall?"

"Can we do something about these before we continue our conversation?" I held up my bound wrists to remind him I still wore handcuffs. "And I'm getting a little tired of smelling like flowery vomit."

He jumped to his feet. "Oh! Yes. Forgive my manners! I suppose I'll have to learn how to pick a lock."

"Uh oh," I said. "How long will that take?"

"Why? Do you have somewhere to be?"

I looked around his room and shrugged. "I guess not."

OVER AN HOUR LATER, GRAHAM WAS STILL DIGGING AT the handcuffs with a wire. We sat across from each other with our hands on the table between us.

"These . . . ridiculous . . . things . . . ." He pushed out his anger between breaths.

I tapped my fingers on the table. "You just need to—"

"This is harder than it looks," he said.

"I don't know. You're making it look pretty hard."

He took a break from the wire to stretch his fingers.

"You didn't learn to pick locks on your island, did you?" he asked. "Which one are you from anyway?"

"Tramore. The farthest one from here."

"And you came all this way to speak with me?" he asked. "To get me to stop the war?"

I nodded. "We need you."

"If you're one of them, why won't they listen to you?"

"Why would they? I can't change their lives."

"What exactly do you need me to do?" asked Graham. "I don't have much to offer."

"Come and meet them." I knew my direct requests could scare him away, but I didn't have time for hints. "Show them you're not your father. Make an alliance and prevent the war."

"What could I offer them in exchange?" He picked up the wire and poked at the handcuffs again. "If the Academy supports my mother, I won't even be king, and the treaty would be useless."

"You've forgotten what I told you. The citizens will take you a lot more seriously when they find out you saved their lives. They will *insist* that you become king."

He held on tight to my wrists with one hand while he struggled with the wire in the other. "And what if I fail? No one will want me as king if it looks like I ran away with an outlaw."

I swallowed. His fears were certainly valid. "Tell them you were kidnapped, and you escaped from the clutches of the evil assassin, Bryn Yarrow."

"I don't know. I'll need some time to think about this," he said.

"There isn't time." I wasn't supposed to tell him too many details in case he told the Academy about the attack, but I needed all the leverage I could get. "They'll launch the boats in twelve days if we don't make it to Tramore by then, which means we need to leave *now*."

His hands paused, resting on mine for a moment. "If the rest of your people want to fight, why don't you want the same?"

"Not all of us think violence is the answer. My father and I would rather see a peaceful solution."

"So you're a diplomat," he said, with just a hint of a question.

"You could say that."

He looked me in the eyes. "You keep surprising me, Miss Yarrow."

You've surprised me more.

"I think it's time to start calling me Bryn," I said.

"Well . . . Bryn," he said, pausing as if to feel the name on his tongue. "You're free. Sort of."

I looked down and realized Graham had released the lock. He slid the cuffs apart and pulled them off my wrists.

"I can't believe you actually did it!" I grabbed both his hands in gratitude, then rubbed my freed wrists. "Thank you."

He smiled. "You're welcome. Now you better hide while a maid prepares your bath."

When I'd washed the prison stench away in his personal bathroom, I changed into some fresh clothing Graham had left me. I didn't care that they were his shirt and trousers. They were clean. And since he was about the same height as me, they fit well enough.

I opened the door that led into his bedroom.

Graham sat on a chair reading the stolen Academy book. When he saw me, he set it down. "My curiosity got the best of me. I had to know what compelled you to risk your freedom to steal this book. It must be incredible."

"I don't know if it is," I said. "I didn't mean to steal it."

He laughed. "Very funny."

I frowned. "I'm serious."

"How can you break into the Academy and accidentally steal a book?" he asked.

"It's very difficult," I said. "It can only be accomplished by the greatest of idiots."

He laughed as if he still believed it was a joke. "All right. You don't have to tell me. You have the right to a few secrets."

Good. I needed a few, but the book wasn't one of them.

I sat on the chair beside his. "You should be reading my other book. It will come in handy for you."

His smile faded. "I . . . I can't go with you. I wish I could, but there's just no way."

The confidence that had built up inside me began to unravel.

"But don't you see how important this is? If you don't come, think how many people will die. They depend on you. *I* depend on you!"

He pushed his fingers through his hair, then buried his face in his hands. "My father also depends on me, and if I leave"— he dropped his hands and shook his head—"I'd never forgive myself if the last thing he knew of me was that I'd deserted Cambria. It would only confirm his doubts."

I couldn't bring myself to argue. This was a subject I knew all too well. I could never let my father down, especially if he were dying. I sank into a chair across from Graham. "I'm sorry about your father."

Three fast knocks sounded at the door.

We both jumped to our feet.

"Hide," he whispered, but I was already on my way.

The knocking came again, louder. I grabbed my things and ducked into the closet, hardly daring to breathe.

Graham closed the door softly behind me.

"Open the door. It's time to start speaking to me again!" Maeve Brennin's commanding voice was hardly muffled, even with two heavy doors between us.

CHAPTER
TWENTY-ONE

I HEARD THE SPRING OF THE KNOB, HIGH-HEELED SHOES clicking across the wood floor, and the door slamming.

"You've been avoiding me," said Maeve.

"Hello, Mother," said Graham in a monotone.

"Is that the tone with which you should greet the queen?" Her voice dripped with condescending sweetness.

He mumbled an apology.

"I hear you disappeared for a few hours today, abandoning your responsibilities at home." Maeve's tone lost its honey all at once. "How dare you? When will you start acting like a king?"

"When will you *let* me? When will you allow me to accept responsibility without swooping down and ripping it out of my hands?"

"Oh, *dear*," said Maeve. Although I couldn't see her, I was sure she was rolling her eyes.

"When will you stop acting like a queen and start acting like a mother?" He said, his anger apparent even in the quiet tone.

I didn't expect him to say something so personal with me

hiding in his closet. My embarrassment tempted me to cover my ears to block out their argument, but my curiosity overrode it.

"Stop this ridiculous behavior," she said. "I didn't come here to listen to unfounded accusations. I came to tell you to stay put and stop leaving this house without—"

"Unfounded?" he asked. "Do you know what's unfounded, Mother? Announcing to the entire city that I have character issues because—" he paused and dropped his voice lower "—because of Ewan's death!"

"You can't deny that. It would traumatize any child to witness his brother's death, especially—"

"Stop!" Graham's voice was hoarse and full of passion. "I have suffered for it every day of my life. Please don't try to make me feel any worse than I already do, because I assure you, it's not possible."

I stayed as silent as I could in the closet, not just to remain unheard, but to catch every bit of emotion in his voice so I could understand what he'd done to make his mother detest him so passionately.

"If I had ever felt as if your heart were truly repentant, I could have forgiven you." The queen's voice was mild on the surface, but a razor-sharp edge lurked beneath the calm. "That's all I ever asked of you—just that one thing."

"How could you know my heart when you haven't even taken the time to look at me?" he asked.

"Thank you for so thoroughly demonstrating the immaturity to which I was referring." The queen's shoes tapped the floor again. "I was hoping to give you another chance to prove that you might be ready for responsibility, but instead, you've shown me you're as unprepared as ever. Now, stay here and don't dare leave this house unattended again!"

The door creaked open, then slammed, leaving the room

drenched in silence. I closed my eyes and wished I could disappear.

Graham opened the closet door and gestured for me to come out before dropping his hands to his side. His eyebrows were low, and his lips were tight.

I emerged slowly, afraid to meet his eyes.

"I'm sorry—" we both began at once.

I stopped and waited for him to speak first. I felt a strange urge to step closer to him, to *touch* him even. My fingers tightened their grip on the book in my hands instead. "I've invaded your home, and your life, for too long," I said. "I'd give *anything* for you to come to Tramore with me, but if you won't, it's time for me to leave." I wasn't pretending to be polite. At that moment, all I wanted was to walk away and never look back.

"And go where? You're an outlaw and a fugitive!"

I leaned against the wall. Leaving would mean abandoning my mission. I hated to let my father down, endanger everyone I loved, and leave Graham to a fate even worse than what I'd planned for him.

"I don't know," I said. "You're right. I'm just so sorry—"

"Don't be sorry. Honestly, it's my pleasure."

"Thanks . . . but I was actually going to say how sorry I am that you have *her* for a mother."

His smile fell from his lips. "Sometimes I think it's my fault."

I wanted to disagree, but I was too uncomfortable with the subject to pursue it further, so I sat in the armchair and opened the stolen book.

WHEN IT WAS DARK OUTSIDE, AND THE HOUSE HAD GONE quiet, Graham snuck to the kitchens and returned with a plate for me. I ate ravenously, reminding myself to be forever grateful for food that wasn't spooned from the gutter.

The Academy's nameless book still lay in my lap. My head was a fuzzy, tired mess, leaving me confused over all I'd read. It illustrated a world so different from this one, with thousands upon thousands of cities, and land that spread for hundreds of miles. New words like *electricity*, *computers*, and *technology* buzzed in my head. I knew Cambria's founders had come a long way for peace and freedom, but history was strangely quiet about the world they'd left behind.

I took the last bite of a warm roll, amazed at how delicious food could be. I stretched and rested my head against the back of my chair, feeling the fatigue catch up with me. My sleep in prison had been about as good as my meals.

"Take my bed," said Graham. "I'll lock the door and sleep in one of the empty bedrooms."

I dragged myself to his bed, too tired to argue. It might look suspicious if the servants, or his mother, found him sleeping somewhere else, but I didn't have long to worry before sleep overtook me.

ANGRY POUNDING ON THE DOOR JOLTED ME FROM dreaming. I shot up, disoriented by the strange surroundings. Faint sunlight glowed around the edges of the long curtains.

"Graham, open the door!"

I stepped to the floor breathlessly, grabbed my bag, and squeezed under the bed. Sure, Graham had the key, but Maeve's banging seemed fierce enough to unhinge the door. If she got one glimpse of me, my mission would be over for good.

"Graham? Graham!" she shrieked. "How dare you try to hide this from me!"

My mouth went dry. Did she know I was here?

"Forging the king's signature is treason, whether or not you're his son!" she cried through the door. Her screams were likely to be heard by every servant in the house. "You foolish boy! I wish you had died instead of your brother!" She attacked the door with both fists, and possibly her feet, like a child throwing a tantrum. "Do you hear me? I wish you were dead!"

She gave the door a final desperate assault and screamed once more before leaving me alone with the relief of silence.

My heart gradually slowed while I waited under the bed. I didn't dare come out until I knew for sure that she was gone. The house was unnaturally quiet, as if each room had been holding its breath with me.

Eventually, I built up the courage to wiggle out from my hiding place. When I stood, another knock, though much softer, echoed through the room. This time, it was accompanied by a whisper instead of a shout.

"It's me. I'm coming in."

The lock clicked open and Graham entered, shutting the door and locking it behind him as he pocketed the key. He dropped another newspaper on the pile already crowding his desk. His eyes were puffy, and his hair was smashed down on one side and sticking up on the other. I imagined that I looked the same, except he was holding a delicious pastry in his hand and I wasn't.

"Here's breakfast." He crossed the room and handed me the flaky bread.

"Is she gone?" I asked, taking a bite.

He nodded. "She had a meeting with the First Immortal she couldn't miss."

"Is your door okay?"

"It will recover," he said, "but I'm more concerned about you."

"Does she know I'm here?"

"Definitely not, or that door wouldn't have remained standing. But you won't be safe here much longer now that she knows about my prison visit."

"And the king's signature," I said.

One side of his mouth turned up in a shy smile. "Actually, she doesn't. I mean, she thinks she does, but she's wrong."

"What do you mean?"

His face lit up. "It wasn't forged."

I watched him to see if I could detect a lie. "So, you're saying the king actually approved my release?"

Graham gestured for me to sit. When I did, he took the other armchair.

"When I found out you'd been captured, I went to see him. I'm not sure why. He doesn't talk much these days." He'd said so little about his father that I'd assumed their relationship was no better than the tumultuous one he had with his mother, but his gentle tone suggested otherwise.

"When I sat next to his bed, he woke up and smiled at me," he said. "Then he asked what was wrong."

This was beginning to seem too personal, but he continued. "I told him I had a friend who'd been wrongly imprisoned. I didn't tell him the details, but he told me to write up his orders and then he signed it. Honestly, he might've been delirious, but I wasn't going to argue."

So, I owed the king my freedom too. I didn't think he had any compassion at all, let alone for a criminal. Delirium seemed the most likely scenario, but I couldn't help but feel strangely honored, though I hardly wanted to admit it to myself.

"Please give him my thanks." My response was hugely inadequate, but I'd never been good at expressing my gratitude, especially when it was most sincere.

"Or you could," he said.

"What?" I stiffened in my chair. "No, no way. I couldn't. I'm sure he doesn't want to spend his last"—I cleared my throat and chose different words—"to spend his precious time with strangers."

"You're not entirely a stranger. I've told him a bit about you —not the outlaw part, naturally—but he knows you're my friend." Graham rested a hand on my arm, reminding me of the awkward fact that we were alone in his bedroom. "You're already in his house. And you'll probably never get another chance to meet him." His face turned solemn.

Everything in me told me not to go, but I owed him so much, and the hand on my arm was heavy and insistent. I looked away, trying not to be swayed by his plaintive blue eyes. My gaze landed on a quill and inkpot on Graham's nightstand. An idea stirred in my mind—an opportunity to twist the rumors to our advantage.

"Fine. I'll go. But I hope you've had my gown cleaned."

He smiled so widely that I had to question his sanity. A dying father. A hateful mother. What allowed him to smile through all that?

"Thank you." He grasped my hand in his, and the heat burned through my skin, leaving me disoriented and confused. About everything.

I TWISTED MY HAIR INTO MULTIPLE BRAIDS AND PINNED them up on my head in the noble style. It didn't seem right to wear a gaudy feathered hat to visit the dying king. I reached back and tightened the corset of the midnight blue gown before finishing the ensemble with the satin shawl. Looking in the full-length mirror on the bathroom wall, I realized it wasn't actually so bad without the hat and the odor.

I glanced at the locked door and picked up the book I'd snuck in here with me, as well as the quill and ink. The Academy's book still had about a hundred empty pages, perfect for someone who happened to need a spare piece of paper. I flipped it open and noticed the first page that marked the book as the Academy's. It could work even better than a blank page.

I tore it out as quietly as possible, hoping Graham wouldn't hear it from the other side of the door. Dipping the quill in the inkpot, I wrote a few words:

Thank you for the second chance. I swear I'll get the job done this time.
Long live the queen.

My hand gripped the quill, hovering over the paper. The note had to be subtle enough to only cast suspicion after Graham disappeared. I hoped the fact that it was the stolen book's page would be enough to link it to Bryn Yarrow because I figured an assassin wouldn't sign her name.

I folded the note and tucked it into my corset before walking out of the bathroom into Graham's room.

His brows furrowed and he tilted his head to the side.

I brushed my hand nervously over my corset. "What?"

"Nothing," he said. "You just look . . . well . . . like a noble."

He checked the hallway for servants and led me out when it was clear. We crept down the corridor with quiet steps, then down a set of stairs. At the end of the hall was an enormous set of carved doors.

I held my breath as we approached and entered the room.

Graham closed the door behind us before going to his father's bedside.

I waited by the door, hesitant and afraid.

Desmond Brennin slept in an enormous bed in the ornate room. Instead of looking grand in his surroundings, he seemed small and forgotten. His hair was gray, his body frail, and the gold-leafed headboard only accentuated the contrast between grandeur and decay. It was hard to believe this was the tyrant who'd destroyed so many lives.

My father would've thought I was crazy if he knew whose bedroom I was standing in. I felt exactly the same way, but it was too late to run.

TWENTY-TWO

GRAHAM TOUCHED HIS FATHER'S ARM AND GREETED HIM gently. The king awoke with watery eyes and a weak smile. His gaze landed on me, but I didn't know if his vision was clear enough to register my presence. Graham gestured me over.

"Father, you have a guest."

I stepped forward toward the king timidly.

The king groaned and pushed himself up a little higher on his pillows. "Who?"

Graham glanced at me. "She's . . . the friend I told you about."

I smiled at the king and dropped into a curtsy, glad Graham didn't give him a name. "Imperator Brennin, I came to thank you. You've done more for me than I deserve."

The king blinked slowly. "What do you mean?"

Graham's face fell in disappointment. Deeper than disappointment.

But then the king reached over and grasped my hand. "My memory does not serve me well at the moment, but you do seem familiar, my dear. I am glad I have done some good for you. It has been so long since I accomplished anything worthwhile."

I swallowed, keeping my eyes on the king's. I didn't know what to say, so I muttered, "Thank you. I'm sorry to wake you."

His grip on my hand tightened and he squinted, studying me. "You do seem quite familiar. Have we met?"

I shook my head.

"You remind me of someone from a former life, perhaps— but, once again, my memory fails me." He released my hand and sank back into his pillow.

I wondered who he was thinking of. He wasn't a good king —or a good person—but at this moment, I couldn't feel anything but pity. His eyelids fluttered to a close as if he had no control over them anymore.

I backed away, giving Graham his space. He stepped closer to his father's bedside, taking the king's pale, veined hand in his.

I looked around the room, searching for somewhere to leave the note I'd written. A bag of doctor's supplies rested on a chair. I backed toward it, but uncertainty weighed down my feet. The doctor would most likely give the note to Graham or the queen without telling anyone else about it.

I glanced back at Graham. He was adjusting the sheets over the king's shoulders. A laundry basket on the other side of the room caught my eye. No one would be digging through that except the servants. And if the stereotype was true, servants loved to gossip. I casually edged my way over and took the note from my dress, dropping it into the basket just as Graham sighed and stood up.

"Sleep well, Father," he said. "I'll visit again soon."

THAT EVENING, I PACED THE FLOOR OF GRAHAM'S ROOM, re-reading the day's news with rising fury.

After only two days in prison, Bryn Yarrow was removed for questioning and has not been returned. The Academy is working to locate the source of the breach . . .

The words blurred and my head spun. For some reason—the Academy's edits, perhaps—Graham's prison appearance hadn't been made public, but after Maeve's tirade this morning, she obviously knew he'd been involved.

I blinked hard and skipped to the next paragraph.

The head librarian of the Irvine Library has a firsthand account from her time working with Yarrow. Mrs. Eleanor Whitting reported the following to the Cambrian Tribune:

"I never liked her. I caught her trying to ingratiate herself with the young heir and dismissed her on the spot. When I witnessed her lurking in Sir Brennin's carriage, it was clear that she had more deadly motives. It's quite possible that only the interference of our dedicated Law Enforcers saved his life that day."

I tossed the newspaper to the floor and crossed my arms, wishing I could take back all the free work I did for that woman in the library.

Graham sat in an armchair, absorbed in the Academy's book.

I'd spent too much time here. If I didn't take Graham to Cael's boat within the next twenty-four hours, Cael wouldn't be able to deliver him to Tramore before the ships launched. I was starting to think I should just get out and save myself while I had the chance. Every time the city's bells signaled a new hour, my hope sank lower.

"Did you know there used to be lamps that worked without fire?" Graham asked. "And machines that rivaled the human mind?"

I'd read about those things in the book the day before and seen the drawings of the strange devices, but they seemed like a fantasy. If we ever had such useful things, why wouldn't we still? My reply was on my tongue when the doorknob rattled.

Graham took a sharp breath and got to his feet, tucking the book under a cushion. I went to the closet and gave him a dramatic salute for luck before shutting myself inside.

"Why is your door *always* locked?" Maeve yelled from the corridor.

Graham turned the lock and opened the door with a creak. He was braver than I would've been.

"To what do I owe the pleasure, Imperatrix?"

The sudden smack of a palm on skin greeted his question. I winced for Graham's sake.

"Don't pretend you don't know," said the queen.

When Graham spoke, his voice was surprisingly calm. "Fine. I know what you came here for."

Maeve groaned. "After all you've done, I can't believe you actually have the gall to dangle a preposition. You're as dense as a commoner. I don't have time for this."

"You always seem to have time for a grammar lesson."

"Shut your mouth and listen." In contrast to her ear-splitting shrieks from earlier, this tone was deeper and more menacing. I almost preferred the screams. "You are on *very* dangerous ground. A prison guard paid us a visit this morning." The crinkle of a newspaper followed her words. "You not only forged the king's signature and removed a dangerous criminal from prison, but after reading *this*, I'm beginning to wonder if you may even be hiding her!"

"I didn't forge—"

"Don't lie to me! The king would never do such a thing without consulting me."

"Honestly, I didn't forge anything. Go ask him yourself if you don't believe me."

"Don't be ridiculous. Our guards say no prisoner was delivered. They did say one of the Ruskins visited, however, which is *very* curious."

I put my face in my hands. She had to be connecting the dots.

"The young Lady Ruskin came to offer her respects to the king."

I dropped my hands, marveling at how naturally he answered. His lying had improved since his last attempt.

"Oh, I seriously doubt it! Everyone knows the Ruskins' loyalty is to the Strouds, not us. The only possible explanation is that she's trying to present herself as an eligible—ugh, it makes my blood boil! Next thing we know, Mara Stroud will be trying to win your affection."

"Why would she? I'm not going to be king anymore."

"Don't change the subject." She managed to keep her voice under control, unlike her outburst this morning, but hatred seeped through every word. "You've brought suspicion on our house. Your foolishness will surely destroy your reputation."

"I didn't have much of a reputation to lose, thanks to you," he said.

"Don't you dare try to blame me!" The shrillness returned for a moment, but then Maeve's voice dropped to her lowest register once more. "Where is the prisoner?"

"I left her in the custody of Enforcers outside the prison. Perhaps she escaped, but I don't know where she is."

I crouched in the dark and waited for her to respond. Did she believe him? Or did I need to get ready to run?

"Even if the king acted without my permission, which I doubt, why would he send *you* to retrieve a dangerous criminal?"

I waited with shallow breaths for the silence to pass. It seemed Graham didn't have a good lie this time.

"Let's pay him a visit. Come with me," said the queen.

Footsteps left the room, echoing down the corridor until I was alone.

I stayed hidden in the closet, anxious for Graham's return. I sat with my knees to my chest, trying to calm my growing fears as the room remained silent for much longer than I'd expected.

I rested my back against the wall, a row of suits hanging in front of me. I debated running while I had the chance, but I couldn't leave without talking to Graham. I tried to tell myself it was okay, that he would be back and then we'd leave together, but I didn't have the ability to believe my own lies.

As the hours passed, my eyes began to burn and I let them close, soon falling into nightmares that seemed pleasant compared to reality.

Footsteps echoed through my dreams until they were right outside the door. I jerked awake, my neck cracking and my back aching. I must've been asleep for hours.

"You can come out now." Graham's voice was quiet and weak.

I jumped to my feet and opened the door. Weak morning light filled the room. Graham sat in a chair with his head back and his eyebrows furrowed above red-rimmed eyes. His hands were clasped over his chest.

My heart sped up. "What happened? Did your father—"

He opened his eyes, revealing the sheen of emotion. A new concern took over, but I couldn't bring myself to ask the question on my lips.

"He wouldn't wake up," he said.

Dread left me empty. I dropped into the chair next to Graham, watching him carefully. "So he's . . . gone?"

"Not yet. He seems to be in a coma. The doctor says if he

doesn't wake up in the next few hours, he's not likely to wake up at all."

Still alive. I ignored my reservations and reached out to pat Graham's hand because I would've needed the comfort if I were in his place. He didn't move or respond, and I let go, feeling the shame in my veins.

He grasped my hand just as I pulled it away, warm and tight in his grip. He smiled weakly. "I'm glad you're here, Bryn."

I wasn't so glad. How soon would guards be here to break down the door? Or was Maeve too distracted by the king's sudden turn?

I stayed by Graham, holding his hand without speaking. I was afraid of the unwanted impact my sympathy could bring, but the overwhelming compassion was too strong. I had to stay here, at least for now. There were some things I couldn't bear to think about. Losing my father was at the top of that list.

"I'm afraid they'll be searching for you soon," he finally said, breaking the silence.

"I was about to leave."

He looked up from the floor and met my eyes. "I'm sorry I couldn't help."

I nodded, trying to keep my misery from surfacing. A sudden urge to tell him everything struck me, but shame—and probably wisdom—held my tongue. No matter what I said, it wouldn't save him. I picked up my bag and put it over my shoulder.

"You're not going back to Tramore, are you?" His eyes lit up with urgency, and perhaps the tiniest bit of hope.

"I have to," I said, "after I say goodbye to my family here."

"The ones in Quarter C, you mean?"

I nodded.

"How will you get into the quarter? And how will you leave these grounds without being seen?"

"I . . . I'll figure it out."

The silence stretched between us. I wanted him to change his mind, but I couldn't ask him to leave now, with his father on the verge of death. I wished I could stay with him. I wished he *wanted* me to stay. But neither of our desires could change what had to happen.

The doorknob clicked. I dashed for a hiding place, but it was too late. A wide-eyed maid stood in the doorway. She looked back and forth from Graham to me, mumbled an apology, then turned on her heel and sped down the corridor.

CHAPTER
TWENTY-THREE

GRAHAM RAN OUT THE DOOR AFTER THE MAID. "MISS Amaia, wait!"

His footsteps caught up to hers in the hall. When they returned, the maid kept her eyes fixed on the floor.

Graham shut the door, locking it this time, though the damage was already done.

"Please forgive my intrusion, sir!" said Miss Amaia. "I thought you were with your father."

She was young, probably close to my own age, but small and frail. Her dark hair was pulled into a long braid under a white cap and her cheeks were flushed.

"I'm not angry," said Graham. "I know this looks rather improper, but I would greatly appreciate it if you didn't tell anyone my friend is here."

She studied my face before turning to Graham. "I'll keep your secret, sir."

"Thank you, Miss Amaia," he said. "You've always been loyal."

Her face reddened even further, and she dropped into a curtsy. "May I be dismissed?"

A spark ignited Graham's tired eyes. "Actually, perhaps you could help. It's not uncommon to have a new maid in the house. Is it possible you could bring us a dress like yours?"

She looked up at Graham, hesitating. "I'll try." She curtsied and left the room, her face pink and her footsteps quick.

"Well." He turned to me. "Are you ready to become a housemaid?"

"Better than a nobleman," I said. I didn't like involving someone I didn't even know, but Graham seemed to trust her.

A few minutes later, Miss Amaia returned carrying a bundle of black fabric with a white apron. As soon as I squeezed my arms into the sleeves and tried to stretch the bodice over my chest, I realized it wouldn't be simple. Apparently, the maid had brought me one of her own, but I had to take what I could get.

I braided my hair and placed a white ruffled cap on my head. I pushed out the air in my lungs in an attempt to secure the buttons on the back of the dress, but the tight sleeves and high-necked bodice weren't making it easy. When I broke into a sweat, I finally swallowed my pride and asked Miss Amaia for help.

She came into the bathroom and buttoned the dress until I could hardly take a breath. I tied on the apron and stepped into Graham's bedroom, begging the buttons to stay intact.

He smiled and nodded. "She looks perfect. Thank you, Miss Amaia."

I raised a skeptical eyebrow.

"I mean it. You have a way of fitting into every role."

"Just not this dress," I said.

"Oh." He took a better look, frowning. "Well, the fit may

not be perfect. Here, take this." He went into his closet and emerged with a black top hat and some of his clothing. "Change into this as soon as you can. The hat might hide your hair well enough to pass for a gentleman—if no one looks too closely."

I picked up my bag and Graham's clothing. For a moment, I was glad I was taking something of his, but then I remembered I'd never be able to see him again. It would be better to destroy any reminders of my failure and forget him. I wrapped the bag, clothes, and hat in a blanket and carried the bundle in front of me. Miss Amaia set two more folded blankets on top of it.

"Be careful," said Graham. He turned back to me, lowering his voice. "I'm sorry. If it weren't for my father—"

"I know. Keep yourself safe and stay out of the fight," I whispered. "I—I won't be able to stop it without your help." I wanted to beg him to save himself, to forget his family and get out of the city, but with his maid nearby, and my fear in the throat, I shut my mouth instead.

The sadness in his eyes deepened. He took my hands in his and I tried to ignore the tingle under my skin.

"Goodbye," he said. "I hope we meet again."

If only. I nodded, but I knew we wouldn't. My heart seemed numb, but my head buzzed with too many thoughts to sort through. What could I say? *Thank you for everything, but I wish I'd never known you because how will I forget you now?* But all I said out loud was goodbye.

I let go of his hands and joined Miss Amaia on the other side of the room, feeling weak and lightheaded. It didn't help that the stupid dress wouldn't let me take a real breath.

I left the room without looking back.

Miss Amaia and I took the stairs to the floor below. A few servants passed us, but none really looked at me. Before we took the second staircase, I caught a glimpse of the queen through the doorway at the end of the hall. She stood beside the king's bed with the doctor, her hands covering her face.

I stopped and stared. I had to remind myself that only yesterday she was a monster who expressed a death wish for Graham, but now she looked so weak and vulnerable.

"Come along," said Miss Amaia.

I jerked my gaze away and caught up to her on the stairway.

On the main floor, we went through the servants' door to the grounds. My breaths were still suppressed by the tightness of my bodice, although I kept my back as straight as possible. My buttons wouldn't hold if I moved the wrong way. Miss Amaia, on the other hand, looked composed and only slightly flushed now.

We passed through the manicured green garden, its hedges and topiaries tightly trimmed. As we approached the guards at the gate, my heart picked up speed. I stayed behind Miss Amaia and kept my face down.

"To what destination are you ladies headed?" one guard asked. I wasn't sure if his tone was suspicious or flirtatious, but I didn't like it either way.

We'd planned what to say, but for once, my tongue was tied. The guards looked me up and down. They weren't the same ones who'd been at the gate when I entered, thankfully, but I became even more self-conscious of the overly tight dress. I lifted the stack of blankets with my things hidden inside higher on my chest. The movement made a button give out. I took in a gasping breath, setting another one loose. I thought I heard it land on the gravel path.

I closed my eyes. *Please don't notice. Please don't notice.*

Fortunately, Miss Amaia kept her composure, along with her buttons. She curtsied and spoke softly. "The queen sent us out to retrieve new materials for Imperator Brennin's comfort. These blankets are not to her liking."

The guard's face grew solemn. "Oh, of course. We wouldn't want to keep them waiting. Go on then."

Miss Amaia walked forward, but with two buttons missing on my back, I was afraid to follow. I pushed out the remaining air in my lungs and took a careful step through the gates. Another button popped open on my back. I went faster, half-expecting the guards to stop me. My dress seemed to get tighter with every breath, and I was sure my bare skin was making an appearance. But the guards said nothing, and I wondered if they were simply too shocked by the rare glimpse of skin to think clearly.

I caught up to Miss Amaia in the street. "I'm about to lose this dress!" I hissed through my teeth.

She followed me as I ran into an alleyway. At least two more buttons popped off on the way. I tried to control my laughter so I wouldn't be standing there naked. It was strange to laugh when I felt so empty inside, but I couldn't help myself.

"I'm sorry I ruined your dress," I said when we were alone, but I was afraid my sincerity was weakened by the wheezing.

"It's only a couple buttons—or ten." She unwrapped my bag and Graham's clothes from the blanket and handed them to me.

I put on Graham's shirt and trousers while Miss Amaia held up blankets to hide me. I tucked my hair into the top hat and returned her damaged dress, hoping it wouldn't get her into trouble.

"Thank you," I said. "You saved me today—and you don't even know me."

"My loyalty is to Sir Brennin," she said, "but I confess I

don't completely trust his judgment this time." She stepped back and fixed a disapproving gaze on my bag.

I had to hide it. I slid it under my white button-up shirt and tucked the hem into my black trousers, making myself look like a nobleman with ill-fitting clothes and a potbelly. "If I may be so bold," said Miss Amaia, "I'd suggest you don't return."

My smile faltered and my insides pinched together. "I won't."

She nodded. "Safe travels, then."

When she walked away, the pain of loss and failure hit me even harder than before. I watched her go, then left the alley.

Cael was waiting in the street, his arms crossed. I figured he'd been watching the house for days, waiting for me to finally come out. He raised an eyebrow at my masculine disguise but didn't comment on it. "So the heir wasn't convinced?"

I shook my head, but everything down to my dragging feet gave away my failure. I walked past him, squinting into the morning sun.

"So that's it?" asked Cael from behind me.

I stopped, knowing I should thank him for getting me out of jail and saving my things, but I forgot my gratitude when I saw his hateful scowl. I dropped my head. "I couldn't do it."

"I wasted a lot of time on you."

"I know." I turned to go, but his next words stopped me before I took a second step.

"Well, that's his death sentence."

My fingers clenched into fists. "I'll talk to my father. To the islanders. We'll think of something else."

He shook his head. "Time's up. And you've already made a big enough mess of things, don't you think?"

I stared at his cold eyes, trying to think of something I could say to make him care. But there was nothing.

"I need one last favor," I said. "I need to say goodbye to the Lenoxes and I can't get into the quarter."

"You don't *need* to say goodbye."

"Yes, I *do*. After that, I'll be ready to go home. No more arguments. Just give me this one last thing, okay?"

He crossed his arms.

"Please. I'll never ask you for anything again."

"Fine." He gestured in front of us. "But you better keep that promise."

"Thank you." My gaze drifted past him until I stared at the Brennin House, at one window in particular. I wanted to force my way in, to march back up there and tell him the whole truth. But instead, I turned around and saved myself.

I avoided the main streets and stayed far from the places Enforcers were likely to be. My long walk took me across the city to the edge of Quarter C, Cael trudging after me. Once there, I hid around the corner of a building and sent him inside the gates. I waited, watching the afternoon sun begin its descent toward the west. People passed by, but no one looked for long at the oddly shaped gentleman I attempted to be.

I'd have to face my father soon and let him see how badly I failed. I considered not returning home so I wouldn't have to witness his disappointment, but I couldn't do that to him, no matter how ashamed I might be.

Etna and Marcus rushed around the corner, startling me out of my dark thoughts. They halted for a moment at my appearance, then continued forward, Cael walking behind them.

Etna stretched out her arms and pulled me into a tight hug. "We were so worried about you."

Marcus put a hand on my shoulder. "You shouldn't have come back, disguise or not. Enforcers are still prowling the quarter."

"He's right," said Etna. "You need to get somewhere safe."

"So do you. I can't bear for you to get caught in the attack. Come with me!"

Etna's eyes gleamed and she shook her head. "It's not worth the risk. Prison would probably kill us faster than anything if we got caught."

I gripped her wrinkled hands, looking into her sad eyes. "Please. I can't leave you two here."

"We'll be fine," said Marcus, looking around the corner. "You should go."

"I'm so sorry." My voice shook and I swallowed to fight the emotion. "I wasted everything your son gave us."

"You're wrong," he said. "Our son would be proud if he were alive to see the life he gave Orrin. And the life he gave you, even if it won't be the same."

Etna wrapped her arms around me again. I closed my eyes, trying to gather in the last bit of calm, but my heart beat too hard to absorb it. I wished they'd follow me to safety, but if they wouldn't, I'd have to try to find another way to save them.

"Goodbye, Grandma." After a long embrace, I opened my eyes and raised my head.

At the end of the street, a lone dark-haired figure in common clothing climbed from a carriage, heading toward the gates to the quarter.

I stared, hardly believing my eyes. My smile widened and my voice went breathless. "He's here."

"Who?" asked Marcus, turning around. "Not your father?"

I shook my head. "Graham Brennin."

"I have to go!" I hugged Etna and Marcus one more time, this time out of joy. "Thank you for everything."

"Goodbye, dear. Come back to us again!" said Etna.

I started to run, but Cael caught me by the elbow. "Get him *out* this time."

"I will," I said. "See you at the boat."

"Can you handle this?" he asked.

"Yes." I wasn't sure if he meant the act of getting out of the city or handing Graham over to him. I also wasn't sure if I could handle either of those things.

"Once I've taken the heir, don't make a single move until your father gets to the cave to bring you home."

I nodded. "I know the plan."

Cael leaned closer, still holding my arm. "Don't mess up."

"Thanks for the concern." I pulled my arm from his grasp and dashed after Graham.

TWENTY-FOUR

GRAHAM WAS ALMOST TO THE GATES. I DARTED BETWEEN citizens, pushing my way toward him. I ran until I was close enough to say his name without the whole street hearing.

"Graham!"

He spun around. His eyes widened, and his eyebrows lifted in surprise. "You're still here."

I took his hand and pulled him around a corner, out of the view of the guard at the gates. "Why did you come?" I asked.

"I couldn't live with myself if I didn't," he said.

An ambitious energy traveled from my heart to my limbs. "What about your father?"

He shook his head. "It doesn't look hopeful. And the doctor told me something he said the last time they spoke."

I waited with hope rising in my chest. His eyes blazed blue under the vibrant afternoon sun and his dark hair was lit with gold.

"He said he wanted me to be happy, to be a better king than he'd been. And thanks to you, I know how."

I covered my mouth. "You'll come with me?"

"Yes," he said, "but I wish I knew how you plan to leave."

My relief burned bright, but my stomach sank with guilt. There was a flip side to every success, and this one was hard to ignore. It would be nice if my conscience could stay out of this.

"You'll see," I said, "but let's get out of here before someone arrests me again."

THE WALK TO THE WESTERN WALL WAS AS MANY MILES AS I'd already gone today, but with Graham, the time went by faster. We picked up our pace, hurrying through the city. We had to make it out before curfew.

Cael was most likely using his uniform as a ticket through the city gates. Graham could've gone through, too, if it weren't vital to keep his departure secret. With the exception of farmers and fishermen, no one but Academy members and the ruling family could venture beyond the wall, and even then, getting off the island was out of the question.

"You left just in time," said Graham. "Guards searched every room."

"I'm not surprised. Your mother is relentless." I imagined Maeve Brennin's disappointment, but it didn't give me the pleasure I expected. All I could picture was the view down the hall to the king's bedside and the queen's hands covering her face.

"She wasn't always like this. Back when Ewan—my brother —was alive, she actually had a heart." His words were laced with bitterness.

I wanted to know what had happened to Ewan, but it would be a shame to open such a painful wound. Besides, I liked secrets where they belonged: buried deep.

I pictured the queen's dejected figure again. "Maybe she still cares."

"If she does, there's no evidence," he said.

"I'm sorry you had to leave your father. My father is everything to me," I said without thinking. I didn't want to give him a reason to stay when we were so close to leaving.

"You speak so highly of him. He must be very good to you."

"He is." I smiled, remembering that I was closing the distance between my father and me with every step. "Without him, I'd be nowhere, and nobody."

"We'd have a lot in common then," he said.

"Oh, stop." I rolled my eyes. "You're one of the most important people in Cambria."

"Not because of anything I've *done*," he said. "You're from a different world than I am. You don't understand what it's like to be born with expectations you can never meet."

I understood more than he knew. My father had very high expectations for me, but it wasn't a problem since he and I had generally wanted the same things.

"This could be your chance to change that," I said, cringing at my ability to mislead and encourage in one sentence. I didn't know how I could still dare to make him believe he'd be making alliances when, in reality, Cael would be making Graham a prisoner as soon as we made it to the shore.

The sun dipped beneath the wall and the windows lit up with warm flickering glows. We kept our pace light and casual to conceal our urgency. I pulled the bag out of my shirt and put it over my shoulder, getting ready to run if we had to.

The noises of the city died down to a hum, leaving us in nearly deserted streets. The quiet darkness, along with the feeling of exposure, pushed me to walk faster. Graham kept pace beside me.

We were approaching the looming wall when the curfew bells rang.

A rhythm began to pound through my veins. I wasn't sure if it was a side effect of my fear or if my ears were picking up on something real.

Graham glanced back. "Someone's coming," he said gravely.

"Run!" I pulled him by the hand.

The wall was straight ahead, but not without barriers. If we could get there first, we'd have an advantage. The Enforcers weren't likely to excel at climbing a sky-high stone wall in the dark.

I raced down the wide street with Graham on my heels. My hat tumbled off and my hair fell around my shoulders. There was nowhere to turn, no side streets, just the fences of the A and B quarters blocking us in on both sides. Our feet pounded over the cobblestones and a gate stood between us and our destination. The grounds of the Third House lay beyond. I ran straight for it.

"We're not . . . going in *there* . . . are we?" asked Graham between breaths.

I glanced back. "No time to go around."

"What about guards?" he panted.

But no one stood in front of the gates. I ran up to the iron-work of the fence and checked the handle.

"I'm sure it's lock—" Graham started but cut himself off when the click of the gate proved him wrong.

I smiled. "Lucky." I swung the gate open just enough to let us through.

Graham held back hesitantly. "What if there are guards inside?"

"It can't be worse than what's behind us."

I turned back and shifted the bolt on the gates before

darting around the hedges. The Stroud house dominated the center of the grounds, its windows dark except one. Graham and I ducked behind a row of prickly bushes just as the Enforcers' torches lit up the night. Their shouts cut through the quiet, and the rattle of the gates was sure to wake everyone within a mile.

"Where have the guards gone?" asked an Enforcer.

I crouched behind the bushes and pushed Graham toward the wall that kept us from freedom.

"What are we doing here?" he whispered, resisting my prodding.

"Just go."

We ran alongside the hedge. The gates clanked and groaned as if the Enforcers were climbing them.

"What is *this*?" A booming voice cut through the calamity.

My heart thudded against my rib cage. I stopped in my tracks and lifted my head to peer over the hedge. A man faced the gates from inside the grounds, his figure broad and imposing.

"Sir Stroud," said an Enforcer, bowing. The others joined him after a moment's delay. "Forgive our intrusion, but we believe curfew breakers may be hiding on your property."

"All I hear are Law Enforcers trying to unhinge my gates!" he shouted.

"But sir—"

Curfew breakers. So they didn't know who we were. I tore my eyes from the scene and ducked below the hedge. We ran on, sticking to the shadows and keeping our heads low.

The argument from behind rose in volume, and I doubted even an angry nobleman could keep the Enforcers from demanding entry. One last sprint across the grounds took us to the base of the looming wall where a large tree grew. We ran behind the tree and I brushed my hands across the stones, confirming that the hidden pair of ropes I'd tied at the top of the wall still hung there. I grabbed the one on the right and handed Graham the other.

"No," he said, shaking his head furiously. "Are you insane? I'm not *climbing* it."

"Yes, you are. Grab the rope."

"No." His expression turned to panic, and he backed away, refusing to touch the rope. "I can't. You don't understand."

I knew he wouldn't like the idea of climbing the wall, especially with his fear of heights. No one would. "Graham." I spoke calmly to keep him from running away. "Graham. You can do this. The rope is secure and there are knots all the way up. It will be simple."

He shook his head stubbornly. "There must be another way. What if I go through the city gates and meet you on the other side—"

"There's no time. And no one can see you leave."

"Does it really matter?" he asked.

"*Yes.*"

"I can't."

I grasped at any argument I could. "If we stay here, they'll find out you're conspiring with a criminal and you'll never be king."

"I'd rather be alive."

"If you don't do this *now*, I'll get captured." My voice rose in desperation. "And they'll never let me out this time!"

He dropped his hands from his face and looked up at the wall.

I put a hand on his shoulder. "I wouldn't have brought you here if I didn't know you could do it."

His eyes locked on mine for several seconds before he finally nodded.

I handed him the rope again. This time he took it.

"Now climb," I said, holding my own rope. "Just move your hands and feet up one knot at a time, got it?"

He reached up, his hands shaking, but his feet left the ground and he moved upward slowly, but steadily.

I started up my own rope, staying at his level.

We had climbed about ten feet when the angry voices grew louder. Torchlight flashed, exposing the tree's silhouette on the wall. We were still hidden within its shadow but wouldn't be for much longer.

Please, no, I silently begged. *Don't let them get to us.*

"Any chance you could speed up?" I asked Graham.

"I'm doing my best!" he said through gritted teeth.

"Try to keep up with me." I started to climb faster, hoping it would motivate him so we'd actually make it out before the Enforcers caught us. We climbed higher, my confidence rising with each stone I passed.

But Graham's sudden yelp dashed my hopes.

My head spun. I looked down in time to see him hit the ground.

I let go of my rope and dropped to his side on the grass where he lay on his back. I leaned over him. "Are you hurt?"

He groaned. "I don't think so." He sat up, glancing around the tree trunk at the torches moving across the grounds.

I pulled him to his feet. "Try again."

"You can't be serious," he said, but he still grabbed the rope.

"Don't let go this time." I started to climb again. "You don't have to keep up with me. Just go at your own pace, okay?"

The firelight grew brighter and the voices rose into a clamor. The Enforcers were close.

I kept by Graham's side until we were level with the top of the tree. Then I held onto my rope with one hand and pulled out a knife with the other. I sliced through the rope just beneath the knot I stood on. Then I swung toward Graham's rope, my knife in hand.

"Are you trying to kill me?" he asked with terror in his voice.

"We can't let them follow." I grabbed his rope and cut it in the same place, watching the severed piece fall to the ground with finality.

Graham looked down, shaking his head before starting to climb again.

We rose above the shadow of the tree, losing our cover.

The noise below escalated. "They're climbing the wall!" someone shouted.

I glanced back to see the fires traveling across the vast lawn, the lights converging as they came straight toward us. We were too high to reach, but their pistols didn't have the same limits.

"Just keep going," I said to Graham.

I looked over my shoulder and realized I was above the rooftops of the mansions. We were halfway there.

"Pistols out!" came an order from the grounds.

"Bryn!" Graham's voice was breathless.

"Keep climbing. They won't shoot."

An ear-splitting shot rang out. Stone crumbled from above, showering me in dust. I ducked my head and closed my eyes. My hands seemed to be frozen in place.

I was wrong.

TWENTY-FIVE

"THERE WILL BE NO KILLING ON MY PROPERTY!" A DEEP voice bellowed.

The reprimand steadied my shaking hands and sent a smile to my lips. I lifted my hand to the next knot. As I did, the rope shifted downward the tiniest bit.

"Bryn, your rope!" said Graham, looking past me.

I looked up. I was nearly dangling by a string. About six feet above me, the fibers were unraveling where the pistol shot must've hit. I tried to swing toward Graham, but the movement made another thread snap. I held on tight, not daring to move an inch upward.

Graham tightened both hands on a knot and pushed his feet against the wall, trying to get to me. His rope caught on a protruding stone up above, keeping him at a distance.

I reached out to him.

He slowly released one hand and reached out for mine, but we still weren't close enough.

Another pistol shot echoed and stone dust exploded on Graham's left.

"Forget it," I said. "Just climb. Now!"

"But—"

"I'll be fine!" I said, hoping it was true. I reached for my knives and pulled out two. I'd climbed with knives before in order to attach the ropes in the first place—but not in the dark under the nerve-wracking threat of pistols.

"I said not to shoot!" came a voice from the ground.

"But, sir, they're escaping!"

"That's not my concern! My daughter is watching from her window at this very moment. I don't fancy her witnessing bloodshed. Kill the defectors, by all means, but not in front of her!"

I gripped a knife in each hand and lodged one into a gap between the stones where the mortar had crumbled. Then I did the same with the other, my arms trembling. My rope snapped and slipped out from under my feet. My body slammed into the wall, but my knives held.

This was suddenly not so simple.

Graham jerked his head around.

I dug in the toes of my boots and moved a knife up to another crack. "See? I told you I'd be fine." I kept moving, lifting one knife at a time, the steel handles digging into my palms.

Graham stared open-mouthed.

I kept it up until I reached the frayed end of the rope. I grabbed hold of a knot with one hand, then pulled myself up and reached the next, returning my knives to my bag once my legs were wrapped around the rope.

"Climb!" I told Graham for what felt like the thousandth time.

He kept going.

I could still hear noises from below, but the wind drowned

out the distant voices so I could only catch words here and there.

"... capture ... the other side ..."

"Go. ... We'll stay ..."

We kept going until there was no more wall to climb.

I gripped the parapet with my fingertips and looked up, my gaze landing on stars instead of stone. I hoisted myself up and over the battlement, dropping into the recessed walkway that ran the entire length of the wall. The ropes were tied to the raised parts of the battlements, the knots as secure as mine always were. I kept my rope attached but started to pull it upward.

"Almost there!" I called to Graham.

Only a few distant torches remained on the ground below. The rest had moved away from the house and into the streets, heading for the city gates.

Graham reached a trembling hand up to the edge of the wall. I grabbed his wrist and helped him over the parapet, but as soon as he stood beside me, he sank to his knees.

"I can't believe I just did that," he said. "And you! Do you climb this wall every day?"

"It wasn't my first time," I raised my voice to keep it above the wind.

"How did you know these ropes would be here?" Graham asked.

"Because I put them here," I replied.

"How? And why in the grounds of the Third House?"

"It's the farthest point to the west in this city. Closest to Tramore." I looked out toward the sea.

Graham regained his breath and reached down for the other rope, starting to pull it up. Since it was twice the length as mine, it took a bit longer.

"Your hands," he said, pointing to the deep red lines in my palms. "Are you okay?"

I nodded, lying to him for what must've been the hundredth time. "I don't even feel it."

He took the rope from me and pulled it the rest of the way up. Then we dropped the end down the other side of the wall, peering into the darkness. Graham stood and reached toward me. After a moment's hesitation, I let him take my right hand and pull me to my feet.

The city stretched on for miles to the east and a waning moon floated over the horizon. The wind howled, whipping against us with enough power to take us off the wall if we weren't careful. It carried the scents of salt, wet dirt, and the sea. The shapes of windows lit the scene below, but it was the pinpoints of light from the sky that made me feel like I was flying. The blanket of clouds had cleared out to reveal the beauty beyond.

Graham's grip tightened on my hand. "This feels like a nightmare."

"It makes me feel alive," I said.

I turned my back to the city. The wind lifted my hair as it rushed toward the misty black ocean. Between the wall and the western shore lay the geometric lines of farmland. The anticipation of escaping energized me, and I itched to move forward, or more accurately, downward.

"Ready for more?" I asked.

"No," he said, "but I'm desperate to get down from here."

I realized Graham still held my hand and pulled it away. "You go first this time."

"This is going to be even harder, isn't it?" he asked.

"Nah. Going down is easy." I didn't believe a word I was saying. "If you fall, at least you'll go in the right direction."

"That's not very comforting."

I gave him the most reassuring smile I could muster. "We'll have to share a rope this time since mine isn't long enough anymore. Would you rather go first or second?"

Graham thought for a moment. "First. That way, if I fall, I'm the only one."

"Actually . . . if that's your reason," I said, "then I'm going first. More motivation for you not to kill us both."

"You sure?" he asked.

"Yes," I said, though I wasn't.

He nodded, his mouth tight. "Okay."

I climbed over the battlements, gripping the rope as I moved downward. Once I'd gone several feet, Graham followed.

We continued down carefully, my hands throbbing. I pushed away my desire for speed and focused on staying alive. As I fixated on what would happen at the shore, my confidence faltered, leaving fear and guilt in its place. As soon as we got to the boat and Cael made his appearance, Graham would discover that I'd betrayed him.

And I didn't know how either of us would survive it.

WHEN OUR FEET HIT THE GROUND, I WISHED I COULD LIE on my back in the grass until the sun came up and forget what had to be done.

"Where do we go now?" Graham asked, still catching his breath and flexing his fingers.

"The shore." I tilted my head toward the west.

We started through a wheat field, running in the dark. We had to get out before the Enforcers found us. The blades of wheat were still green and soft, not yet ripened into the prickly yellow stalks they'd become.

Next came an orchard with fruit hanging from the tree limbs. *Pears.*

I made a beeline for the fruit, stuffing as many as I could into my bag and sinking my teeth into another. The Cambrians couldn't keep me from their delicacies any longer.

"Stealing again?" Graham asked. "You really are a criminal."

We emerged from the cover of the orchard and continued through farms and pastures. Occasionally, we passed a stable or farmhouse, the few inhabited places outside the wall on this island. Horses and cows woke and lifted their heads as we went by, but the night stayed quiet and still.

Eventually, the black shoreline came into view. I ran on, aiming for a hill that rose up near the water's edge.

"I don't see a boat," said Graham when he caught up to me.

"That's the idea." If we left a boat in plain view, Enforcers would either destroy or confiscate it.

I led Graham down to the rocky shore beside the round hill.

"You do know I can't swim," he said.

"You won't need to. Just get ready to wade—that is, if your noble sensibilities can handle a little mud."

"Be nice," he said. "It's my first time out in the big world."

His words nearly stopped me in my tracks. He didn't deserve this. Whatever this thing was that had grown between us was about to be dashed like a boat on the rocks.

Taking my bag off and lifting it high, I climbed down the rocky shore and jumped into the water, gasping from the cold. My boots caught between the rocks as I trudged forward through the waves and rounded the seaward side of the hill. The dark eye of a cave greeted me. It was only accessible from the water, leaving it hidden to anyone on land.

I glanced back to see Graham following me through the

water and into the cave. I splashed forward into the darkness, stumbling onto the rocky ground, then squinted at the back of the cave, waiting for my eyes to adjust.

The outline of a sailboat revealed itself in the moonlight.

Beside it was a man.

CHAPTER
TWENTY-SIX

THE MAN STEPPED TOWARD ME.

I froze at the sight of Cael's shadowy figure. It was time to hand Graham over.

Graham waded out of the shallow water, joining me in the cave.

As my eyes continued to adjust, the white on Cael's uniform contrasted against the darkness. Something metal glinted in his hand.

I remembered the pistol I'd given him, and panic gripped my heart.

Graham spoke, his voice soft. "An Enforcer?"

I pushed Graham behind me, standing between him and Cael. I couldn't keep my eyes off Cael's hand.

"Move," Cael growled.

I knew I should. I knew the plan. This was everything I'd fought for. But the fear of what Cael might do to Graham once I moved out of his way consumed me.

Cael lifted his arm toward Graham.

I swung my bag hard at Cael, the books inside colliding with his head. The impact reverberated through the cave. He smashed into the rocky ground and went still.

I leaned over him, shocked at what I'd just done.

"Did you just *kill* a Law Enforcer?" Graham asked.

"No!" I shouted. "I . . . don't think so." I reached down and touched two fingers to his neck. A pulse beat beneath them. Next to his hand lay a pair of metal handcuffs. Not a pistol.

"He's alive," I said.

Graham breathed in relief. "What now? Is this your boat?"

"Yes," I said.

I was supposed to let Cael take Graham in this boat, then wait here for my father so we could go home together, but with Cael stretched out unconscious on the ground, that was obviously not happening.

I opened his jacket and removed the pistol tucked into his belt. It would be best if Cael didn't have a weapon when he woke up. The waves lapped at the rocks beneath him, rising around his prone body. The tide was coming in and he could drown if we left him there.

"Help me move him to higher ground," I said.

We picked him up, me at his head and Graham at his feet, then shuffled upward, carrying Cael around the boat to the back of the cave. We set him down on a large flat rock, eliciting a groan from his throat.

My head clamored with the noise of indecision. When Cael came to, he'd be angry enough to do just about anything. I couldn't wait here and see what happened. Even if he'd only been trying to handcuff Graham and not shoot him, I didn't trust him.

And I wasn't ready to let Graham go.

I looked back at the boat. It leaned to the side, beached in only a few inches of water on the cave floor. It wouldn't be easy to get out and I wasn't sure I could sail all the way to Tramore on my own. I'd never sailed without my father.

I turned to Graham.

He looked back at me with a question—and trust—on his face.

I had to change the plan. It wouldn't stop the inevitable betrayal, but it would delay it. I'd stay with Graham. I'd stay in control. I had to take what I could get.

I lifted my chin, making up my mind. "Help me." I stood and removed the anchor from the ground and hefted it onto the deck, along with my bag.

We pushed on the sailboat with all our strength. It nudged forward slightly, but the next wave set it back to where it started. We pushed again, but the incoming tide was forceful and relentless.

"Come on!" I shoved the boat angrily. It moved, but once again, the waves pushed it right back. I looked back at Cael. He couldn't stay unconscious for much longer. He'd likely find a way to come after us, but I hoped to at least have a good head start. And if we didn't start sailing now, we wouldn't have a chance of getting away from the Enforcers who had to be searching the island for us.

"Maybe we could pull it instead," said Graham.

I nodded, then climbed onto the tilted deck and found a rope. I attached one end around my waist and waded to the prow, tying the other around a cleat. Then I waded to the edge of the cave, the water at my chest, and looped the rope around a boulder outside the opening, using it like a pulley. Letting it take most of the pressure, I planted my feet in the sandy seafloor and gripped the rocks to pull myself forward. I made a few inches of progress, but the waves fought hard against me.

With a sudden yank, I lunged forward, my entire body falling under the powerful waves. They crashed over me, pinning me beneath them for a panicked moment. I kicked up hard, taking a desperate breath when my head broke the surface.

The boat now bobbed on the water.

Graham stood behind me with the rope in his hands.

I coughed the seawater from my lungs. "Thanks," I managed to get out between coughs.

We tugged the rope together, bringing the sailboat all the way out of the cave. I climbed aboard, hoping I could handle this thing without my father. The sea was so powerful, and I felt so small. Mist hung over the water and the faintest pink light shone through the vapor. We were almost too late.

When the sun came up, the Enforcers would find us.

I reached toward Graham and helped him clumsily climb over the edge of the boat.

He landed on the deck with a thud and lay there catching his breath before propping himself up and getting to his feet, almost falling back to the deck again when a wave lifted the bow.

The tide was against us, but the wind was at our backs. I released the sails. They caught the wind and hung on, carrying the boat westward. We repeatedly glanced back at Cambria, watching for a glimpse of the black and white uniforms that would prove we'd gone too slow.

Thoughts of my father weighed me down. When he discovered I had taken Graham on my own, he'd be furious and wild with worry, but I couldn't imagine what steps he'd take next. Would he and Cael both go after us? Would he stop me?

"Can I help?" asked Graham.

"No," I snapped, unable to control my tongue as the consequences of my actions sank in. I'd gotten us into a situation I couldn't control and I just wanted to figure it out in peace.

Graham was quiet.

I should've apologized, but I was too stressed and exhausted to hang on to any virtues. A tiny bit of relief joined my fear when the green island with the scar of the city wall disappeared into the fog behind us.

The cloudy sky lit up gradually, like a fire burning behind a curtain. The sun flashed off something in the distance behind us and the angular shape of a sailboat appeared through the fog. My eyes shot to Graham, but he was looking the opposite direction. It was probably just a fisherman, I told myself, but my instincts told me we weren't so lucky.

As we sailed, I showed Graham how to angle the sails to catch the wind so we would stay on course. He'd learned the basics from my father's journal but putting it into practice was something else entirely.

The boat's deck was narrow, with sleeping cabins on each end with doors just large enough to crawl through. The center was lower than the bow and stern, which were above the two cabins, and the deck had a hatch for storage. It held a few water barrels, dried seaweed and meat, fishing supplies, and navigation instruments.

"Where's the bathroom?" asked Graham from his perch on the bow.

I gestured to the ocean. "It's all yours."

His face reddened. "This will be a bit of an adjustment."

I smiled. "Are you wondering where the maids are, too?"

"No, I didn't expect . . ." He laughed when he realized I was making fun of him. He flipped through the maps in the journal and rotated the compass. "I've never seen one of these. It's incredible."

"I know." I loved the feel of the smooth, round brass compass. It signified adventure and freedom—like holding power in your hands.

He turned to a page with a map of Tramore, the farthest island to the west. "So, this is your home. Do you have a lot of family there?"

"Some. My father. My aunt and uncle. There are plenty of islanders there, but most aren't relatives."

"I wish we could go to all the islands."

"That's not an option," I said. "Not if we want to stop the attack in time."

As long as we were able to catch an occasional fish, we wouldn't have to stop at any islands along the way. We had plenty of water and a decent amount of food. If we stayed on course, we'd get to Tramore in nine days. Right as the islanders set sail for Cambria.

Graham looked up at me. "I'll do whatever it takes to avoid a war."

"So will I."

I reached for the backstay, securing the sail more tightly to the stern and angling it against the changing winds. On my order, Graham walked shakily across the deck and rotated the tiller, pointing us to the west.

"Help yourself to the food," I said, gesturing to the storage hold, "but it won't be what you're used to."

He was quiet for a moment, watching the ocean below him. "None of this is what I'm used to," he finally said. "That's what I love most about it."

I stayed quiet. When we got to Tramore, he'd realize none of this was as good as it seemed—me, most of all. I sat on the lower deck, resting my back against the door to my cabin. My eyes grew heavy. I tried to fight it, but the peaceful sounds of the sea lulled me out of consciousness.

I AWOKE TO THE WIND WHIPPING AT THE SAILS, WATER slicing past the bow and rudder, and the occasional seagull's call. I sat up abruptly, realizing I'd left Graham alone on navigation duty. He sat where I'd last seen him, manning the sail while studying the book and compass.

"Did you sleep well?" he asked.

"Eh." I rubbed my kinked neck. "Are we going the right way?"

"I think so. I've kept us heading due west."

The sun was directly in front of the bow, and so low in the sky that it seemed to rest on the surface of the ocean.

"Is that an island?" asked Graham.

I squinted into the glare of the setting sun until my eyes watered and the light forced them shut. Behind my eyelids, red and black blotches crowded each other out. When I opened them, the spots faded away. All except one.

I blinked again, but the dark mound on the horizon remained. "That's Argal."

Graham dropped his book and dashed to the bow. Shielding his eyes with one hand, he let out an uncharacteristic laugh of triumph. "It's real. It's actually real."

I laughed. "What did you expect?"

"I don't know. Seeing it for myself is an entirely different experience than reading about it. It's still hard to believe there's more to this world than the city."

We looked out at the horizon together, our eyes on the island.

"Looks like you kept us right on course. Good work, Graham."

He flashed a wide smile that contained more confidence than I'd ever seen in him. I had felt the same way when my father let me sail for the first time. I hadn't expected it to be so addicting, not only sailing itself, but the exhilaration of freedom and power. I wondered if the feeling would change him.

I hoped it wouldn't.

The boat carried us past Argal from a distance. Graham's eyes stayed glued to the island until it was out of sight. Then he looked back at me with exhaustion.

"Time for you to sleep," I said.

He nodded wearily before handing me the compass and heading toward a cabin.

"What is this for?" He pointed to a padlock on the door's latch.

I swallowed. Cael had planned on locking Graham up while he sailed. I couldn't think of a lie fast enough, so for once I told the truth. "It's for you. To keep you out of the way."

He laughed heartily before climbing into his cabin for the night.

I stared out at the grandeur of the shimmering ocean and put my hand on the tiller. I'd have to lock away my feelings to get through the next nine days.

GRAHAM STUDIED THE MAPS AND GUIDES IN MY BOOK THE next day as we sailed under the gray sky. The ocean churned and the clouds darkened, worrying me.

I picked up the Academy book, the wind ruffling the pages. There was plenty I hadn't read yet, even considering that the book was left unfinished. "Well, since you basically know how to navigate this thing, I'm sure you won't mind if I get lost in a book," I said.

"What if I accidentally take us back to Cambria?" he asked.

"Then we'll get more pears."

"Seriously, Bryn. I don't trust myself in this wind."

"I trust you," I said. And oddly enough, it wasn't a lie.

I flipped through the book, scanning what I'd already read. So many drawings of objects that meant nothing to me. So many strange words—and I'd been so sure I knew them all. The only familiar parts were from the history I'd learned long ago: glorifying Kendrick Irvine as a savior who led his people to the land that would become Cambria.

But then I found something I couldn't possibly believe.

We must continue forward with our mission to keep this kingdom pure, as Irvine envisioned. Our forefathers strived to create a utopia separate from the world, and we were able to achieve it by eschewing the evils associated with technological progress and returning to a more naturalistic and enlightened time. We have thrived in a glorious century of peace while the majority of humanity suffered, destroying themselves with technology, corruption, and war. Only through continued isolation can we protect our language and culture from the unwelcome influences of other surviving civilizations.

MY BREATH CAUGHT AS THE POSSIBILITIES OVERWHELMED me. We all knew our civilization was the only one to survive the rising sea levels over a hundred years ago. It was a fact. Indisputable. And yet . . .

"You look upset," said Graham.

I shut the book. "You've finished this, haven't you?"

He set down the compass. "Yes, but I was waiting for you to read more before we talked about it. I thought you wouldn't believe me."

I laughed, embarrassed by the accuracy of his guess. "I don't believe it. Not really, anyway."

"It doesn't seem so unbelievable to me. In the past week, I've realized there's so much I don't know about the world."

"But—" *I thought I knew it all.* I didn't dare say it. It suddenly struck me as incredibly naive, so I switched directions. "It's not your fault you weren't informed. They only told you enough to make sure you carried on tradition."

He nodded, then frowned. "How is it you understand Cambria so well? I've lived there for a lifetime and I'm only beginning to unravel my misconceptions. Yet, you're an outsider and you seem to see it clearly."

"Well," I said, "my parents lived in both Cambria and Tramore, so I guess that gives me a unique perspective."

A gust of wind angled the boat off course. Graham checked the compass, re-adjusting us toward the northwest. He should have been born into a different life. He fit in much better when he wasn't restrained by city walls.

I looked at the sky, realizing the dark clouds had turned heavy and ominous. A storm was imminent.

"So, were your parents banished?" asked Graham.

I hesitated, knowing my answer would create further questions. "No. My father's parents were outlawed. He was born on Tramore."

"You talk a lot about your father. What about your mother?"

"Well," I said, speaking slowly, "she's dead."

His eyebrows lowered. "I'm sorry. This is why I avoid asking these kinds of questions. I know as well as anybody that family can be the most complicated subject." He slumped his shoulders and rested his chin in his hands.

"It's okay. She died years ago. It was the worst time of my life, but my father got me through it. We got each other through it, really."

He sat up straight again, but his eyes swam with concern.

"I miss her, obviously, but I've gotten used to it." I flinched as the boat dipped to the side and water sprayed over the deck. The wind speed was increasing, as well as the size of the waves. "It's my father I'm worried about. He's never considered moving on. They really loved each other. In fact—" I cut myself off as another wave splashed my feet. I felt uncomfortable giving away so much truth. I didn't know if I should say it, but something prodded at me to continue. "He was an islander, but she was a Cambrian."

Graham's eyes grew wide. Before he could speak, the boat dropped into a trough between the waves and the deck tilted wildly. We grabbed the mast to keep from falling overboard.

"Help me with the sail!" I cried.

We loosened the stays and tied the sails until they were secured against the mast. The sea churned, dark and angry. Sharp raindrops hit my face.

"Secure the cargo!" I said. "Where's the compass?"

Graham lunged to the front of the boat. He opened his cabin door and shoved the books and compass inside. A wave lifted the bow. Graham held tight to the doorway and I gripped the mast. The next wave rose above us, the crest beginning to curl. It would wash us off the deck, no matter how tightly we held on.

"Get inside!" I shouted.

He squinted into the distance, not responding to my shouts, while his face filled with dread.

"Graham, get in!"

I dashed over and pushed him toward the door as the bow dropped again.

Just before I dove into the cabin, I saw what he'd seen through the heavy sheet of rain: another boat.

TWENTY-SEVEN

I SLAMMED THE CABIN DOOR AS A WAVE ENVELOPED THE deck.

Graham's mouth moved, but the sound was lost to the storm. Still, I knew what he was trying to say. Someone was following us. I didn't know if it was Cael, the Enforcers, or maybe even my father, but either way, I wanted to stay far ahead of them.

We pressed our hands into the ceiling to brace our bodies against the violent waves. The boat rose and plummeted, rolling the cramped cabin, and us, in every possible direction. At first, I tried to keep a space between Graham and me, but the constantly angling deck made it impossible.

Thunder added its roar to the ear-splitting torrent and waves slammed incessantly against the hull. I thought I couldn't be seasick, but this time I fought hard to keep nausea from overtaking me. One glance at Graham's face proved he felt the same.

The storm roared for so long that I began to imagine ending

up on the shores of a strange new land—if one really existed. We could lose our world completely.

I squeezed my eyes shut to fight the nausea and pushed my arms harder against the ceiling, grasping at whatever bit of control I could reach.

When the downpour quieted and the waves calmed, I peeled my eyes open and let my arms relax. My whole body ached.

Graham had his eyes squeezed shut and his face was sallow. He groaned and peered through one eye.

"I think it's over," I said.

He put a hand over his mouth and escaped the cabin in a rush.

I stayed where I was to let my churning stomach ease up. Stretching out on the mattress, I whimpered when my muscles and joints moved out of their cramped positions. When the deck became level, I crawled out. Through the clouds came the faint glow of the late afternoon sun.

Graham knelt at the edge of the deck, leaning over the water, which seemed closer than it should've been.

"Feeling better?" I asked.

"Yes, thank you."

I rolled my eyes. "You don't need to be so polite at a time like this. It's okay to be honest."

"All right, then. I'm terrible. How are you?"

My gaze landed on the deck. The hatch door had come loose from its hinges and was cracked down the middle. "You've got to be kidding. No!"

"What?" asked Graham, turning around.

I crouched and examined the damaged hatch. The hold

was empty, except for one barrel and a pool of seawater. I dropped my head in my hands and groaned. "We're dead."

Graham knelt beside me. He reached into the water and picked up the barrel, then took a sip. "Still fresh."

"Well, that's something. But it will only delay the inevitable —unless we can get back to land within a day."

"There's something else," he said. "Before the storm, I saw—"

"A boat," I said. "I know."

"Do you think they're after us?"

I nodded. *Someone* definitely was.

"Maybe the Enforcers have caught up to us. Or maybe my mother sent out a search party. Unless, of course, she's thrilled I'm gone."

If she was being blamed for his disappearance, as I'd tried to arrange, she wouldn't be so thrilled. She'd be trying to prove her innocence by finding Graham—which I couldn't let happen.

"Whoever it is, that storm must have separated us," I said. "There's no sign of them now."

He nodded, his disheveled hair falling over his forehead. With his unshaven face and tanned skin, he was beginning to lose the resemblance to his former self. Even his blue eyes reflected a new ruggedness.

But why was I looking? I dropped my gaze. We were lost in the middle of the ocean and the color of his eyes meant nothing.

"We're sitting too low in the water," I said. "Let's get this hold cleared."

"How?" He looked around. "We've lost all our tools."

I sagged against the rim of the boat. Maybe I'd have to come to terms with this whole death thing. But then I remembered something. I crossed the deck and opened the cabin door, emptying my bag of its contents.

I brought it out and held it up. "It's sharkskin. Watertight."

He smiled. "Smart."

I dipped the bag into the water filling the hold and dumped it overboard before going back for another.

Graham and I took turns on water removal duty until we were thoroughly exhausted. By nightfall, we'd finally finished clearing most of it out. The sails were up again, the canvas curving against the wind.

We sat on the prow and waited for the clouds to clear so we could use the stars to regain our bearings and find the nearest island. To get a precise location, I needed a sextant, but it had been washed away with half our supplies.

A cloud thinned, revealing a patch of starry sky. "There," I said, "the—"

"North Star," Graham interrupted, then lifted his shoulders in a humble shrug. "I've studied astronomy. I may not have understood the practical use of it—those books weren't the type you'd find in Cambria—but I was fascinated all the same. I can identify most constellations."

I smiled. "Maybe you should be teaching me instead."

"I'm sorry. I wasn't trying to act like a know-it-all."

"I meant it. Besides, you're a noble. You were born a know-it-all." I held my thumb out to the horizon and measured roughly up to the North Star. We seemed to be at about the same latitude as before the storm. But for the longitude . . .

"The closest island is Gellor, isn't it?" asked Graham, his arm extended toward the stars, making the calculations along with me.

"Yeah. It looks like the storm pushed us south, but if we continue northwestward with the wind—and if we're lucky—we'll make it to Gellor before . . ."

"Before we die," said Graham.

"Exactly."

"We'll get there," he said.

"How do you know?"

"Because I trust you."

I frowned. That didn't give me any comfort.

"And," he said, "we still have our compass."

I had to laugh at his optimism. It was better than nothing, but our water supply was the real problem.

"So . . ." He fidgeted with the compass, brushing a finger over the glass face. "If your mother was a Cambrian, how did your parents meet?"

I looked around at the blackness I floated in, absorbing the desolate comfort of the nighttime sea. I normally wouldn't have wanted to answer personal questions, but the thought of talking about my parents seemed nice. "My father got his hands on a boat and climbed the wall into the city."

"He sounds like you." A half-smile played at his lips.

"Just wait." I smiled, too. "Then he impersonated a noble and met my mother at an Academy ball."

"Your mother was a *noble*?" He laughed. "This really was a scandal."

"You have no idea." I beamed with pride.

"So, what happened?"

I shrugged. "They fell in love." I had no intention of telling him the entire story. "Her family wasn't thrilled, to say the least. She chose a man who was the complete opposite of the Cambrian type."

"The Cambrian type," he muttered, staring down at the deep black water. I followed his gaze, watching the choppy reflection of the waning half-moon ripple across the surface. When I looked up, he seemed closer. I flinched, fighting the urge to run.

But it wasn't exactly uncomfortable.

"When I'm king, I'll have no choice but to marry 'the Cambrian type,'" said Graham.

"Any favorite Cambrian ladies?" I asked with a wink.

"Eh . . ." Graham made a face. "Not particularly. Besides, if I did have a favorite, she'd have to be an Immovable or in Class A for it to be legal. And of course, my mother would certainly torment anyone who didn't earn her approval, which would leave me with even fewer options."

"I guess that rules out Mara Stroud, then," I said. "Your mother clearly despises her —oh, and the Eleventh House, too. So they're no good."

"No one is." He laughed. "Not to both my mother and me, anyway."

"I can imagine," I said. "Nobles have impossibly high standards—except my mother, obviously."

"Their story makes me realize how ordinary my parents are," said Graham. "Take away their titles and you're left with nothing but a marriage of convenience."

"If you took away their titles, they might've had the opportunity to marry for love instead of convenience," I said, surprised to hear myself defending them. "In some ways, kings and queens have less freedom than everybody else."

Graham nodded. "That's true."

"Maybe, in another life with different choices, your father could've been the kind man I glimpsed. When we *feel* we have no choice is often when we make the worst decisions."

The moonlight cast a shadow from his messy hair over Graham's face. He sighed and dropped his head.

I wondered if I shouldn't have said that about his father. It was too sensitive of a topic. We didn't even know if he was still alive.

"I'm sorry," I said.

I looked up at the stars again but was shaken from my focus

when I felt his hand on mine. My eyes shot wide open. *What was he doing?*

But apparently, he couldn't read me as well as the compass. He moved his fingertips down my hand, oblivious to my panic.

I was as still as a sail without wind.

His fingers slipped between mine.

I closed my eyes and wished I were anywhere but here. Prison, the aqueducts, chatting with the queen. Any of those would be a relief in comparison.

Then pull your hand away! I told myself, but my body didn't want to. The warmth of his hand was paralyzing. Intoxicating.

Relax. It doesn't mean anything, another part of my mind argued.

He must have finally picked up on my stillness, or the fact that I hadn't taken a breath in the past thirty seconds, because his hand lifted and he got to his feet.

I let out the air I'd been holding.

"I'm sure you're tired," he said. "I'll keep an eye on things."

I nodded and jumped up awkwardly. "Uh, thanks. Wake me when you're ready to sleep."

"Goodnight, Bryn."

It was his turn to rest, and we both knew it, but I could hardly bring myself to say another word. I mumbled goodnight and crawled into my cabin, but I didn't feel as tired as I should have. My heart was beating too fast. Warm energy burned in my hand and my emotions seemed crammed into a box tighter than this space. Nothing fit. Nothing felt right. Each day since I'd met Graham, another layer of guilt had settled in my stomach. It was getting heavier by the hour.

I squeezed my eyes shut, wishing I could force out tears, but they remained bottled up inside—my first symptom of dehydration. I needed something to release the pressure in my heart, so I focused hard, replacing my doubts with thoughts that would push me forward.

My family. My people. My mother.

My father.

It didn't matter how hard this was. I repeated my motivations through my mind until the doubts eased just a little. Regardless of what I'd just told Graham about bad decisions, trying to continue on to Tramore was my *only* choice.

CHAPTER
TWENTY-EIGHT

WHEN I OPENED MY EYES, I KNEW I'D SLEPT TOO LONG. I shot out to the deck, the unforgiving sun already high. I turned back toward my cabin to see Graham sitting on the stern above it, his hand on the tiller and his eyelids drooping.

He blinked. "Good morning, or afternoon, I suppose."

"Have you been awake all this time?"

He stifled a yawn. "Yes, but I'm fine."

I laughed. "Liar. You're exhausted. Take a drink." I gestured to the barrel.

"No, thank you. I drank not long ago."

I frowned. "Are you sure?"

"Yes." He smiled to reassure me, but a red line appeared in the center of his cracked lips. "Perhaps I'm a little tired."

"Good. Go to sleep. Now."

"Yes, Imperatrix."

"Shut up." I took the compass from him and he went into his cabin. I should've thanked him for the sleep, but I could hardly look him in the eye.

I drank only when I couldn't swallow without the moisture.

There was little cloud cover and no rain now that I wanted it. Until we made it to an island, our water supply would have to do—and we'd already finished half the barrel.

I kept sailing northwest, as I hoped Graham had, but the view throughout the day was the same. Ocean on every horizon, with a few stray clouds drifting through the sky. The sun was the only thing that changed as it fell lazily toward the sea.

Alone on the deck, I waited, watching for a sign of land. When night fell, the vast blackness surrounded me. I kept sailing, my body weakening, each hour more hopeless than the last.

By late afternoon the next day, the dryness in my eyes turned to a burn. I sat on the deck, taking cover in patches of shade cast by the sails. I picked up the water barrel and was about to take a sip when I realized it was almost completely empty.

I'd been drinking while Graham slept for hours. He'd gone too long without water.

I squeezed into his cabin and nudged him. "Hey, when's the last time you had a drink?"

He squinted through one eye and groaned. The crack in his lip was deeper now.

I lifted his head and put the barrel to his lips, pouring water into his mouth before he could stop me.

He drank a little, then pushed it away. "I'm fine . . . don't need it."

I thought back on the past two days, racking my brain for a memory of him drinking anything. All I remembered for sure was when he took a sip to taste the water after the storm.

"What are you trying to prove?" I poured the last of the water into his mouth, making sure he swallowed before closed his eyes again. I pushed away the empty barrel and reached for Graham's hand, holding it without fear this time. Maybe because I didn't expect him to remember. Or maybe because I thought it could be my last chance.

The sun set in a blaze of red sky, leaving us alone in the nothingness. I huddled by Graham in his cabin, hardly bothering to adjust the sails. I wasn't sure I even knew where to go anymore.

He slept fitfully, squeezing my hand and muttering broken phrases. "Didn't mean to . . . please forgive . . ."

"Just relax," I said for what felt like the eightieth time.

"Bryn?"

I shook my head. "It's okay. Don't talk."

His voice was dry and raspy. "Thanks . . . for coming to see me."

I let go of his hand and pulled my legs to my chest.

"Can I tell you a secret?" he asked.

I buried my head in my knees, trying to block out his deliriousness in case it was contagious. I couldn't afford to start telling secrets. I'd much prefer to die with them unsaid.

But his slurred voice broke through anyway. "I only kept going to the library . . . to see you."

"Stop talking. Save your energy."

"I hadn't felt happy in so long," he whispered, "not since . . ."

I covered my ears and climbed out of the cabin. I couldn't hear it. Not if it was real. Not if it wasn't. I walked across the deck to the bow. Only a sliver of red remained on the horizon, hanging on stubbornly. The rest of the sky was alive with the deepest shade of blue.

I watched the water pass by, finding comfort in the constant flow. The world didn't care what happened to us. It would go on turning without a hitch. It was the people who would suffer when we didn't make it to Tramore in time.

And my father. He wouldn't be able to stay out of the battle. He'd fight for his family until his dying breath.

I looked back at Graham. I itched to go back, to stay with him, to keep him from being alone ever again. It hadn't crossed my mind that he'd save the drinking water for me. I realized, with shame, that I wouldn't have thought to do it for him. My selfishness won out, like it always had.

I'd die selfish.

And Graham would die because of my lies.

Just before the sky darkened from blue to black, my ears picked up a change. A tiny shift in the same old sound of water lapping against the boat.

Waves breaking on land.

I rushed to the tiller, directing us toward the sound. But as we got closer, my heart sank. It was only a rocky mound, nothing but a few boulders.

But it triggered a memory.

My father's maps. I'd studied his journal for so long. I knew of a place like this off the southern tip of Gellor. I rotated the tiller the other way, steering us toward the north. It was just a matter of making it there before . . . I shook my head to avoid the thought.

"Graham!" I hopped back to the cabin and leaned through the doorway. "You'll be okay. Just hang on."

He didn't move. The only sign of life besides his raspy breathing was a furrow between his brows.

I KEPT THE BOAT ON COURSE TO THE NORTH, BUT THE weak breeze barely lifted the sails. My strength had become as dim as the night.

I fought the pull of sleep, afraid to close my eyes for more than a few seconds. The dryness in my throat made it hurt to breathe. How much worse did Graham feel? I'd never imagine myself as stronger than him again. I laughed aloud, feeling a strange urge to tell him—to tell him that and more—but I stopped myself, recognizing it for what it was: the beginnings of delirium.

With my weakness came anger, and a desire to blame everyone who'd gotten us here. Cael. The king. The outlaws. The storm. I could blame them all, but it was a lie. This was my fault. I'd practically murdered Graham myself.

The compass fell from my hands and rolled across the deck toward Graham.

I went after it, ending up on my knees by his door again. I clutched it in my hands and looked at Graham's face. If we were going to die, it didn't matter if he knew my secrets.

"Graham." His name scraped against my tongue and I moved closer to him. "I'm sorry. I'm so sorry. I'm not who you think I am . . ." My voice gave out and I leaned over, pressing my forehead to his.

The next thing I knew, I was riding in a carriage through Cambria. It took us through the winding streets, higher and higher, up toward the Academy. My father sat beside me, beaming with a pride I'd only dreamed of.

I looked to my other side, surprised to see my mother there —alive. I smiled at her, expecting her to glow with pride as well, but her warm, copper brown eyes hardened.

Cael sat there, too, dressed in a distinguished suit. My parents also wore noble clothing. I looked down to see what kind of finery I was wearing, but it was only a man's shirt and trousers. They were dirty and torn, stained with something that looked like blood. I wasn't meant to be here.

"Stop the carriage!" I wanted to say, but when I opened my mouth, the rush of waves was all I heard.

Waves. Not the random rippling of water on the hull, but consistent, regular ones.

I lifted my head from my disorienting dream to find myself lying next to Graham in the cabin. *Was I dreaming? Or am I dreaming now?* And what was this pounding in my head? If I could just have a nice drink of water, I could make sense of it all.

The boat crashed with a jolt. *Need to get off.* I couldn't remember why, but it seemed like the right thing to do.

Wait.

Graham breathed erratically, like he couldn't catch a decent breath. I wanted to stay with him, but—

Get water, my mind whispered.

I pulled away from him and crawled out of the cabin to the edge of the boat.

My eyes glazed over as I returned to Cambria and saw my father beaming at me. Then Cael took his place, his satisfied smile cruel and mocking. I'd done something terrible and he knew it. My mother appeared next, her disappointment a strong contrast to Cael's pride. She, too, knew what I'd done.

I reached for the door of the carriage and dropped to the hard cobblestones, trying to grasp at a memory that remained just out of reach. I looked down. I stood in a few feet of water on a rocky shore. I stepped forward, moving onto the land, but after a few steps, my legs couldn't carry me. My heart fluttered unevenly within my chest as if it had forgotten how it used to beat. I had to get water. But how could I, when ten steps seemed like ten miles?

The city streets returned, and my father stood in front of

me. A brass goblet materialized in his hand.

"Please. Let me drink." I reached for it, fumbling for a grasp.

Cool water went down my throat, stinging, but life-giving, all the way to my belly. It seemed so real.

"Thank you, Father," I said. "Don't forget about Graham." Yes, that was his name. How could I have forgotten?

"Father?"

The voice jerked me back to reality. The goblet became a barrel and my father disappeared, along with the city. The vision plunged into darkness.

"Where am I?" I asked, blinking my dry eyes.

"Gellor," the irritated voice said.

"Are you . . . Cael?" I squinted, not sure if I was hallucinating.

"I'm definitely not your father."

I was too grateful just then to hate him. He had water. That was infinitely more valuable than kindness.

Cael brought the barrel to my lips again.

"No." I pushed it away. "Take it to Graham." At that moment, I didn't care if he saw Cael. I only cared that he survived.

Cael pulled back the barrel but didn't stand. Instead, he sank lazily to the rocky shore, smiling with tight lips. "Hm . . . no. I don't see any reason to do that."

"What?" I was too weary to put the anger behind my words, but I felt the burn of fury all the same. My hatred for him returned, stronger than I would've thought my body could contain.

"You changed the plan on me," he said. "You bloody *knocked* me out and took my boat. I had to steal one from a fisherman to come after you!"

"I thought . . . I thought you'd kill him."

"I wasn't going to!" he shouted. "But now that you've done this"—he gestured with both arms at the situation—"I think it's fair if I make a few changes to the plan myself."

"No," I said, reaching for the barrel. "You can't let him die."

"Yes, I can," said Cael. "It will save *so* much trouble. We could just go home. The job would be done."

I gripped his shirt, a sudden surge of energy in my veins. "Help him." I shook him and shouted in his face. "Help him!"

He peeled my fingers off the fabric. My shaky arms couldn't fight back.

"Well," he said, "I've hardly slept in days, so it's time to say goodnight. You should have enough strength to find more water when this is empty, as long as you don't waste any on him." He stood up, brushing off his clothes. "I'll be watching you. So, do the right thing, okay?"

He walked along the shore, into the darkness.

"Come back!" My voice was hoarse and desperate, but I didn't care. I wasn't strong enough to get the barrel to Graham on my own. "You can't do this. If you walk away, you can forget your reward!"

"Oh, yeah?" He turned, shaking his head. "Do you think I'll keep your secrets if you don't follow through?"

He wouldn't. I'd always known that. My threats were meaningless.

"Also—" Cael reached for something in his belt. "If he does live, and you don't finish the job, I will. And I'll do it the way I've always thought it should be done." Moonlight revealed a pistol in his hand.

I shook my head. I'd taken his pistol when I knocked him out and couldn't imagine how he'd found another one, but I didn't doubt he'd use it. "No. I'll do it!"

"Good." He tucked the weapon into his belt and turned around, fading into the night.

CHAPTER
TWENTY-NINE

I reached for the water barrel Cael left behind and forced myself to stand on trembling legs. The rocks scraped and trapped my feet in their crevices. I stumbled to the ground. Sharp rocks tore my knees and I dropped the barrel. Crawling forward, I wrapped my arm around it again and continued across the moonlit shore.

Each step sent a bolt of pain through my head. My burning eyes fought to stay open, even in the darkness, and my vision dimmed until I couldn't tell if they were open or shut.

I need more water, I thought.

No, a voice in my mind argued. *Graham won't have enough.*

If I don't, we'll both die.

He might already be dead.

Don't you dare.

Please.

Don't.

I uncorked the barrel and took a sip. The smooth flow enlivened me enough to move my feet a few more steps. My vision cleared to reveal glossy black water up to my knees.

I trudged through the water to the side of the boat. The barrel wasn't hard to toss onto the deck, but my weakened body wouldn't be so easy. I reached my hands up and gripped the boat, but my fingers felt limp. I lifted my feet out of the thigh-deep water, searching for footholds in the wooden hull. My arms shook, and my heart pounded so fast that I thought it would burst.

My body felt broken and useless. I dropped back into the water and screamed with rage. The sound ripped through my dry throat and I tasted blood. I waded to the other side, keeping my hand along the hull. It brushed against something coarse. A rope. It hung into the water, connected to the anchor. I couldn't even remember dropping it.

I planted my feet on the anchor and pulled myself up the rope until one knee made it over the edge, then the other, and I collapsed onto the deck, gasping for breath.

I picked up the water barrel from the deck and took it into the cabin to Graham's side. His body was still. Only his weak breathing kept me from a panic.

I reached over and brushed the hair off his forehead. "Graham, wake up."

I propped his head up on my knees, putting the spout to his mouth.

He didn't wake. The water ran down his face.

"Just drink it! You're not allowed to die!"

He stirred, but his eyes wouldn't open. I lifted the barrel and tried again.

And this time, *this time*, he swallowed.

He gulped it down. I kept it at his lips, trying to make him drink more, but he soon closed his mouth and fell back asleep. I'd get more water for him after I slept. He breathed more calmly now. I took one more drink and set the barrel down, then finally let myself lie down beside him, not even bothering to keep space between us like I'd always done.

I rested my head on his chest, if only to hear the glorious sound of his heart still beating. Touching him like this felt like trespassing into a forbidden place I shouldn't even dream of going, but right now, nothing mattered except that he was alive. I longed to be closer to him, to feel him breathe and to keep him breathing. Not only could his body still give in to dehydration, but Cael was out there, and now I was one hundred percent certain I couldn't trust him. I fell asleep with my ear to Graham's heart and my arm draped across him protectively.

I awoke to a warm hand on my forehead. My eyes fluttered, squinting against the morning light. Though I'd probably only gotten a few hours of sleep, my body felt dramatically different—almost like my own again.

Graham leaned over me. "Time for some water." He had a raspiness to his voice and the split in his lip was still visible.

He handed me the barrel and I sat up to drink, my memories of the night before haunting me, from the dehydration to the fact that I'd spent the night practically wrapped around Graham. I could only hope I'd moved farther away before he woke up and saw me like that. If not, I'd blame it on the delirium.

I finished off the last few drops of water and climbed out of the cabin after Graham. Now that it was daylight, I could get a real look at this island. Beyond the gray tide pools on the shore, it was lush and green, covered in hills and forests. Two hills taller than the rest stood near its center. Birds soared above the canopies of the trees and the scent of greenery made me want to close my eyes and breathe it in.

"Where'd you find another barrel, anyway?" he asked, looking at the one I held.

"Oh." I cleared my throat. "Uh, I found it washed up on the shore last night."

"Wow," said Graham. "It must be one of our lost barrels. How fortunate that it ended up in the same place we did."

"Well, that's how currents work," I said, hoping to stave off any potential suspicion. "But it's time to get some more water. And food. I'm starving."

Graham eagerly reached into his pocket and pulled out a silver fish between his thumb and forefinger. "Oh, that reminds me, I caught a fish!"

I took it from his hand and laughed, but it came out more like a dry cough. "Did you intentionally catch the tiniest fish in the ocean?"

"Excuse *me*," he said in the tone of a nobleman, "I thought you'd be impressed, considering that I caught it with my bare hands now that our net is gone."

I smiled and glanced at the craggy beach. "It was washed up in a tide pool, wasn't it?"

"Yes. Yes, it was." He sighed. "I must say, I'm glad you're alive to mock me."

I smiled. "And I'm glad you're alive to be mocked." I hadn't forgotten the depths of my fear last night. I ducked my head and turned away, toward the island, in case my eyes revealed the emotion swimming beneath the surface. If he knew how I felt, we had a whole new set of problems.

We shared a minuscule portion of fish, then lifted the anchor and set sail, staying close to the shores. I didn't dare leave the boat completely exposed while we fetched water. Since boats were forbidden among islanders, they were rare and extremely valuable–cowries, on the other hand, were abundant and worthless outside the wall. Boats were freedom.

I hoped I might also keep Cael from finding me and my boat again, but he'd proven himself to be far too good at stalking me.

The rocky beaches gave way to lush mangroves. We found a large enough opening in the tangled roots and branches and hid the boat among the trees. Then we picked up our barrels and left the mangrove for the shores of Gellor.

As we entered the lush forest, Graham's eyes were full of wonder and his mouth gaped open in an astonished smile. "I'm on non-Cambrian ground," he said. "This might as well be a new world."

Something in the tone of his voice urged me to pause and listen. I should've moved on, but for the first time, I wanted to be right where I was. I could almost imagine we were two ordinary people, without the ropes binding us to our duty.

"Is something wrong?" he asked.

I shook my head to shake away my thoughts. "No. But we'll have to be careful to avoid the islanders. They won't welcome a Brennin with anything but a spear."

"Are they really that violent?" asked Graham. "Your book doesn't portray them that way at all."

"Well, that's because my father was one of them."

"Your father?" Graham asked. "That's *his* journal?"

Oh. I frowned, remembering I hadn't ever told Graham where the journal came from. But I guess it didn't matter now. "Yeah. He wrote it."

"Why didn't you tell me?"

"You never asked."

"Yes, I did!" said Graham. "I asked a million questions about that book."

I smirked. "Yeah, that's true. You definitely did."

We hiked uphill through the thick forest, wary and alert for signs of islanders. I kept my bag open and my knives ready.

Mixed in with the rustling wind and bird calls came the sound of running water. The bushes and trees grew closer as we followed the sound. My hair caught on branches, tangling and slowing me down. Brambles scraped our hands and clothes, but I didn't mind so much when I noticed the blackberries.

I stopped, set down my barrel, and popped a few berries in my mouth. They were tart and firm, and the juices stung my dry tongue and lips. I still couldn't resist eating another.

I handed some to Graham.

"What exactly happened last night?" he asked, taking the blackberries.

I choked on a berry and nearly swallowed it whole. "You mean, besides you almost dying?" I was afraid of what he might remember. He was too full of questions this morning. "We sailed for hours. I'd nearly given up when I saw some rocks that put me back on course. Eventually, we came here."

"I'm glad you held yourself together better than I did."

I shook my head angrily. "Don't try to pretend it was by chance. You weren't drinking any water."

He put his barrel on the ground. "It ended up being a good strategy."

"*Strategy?*"

"Sure." He lifted his head and looked me in the eye. "If we'd shared the water, neither of us would've been capable enough to find land."

I stared him back in the eye. I knew a lie when I heard one. "There's no way you could have known that. You almost killed yourself."

"I'm sor—" Graham started to apologize, then stopped. "No. Actually, I'm not. I'd make the same choice again."

"Then you'd die." I felt a heat rising in my face. "I couldn't do it on my own. I barely made it off the boat before—" I cut myself off, swallowing my words.

His voice was quiet and curious. "Before what? You brought back water, didn't you?"

"I . . . yes," I answered lamely. "But I only just made it back to you. We both nearly died."

"I *am* sorry about that." He took a step closer to me. "Is there anything else?" he asked.

"Anything else?" I asked, my heart racing.

"Anything that happened last night, I mean. I thought I heard you shouting at someone."

I froze. "No, nothing. I was a bit delirious. I may have been shouting, but not *at* anyone."

"Well, whatever happened," said Graham, "thank you for saving my life."

The fears from yesterday were still so fresh and painful. I thought of his lifeless form on the deck and I shuddered, reaching for his hand without thinking.

His surprised eyes shot to mine and he squeezed my hand. "Oh, that reminds me of my biggest question."

I felt my face heat up as I realized what he meant.

He smiled. "Did I wake up with this hand across my chest or was that nothing but a fantasy?"

I stared back at him, this question somehow the most terrifying of them all. I should've let go of his hand and pulled away, told another lie, laughed it off, *anything*. But we both stayed where we stood, my helplessness revealing the truth.

He laced his fingers between mine. All the energy in my body seemed to flow to the tips of my fingers, making the touch almost unbearable. I still didn't pull away.

My eyes remained locked on his, afraid of what he'd do next, terrified of what *I'd* do next. On the outside, I was stone. Inside, my veins pulsed, my mind raced, and I fought a hidden battle without knowing which side I was on.

He lifted his other hand up my arm, to my shoulder. My

skin shivered with anticipation. He brushed the hair off my neck and my eyes closed against my will. I leaned my face into his hand, wishing he'd stop but waiting for more.

I was about to give in and find out what *more* would feel like when my mental battle was sealed with a single thought: *If you don't finish the job, I will.*

My hand slid from his and I backed away, my eyes flashing to the trees around us. Cael could be watching. His threat was nothing to take lightly.

Graham's eyebrows pushed together, confused and questioning.

Guilt and fear filled the space in my chest that had been blazing with life a moment earlier. I looked at the ground.

"Did you hear that?" Graham said, his gentle tone transformed to urgency.

I straightened up and listened, my ears alert.

A dog's bark echoed through the woods. If dogs were close, so were people.

THIRTY

"Come on," I whispered.

We continued through the forest as quietly as we could, but the dense trees and underbrush weren't making it easy.

We heard the dog again, closer now.

The forest opened up to reveal a silver river gleaming at the edge of the tree line. I took my barrel and stepped to the water's edge, placing it on its side in the cold current.

Graham leaned close and put a hand on my shoulder. "Look up."

I lifted my gaze from the water. A large brown dog growled at us from the opposite bank.

The barrel slipped out of my hands with a splash.

The dog barked fiercely, and I thought I heard a shout.

I reached out and caught the barrel before the current swept it away. "Fill your barrel!" I said to Graham. "We need both."

The dog continued barking at us with no less energy than before.

As Graham set his barrel in the water, a woman stepped

out of the trees beside the dog. Her face was rugged and brown, framed by long black hair streaked with gray. She held an axe in her hand.

"Who are you?" she asked, her voice deep and commanding.

The dog howled.

She touched her hand to the dog's head, quieting the howl. "Answer me!"

Graham and I looked at each other. I started to reach for my knives on instinct, but the truth was that I had no desire to hurt this force of a woman. I just didn't have a clue what to say.

"This is Bryn Yarrow, ambassador of Tramore," said Graham, finding his words when I couldn't. "And my name is Graham Brennin. We're here to offer you peace."

I cringed, wishing he weren't so damn honest.

The woman's sharp eyes narrowed. "Graham Brennin? The heir of Cambria?"

He nodded. "Yes."

"What an unexpected surprise." Her face remained firm and distrusting. "Come with me, then. I want the rest of the village to hear whatever it is you have to say."

"Thank you," said Graham, stepping forward into the shallow river.

I grabbed him by the shoulder. "What are you doing? We don't have time for this. Let's go!"

"It's too late now," he mumbled, glancing at the woman and the dog, then back at me. "We can't say 'never mind' and run away."

"Then let's not say anything. Let's just run away."

"Are you coming or not?" asked the woman.

We both looked at her. I nodded, intimidated by her power. Something about this woman demanded respect. Not in Maeve

Brennin's style, but in a way that made me believe she deserved it.

"Leave your weapons behind," she pointed at my bag.

"What makes you think I have—"

"Leave them," she said, lifting the axe and resting it over her shoulder. "I saw the way your hand hovered over that bag."

I stepped back to the bank and hid my bag in a bush and set down our water barrels, taking note of every detail of our surroundings so I could find it on the way out. Then we crossed the river.

THE FOREST OPENED UP TO FIELDS AND COTTAGES appeared up ahead. They'd been roughly built with stacked stone bases, timber frames, and thatched roofs. We stepped onto a dirt path that led to the cluster of tiny houses. The dog ran on ahead of us.

Figures moved around outside, going busily about their lives. Graham sped up as if the mere sight of humans energized him. I lagged behind, uneasy about strolling in pretending we had something to offer these people.

We passed the first home. The first villagers looked our way, abandoning their work to stare.

I forced my mouth to lift so I might pass for a real ambassador, as Graham claimed I was, but I wasn't sure it looked like a real smile. *Be charming*, I thought, trying to put sincerity into my expression.

Graham's smile was as natural as any I'd seen. His back was straight, but somehow the stiffness had dissolved, leaving confidence in its place. His jaw was shadowed, and his dark hair was anything but the perfectly combed style it once was, but it only added an air of boldness. He looked comfortable, approachable, and even a little bit regal.

A group of children sat in rows on the ground, writing in the dirt with sticks. When we came closer, a few dropped their sticks and gaped. I smiled at a little girl with sun-browned skin and white-blonde hair.

"Keep writing, please!" a young man with shaggy red hair ordered. "I didn't tell you to stop."

"But, look," said the blonde girl, without taking her eyes from me. "There's someone *new* here."

The other children spun around, jumping to their feet to get a better look.

The teacher's head shot up and he narrowed his eyes. "Who are these two, Rowan?" he asked the woman we followed.

"Come to the square," she said. "You'll see."

I followed Rowan away from the children, with Graham close behind. The red-headed teacher stayed behind us both, his suspicious glare making it clear we weren't welcome.

Rowan led us to an open space in the middle of the cottages. My boots landed on smooth stones. The ground was paved with them, almost like a street in Cambria. Benches lined the edge of the open space, and a blackened fire pit marked the center. It still smelled of smoke.

Rowan crossed the paving stones to a bell hanging on a pole. She pulled a rope, sending its tolls through the quiet village. It sounded strange and unnatural here, like the city was leaking into the outside world.

"Sit." She gestured to a bench in front of the fire pit.

I reluctantly obeyed. She wasn't warm or welcoming, but that wasn't what bothered me. Being around her made me uncomfortably aware of my own failings. She was the kind of person my father wanted me to be— authoritarian and always in control—but in reality, I was so far from that.

The villagers gathered, their voices rising as their numbers grew. When the benches were filled and surrounded by observers, Rowan addressed the crowd. "We have visitors. Bryn Yarrow, who claims to be an ambassador from Tramore"—she appraised me from the corner of her eye before turning her gaze beside me—"and Sir Graham Brennin."

The crowd went quiet for a beat, as if drawing a collective breath. All eyes fixed on Graham.

Then the noise returned, loud and angry. The clamor of voices made each word indistinguishable from the rest. I wished Graham hadn't been so trusting.

Rowan rang the bell again, quieting most of the voices but not all.

"Cambria's precious heir?" said someone behind us.

"What business have you got here?" a man asked. "Come to pick up a fresh steak for a royal banquet?"

"Here to make sure we're workin' hard enough?" a woman with a baby on her hip asked. "You're welcome to chop down trees for a day to find out."

Graham's face reddened. "Excuse me," he said, his voice unsure. "I—"

"The little heir is out to see how much more he can take from us. Or is it king now? Has your father been nagged to death by the queen yet?"

"Nah. He's brought his lady to impress 'er. 'Look at all the slaves I got, m'lady. Aren't I the perfect tyrant?'"

"She's from Tramore?" said a voice behind me. I turned to see the red-headed teacher who followed us here. "Why would she be with the heir? He must be manipulating her. She's hardly said a word after all, so—"

"Oh, I'll say a word, ginger!" I shot to my feet and faced

him. "None of you have a clue!" I pointed at Graham. "This man isn't his father. He's not like any king before him. And if you'd *listen* to him, you might end up with something more than a head full of tripe." I glared at the teacher for too long before taking a deep breath and sinking back to the bench.

Whoa. What happened to my attempt at charm?

But at least everyone was quiet.

Graham stared at me wide-eyed, then lifted his chin and stood. "Well, now that I've had a proper introduction, let me explain myself. I know you don't trust me—and I don't blame you—but we're here to help. There's a war brewing among the outlaws." He paused, appraising the crowd. "I imagine you're aware of it."

Fearful eyes shifted, some to Rowan, others to me.

"We weren't," said Rowan, "but it doesn't sound like a bad idea."

The crowd laughed and some cheered.

I frowned. Based on what my father told me, I was under the impression that all the islands were uniting for the attack, though it would be led by the people of Tramore. Either Rowan was lying—which was perfectly reasonable, given the fact that she was talking to the heir—or the news of the uprising hadn't yet made it to Gellor.

Graham tried to keep the surprise from his face, but the lift of his right eyebrow revealed it, at least to me. Still, he had to continue. He'd been trying to pretend we'd come here for an important reason, so if he didn't say something impressive, I doubted these people would just let us walk away.

"I've recently begun to learn more about your people," he finally said. "I've seen how much we depend upon you, and yet, you've been isolated, banished, and perse-cuted by Cambria. I understand why war may seem appealing." His eyes were as clear and honest as his intentions and his words were every bit as persuasive as a king's should be.

He looked at me and I nodded, urging him on.

"It's my duty to protect the people within and outside the wall. Instead of war, imagine how we'd benefit from an alliance. Let's make a pledge for peace."

"An alliance?" The red-headed teacher spoke with as much skepticism as before. "So, we promise not to join in an uprising —and then what? You let us continue our miserable lives? You're not really giving us any options, are you?"

"Don't forget who he is," someone in the crowd shouted. "We can't trust him!"

"Sorry, Brennin." The teacher stepped forward aggressively. "But honestly, how could this possibly benefit us?" His messy red hair shadowed his face and his mouth tightened.

"Excellent question," said Graham. He stepped closer to the man. "You work so hard, only to have the city snatch it all away and leave you with barely enough to live on. How would you like to be compensated for your work?"

Low mutters buzzed around us. The teacher gritted his teeth.

"You want to educate your children," said Graham. "What about books? Materials for learning? I can provide that."

The man stepped back. "Is that what you think we want most? The Academy's books? Biased education?" He shook his head. "Then you're out of touch—like every other noble."

Graham frowned.

I looked at the red-haired teacher. There was a tangible air of loneliness and loss about him. His gloomy eyes reminded me of Graham's when I'd first met him, but brown instead of blue, and with an undertone of fury. Graham had been alone, with hardly a friend. He'd lost his brother, and he still suffered from the pain.

I knew what these people wanted.

"You've lost someone, haven't you?" I asked.

The man's eyes shifted, but he didn't answer.

"There are people you love in the city," I said. I raised my voice to address them all. "Many of you had to leave behind family and friends when the Academy banished you to this island. What you want most is to see them again." I looked back at the teacher, noticing a softness in his eyes. "Am I right?"

Graham smiled at me and mouthed a thank you. "If you promise to keep the peace," he said. "I'll do everything in my power to allow those who desire it to come back to the city. If I become king—"

"If?" Rowan interrupted. "Why would there be an *if*?"

"Well, it's complicated." He bit his lip. "But your alliance would help secure my position. The last thing the Cambrians want is a war."

"What about criminals walking through your gates?" said a woman in the crowd. "Or worse, the *uneducated*. Your words sound nice and all, but I know the Academy. They'll never let us be with our families."

"It's true that I wouldn't be the only one with the choice," said Graham, "but I can promise you I'd never let those Immortals rest until each of you has been given the chance to be with the ones you've lost."

Some villagers nodded. Some still looked suspicious. But not one of them argued.

Graham turned and smiled at me.

Pain rose inside my chest. No, pain was too nice a word for it. Agony. An awareness that all Graham had said—all I'd wanted to be true—were only words. Empty promises. He'd never get a chance to fulfill them. But, as usual, I had no choice but to bury my feelings and put on a false smile.

I went to Graham's side. "Nice speech. Now, can we go?"

He looked around. "So soon?"

"We can't leave our boat for too long. We need to get sailing."

He bit his lip. "I suppose you're right, but I'm so incredibly exhausted. Would it be possible to rest before trudging through the forest again?"

I wanted to say no, but the truth was that I was exhausted, too. We still had to recover from our dehydration, and resting here on land sounded very appealing. As long as we were in the village, it was unlikely Cael would make an appearance. "Okay. If they're not going to kill us, I could use a little rest."

CHAPTER
THIRTY-ONE

The villagers fed us, and Rowan let us sleep in her house for the rest of the day. We woke in the evening and returned to the village square, taking a seat on rustic benches and tree trunks around a glowing fire. The light flickered on the faces of those who hadn't yet gone home.

Graham spoke with them, looking excited to finally be meeting some outlaws. I wished I were capable of being comfortable with crowds the way he was here. But I stayed back, focused on the sound of the crackling fire, trying to absorb a bit of peace into my heart. I couldn't help but feel alone, like a tiny fish in the wide ocean.

Someone sat on the bench beside me. Out of the corner of my eye, I saw a thick head of hair lit up to bright orange by the fire. I pretended not to notice him.

"I can't help but wonder," he said quietly, "why a girl from Tramore wants to help the heir make peace treaties."

I wasn't in the mood to talk, but I took a deep breath and looked at him. "Too many people will die if we attack."

He nodded. "But maybe that's the price of freedom."

"How long have you been here?"

His brown eyes shone in the firelight. "Three years."

"You haven't seen your family for three years?"

"No. Or"—he looked at the ground—"the woman I loved."

"I'm sorry," I said. "I hope you can find them. And her."

"So do I, but even if I did get back to Cambria, it wouldn't help me see her again."

I twisted my hair and looked back at the fire. "Why is that?"

"Last I knew, she was in prison."

An idea flew into my head. I searched his face, looking for something to confirm my suspicions. *Prison. Three years ago. He had red hair like mine*, she'd said. I shook my head in disbelief. "Is your name Lachlan?"

His eyes narrowed. "Who are you again?"

I felt a thrill as if I'd found a missing piece of a puzzle. "My name's Bryn."

"Right, but . . . have we met?"

"No, but I know Cait."

The pride, anger, and bitterness in his face melted away. "Has she been outlawed too? Is she on Tramore?"

"No. She's still in prison."

His smile faded, but his newfound enthusiasm remained. "But you met her? How?"

"Well, it's kind of a long story," I said. "Let's just say I found a way to upset the Academy."

His smile filled his face. "You saw her in prison, then. And she's okay?"

"She's fine. Extraordinary, actually. What Cait did for you was selfless and brave. I don't know how you dared to lose what you had. If someone risked everything for me like that, I'd—" I stopped and felt a blush color my cheeks. Hadn't Graham saved the water for me? I couldn't finish my sentence without becoming the world's biggest hypocrite.

His smile fell, the lines of his mouth revealing his grief. "I know. Don't you think I regret it every day? I was trying to be *noble*, to do the right thing. But it turned out to be the biggest mistake of my life."

"She thinks you're still in the city. How'd you get banished?"

"After Cait turned herself in, I tried to take the blame. I told them she was innocent, that I'd bribed her to cheat for me. So they decided we were both guilty." He shook his head. "I couldn't let them banish me without trying to see her one more time, so I fought the guards to get to her. I was inside the prison doors when they shot me. Next thing I knew, I was in a boat with a bullet wound in my shoulder."

"She has no idea," I said.

He dropped his head. "I wish she knew. Even if I never see her again, I wish she could know I tried."

I nodded but stayed quiet. In the fire's glow, the gleam of his eyes became a mirror, and all I could see was myself. I mulled over what he'd said.

Trying to be noble.

Biggest mistake of my life.

ALL THE VILLAGERS HAD RETURNED TO THEIR COTTAGES when night came, and a crescent moon floated in the east. In only four more days, the moon would be in complete shadow and the islanders would launch.

I sat huddled on the bench, feeling strangely cold, even with the fire glowing near. My heart was stretched two ways, filling me with fear over what my next action would be. Whatever I chose, at least one half of my heart would feel the pain.

Graham came back to the bench and sat beside me. His presence chased my thoughts back to their caverns.

"Are you feeling okay?" he asked.

"I'm fine. Just tired."

"That man you were talking to—Lachlan—is giving us his home for the night. If we want it."

I rubbed my arms and nodded. "I do."

"Are you cold?"

Before I could answer, he put his arm around my back and pulled me closer. I didn't mean to let him. I didn't deserve his warmth. But all the resistance was in my mind alone. My body welcomed the touch and I rested my head on his shoulder, hating myself for my weakness.

"Thanks for speaking up earlier," he said. "They really listened to you."

"Me? I did nothing more than lose my temper. You're the one who earned their respect."

"But you understood them. You knew what they wanted."

"Only because I know others like them."

"Is your island the same way? Full of people whose families have been torn apart by Cambria?"

"Not so much now. They stopped sending people to Tramore years ago. Too far away, I guess, and not enough resources. My grandparents were some of the last citizens banished there."

He moved his hand along my back, softly, as if he were afraid I might notice. Maybe he was trying to warm me, but it sent a tingle of chills up my neck instead.

"What did they do?" he asked.

"Their story is in my father's book," I said. "Remember the couple who secretly kept their Class D brother in their home when his own burnt down?"

"Yes! That was them? Your father never wrote that it was his own parents."

"I know. He tried to keep his journal anonymous in case anybody ever found it."

He shook his head. "I'll be so intimidated when I meet your family."

"Well, you won't be meeting *them*. They died before I was born. But it seems like you don't need to be intimidated by anyone. You've won everybody over so far."

He looked at me, his face only inches from mine. "Everybody?"

I tore my eyes from his intense blue ones and looked back at the dying fire.

He moved his hand to my shoulder. "Have you realized that if we're able to change the law, you could live in Cambria? We both could."

For a moment, I let myself imagine that future. No war. No restrictions. Just us living normal, peaceful lives. What would it be like to wake up every morning and know I could be myself that day? No more hiding, lying, pretending. Just me. With Graham.

"You're smiling. Does that mean you'll consider it?"

My smile fell and my thoughts slipped away as I woke from my daydream.

"No." There was no reason to lie this time.

He took a sharp breath and dropped his hand from my shoulder before standing. "It's getting late."

I nodded and left the bench, giving one last look at the dying coals before heading into the night.

WE SAID OUR GOODBYES EARLY THE NEXT MORNING. WHEN the village ended at the fields, we headed into the forest.

"Wait!" someone shouted as we entered the trees.

Even before looking over my shoulder, I knew who it would be.

Sure enough, Lachlan ran toward us through the field.

We stopped and let him catch up, though I was tempted to run instead. "Please," he said, "let me go back with you."

A lump rose in my throat. Graham stared open-mouthed, reminding me I hadn't told him Lachlan's story. I knew what he would say, but I wouldn't do it. It wasn't remotely an option.

"Please. I need to find Cait," said Lachlan.

"Who's Cait?" asked Graham.

"A friend from prison," I said. "She and Lachlan were . . . engaged?"

"Nearly." Lachlan fidgeted with his ragged sleeves. "Look, I have to go back with you. Maybe you can use your authority to let me see her. If you just—"

"We can't take you," I said. "I'm sorry, but we're not going back to Cambria yet."

He gripped his fingers into fists and clenched his jaw. "I thought you understood. You acted like you cared. Was that a lie?"

"No!" How could he accuse me of being insincere when I'd felt his suffering, and Cait's, so personally? "We have work to do, that's all. I want to help, but it's not an option!"

Graham turned to Lachlan. "Will you excuse us for a moment, please?"

Lachlan shrugged and walked off into the field, resting his hands on his hips in irritation.

"Would it be such a problem if he came to Tramore with us?" asked Graham once we were alone. "If he calmed down a bit, he might even be able to help our cause."

"It would be terribly unwise. For his sake and ours."

"But—" his eyebrows drew together, and he searched my

face as if he'd caught a glimpse of a secret floating too close to the surface. "Why?"

An anchor's weight of guilt pulled on me. "Do you want to run out of water again? We already lost our food and half our barrels–and there's no way I'm taking anything from these villagers who have barely enough."

"What about on our way back to Cambria, after visiting Tramore?" Graham asked. "We could get more food and water there, couldn't we?"

I closed my eyes and took a breath. If I didn't allow it, Graham could get more suspicious. But I hated to make another promise I didn't intend to keep.

"Fine." I let the air out between my lips, giving in to another lie. "But I want you to tell him."

"Thank you."

I looked away. I didn't want to see the joy on Lachlan's face when Graham told him we'd come back for him. It would only end up as a painful memory.

Please tell me I'm doing the right thing.

THIRTY-TWO

THE SAILBOAT GLIDED SWIFTLY OVER THE WAVES, CARRIED by an insistent westward wind. Time passed by relentlessly, falling between my fingers like sand, just another element out of my control.

Graham stood behind the sail again with my book in his hand. He'd soon know this boat as well as I did, as obsessed as he was with mastering sailing. I sat on the bow, facing the oncoming sea, and re-opened the Academy's book.

For this purpose, the Academy has pledged not to reveal the possibility of the existence of other societies or the technologies they possess. Our banished traitors would surely attempt to venture out into the world, attracting the notice of foreigners who would harm our great establishment. Perhaps even the unsatisfied minority within Cambria's walls would grow restless with ignorant curiosity. Such is mankind.

If the day comes when our citizens no longer respect the edicts of Kendrick Irvine, or if they express an unhealthy interest in the outside world, the Academy has sworn to protect our society at any cost, including

---

THE BOOK ENDED MID-SENTENCE, LEAVING HALF A PAGE OF glaring white. I turned the page, and the next, but each one after this point was blank. The breeze whipped through my hair, making a mess as tangled as my mind.

Graham's voice came to me, but my ears pushed it away to avoid letting more noise into my brain.

After a moment, I looked back at him. "What was that?"

"I asked how soon we'll see Ash Island."

"Before the end of the day," I said.

"Your father didn't write as much about that island as the others. Are there a lot of people there?"

"No," I said. "According to rumor, they like to kill each other off in competition for the island's limited resources. And according to fact, they're Cambria's most dangerous criminals. I'd never go anywhere near there."

"I'm realizing that people are rarely as heartless as we make them out to be."

I looked over my shoulder at him. "These people are different. They'd murder their own mothers. And some of them probably did."

"But you haven't met them," he said.

"No. And I don't want to."

He shrugged. "Maybe they're not that bad."

"Trust me. Even with your charm and good looks, they'd roast you alive."

One side of his mouth turned up. "Good looks?"

I tried to laugh it off to hide my embarrassment. "For a noble."

His smile expanded to both sides of his mouth. "Thanks."

My anxious fingers twisted through my hair. "Don't get a big head over it."

"Speaking of looks," he said, "your hair is lighter."

I abruptly pushed my hair behind me. "That's what happens when you're on a boat in the sun for days."

"Yes, I know." He took a step back and tilted his head, analyzing me. "But it's quite a difference. I wouldn't even call it brown anymore."

"Well, look at you," I said. "You're not the pale, perfectly groomed gentleman I met in the library."

"I'll take that as a compliment."

His open smile was an invitation, but I couldn't suppress my anxieties enough to accept it. Time to change the subject.

"Have you missed your family?" I asked.

Graham rubbed his scruffy chin. "I'm ashamed to say I've been trying not to think about them."

"Too painful?"

"Partially." His eyebrows furrowed. "Definitely, when I think of my father. Do you think he's still alive?"

"Yeah, I do." I wasn't sure why, but I believed it.

"I want to be by his side when he leaves this world. I need to be at the shore to say goodbye when his body is sent away on the pyre. To know he's been set free."

Something pricked at my eye. I looked away, out at the water and sky, trying to focus on anything I could to fend off the guilt and sadness.

"But I haven't been mourning all this time," he said. "How could I, when my life finally has some excitement? I could never be too sad while spending my time with someone like you."

If I'd been a halfway decent person, I wouldn't have felt the thrill his words gave me. "Let me guess," I said, surprised at the lack of emotion that bled into my voice. "You haven't spent much time missing your mother, have you?"

"A bit more than I would've expected, to be honest."

"Maybe being away from her has made you aware of her virtues."

Graham reached over to tighten the mainstay. "I'm afraid it seems to be the opposite. I wonder now if she was wrong about everything, even what I always believed to be true. Still, when I think of the way I left her. . ." He smiled, but this time the expression carried more sadness than joy. More weariness than amusement.

"Time to take a break." I stepped down from the bow and took the book from his hands. "Go catch a miniature fish or something."

Graham looked down at my feet. "Bryn, look!"

I followed his gaze to the hatch. Water bubbled up from the cracks, spilling out onto the deck.

"We have a leak!" I shouted. "Quick, help me."

Only then did I notice how low the hull sat in the water. I opened the hatch. It was almost completely full, our barrels floating in seawater. Apparently, the storm was still doing its damage.

"Where's your bag?" asked Graham. "Can we bail it out again?"

"It wouldn't last," I said. "We have to repair it."

"How?" he asked.

I looked up at him, ready to eat my own words. "We have to stop at Ash Island."

THE SAILBOAT GRADUALLY SANK LOWER AS THE DAY WENT on until we were forced to sacrifice one of the water barrels to bail out the seawater. But it hardly helped. The water came in as fast as we took it out.

By evening, the single flat-topped peak of Ash Island loomed like a threat. Its black shores glittered with coarse particles that reflected the low golden sun. We directed the boat toward a small cove.

"It's beautiful," said Graham.

It might've been, but I couldn't see it, not when I was dominated by fear.

"We need to look for some materials to patch the boat," I said. "And we should really get more water."

We hit the black sand and jumped out, pulling the boat as far as possible onto the shore. We tipped it on its side. Water seeped out of a small crack in the hull.

"There's the culprit," I said. I hoped stuffing it with resin or clay would be enough—and that we could find some. It only needed to hold for another day or two to get us to Tramore, so I'd take my chances with what we could find close to shore. I meant what I said to Graham. I *really* didn't want to meet the outlaws here.

"We'll have to stay close to the boat," I said. "It would be idiotic to leave the most valuable object for miles unattended."

"Should we split up?" asked Graham. "That way, I could search for water and you could stay close to get . . . whatever it is you need."

"Splitting up doesn't seem like a good idea." I shook my head, terrified at the thought. I didn't want to separate, but it would get us off this island faster if we did. Or it would kill us faster. One of the two.

"Will you miss me?" asked Graham, his eyes sparkling like the sand he stood on.

I wouldn't answer that question with honesty. "Don't flatter yourself. I just don't want to lose my peace offering."

His eyes peered through me as if he were starting to see straight through my lies. Then he hoisted the barrel under his arm and stepped back. "I'll be careful if you will."

"But—" I wanted to argue and make him stay with me, but the light would fade soon, and we needed to get off this island. "Fine. But if you haven't found any water by the time the sun sets, come straight back. And take this." I picked up my bag and handed him a knife.

He took it, keeping the sheath on the blade, and turned away hesitantly. When he spoke, his voice carried a hint of a question. "Goodbye."

My fears almost pushed me to say more than I wanted, but I resisted the urge and smiled. "No need for goodbyes. You'll be back in no time."

He stared at me for too long before nodding. "You're right."

"I know."

I took my bag and headed to the tree line, but I kept my eyes on Graham until he crossed the black sand and disappeared into the woods.

I regretted letting him go the moment I lost sight of him.

CHAPTER
THIRTY-THREE

THE CLOSER THE SUN VENTURED TO THE HORIZON, THE more I feared I'd made a huge mistake. The solitary peak cast strange shadows on the island, making the black shores even blacker. My eyes constantly searched the rocks and trees for some material I could work with and my ears stayed pricked for the smallest sound. So far, it was still and silent, not even touched by the wind.

I carried three knives. I scraped some bark from a tree and took it back to the boat to see if it might help patch the crack. The island was filled with scraggly trees and mounds of black, crumbling rocks. No cork, clay, or resin to be found.

I stopped by the boat and stuffed the crack with the spongy bark. I frowned as I put it in. Without something sticky, it wouldn't hold.

I looked at the peak of the island, my anxiety for Graham demolishing my focus. If he didn't get back before the sun went down, I'd go after him. I turned back to the boat, trying to force myself to think, but as I did, something across the water caught my eye.

A white sail bobbed over the waves in the distance, coming in from the north. It had to be Cael. Normally, the thought of him showing up infuriated me, but this time it gave me hope. If I couldn't fix my own boat, maybe I could steal his.

The boat vanished around the curve of the island and I returned my gaze to the trees. A shout broke the stillness, echoing off the mountain and rebounding back.

Graham.

I sprinted toward the sound, knives in hand.

Yells rang out from somewhere on the mountain—or was it just echoing from there? I darted into the trees, but the voices seemed to come from the other side now. I stopped and suppressed my rapid breathing so I could listen.

A shout from my right. No, left. They echoed off the rocks beneath my feet and the black cliffs ahead. Panic took hold when I realized I wouldn't find him soon enough.

But I could make sure they found *me.*

I climbed to the top of a giant black boulder and shouted with all the volume I could muster. A flock of birds took flight from the surrounding trees, screeching as they flew over me. The islanders couldn't miss me now.

Sure enough, several shouts rose up at once, the words unclear, but the intent obvious.

I reached for my belt and drew a knife, letting the sheath fall to the boulder at my feet. I held the steel between my thumb and forefinger and lifted my arm.

The shouts consolidated and came closer. I turned to greet them.

One by one, men came into view on the rocky ground below me, holding up crude clubs and spears. They were mostly shirtless, with ragged clothing and long hair. They were exactly the kind of barbarians that every Cambrian pictured when outlaws were mentioned.

Next came Graham. Alive. But the three spears at his back threatened to change that.

"Bryn!" He stumbled over the rocks.

"Shut it!" A man with dirty gray hair tied back in a ponytail nudged him with his spear.

I launched my knife at the man's feet.

He jumped back and dropped his spear as the knife pierced the place he'd been standing.

The gray-haired man picked up the knife and smirked. "Missed, blondie."

I yanked the other knife from my belt. "That was just a warning."

"Ah, you don't wanna do this," he said. "I'd hate for word to spread tellin' that I was killed by a *girl*."

A skinny boy with a sparse patch of hair on his chin snorted. "That wouldn't do no good for your rep, eh, Keane?"

"Spear up, Nevin!" Keane ordered.

The boy jumped and pointed his spear at Graham's back again.

I gripped the knife tighter. "Let him go or one of you dies."

"Mind if I choose which one?" asked Keane.

"I've already decided." I lifted my knife and prepared my aim.

"Me?" Keane pointed at his hairy chest. "Nah, I don't buy it. If that was the case, you wouldn't've aimed at my feet the first time."

A regretful thought drifted through my mind. *I should've killed him.*

No. I couldn't. *No one dies.*

And yet. If it saved Graham, maybe I could. I drew my arm back and imagined a wooden target in place of the man's chest. But the moment before I sent the knife flying, I made the mistake of glancing at Graham. He looked up with pleading eyes and shook his head. His mouth moved soundlessly, begging me not to do it.

I sighed and let my knife fall.

"Ha!" cried the boy named Nevin. "We scared 'er good."

"Time to hop down from that rock, blondie," said Keane. "You lost."

They had me surrounded. Keane signaled at two men. They grabbed my arms and held them tight behind my back.

"Don't hurt her!" said Graham.

Keane laughed and rolled his eyes. "Sir. Madam," he said, switching to a pretentious nobleman's accent. "I'd be greatly obliged if you would deign to join us at our humble abode."

The men forced us uphill toward the mountain, their spears leaving no room for resistance. The sunlight had nearly faded, leaving only a pink glow in the sky behind the black peak.

Each time Graham glanced back at me, a spear dug into his back to prod him forward.

"Almost there," said Keane.

I searched the landscape on each side. There were no signs of houses, a village, or anything man-made. I was beginning to believe they'd hiked us up here just to drop us off a cliff for their amusement. They'd probably killed before. They were on this island for a reason, after all.

We headed straight for the side of the mountain. I squinted, making out a dark shape in the dim light. Straight ahead, black on black in the mountainside, was a wide crevice.

"You live in *caves*?" Graham mumbled before they forced him through the opening.

They shoved me through next, scraping my shoulder against the jagged rock. The ground angled downhill, and goosebumps sprung up on my body as the temperature dropped several degrees. My view filled with black. I stepped blindly through the dark, the pressure from the spear never letting up.

Eventually, the flicker of fire broke through up ahead and the tunnel expanded into a wide cavern. Stalactites as sharp as their spears covered the ceiling. Rustic sconces in the wall shone firelight on sheets of grass lining the black floor. A pile of wrinkled mushrooms littered one corner.

Even with the nearby fires, I shivered in my wet clothing. The other islands offered at least some degree of civilization, but not this bleak place. It reminded me of prison, only colder.

The men shoved Graham to the floor. When the hands holding my wrists loosened, I wrenched out of their grip and dashed forward, reaching for the spear of the man in front of me. But just as my hands touched his weapon, a sharp point pressed against my ribs. I gasped and let go.

Keane stepped forward. "Not very polite for a waller, are ya?"

I backed away from the spear and dropped to the ground beside Graham, rubbing my side. I looked around, trying to see how many there were. I counted twelve.

Keane leveled his glare with mine. "Time to tell us what a couple of Cambrian snobs are doin' on our island."

I stared back. I had no intention of telling him anything.

"We ain't wallers," said Graham.

I looked at him from the corner of my eye, hiding my surprise at his convincing accent.

Keane looked skeptical. "Away with ya. Sounds like a whoppin' cod to me."

Graham spoke again, his accent seamless. "We're outlaws like the rest of ya."

"Then how'd'ya get that fancy floater we saw sailin' in?"

"Fancy?" I asked. "It's nothin' but scrap."

"Nevin, you're the man that spotted it," said Keane. "Did it look like bleedin' scrap?"

The scrawny boy with the patchy stubble scratched his head. "Uh, I dunno. It was far away, comin' in from the north, but it looked like it were a city boat."

Graham glanced at me at the mention of the word *north* but stayed quiet. We'd come in from the east and he hadn't seen Cael's boat like I had.

I laughed. "Can't trust a word from that hairless twit. We're from Tramore."

"Tramore?" Keane furrowed his brows. "Whaddya think, men? Pond-hoppin' outlaws? Or bloody liars?"

The men stared us down with anger in their eyes, but Nevin looked unsure.

Their leader continued. "I dunno 'bout the rest of you, but I'm pickin' up a whiff of *nobility* here."

I kept my breathing steady and my mouth shut.

"Are y'all men on this island?" Graham asked.

"We're askin' the questions," said Keane.

I wanted to stall them and avoid the accusations. "More like boys." I gestured at Nevin. "This guy can't even grow a beard."

The boy looked unaware for a moment before reaching up to touch his chin. "Hey, that ain't very nice."

Keane looked at Graham. "Course we're all men. If they let us make babies here, we'd raise 'em up to be the biggest threat Cambria ever saw."

I hadn't known that, but I was glad—for the sake of the hypothetical women. I wondered, not for the first time, what these men's crimes might be.

"Let's get to the point." Keane crouched down in front of us. "It don't make a drop of difference whether yer wallers or Tramorians. Just tell us where the boat is and you're free."

Graham frowned, shaking his head.

Whether or not I talked, they'd find it eventually. I wondered why they were even asking. I could think of just one reason—there were more criminals here than the ones in front of us and they wanted to get there first.

"How many men are on the island?" I asked.

Keane shrugged. "More yesterday than today is all I know. Let's just say you're lucky you met us and not the other guys."

I bit my lip. If they tried to take my boat, they'd see the crack and probably kill us out of disappointment. Still, it could give me time to find Cael's, but I didn't trust him not to hurt Graham. And if they took Cael's boat . . . well, I could live with that as long as I found a way to fix my own.

"The boat's yours," I said, "if you swear not to hurt us."

Graham squeezed my hand and shook his head. "There might be another way."

"This *is* the other way," I whispered in his ear.

"I thought you had more fight in ya," said Keane. "Makes me think you're planning on tellin' us wrong cuz you 'spect you can get to it first. That ain't gonna work. We know every bloody rock on this island."

"I'm not. I got what I want," I said. "To ditch Tramore. Our parents. To be together without anyone controllin' our lives." I wrapped my fingers around Graham's to sell it.

Nevin wrinkled his nose. "There's naught but mushies to eat here, so ya know."

"We'll live," I said.

"Maybe." Keane narrowed his eyes. "Look. I dunno what you're playing at, but I'll pretend to believe you. Tell us where you roped it and we'll leave this whole place to the two of you," said Keane, gesturing at the cave walls.

I swallowed. I'd have to take a gamble, but I'd seen the boat well enough to guess where it might be. "Northwest edge, where the shore makes a sharp turn."

"And if it ain't there?" asked Keane.

"We need water," I said. "Point us to that and you'll know where to find us."

Keane pointed at the ceiling.

I looked up, seeing nothing but darkness.

He laughed. "No, no, the mountain. Out, then up. Can't miss it."

Graham stood, pulling me by the hand.

"Lower your spears, men. And get moving," said Keane. He took a short branch from the ground, lit it with the flame from the wall's torches, and handed it to me. "You'll be needin' this."

I accepted the torch, taken aback by the gesture. It seemed almost polite.

Graham retrieved the barrel the men had taken from him and went up the tunnel after them. I followed with Keane behind me. The dark sky appeared, and Graham stepped outside.

I stopped before exiting the tunnel and turned around, watching Keane's face in the torchlight, wondering whether I was crazy for thinking I might be able to trust him. One weight on my conscience needed to be eased. "Listen," I whispered. "If there's someone at the boat, tie him up—tight—but don't kill him."

"You said it was just the two of you," said Keane.

"Not exactly." I glanced back. "But please, try not to kill him, as tempted as you'll be."

He lowered his voice. "I'm not quite the barbarian you think I am." His accent sounded Cambrian now—high-ranked Cambrian. "I don't kill every man I see."

My mouth fell open as I realized I'd possibly found a friend in my enemy. "Trust me. It's not you—it's him."

"You know, if there's room, maybe the men would tolerate you two taggin' along. It's your boat after all." He winked. "Just don't tell 'em I said that."

"Thank you," I said, though I really hoped I wouldn't have to take him up on that offer. "You're a good man."

Keane cleared his throat and spoke louder. "Now that's takin' it too far, blondie." He squeezed past me and left the cave, catching up to his men who ran downhill toward the northwest carrying their torches.

I emerged from the tunnel, lighting up the cliff face with my torch.

Graham was standing closer than I'd expected. He waited at the entrance, studying me curiously. He couldn't have heard the hushed conversation, but my fears didn't abate.

I turned my smile to an innocent one and stepped to the edge of the hill.

When the lights from the men's torches were distant specks, Graham turned to me. "Will you please tell me what just happened? You didn't move the boat, did you?"

I could only smile. If Cael lost his boat, we'd finally be able to get away from him. New possibilities opened up in my head and my heart.

"I have to assume you don't actually want to be marooned on an island with me for the rest of your life," he said.

"It won't be so bad."

His eyes grew wide.

"I'm kidding! Nothing could get me to stay in this hell hole. I'll explain on the way. Let's go."

CHAPTER
THIRTY-FOUR

THE MOON HADN'T RISEN YET, SO ONLY THE TWINKLING stars lit the sky. We followed a narrow pathway that wrapped around the edge of the peak. I led the way with the torch, keeping close to the face of the mountain and away from the black void that would take us to our deaths if we took a wrong step.

I explained to Graham how I'd seen the boat sail in. I didn't tell him it was Cael's, but now I wouldn't have to. We could leave the island without him following. Maybe I didn't have only one choice. Maybe I could think of a plan that didn't require betraying Graham. Maybe I could let my heart feel, without blocking the feelings I'd fought so hard.

"Do you think it's the Enforcers?" asked Graham.

"It's possible," I said, "but I'm not worried. The islanders would dominate them."

"What if they take your boat after theirs is stolen?"

If it really were Enforcers, I'd have the exact same concern. "We're fine for now. The boat isn't patched yet. It wouldn't get far if they tried to sail away with it."

My answer seemed to satisfy him. He switched the barrel to the other arm and followed close behind, keeping to the light cast on the ground by the torch.

"It's hard to believe the only water source here is at the top of a mountain," I said.

"I couldn't find anything along the shore," said Graham.

"Strange." I stepped over a fallen log in the pathway. "Can't say this is my favorite island."

"There's a mysterious beauty to it," said Graham. "I could see you fitting in here."

I laughed. "Because of my criminal history?"

"That's not what I meant."

"What about you?" I asked. "Could you ever imagine living here?"

"I'd have to get better at climbing, and swimming . . . and everything, but even so, I'd always feel too ordinary to belong."

"I think you've done enough to be considered officially un-ordinary."

"Thanks. That's the nicest thing you've ever said to me."

I looked over my shoulder at him. When I saw his playful smile, my own widened.

"You seem . . . happier," he said. "I don't think you've mocked me in the past hour, for one thing."

"Am I that bad?"

"Absolutely."

I laughed. I *was* happier. It didn't make total sense. I didn't know how we'd get my boat fixed or when we'd leave this island, but I felt sure we'd be okay. Knowing I had an ally in Keane gave me another layer of security.

The path widened and Graham moved to my side. "Something else is different, too. It's the way you're . . ." he paused and looked me in the eye ". . . the way you're looking at me."

I would've denied there was anything special about the way

I was looking at him, but the problem was that I could feel myself doing it at that very moment. I wanted to take in every detail of him, to know him to his core, and judging by the way he looked back at me, he felt the same.

It became so pleasantly uncomfortable that I finally forced myself to pull away and continue up the path. My breath caught in my throat when I rounded the final corner.

The path had delivered us to the top of the peak. I hadn't known what to expect, but it wasn't this. A vast, black lake, as still as a mirror, spread out before us, floating above the rest of the world. It reflected the entire night sky as if a piece of the heavens was caught in the mountain's grasp.

"Incredible," said Graham.

I reached my hand down and broke the peaceful glass. "You won't believe this, but it's *warm*."

He set down the barrel and crouched beside me, dipping his hand into the lake.

I propped up the torch between some boulders. "Time to learn how to swim."

WE FLOATED IN THE CENTER OF THE LAKE, WITH NOTHING but underwear on us and stars above us. Back in Cambria, I never could've let him see me like this. But here in the dark, on an island that was as far from proper as possible, it felt almost natural.

It had definitely taken him longer to get comfortable with our minimal clothing than the water itself. He could already stay afloat just fine and was practicing every stroke I'd taught him.

"I've learned so much since I met you." His voice was

muffled through the water covering my ears. "Lock picking, stealing, climbing, sailing, swimming . . ."

"Lying," I blurted out. That new skill of his surprised me the most.

"Well," he said, "it's easy when you're learning from the best."

I laughed to stave off the guilt that hadn't lost its grip on me. He couldn't possibly know how much I'd lied, but his words stung all the same. "I hope I haven't been too terrible an influence on you. Your goodness is . . . refreshing. Like you have nothing to hide."

He was still except for the movement of his feet in the water. The silence between us widened into a gulf. I'd said the wrong thing, but I wasn't sure why.

"Graham?"

His sigh reached me even through the water covering my ears. "I wish that were true." He rolled over and swam away.

I stayed where I was, letting my feet sink until only my head was above the surface. I longed to know what he was feeling, but it seemed right to give him space.

When he reached the rim, he looked back and gestured for me to come closer.

I swam over, eager to be beside him again. Once I got to the edge of the lake, I put my hand on the rim beside his. The ground was still far below our feet.

"If I tell you," Graham said, his soft voice drifting over the silent lake, "you'll no longer look at me the way you are right now."

I dropped my eyes to his chest, my head buzzing with confusion. "Honestly—" I paused, preparing to admit more than I should. "Nothing can change the way I feel about you."

"Bryn." He shook his head, his eyes as solemn as I'd ever seen. "Why do you think my mother hates me so much?"

"Because she's evil."

"Please." He closed his eyes for a long breath. "Don't make me say it."

A memory surfaced. Graham's room. The queen's furious voice. *It would traumatize any child to witness his brother's death.*

I covered my mouth. "Your brother?"

He nodded almost imperceptibly. "It's my fault he's dead."

I stared, speechless. The warm water couldn't stop the chills from running down my spine.

When he spoke again, his voice was almost as quiet as the lake. "I was ten years old. Ewan was twelve."

I waited, afraid anything I said would be all wrong. I never knew how his brother died, but I hadn't imagined Graham could've been a part of it.

"He'd do anything to make me laugh. As I got older, I started persuading him to break rules for my entertainment. It started with little things, but eventually, I was getting him to jump from moving carriages and sneak into the streets with me at night. Whatever I said, he did. And I never stopped to think of the consequences."

He took a deep breath and lifted his eyes toward the stars. "One night, I climbed out a window onto the roof. I wanted him to come too, but he was afraid. Then I . . . I called him a coward." He rested his hand over his eyes before pushing it back through his hair with an aching sigh. "I shamed him into following me. So he did. We were at the highest point when he stepped on a loose shingle and slipped."

My heart resumed its pounding after a moment as if it had quieted to hear his confession. I moved my hand from the black rim and put it over Graham's, trying to tell him what I couldn't with words. But it wasn't enough. Not even close to enough.

"When I saw him hit the ground—" his voice faltered, and

he paused for more breaths "—I wished it had been me. It should have been me. I wanted to die—and I think a part of me did."

His pain overflowed right into me. I shook my head to erase the vision he'd been forced to relive every day. How could he possibly heal from that? Yes, my mother had died, but it was slow, peaceful, and most importantly, not my fault.

"Graham," I said, at a loss for words. "I'm *so* sorry."

"So am I," he said. "Eternally."

I tried to let it go, but I couldn't fight the rising passion. "What happened was awful—beyond awful. A nightmare no child should have to live. But that's exactly it. You were a child!" I moved my hand to his shoulder and looked him in the eye. "It was an accident, Graham. Your mother was wrong to blame you."

"I want to believe you, more than anything. But if I didn't do something wrong, why do I feel so much remorse?"

I looked down at the still water. "I don't know."

"I'll never shake the remorse. I'll never stop blaming myself. But these past few weeks with you have shown me what it's like to feel anything other than completely alone." He reached his hand up to my cheek.

My gaze shot back to him. My body flowed with too much energy to separate my emotions from my logic and keep them contained where they belonged. All I knew was a desire to lighten his pain, to clear his remorse, to let him know he was good.

I didn't notice when the distance between us disappeared, but I found myself mere inches from his face. The inches were still too much.

Graham slid his hand under my chin, his eyes glancing toward my lips.

I searched for the strength to stop. I tried to direct my

energy into logic. I told my hands to stay put, but they moved up his neck and twisted into his hair instead.

He leaned his forehead head onto mine, his breath keeping pace with my own. When he brushed my lip with the tip of his finger, I lost all resistance and kissed him.

He kissed me back with more certainty than I could've dreamed of, his mouth shamelessly exploring mine as if he'd been planning in precise detail exactly what he would do to me if he ever got the chance.

Chills traveled through my body, yet everything was warm. I'd wanted this for much longer than I'd consciously realized, and now I feared I would never get enough.

Wait.

This isn't right.

He doesn't know.

I pulled back. I didn't deserve this, not if I still couldn't be honest with him. I should've said I was sorry, told him I'd made a mistake, and swore it would never happen again.

But then he reached around my back and pulled me against him, my thoughts immediately fleeing as I fell completely under his control. He kissed me again and I wrapped my arms around his neck to pull him even closer. For a moment, as I became hopelessly lost in the intoxication of his lips and the heat of his skin, he was just Graham—and I could pretend I was a girl without any dangerous secrets.

I didn't want to let go. Not ever. But the guilt in my heart raged. Did any of this mean a thing if he didn't truly know me? I opened my eyes and pulled away, sending ripples across the dark lake.

His mouth angled downward, his smile gone as quickly as the kiss. "What is it?"

I looked away, afraid to meet his eye. "We've been here too long."

He was quiet as if trying to detect what had caused the sudden change. "Did I do something wrong?"

I shook my head. "I just need a minute."

I turned away and swam across the dark waters alone. For a few short moments, everything had felt perfect. But now my heart felt as cold as my lips.

CHAPTER

THIRTY-FIVE

THE FAR RIM OF THE LAKE GAVE ME A QUIET PLACE TO think. It was time to find a way to set things right. If Cael couldn't follow us, maybe I could save Graham. But how could I stop the attack if I didn't deliver him to Tramore as promised?

I rested my arms on the rim and dropped my cheek to the cold black rock. It would have been worlds easier if I could at least decipher what was right.

A whisper hissed in the dark. Fear jolted through me and I raised my head.

A figure crouched in front of me. Even in the dim starlight, I recognized his arrogant posture.

Cael wasn't with his boat.

"I'm glad *one* of us is having a good time," he said.

I glanced at the other side of the lake. Wisps of steam rose from the surface so I could barely see Graham at all, and he was definitely too far away to overhear us. "It's not what you think."

He snorted. "Unlike that idiot, I can see through your lies— and you've managed to convince me you can't fulfill your side of the bargain." He lifted his face from the shadows, every angle of his face harsh with contempt. "Congratulations."

My face grew hot and my muscles tensed. I hoisted myself out of the water, the cool air hitting my exposed skin. I tried not to cower as I faced Cael in only my underwear. "If you hurt him, I'll make sure you *never* get what you want, even if it means I don't either."

"Then I'll make sure everyone knows who Bryn Yarrow really is."

"I don't care."

He laughed softly and shook his head. "Your father certainly will. But anyway, I came here to tell you Enforcers are searching the island."

"What?" My question was nearly soundless.

"Their boat's anchored to the north. I'd recommend getting out of here. Now."

So I hadn't seen Cael's boat. And I hadn't gotten rid of him. I'd done something much more dangerous. I looked down the mountain, searching the shores for a sign of the Enforcers, but I saw nothing. The island was dark and quiet.

Except—

A tiny glow of orange light drew my eyes back to the eastern shore. The light grew larger and brighter. Something was burning.

"No, no, no, no. It's my boat!"

Cael swore. "Mine will be next." He jumped down, landing hard on the path below and sprinting down the mountain.

"Bryn!"

I glanced back. Graham ran around the rim toward me just as Cael disappeared from view.

"I heard your voice," he said as he came closer. "What happened?"

I stared down at the blaze past the shore, hardly daring to blink. "Enforcers. They're burning our boat."

"What?" His eyes traveled down the mountain until he saw it too. "How do you know it's—" He took a deep breath. "What should we do?"

I tore my eyes from the distant fire. Cael's boat was still here, somewhere, but I wouldn't take Graham anywhere near him.

My boat was on fire.

Enforcers were here for us.

I swallowed and looked at Graham. The memory of pain lingered in his eyes. I didn't know how I'd save him yet, but I would. For now, we had to get off this miserable island.

"We might be able to catch up with Keane," I said.

"Keane? Isn't he part of the problem?"

"He said something that made me think he'd be willing to help us. I'm not sure if he meant it, but it's the best chance we've got."

"Then let's go," he said, his trust in me still strong.

We threw on our clothes. Our torch had long burned out so we'd have to navigate through the dark.

We took the curved mountain path, eventually passing the crevice that led to the cave. From there, we tried to head north in the direction Keane's group had gone. We were going much slower in the darkness than I would've preferred. With all the veins of black rock and tangled bushes poking through the ground, running meant falling.

I hoped Keane and his men were okay, that I hadn't sentenced them all to death by sending them to steal the Enforcers' boat. Yes, the islanders were probably stronger and tougher than the Enforcers, and certainly dangerous with their spears, but the Enforcers had something the islanders didn't: guns.

But my burning boat told me the Enforcers didn't know about Keane's plans yet. They wouldn't have destroyed the only other way off the island if their own was under threat.

A speck of light appeared in a patch of trees up ahead.

I stopped and crouched, Graham joining me behind the bushes.

I peered through the foliage. "There's someone down there."

"Keane?" asked Graham.

A voice cut through the quiet night. "This place is dreadful. I'm sure there's nothing to find here but barbarians and mushrooms."

"Keep your pistol ready," said another man.

They came closer, crashing through the undergrowth as if they wanted the whole island to hear.

We hid quietly in the bushes and waited for them to pass. The flames of their torches became smaller as the men walked away.

Graham leaned close and whispered in my ear. "We can use them to find the boat."

"But I'm not sure they're even on their way—" I stopped, realizing what he meant. "That might work."

"The problem is that they're most likely looking for me," he said. "I can't be recognized."

"They wouldn't look twice if you were an outlaw," I whispered.

"But I'm not."

"They won't know that." I peeked over the bushes, searching for the torches, but they'd moved out of sight. "You know I'd do it, but there aren't women here, remember?"

"Maybe that's not common knowledge. We didn't know."

"But they're Enforcers. They'll know. Just trust me, okay?"

He sighed in resignation. "I always have."

"Then take off your shirt," I said.

"What?"

"You'll be more convincing."

After a moment's hesitation, he lifted the shirt over his head.

I dug into the ground with my fingers, coating them with mud. I reached for his face and smeared the mud over his cheeks, forehead, and chin.

He shut his eyes and mouth while I painted with my fingers. One last stroke down the bridge of his nose and I was done. On impulse, I stamped two handprints on his bare chest.

"There," I said. "Perfectly uncivilized."

His eyebrows lowered and his eyes became solemn. "If something goes wrong, I want to tell you"—he paused and started again—"I want to thank you for all you've done."

A tug of guilt pulled at me, but I kept my mouth shut.

He leaned in and pressed his lips to my cheek. "Sorry about the mud." He brushed off my face. "And sorry about . . . that."

It took me a moment to come to my senses. "Do you know what to say?"

He smiled. "I have an idea."

Graham got up and ran in the direction where the torches had vanished. I followed quietly behind, keeping to the shadows. I trusted him to do this. But my fear kept one thought active in my mind: they had pistols and we had nothing.

THIRTY-SIX

THE GLOW OF TORCHES CAME INTO VIEW AGAIN. I SLOWED down and stayed to the side of the Enforcers, trying not to rustle the bushes.

Graham walked straight up behind the men. "Evenin'."

They spun toward him, their backs now to me. One pointed his pistol at Graham's chest. I gripped the bark of the tree I hid behind. I wasn't sure I had the self-control to stay out of it, not with Graham's life at risk.

"Stay back, criminal," the man with the pistol growled.

Graham raised his hands and gave them a polite smile. Almost too polite. "No need for weapons, wallers. I ain't armed."

They stepped closer, inspecting him in the torchlight. Fortunately, they didn't see past his accent or the dirt streaked across his face and chest.

The man with the pistol lowered it but didn't put it away. "You haven't seen any visitors here lately, have you?" he asked.

"Visitors?" said Graham. "Someone you're lookin' for in particular?"

The men looked at each other. One shrugged and the other continued.

"A couple of nobles have gone missing from Cambria. In all likelihood, they've been assassinated, but the Academy sent us to search on the slim chance they defected."

"It's a fool's errand if you ask me," said the other man.

"Oh?" Graham sounded genuinely surprised. "I'd be more willin' to tell you what I know if you tell me what you know. Who are they?"

The man with the pistol narrowed his eyes. "We're searching for Sir Graham Brennin and Lady Mara Stroud."

I gasped, then clapped my hands over my mouth.

Graham's face clouded into a distant unreadable expression. He looked past the men and straight toward my hiding place. I didn't know if he could even see me in the dark, but I felt entirely exposed.

But then his gaze returned to the Enforcers and he smiled, nearly extinguishing my fears. "Haven't seen 'em."

"Then why did you say you would tell us what you know?" The man aimed his pistol at Graham again. "Is there something you're hiding?"

"Well," he said, "I could be wrong, but it looked like someone's stealin' your boat."

The men swore and took off at a run, pushing past Graham.

This was the chance we'd been waiting for, but I couldn't seem to move.

Graham followed at their heels, staying near the two bouncing flames in the dark. I pulled myself together and chased after them.

We ran until the faint glow of impending day lit up the eastern horizon. The Enforcers didn't stop until they left behind the trees and black rocks for the coarse, dark sand at the shore. They crouched to the ground, gasping for breath.

I hid in the thin trees.

Graham ran past them, splashing through the water. He dove in when it was deep enough. A boat much larger than mine was anchored a good distance from the shore.

Relief flowed through me until it crashed into the dam of my fears. We didn't know who was in control of the boat. Graham had most likely gone ahead to find out if it was safe. I should've been the one to take the risk.

The Enforcers waded into the ocean and pulled out their pistols.

Graham still swam toward the boat. He knew what to do, but struggling past crashing waves wasn't like gliding through the still glass of the mountain lake. I stood up, hardly caring if I was seen. I had to make sure Graham was safe. Several figures moved about on the deck of the boat. I couldn't tell if they were Cambrians or islanders.

The Enforcers stepped into deeper water and lifted their pistols toward the boat.

I took my chance and left the trees, running across the shore. I reached the water and dove in. The waves fought against me, but I pushed back harder. I held my breath and swam under, trying to remain invisible to the Enforcers. The saltwater stung my open eyes and I pushed against the dark rocky ground to move faster.

The muffled sound of gunshot forced me to lift my head out of the water. I pulled in a desperate breath and searched for Graham. The morning light revealed his shirtless figure climbing a rope ladder into the boat. The man up on deck had a ponytail.

I ducked back under and swam with all my strength, finally reaching the deeper water. Another gunshot renewed my fear and panic. I looked up again and saw that Graham had made it into the boat.

He was okay. For now.

Don't stop. Just swim.

My clothes felt so heavy, pulling me, slowing me down. I had to get there before someone got shot. And especially before the other Enforcers on the island were lured by the sounds of a fight.

I swam on, lifting my head only for much-needed breaths.

A pistol cracked.

I kept swimming.

Just when I thought my arms and lungs couldn't take any more, a large shadow loomed over my head. I lifted my head to see the boat right in front of me.

"There she is!" Graham shouted from the deck.

"Get to the other side!" Keane yelled.

I swam toward the dark hull, trying to find my way behind the boat, somewhere safe from the bullets.

Crack.

Another blast erupted from the pistol. I looked up to see it find its target. The figure behind Graham reeled and fell from the boat headfirst. He hit the water hard and the splash sprayed over me. He sank beneath the surface.

I dove again, this time toward him, but he was sinking fast. I kicked fiercely, deeper and deeper until I could hardly see. Then, finally, I felt an arm. I grabbed him around his waist and kicked up toward the sky, my heart pounding against the captive air in my chest.

I broke the surface and sucked in an urgent breath. The boy's face came out of the water. The first thing I noticed was the patchy stubble on his chin. Then the eyes that stared unblinking at the sky. Then the blood. The side of his head flowed red.

A scream echoed through my ears and the taste of salt filled my mouth. Nevin slipped lower in my arms. I gripped him tighter, coughing the water from my lungs.

"Let him go!" Someone from the yelled. "He's already—"

No! I didn't have the breath to shout back, but I couldn't let him go. I pulled him with me right up to the edge of the boat, the weight of his body dragging me down. My head went under again and I came up choking. I searched the side of the boat, but the ladder was gone.

Graham shouted from the deck. "She needs the ladder!"

Another angry shot fired, thudding into the hull above me.

The other side of the boat might as well have been miles away for all the strength I had. I still held tightly to Nevin.

The rope ladder splashed into the water beside me. I reached up and grasped it, my hand covered in Nevin's blood.

"Pull us up!" The shriek that came from my mouth didn't sound like my own.

"They'll shoot!" Keane yelled.

My body began to seize in shock and panic. Even if I hadn't been holding Nevin, I didn't think I could stay afloat. A wave enveloped me and my hand nearly slipped off the rung.

"She'll drown!" Graham shouted from above.

The ladder finally began to lift. I gripped it as tightly as I could, holding Nevin with my other arm. My knuckles went white and my arm struggled to hold the extra weight. Graham and Keane leaned over the side, ready to grab us.

The pistol fired again.

Pain burned through my left side.

My body went weak all at once. I didn't remember letting go of Nevin, but I looked down to see him disappear under the grasping pull of the waves. The rope fell away from my other hand. I hit the water and kept falling. My arms still reached for what I used to hold.

I told my body to fight. I begged my legs to kick. But the fire between my ribs overpowered me and I could only fall.

As I drifted into darkness, I held on to two thoughts.

The first: I would never make my father proud.

The last: Now Graham could be free.

CHAPTER
THIRTY-SEVEN

I THOUGHT THERE WOULD BE NOTHING LEFT TO FEEL. I was dead. No one could save me.

I was sure.

But in my waning consciousness, I felt something wrap around me. I thought I floated up instead of down. The pain in my side flared up and I wanted to fight whatever held me.

The next thing I knew, I was on a hard surface coughing violently. My lungs were too full of water to accept the air. But little by little, liquid went out and oxygen came in. Each cough felt like another shot in the ribs. Sharp, persistent, burning torture.

My mind tried to escape the pain, but disorienting images and sounds remained. Coughing, gasping, vomiting, searing pain, arms around me, blood everywhere, voices I knew, voices I didn't know, wind on my face, and someone calling me by the wrong name.

When I finally cleared my lungs, I collapsed and squeezed my eyes shut, wishing I wouldn't have to wake and bear this pain again.

I NEVER SEEMED TO GET WHAT I WISHED FOR.

I opened my eyes to see Graham's face. His mouth was set in a straight line. I tried to smile, but I didn't know if it worked. I lifted my head, but the movement reactivated the pain. I was on a hard mattress in a small room with planked walls, a wool blanket spread over me.

"No, no, don't move." Graham's voice was tired and inflectionless, and his brows held a deep furrow. He wore a crisp white Law Enforcer shirt he must've found on this boat. But it was something in his expression that held the true change. "The bullet wasn't too deep, but you need to rest."

"The bullet?" It took a moment for the memory of the pistol shot to return. "Who took it out?"

"I did. But be careful. The bleeding hasn't stopped, even with the bandage."

I moved the blanket off myself and gingerly touched my waist and tried not to imagine Graham digging in the wound while I slept. I wore a new shirt too, but it was already bloodstained on my left side. "You dove after me, didn't you?"

Graham nodded, his blue eyes intense.

"Did you get Nevin? Was anyone else hurt?"

"No. No to both. We couldn't save him," he said. "But we've been on the ocean since yesterday. It's all right now." The furrow between his brow didn't fade.

That meant the new moon was tomorrow night. The islanders would set sail for Cambria the morning after. The thought left me defeated.

"Are you all right?" I asked.

"I didn't get shot," he replied flatly.

That wasn't exactly what I'd meant, but I didn't want to ask again in case I received an honest answer.

"Where are we going?" I asked.

"I told them our boat was burned and that we changed our minds about running away, so they're taking us to Tramore. Nice of them, isn't it?"

"What?" I sat up, ignoring the fire radiating through my torso. "No. You—we—can't go."

"Why not? Your family's there, aren't they?" he asked.

"Yes . . . but . . . ." I stumbled over my words, still unable to set the truth free.

"And they're about to sail for Cambria?"

I bit my lip and nodded.

"Then we have to go." He slouched on the edge of the bed, resting his head against the wall. I'd never seen him look so tired. "Besides, you need help."

The door swung open and Keane nudged his way through the low doorway. He wore an Enforcer's uniform, giving him a completely different look.

"Hey there, blondie."

I smoothed my hair self-consciously.

Keane crouched down and spoke softly in his noble accent. "Words aren't enough to tell you how much I appreciate what you tried to do for Nevin."

I gulped. The image of Nevin's staring eyes and the blood on his face reappeared in my mind, a nightmare I couldn't forget.

"I know he didn't mean anything to you." Keane's voice cracked. "But he was the closest I had to a son."

Tears stung my eyes, but I sniffed and willed them not to fall. "I'm so sorry I couldn't help." The apology was inadequate, but I was afraid I'd lose the battle with my tears if I said another word.

"I know." He stood and walked to the door, then stopped,

resting his hand on the doorframe. "You were pretty clever back there, sending us to an Enforcers' boat and all."

I blushed. "I swear I didn't know."

"When I saw it, I doubted it was yours, but I ordered my men not to kill anyone on board, as you asked. The man surrendered pretty easily. Turns out he's just the cook."

"Thanks." I nodded quickly so he wouldn't say anything else.

Keane left, shutting the door behind him.

I became suddenly aware of Graham and what he didn't know. Or might know.

He kept his eyes on the floor.

I should've tried to explain, but I was finished with lies and had no energy for the truth. I wanted to reach for him, to hold his hand, to go back to the way things were. But I didn't deserve any of it.

"We should be to Tramore by tomorrow." He stood and went to the door. "I'll let you sleep."

"What about you?" I wasn't ready for him to leave me. "Have you slept?"

He shrugged and left the room without saying goodbye.

THAT EVENING, I FOUND MY WAY TO MY FEET AND LEFT the cabin for some fresh air on the upper deck. On my way down the hallway, I had to stop and lean against the wall while waiting for my blurred vision to solidify. I slowly climbed the ladder to the deck, fighting the lightheadedness.

Men dotted the boat, some adjusting the sails, others resting or looking out to sea. They were all dressed as Enforcers, though their unkempt hair and overgrown beards easily gave them away. A sailboat this size was too complex to be navigated by only two people, so we were lucky to have them on our side, regardless of whatever crimes they'd committed.

Graham stood on the bow in his new Enforcer clothing, looking down at the deck as the boat glided toward the setting sun. He pointed at the sails and gave an order to one of the men. Was he the one teaching them how to sail?

I crossed the deck toward him.

He dashed to my side. "What are you doing on deck? You'll bleed to death."

"I'll recover. I always have." A wave of dizziness hit me, and I gripped the rail with one hand, groaning. "My father always says the quickest way to heal is to ignore the pain."

He raised an eyebrow. "I'm not sure I agree with him."

"You don't have to," I said, "but I do."

"About everything?"

I hesitated, trying to make sure my answer wasn't just what I wanted to be true. "He's the smartest person I know, so yeah, I think so."

"So he's smart." He looked me in the eye. "But that doesn't make him right. Look at Cambria. The Academy. So intelligent —and so wrong."

My eyes itched to escape from his intense stare, but I didn't want him to see it as a surrender, so I kept mine focused on his. "Don't compare my father to the Academy. Everything he's done has been to improve the world. But sometimes it doesn't go how you plan. Sometimes, despite your best efforts, terrible things happen." I stopped and took a deep breath, blowing it out slowly to stave off the pain in my side.

He was silent.

I waited for him to speak, but he only looked out to sea. I used to know that expression, but his sadness had evolved; it was compounded by a layer of distrust that hadn't been there before. Something had broken between us.

I stood by him, mentally debating what to do or say.

In the end, I turned and walked away slowly, mourning the loss of something I wasn't sure I ever really had. Before I climbed beneath the deck, wincing with each movement, I checked to see if he was looking my way, but he hadn't moved at all.

A question dominated my mind: *Does he know who I am?*

And if he did, why would he still go to Tramore?

When my feet hit the floor of the lower deck, I couldn't tell which way was up. A bright red blot expanded across the side of my shirt. Fuzzy black spots layered themselves over my vision until I saw nothing. I clutched the ladder and sank to the floor, my stomach churning and my face unbearably hot.

"Whoa, there," said a man's voice.

Hands pulled me up and supported me down the hall and back to the cabin. When I was lying down, my vision gradually cleared and my head cooled. Keane was crouched beside me.

"Thanks," I muttered.

He stroked his beard, studying my face. "How'd a girl like you get herself into this mess?"

"A girl like me?" I started to laugh, but it turned to a groan and I clutched my side.

"You're not really from Tramore, are you?" he asked.

I lifted my head from the mattress and blinked. "What makes you say that?"

He tapped the side of his head. "I spent most of my life among nobles. Even a really good accent isn't enough to hide who you are."

"Did Graham say something?"

Keane laughed. "He didn't tell me, if that's what you mean.

But for those who know where to look, you've got noble written all over you."

I swallowed. "There's nothing noble about me."

"Huh." He pursed his lips. "If you say so."

I stared, afraid of what he knew, and what he might do about it.

"Don't get all wide-eyed on me, blondie. I won't tell a soul."

I relaxed and rested my head again. "I doubt it makes any difference now."

"How about some dinner?" he asked, changing the subject. "This boat has the best food I've seen in years."

My stomach sickened at the mention of food, but I needed the strength. "Thank you."

I stared at the low wooden ceiling. My heart pounded, every beat counting down to the biggest mistake of my life. The inevitable would come soon enough.

I was powerless to stop it.

CHAPTER
THIRTY-EIGHT

After a long, feverish sleep, I climbed to my feet and went up on deck.

An orange glow lingered in the sky, but the sun was gone. It was evening again but a whole day later than the last time I'd seen the sky. The familiar outline of a lush forested island was silhouetted in the fading light.

Tramore. Right now it seemed darker than Ash Island.

Keane patted me on the shoulder. "You get back to your family."

"She will." Graham walked up behind him in his Enforcer clothes, carrying a large fabric bag and a water barrel. "I'll make sure of it." He sounded upbeat, but he didn't look at me.

We said goodbye to the men and tossed the rope ladder down. Graham was still talking to Keane when I began climbing.

"Wait!" said Graham. "You shouldn't be—"

I kept climbing, then let go of the rope and splashed into the water on my own. I swam for the shore, but every stroke of my left arm stretched the wound in my side and slowed me down.

Graham landed in the water behind me, his barrel splashing down beside him. Keane tossed down his bag and Graham caught it, placing it on top of the floating barrel to keep it dry. It didn't take long for him to catch up to me.

"What are you *doing?*" he asked.

I didn't have the breath to answer. Just swimming took all my strength.

His voice was heavy with frustration. "You're not even trying to be careful!"

My feet hit the soft sand and I stood up, wading to shore. Fresh blood soaked through my shirt.

"I'll be fine." My attempt to sound convincing was lost to the whimper in my voice. I took a step on the smooth sand, heading toward the trees.

Graham reached for my shoulder, stopping me. "You need a new bandage."

"I didn't bring one."

"I know," he said, "but I did."

I covered my face and avoided his glare. "Thank you."

I half-sat, half-collapsed on the ground. He knelt and opened the bag he brought.

I reached out a hand. "I can do it."

"No, sorry. I don't trust you."

I glanced at his face, looking for the smile I expected to accompany his words, but his eyes were solemn in the dim light.

Graham gathered fallen sticks and started a fire using supplies he'd brought from the boat. I came as close as I could to the fire's heat, wringing out my wet hair as I shivered.

He sat on the sand beside me, preparing the bandage. My heartbeat was quickening by the moment. I hadn't yet looked at my wound. I gripped the hem of my shirt, afraid of what I'd see.

"It's okay," he said. "There's nothing improper about showing skin when there's a gaping wound involved."

I forced my hands to relax, then lifted my shirt enough to reveal the bloody bandage.

He pulled at the edge of the fabric, unwrapping it from my waist. His hands were soon red. When it was off, his eyebrows lifted, and his mouth fell open.

I took a deep breath and looked down. Every ugly color had come together to create a blotchy bruise on my entire left side, complete with angry red veins branching from the dark hole in the center. I squeezed my eyes shut and tried to un-see it. "All right. I'm glad you're the one doing this."

I suspected it made Graham sick too, but he didn't show it. He gently dabbed at the wound with a cloth.

"You should be a doctor," I said. "If you weren't going to be king, I mean."

He set the towel down. "*Am* I going to be king?" he said so softly that I wasn't sure he meant for me to answer. He lifted a new bandage and started wrapping it around my waist.

I gripped the ground to fight the pain, but the fine sand slipped through my fingers, giving me nothing to hold.

He reached the bandage around my back. "I know it hurts, but you'll heal fast."

I gritted my teeth. "You don't have to lie to me."

He tugged the fabric tighter and secured it. "That should mean you don't have to lie to me either."

I shook my head. "I won't."

"Really?" He paused and looked up. "Are you ready to tell me the truth now?"

I dropped my eyes. Which truth? The truth about who I really was? The truth about how I'd used him? Or the truth that he'd won me over so completely that my heart had written an entirely new definition of loyalty?

I was done with lies, but not brave enough for the truth, so I took the easy way out and uttered the most cowardly words of my life. "You shouldn't have jumped in after me."

"Excuse me?" He finished the bandage and pulled his hands away. "You were shot while trying to rescue Nevin. Now you're suggesting I should've let you drown?" He shook his head.

I looked down at my hands. "I'm sorry."

He stood and scanned the shoreline. "Which way to the village?"

I moved to stand. "It's . . . ." My head seemed to drain of blood, and I collapsed in the sand.

He knelt in front of me. "Do you need more time?"

"Yes. *Yes.*" I couldn't change what would happen, but I could delay it a little longer. Tonight would be the new moon, which meant they wouldn't set sail until morning.

His blue eyes lit up with gold from the fire. "If we wait, it could get worse."

"If we walk, it could get worse."

"That's not what your father would say."

I sighed. What would my father say? "Maybe he was wrong."

Graham's frown softened. "So you're choosing my side now?"

I wanted to. I *longed* to, but the war wouldn't go away if I didn't follow through. And my father would never have the daughter he deserved. No matter what I chose, it would be wrong. "I'm not sure I have a choice," I finally said.

He leaned closer. We didn't touch, but I shamefully wished we did.

"I was never desperate to be king," he said.

His words took me off guard. I felt dizzy in two ways.

He pressed his lips together and his eyes bore into mine. "It's possible that you could've convinced me to give it up, to run away, to find a new life. Someone else could have taken the throne."

I stared at him, my gaze burning with remorse I couldn't hide. I blinked and tried to cool the fire, but it was too late. Guilt was like love. It could remain hidden for the longest time, but once it made an appearance, there was no stopping the world from seeing it in the smallest of glances. I turned my head down so my hair covered my face.

Graham moved the strands away and tucked them behind my ear. The touch sent another layer of goosebumps over the ones I already had.

"Or we could've stayed in the city," he said. "Together."

"That wouldn't have stopped the war."

"Is it really about the war?" he asked softly. "If so, you could've given me a chance to make the alliance. A real chance, I mean."

I swallowed, too cowardly to speak.

"But that wasn't what you wanted, was it?" he asked.

My voice was as weak as a plea. "It was never about what I wanted."

"You told me once to do what I want. Why won't *you*?"

I looked away, into the fire. A piece of firewood crumbled and cracked apart, shooting embers into the air.

I hadn't noticed the hair that had fallen in my face again until Graham reached over and swept it around my back. His hand stayed there, too close to my nervous pulse. His lips brushed against my forehead.

I closed my eyes and ached for more.

His hand moved up my neck and his fingers slid under my hair. But then he stopped, hesitating.

I was afraid nothing would happen if I waited—that he'd leave and never touch me again. I'd miss my last chance. I fought the pain of my wound and leaned toward him. When I put my hand on his face, the rough texture of his cheek reminded me how much he'd changed. I closed my eyes and leaned even closer. He should have pushed me away. He shouldn't have let me kiss him. And he especially shouldn't have kissed me back.

But he did. And he held nothing back.

The sweetness and passion of his kiss nearly tricked me into believing nothing was wrong. I tried to make it last, but, like everything else between us, it ended too soon.

He pulled away with a sigh, his lips grazing mine one final time before he turned toward the fire.

I stayed back, in the dark and cold. "I get the feeling that won't happen again."

He didn't look at me. "Maybe if we were different people."

He was right, but that didn't stop the sting of his words from piercing me deeper than the pain in my side.

MY NIGHTMARES HARDLY LET ME REST. FROM THE moment I closed my eyes, I was assaulted with one impossible decision after another. Every dilemma led me to the same place, to the same choice. I wanted to wake, but my mind wouldn't let me. Intense cold and heat surrounded me at the same time, and both were unbearable. I tried to scream, to break through my cage, but it sounded only in my head.

In my agony, I felt something real. I finally peeled my eyes open.

Graham's hand touched my forehead. "You're feverish."

I tried to deny it, but my voice didn't work.

"Time to find help."

"No." I found my voice and moaned. "No, just stay. Please stay."

I closed my eyes, only to see my nightmares resume. Something lifted me. The pain in my side forced out a cry.

"It's okay," he said.

I tried to fight his arms. I didn't want to go. I couldn't let him.

"Put me down," I said. "Leave me here. We can't go."

"You might as well stop struggling and tell me how to get there because it's happening whether you want it or not."

"No." I tried to find the ground. "I won't tell."

My struggles forced him to set me down.

His voice was full of frustration. "Do you *want* to die?"

"If it will save you."

"I—" he began, then paused and softened his voice. "I understand the feeling."

No, not again. Don't risk everything for me again. "You don't understand."

"Yes, I do." He lifted me again, and I couldn't stop myself from crying out in pain.

I pushed against him, but my strength was gone. His hand was cold on my arm. He had always felt warm before.

He took a step.

I squeezed my eyes shut and lingered between dreams of pain and the agonizing reality. My last hope was that he wouldn't find the right path.

I woke on the ground in the dark forest. I had no idea how much time had passed, but the night wasn't as dark. I lifted my head.

Graham was lying right beside me on the dirt, breathing soundly, his body against mine. He'd hardly slept at all in the past few days. He must've been unable to fight it.

Perfect.

I smiled weakly and sat up, slowly moving away from him.

He stirred.

I held my breath.

But he only shifted in his sleep and was peaceful again.

I forced myself to my hands and knees, then to my feet. I stood, looking down at him while regaining my breath. I had to save him. And I had an idea.

I searched for the bag Graham brought from the Enforcers' boat, then realized it was pinned under his sleeping body. I didn't dare move him. Even if I could, there wasn't likely to be paper and ink. I tore a stick from a tree and tried to write in the dirt, but the rocky ground was too uneven and he'd probably step on it instead of reading it. No, too risky.

I sighed and felt blood gush from my wound.

That could work.

I lifted my shirt and tore a piece off the bandage around my waist.

CHAPTER
THIRTY-NINE

Hope alone drove me on. Never mind the dark, the burning fever, or the blood flowing from my poorly bandaged side. This was my last chance to make the right choice.

I headed uphill, to the north.

My fingers were stained red, but I hoped the map I'd smeared across the bandage could save Graham. As long as he followed the directions written in my blood, he'd end up on the opposite side of the island, far from danger.

My progress was slow, but the longer I walked, the more numb I became to the pain. Maybe my father *was* right. Maybe I would heal faster if I tried to forget.

I focused on making it from one tree to the next. When I went over the first hill, I told myself there was only one more. Eventually, it would be true.

I stumbled over and over again. It was getting harder to control my feet. The flow of blood was hot on my skin, but my guilt was lighter than it had been in weeks—but far from gone. It would never be gone. Branches scraped at my face and arms as I trudged through the trees. My vision seemed to fade, even as a faint blue lit the sky. I put all my strength into taking another step. And then another.

I finally climbed the top of the last hill when a sliver of sun broke the horizon. A village was nestled along the shoreline below. I picked up speed on the way down. I knew I could make it now.

Blood covered my whole left side. It ran from my hip to my leg, to my feet. I stumbled again, this time ending up flat on my face. Through the foggy echoes of my head came faraway shouts.

I tried to push myself up to meet them, but there didn't seem to be a difference between up and down.

"Help!" a woman yelled. I thought I recognized her voice.

A moment later, I felt hands on my back, turning me over. The woman called my name again and again. I opened my eyes to see my aunt Elin and her husband, Oliver. My father's brother.

"I'm here," I said. "Don't attack . . . I'm here."

Elin gasped. "Look at all that blood. "

"But where's the heir?" asked Oliver. "Your guard got here a few hours ago sayin' you'd set sail with him yourself. Shouldn't he be with you?"

Not Cael again. I groaned but didn't answer.

They glanced back the way I'd come.

"Honey," said Elin, "who did this to you?"

A cloth pushed against my side, aggravating the pain. I tried to swat it away.

"Was it Brennin?" Elin put her hand on my face. "She's got an awful fever."

"Where is the heir?" Oliver asked again, shaking me gently.

"He's . . . he's dead," I finally managed to say.

"I guess we won't need to hold him hostage then," said Oliver. "Makes our lives easier."

They spoke quietly to each other and lifted me under the arms. I was beginning to go under when the last sound I wanted to hear broke through my fading consciousness.

The voice came from somewhere up the hill.

I opened my eyes.

"Is she alive?" asked Graham.

No. It can't be.

"Looks like he survived," said Elin.

"He's covered in blood, too. Must've been a bad fight between 'em."

Through my exhaustion, I couldn't grasp what Oliver meant. They pulled me down the hill, but I dug my feet in and resisted with an energy I thought I'd lost.

"Stay back!" Elin shouted over her shoulder.

"No," I mumbled. "He's not—" *dangerous*, I wanted to say, but the word got stuck in my throat.

I turned my head. Graham rushed down the hill, his Enforcer shirt and hands red with my blood.

Elin put two fingers in her mouth and gave an ear-splitting whistle. Within seconds, a handful of villagers appeared from between the houses and started up the hill toward us.

Cael was in the lead. His face hardened when he saw me. He ran past with a hungry gleam in his eyes.

"Don't hurt him," I tried to say, but it came out too weak to be heard.

I pulled away from my aunt and uncle. The islanders sprinted toward Graham, but he didn't stop.

I gathered a breath and shouted with all my remaining strength. "Run!"

Cael reached him first and smashed his fist into his stomach. Graham reeled back and doubled over.

I screamed, but Elin and Oliver held my arms back again, taking me with them.

Cael slammed his fist into Graham's face. Again and again.

I couldn't pull my eyes away.

Graham fell to the ground, his face spattered with blood.

They pulled me behind a house, and he disappeared from my view.

"Stop." My pleas were weak and useless. "Please stop."

They pushed me inside the house and put me on a bed. Elin rested a hand on my shoulder, and I sank down helplessly, my vision spotty and clouded. My heart still pounded furiously.

"Calm down or you'll bleed to death."

I gasped as Elin pressed a cloth to my side. I wanted to fight, to get out, but even the hand on my shoulder was too over-powering for me. Elin stepped over to me with a strip of cloth and some water in a wooden cup. She propped my head up and brought the cup to my mouth. I gulped it down.

"Get the medicine Orrin gave us," said Elin, removing my soaked bandage and wrapping the fresh cloth around my waist with deft fingers.

I perked up at the mention of my father's name—at least one of his names.

"Here," said Oliver, handing her a brown glass bottle.

They poured a few drops of the foul-tasting liquid into my mouth and I swallowed, gagging at the taste. It was followed by more water.

Shouts came from outside, but I couldn't hear the words.

Oliver squeezed my hand and left the house in response.

My aunt leaned over me, her cropped dark hair framing her brown face and serious eyes. "What happened? What did he do to you?"

"It wasn't him. Enforcers found us," I whispered, "on Ash Island."

"So he didn't hurt you?"

"No." I shook my head, then winced at the pain. "He's the reason I'm alive."

Elin's eyes widened.

I sat up, but she pushed me back down. "Let me get to him," I said, pushing her hands off. "Let me see him!"

"Be calm. It will be okay."

Her hands pinned my shoulders against the mattress, but I didn't calm down. Instead, my ragged breaths shook my body. "The plan was only to capture him!"

"I know, but when we saw you like this, we thought—"

I squeezed my eyes shut and tried to focus. "Cael wasn't supposed to hurt him! I'll kill that man . . ." I squeezed out of Elin's grip and dropped my feet off the bed.

"Honey, you're losing blood," said Elin, reaching for me.

I shoved her hands away and stood up. "I'll lose even more if you won't help me."

She shook her head before coming to my side. "You're as stubborn as a Yarrow."

I held onto her and we left the cottage.

In the sun, my vision blurred, and my ears grew hot. She probably wouldn't have to make me lie down. I'd be on the ground soon enough. I looked down at the shore. Either my eyes were giving out or there was only one boat in front of me.

"Where are the boats?" I asked. Since I'd only gotten here just before they planned to launch, I expected the shore to be filled with them, but it was calm and quiet. "There should be boats."

"Don't worry," said Elin. "Cael's boat is here to take you home."

"No, not Cael's boat." I faced her, grabbing her shoulders to steady myself. "Where are the boats?"

"Honey," she said softly, "you're feverish. We need to get you—"

"No." I shook my head, looking back to the shore to see if my eyes were playing tricks on me, but there was still only one boat. "The attack! You're attacking Cambria!"

"What on earth are you going on about?" asked Elin.

"The *war*," I said firmly, trying to get it through her head.

"What war?" asked Elin.

The genuine confusion on her face silenced me. Then it terrified me. I took a few long breaths, trying to stave off the panic. I gathered my strength before I spoke again. "You don't know about it." The reality smashed into me and I felt my world fall out from under me. "It wasn't real."

Elin stood there, silently supporting me so my body wouldn't collapse as everything inside of me had.

"My father lied." I stared vacantly at the single boat on the shore. "None of it was real."

"Honey . . ." Elin began.

My head whipped around at the sound of rising voices.

Cael and Oliver dragged Graham between them through the village. Graham's head hung down and even more blood stained his clothing.

Elin and I started forward to meet them, but they turned, pulling Graham between two houses. We moved faster, following behind them. The space in front of us opened to a clearing at the edge of the village. In the center was a pit.

They took Graham to the edge and threw him in.

"*No!*" I screamed.

I yanked away from Elin and stumbled, then dove, to the ground. I crawled to the edge of the pit and looked down.

Graham lay at the bottom.

I screamed his name.

He moved, slowly rolling over, then got to his knees. He looked up at me, his face bruised and bleeding. One eye was swollen shut.

"Graham." I breathed his name. "I'm so sorry." I knew it was inadequate. I could say it a thousand times and it wouldn't make the slightest difference. Not after all I'd done.

"Tell the truth," he said, his voice low.

A wave of dizziness hit, making me grip the ground to keep from falling in. I didn't know if it was the words themselves or the steel in his voice that hurt more. Even with the distance between us, his blue eyes bore through me, all the way to my shameful soul.

"Why are you still here?" he asked.

"To make sure you're safe," I whispered.

"Safe behind bars? Don't worry. I won't be returning to Cambria to steal your throne."

I stared at him, stunned. "You knew. And you still followed me. Why?" I choked on my words and hot blood burned my waist. "Why didn't you save yourself? *Why did you come?!*"

His face turned dark and somber. "You said there was a war."

"But Graham . . ." My breath caught. I wasn't sure if what he'd said was an accusation or if he still believed there was a war. If he did, he would learn the truth soon enough. And he'd know that he abandoned his duty, left his father on his deathbed, and got beaten and thrown in a pit for nothing. For absolutely *nothing*.

I sank to the ground, the ache in my heart more agonizing than the pain in my body. Someone pulled me to my knees gently. "Time to go," said Elin.

"Get him out," I said.

Elin didn't speak.

Oliver looked either regretful or uncomfortable, I couldn't tell which, but he made no move toward Graham.

Cael simply shook his head and folded his arms, his knuckles bloody.

I wanted to beat him like he'd beaten Graham. I wanted him to feel all the pain he'd caused. I looked at the pistol in his belt and tried to stand.

I fell back to the ground, the tears burning my eyes. "Get him *out*," I said again, but my voice had grown so weak that it had no strength behind it. Still, they had to understand. If the war was only my father's lie, they had no reason to keep Graham trapped in a pit.

"We promised Orrin we'd keep him here," said Oliver, "so he stays."

"But why?"

"So you can be queen," he said as if it were the most obvious answer in the world.

I leaned over, peering back into the pit. Elin held onto me, but I wished she didn't.

"We're done here," said Cael.

"Wait," I said, reaching toward Graham.

He stared up at me. "Goodbye, Mara."

I'd never heard my name spoken with so much bitterness. My hand still reached out, but I couldn't get to him.

Cael picked me up in his rough arms and pulled me away from the one person I'd ever been willing to die for. Desperation raged inside me and sobs wracked my body, but even this much passion couldn't overcome the weakness. I finally gave in to the darkness and lost my grip on my broken world.

CHAPTER

FORTY

I woke to the rise and fall of the boat on the waves. The lower cabin of the fishing boat was dark, but a bit of sunlight streamed through the hatch in the ceiling.

I lay on my side with my legs pulled up to my chest. Nine days had passed since I'd left Graham on Tramore. I'd slept through most of them and we'd be back to Cambria by tomorrow.

The medicine had cleared up my infection and my wound was healing, but I still felt dead inside. *My father lied to me*, I repeated to myself for the thousandth time. I couldn't believe that he wanted me to be queen so badly that he'd invented the whole war and manipulated me into fighting my way to the throne. Getting rid of Graham would force the crown to pass to the Third House—and therefore, me—but I never would've done it if I hadn't believed so many lives were at stake.

He'd even pretended he didn't *want* me to take the risk. For years, he'd been predicting the islanders would soon gather an uprising, that it was only a matter of time. After the two of us had secretly sailed to Tramore the previous summer, he'd told me, on these very waves, that it was finally happening. They'd even set an exact date.

And then he'd said, so casually that I never would've suspected a thing, that they'd call it off if I became queen.

So I formed my plan.

And I took every fated step that led to this moment.

I groaned and rolled onto my back on the hard, wooden floor, my body rising and falling with the boat and the waves.

The hatch in the ceiling opened and Cael climbed down a ladder. "Time to pull yourself together. We'll be home soon." He squinted at me under the sunlight from the hatch. "At least that mousy brown dye has faded from your hair in time."

I ignored him.

"Clearly, we'd both rather pretend the other doesn't exist, but you can't completely avoid me when I'm First Immortal," said Cael.

"Yes, I can."

"Not in public. Think how suspicious it would look if you selected a man you clearly despise. So, can we both agree to just pretend?"

I met his gaze. I was used to pretending. I was still pretending I didn't know about my father's lies, and I suspected Cael had *always* pretended not to know. "I can do that."

"Good." He nodded. "Oh, and that reminds me. I wasn't pretending to be an Enforcer. I became a member of the Academy so that my selection as Immortal would be convincing."

Back when I had smaller concerns, it would've made me furious that Cael had gone against my direct orders and sworn an oath of loyalty to the Immortals and the king by joining the Academy, but now it hardly made an impact. At least now I knew where he'd gotten the uniform and the second pistol.

"That was risky," I said. "You can't get a job like that and take off for three weeks and expect them not to notice."

"The Eleventh House is always overlooked. A Ruskin's disappearance won't be nearly as suspicious as yours if they noticed," he said. "Of course, you never made the habit of leaving your house anyway. But if the king died—"

"The Enforcers on Ash Island were looking for me," I said, realizing I had to tell him. "They know I'm missing."

Cael rolled his eyes. "We better find a way to explain your absence, then."

He was right. If I just showed up outside the wall after Graham's disappearance, all suspicion would immediately jump from Maeve Brennin to me. And I refused to let that happen when all I wanted was to get back to Graham.

"I have an idea," I said, "but I'll need a gown." I told Cael my plan and he went up on deck, leaving me alone in the creaking cabin.

The truth was that I had a lot of ideas, but I wouldn't be sharing them all with him—or with my father. Even if I had to do it alone.

Graham wasn't the only one I'd failed. I remembered the promises I'd made to Lachlan and Cait. I said I'd get her out of prison, and I still meant to. I could help them both.

"I'll fix it," I said out loud to no one. "I'll fix everything."

I had to repair all the damage Bryn Yarrow had done. A better person could rise in her place.

WE PULLED THE BOAT INTO THE CAVE ON CAMBRIA IN THE rainy gray afternoon the next day. Cael left for the city while I waited.

When he returned to the cave, hours later, he wore a clean

uniform and held a ruffled red gown. It was one of mine that I'd never worn. "Your father wants to see you, but he'll have to wait until they bring you home to avoid suspicion."

"Of course," I said in a monotone.

"Also," said Cael, "the king's dead."

I was quiet. I could only think of Graham.

Cael unrolled the dress, then pulled out his pistol and shot a hole in the left side, right where my wound would be when I wore it.

I took off my bandage and changed into the dress, my side aching, then wove my hair into braids and pinned them up on my head. We left the cave and walked for about half a mile until we came to a rocky headland. The fishing marina was on the other side.

I nodded to Cael, who headed up the opposite way, and waded into the water. The red dress billowed up, absorbing the seawater as I went deeper. The layers of fabric weighed me down and I was afraid it would drag me to the bottom of the sea if I tried to swim, so I was careful not to go too far. I ducked my head under the water to get my hair wet, then came back up, the water at my neck.

I waded around the headland and aimed for the marina. As the water grew shallower, I crawled along the sand.

When I made it to the beach, I collapsed on my belly, breathing hard.

It didn't take long for the shouting to start.

"Look!"

"Is that a . . . noblewoman?"

Hands turned me over. I squinted up at them, my face contorted with pain. I didn't have to pretend to feel it.

"What happened?" a fisherman asked, examining my side. "Were you shot?"

"What's your name?" asked another.

"Mara Stroud," I mumbled.

"Stroud?" Another man asked, joining the first. "Enforcer, come here!" he yelled.

Cael ran toward us from the marina as if he'd simply been on a routine patrol. He crossed the sand, then leaned over me. "She's in bad shape. Looks like a pistol shot."

I nodded.

"Who did this to you?" Cael asked a little too loudly.

The fishermen leaned in, listening closely.

"The queen's assassin," I whispered.

Their faces revealed their shock.

"Yarrow?" one man asked.

"What about the heir?" Cael asked. "Have you seen him?"

I looked at the three men, my face grave. "She shot him, too. But he didn't survive."

They were silent. More fishermen and Enforcers gathered around me. Cael repeated what I'd said, over and over again, reinforcing the story until no one could doubt it was true.

They picked me up and carried me up the shore and through the city gates, the hinges groaning as the giant doors swung open. I looked over my shoulder, giving a final glance to the sea before we passed through the enormous stone archway into the city that would soon be mine.

CHAPTER
FORTY-ONE

THE CARRIAGE TOOK ME AND CAEL THROUGH THE STREETS, stopping when we reached the front gates of my house. Night had fallen and burning street lamps flanked the iron gates. My father ran across the grounds to meet us. He had the same long stride, blonde hair, and firm jaw as always, but he felt like a stranger.

My heart was torn, conflicted. I held so much anger, but somehow, it wasn't enough to drive out a lifetime of love.

He picked me up in his arms and pulled me out of the carriage.

I wanted to fight him, to speak my hatred, but all I could do was cry. I buried my face in his neck and let him carry me up the path and into our house.

Cael stayed behind.

My father took me through the entry and into the bedroom closest to the front door and laid me gently on the four-poster bed. I forced myself to stay calm and hide my anger. I couldn't let him realize I knew about his lie or he'd stop me from going back to Graham.

"Are you okay?" he asked. "I mean, I know you were shot, but . . ."

Apparently, neither of us knew what to say.

He sighed. "You know, you almost ruined the whole plan when you left with the heir. But now"—he gestured at me—"you're able to use it to your advantage. By the time the rest of the city hears, they'll be convinced Maeve Brennin is guilty."

"How did they find out I left?" I asked. I'd always been so private and reclusive that I couldn't imagine someone missing me.

"When the heir disappeared, most of the city suspected Maeve—that note you planted was an excellent touch—but some, as well as Maeve herself, obviously, thought we had something to do with it. The Academy came to question us. I couldn't cover for you when they insisted on searching our home, so I gave them a sob story and told them you'd gone missing."

"It seems like that would've made me look more guilty," I said, "especially since they caught us climbing the wall here."

He nodded. "The speculation has been insane. Some people said maybe you'd been dead or gone for years, since no one had seen you in so long, and that I was hiding it so I wouldn't lose my status and get kicked out of this house. There've been all sorts of ideas, but the Ruskins and I have been planting rumors and influencing the papers as much as possible in our favor."

So the path to the throne was clear. I didn't want it, but I had to hide my true feelings from my father. I'd have to put on a face for all of Cambria and let them make me queen. At least for a day.

"I'm tired," I said, pulling up a quilt.

"Of course you are." He stood up, nodding. "Well, done, Mara. You stopped the war."

The blood seemed to stop inside my veins. The words rose in my throat, itching to call him out on his lies, but I stayed quiet so he'd think we were still on the same side. In the past, I would've been glad to hear even the tiniest bit of praise from him, but praise wrapped in lies gave me no joy.

When he left the room, I promised myself I'd never work for his love again.

In the morning, I picked up the day's newspaper off the front steps and went up two flights of stairs to the bedroom at the end of the hall. In the Brennin's house, with its identical floor plan, this would've been Graham's room.

I sat on the wood floor of the vacant room, my body still aching. Dust danced in the air, lit by the sunlight from the east window. Though I'd lived in this house for my entire life, other than a few summers on Tramore, I'd hardly entered this room. Now that I was in here, I felt as lonely as a boat lost at sea. But it was better than facing my father.

I set the paper on my lap, the smell of fresh ink meeting my nose, and looked at the headline. *Our dearly departed Imperator.* I read the article and saw that the funeral was tomorrow morning, followed by the ocean burial.

Thanks to me, Graham wouldn't be here to mourn him.

I could go in his place. It would be very uncharacteristic of me to show my face at a noble's event, but I felt that I owed it to Graham.

Sir Graham Brennin assassinated was the next article. Even though it wasn't true, I could hardly look at the words. They'd soon be planning a funeral for him as well.

Right beside that article was one about me. *Lady Mara Stroud survives assassination attempt.* It was definitely the most positive thing ever written about me. Before being found on the beach, I couldn't have been more unpopular, but this had created sympathy in the eyes of the public. The article ended by announcing the coronation was scheduled for the next evening if my health permitted.

"Mara?" My father's shout came from somewhere downstairs.

I dropped the newspaper with a sigh and left the room, heading down to see what he wanted.

My father stood at the base of the second stairway. He was dressed in his noble suit and he held a wine glass in his hand. "Etna's at the gates. She wants to see you."

"Can't the guards just let her in?"

"You're not queen yet," he said, "though even queens are subject to the law. And I'm not willing to bribe the guards to take a break when it's not essential."

"Fine. I'll go."

I quickly dressed in a blue gown and braided my hair up on my head before venturing through the front hall and out the door. I crossed the grounds to the gate, the hem of my gown swishing against the long wet grass. The lawn was quiet and secluded, hardly different from the last morning I'd spent here with my father the day I'd left for the city. Leaves rustled in the cool breeze as I passed beneath the trees, and the flowers spread their scents around the garden. But none of it gave me any pleasure.

Etna looked even smaller than usual as she smiled from the other side of the gate. It was strange to see her as myself again. For many months, we'd avoided visiting each other so there wouldn't be any suspicion on the Lenoxes if something went wrong.

The guards bowed and opened the gate for me. I stepped into the street.

Etna put her arms out wide and pulled me into an embrace. "My dear girl."

I hoped she wouldn't ask questions. Saying my thoughts out loud wasn't something I dared to do just then, but I knew I owed it to her, after all she'd done.

She pulled back and took my hand, leading me along the outside of the fence, away from the guards. "Are you all right?" She shook her head and sighed. "I'm sorry. Of course you're not."

I tried to smile, but my eyes burned instead. I turned away, toward the high stone wall at the back of the grounds.

"Cael brought a message from your father this morning. I came as soon as I could."

"Thanks," I said. "It's so good to see you."

She reached a hand up to my face and brushed my hair out of my eyes. "But you're not happy."

I hated to disappoint her, but she deserved the truth—or at least part of it. "Remember the last time we were together? "I spoke in a whisper as if my father might overhear me from inside the house. "I'd give anything to go back to that moment—after meeting Graham, but before betraying him."

Her sad brown eyes understood so much. "But you would've been forced to live in hiding. And you couldn't have stopped the war."

I sighed, leaning against the iron fence. My father had thoroughly deceived Etna, too. It made me angry, but her sincerity gave me some relief that she hadn't been in on the lie. "I'd gladly disappear for the rest of my life if it meant he could be free."

Etna's lips pressed together, and she looked up at the sky. "Did you know my son was in love with Isla?"

I couldn't keep my eyes from widening. My father never told me that he and his best friend had both loved my mother.

"When Evander was dying, he gave Orrin and Isla his blessing. He made your father take his identity so it could happen, even though the jealousy had nearly torn them apart before."

I reached for Etna's hand. I had known Evander Lenox gave his name and Class A rank card to my father so he could hide his outlaw status and marry into the Stroud family, but my father had kept the rest of the story to himself.

Etna's voice shook. "Do you know what I think?" She paused and swallowed. "I think Evander would have done the same thing had he lived. That's the way he loved." She squeezed my hand and made her voice even softer. "And I think that's the way *you* love."

"Is it?" I didn't know if what I felt could be contained in one small word. Was one enough to save him?

"So?" asked Etna. "Are you going to make it right?"

My mouth went dry. No one could know my plans. "You know my father won't let me leave."

"Does he know how you feel?"

"Oh, no." I shook my head. "No way."

"Why don't you tell him?" asked Etna.

"I can't. I just . . . can't. And even if I do go back, Graham will never forgive me."

"Maybe not. I don't know. But I seem to recall your father saying the same thing about Evander."

I longed to confide in Etna, but I couldn't risk her telling my father. No matter what had happened in his past, I couldn't trust him. And anyway, he hadn't been the hero of that story. Not then, not now. All he had was a hero's name.

CHAPTER
FORTY-TWO

I wandered the grounds after Etna was gone, my mind churning. I wished I could run, leave now, forget the coronation. But there was too much to do and not enough time.

When my mind was made up, I went inside to my bedroom on the ground level that faced the front gates. There, I found a pearl clutch. It wasn't as useful as the sharkskin bag I'd lost, but everyone would expect me to look like a queen.

Next, I visited the kitchens and took an empty glass jar, sliding it into my clutch. I left through the servants' door, though no servants had used it since my mother died because my father preferred the privacy. The guards opened the gates for me, and I left as the noonday bell rang out nearby, loud and clear, propelling me into action.

I waved down a carriage and climbed inside, giving my directions to the driver.

As we drove through the city, I peered through the sheer white curtain, feeling vulnerable and afraid. I'd gotten too much attention as Bryn Yarrow. Sure, my hair was pale blonde now instead of brown. My gown looked nothing like my drab dresses, but how much could I really hide?

Eventually, the carriage came to a stop in front of an unremarkable rectangular brick building, one I'd only seen before while handcuffed.

"Wait for me," I told the driver.

My heeled shoes clicked across the cobblestones. Before opening the door to the prison, I lifted my head and took a deep breath, forcing my most noble expression to my face. I slowly pulled the handle, my heart beating in my throat. A rotten smell wafted through the door.

Thankfully, the first face I saw was unfamiliar.

A guard behind a desk jumped out of his chair and bowed. "Good day. How may I be of service, Lady—?"

"Stroud," I said,

He glanced at my waist, but my gown covered my bandage. "Oh! Lady Stroud." He bowed again, more deeply this time. "How do you fare on this fine day?"

"My injury has improved," I said, wishing everyone didn't know about it. "Thank you."

"Well," he said, "how may I ever be of service to you, milady?"

"I believe there to be a prisoner residing here by the name of Cait. Bring her to me, please."

His mouth turned down. "Yes, Lady Stroud. Please wait one moment."

He turned out of the room and went down the stone steps into the foul prison air. I fought the urge to wring my hands together but had to keep my nervousness invisible. I thought of Al, wishing I could bring him with me, but I knew he'd be released soon enough, and I was already taking a risk.

The shuffling of feet dragging on stone sounded from the

stairway. A matted head of red curls appeared. I smiled, then hurriedly wiped it from my face, pursing my lips like a noble instead.

Cait lifted her head and appraised me with fearful eyes.

"Remove her handcuffs," I said.

Cait's eyes grew even wider and her mouth fell open. She backed away from me as if she'd rather go back to her cell.

The guard hesitated.

"Do it." I pulled my eyes from Cait's and looked down my nose at the guard. "I need this woman as my servant. Please return her rank card and let her go."

The guard looked back and forth from me to Cait. "I believe her sentence was intended to be much longer."

"You wouldn't want to lose favor with your new queen," I said, lowering my voice the way Maeve Brennin did. "Would you, sir?"

"No, Lady Stroud," he said.

"You might as well address me as Imperatrix. My coronation is tomorrow, after all."

"Yes . . . Imperatrix." He hurried to a cabinet and unlocked a drawer, flipping through the leather cards inside.

Cait waited in the center of the room, her eyebrows furrowed. Her clothes were blackened and dingy, and smudges dotted her face. I wished I could offer her a smile to tell her she was safe.

The guard handed Cait her Class A card.

"Come with me," I said.

The guard opened the door for me, bowing stiffly as I went through.

"May my deepest gratitude be with you," I said to him.

Cait obediently followed me to the waiting carriage. I showed her rank card to the driver and she climbed inside. I got in and sat on the opposite seat.

When the carriage began to roll, I dropped my noble accent and smiled. "Good to see you again."

Cait's gaze locked onto my face, finally seeing me. This time, her mouth lifted, and a light sparked in her eyes. "No way. I didn't recognize you!" She shook her head in disbelief. "Bryn?"

"I told you I'd get you out of there."

She laughed and shook her head again, her eyes welling with tears. "I can't—thank you! But you're . . . you're—"

"Queen?"

She shut her mouth and nodded.

"Well, not until tomorrow," I said.

She glanced out the curtained window, then back to me. Her tangled hair shadowed her face, still thick with dirt and grime. I thought I'd been filthy when I was in prison, but she'd been in there for so long that she'd probably forgotten what it was like to be clean.

"But how—why . . ." She covered her face with both hands as her voice trailed off.

"I'll explain. I need your help," I said, "and so does Lachlan."

She set her intense brown eyes on mine. "Lachlan?"

I nodded.

She flashed a smile that was only dimmed by the plaque on her teeth. She was going to need a lot of work to pass as a royal servant.

"We have a lot to talk about. But let's get you some food and a bath first."

Just before curfew, Cait and I arrived at the gates to my house. She wore a clean black maid's dress and no longer smelled like death, but my heart pounded anyway. Cait glanced at me nervously before taking her rank card from her pocket. She brushed her hair back, the red curls now free of grease and dirt, and presented it to the guards with shaking hands.

"This is my new maid," I told the men. "It's time I live as a queen should."

"Indeed, Imperatrix," said one guard, before bowing and swinging open the iron gates.

"I will also be hiring more guards soon," I said. "My assassination attempt has had me up at night with dread and I fear there will be another."

"To your health," one guard said.

"Thank you."

The men bowed again as we passed and continued toward my house.

"This is crazy," Cait whispered.

"I know." The weight of the full jar in my pearl clutch wouldn't let me forget it. "I hope you're crazy enough for it."

She laughed. "I impersonated a man and cheated on a ranking test, remember?"

"True." That's how I knew I could count on her.

We went in the doors quietly, but my father didn't seem to be around. He was probably celebrating at the Ruskins' mansion. The coronation was as big of a deal for Cael's family as it was for mine, and my father treated Cael like a son these days. Sometimes it seemed as if he liked him more than me.

Cait and I hurried through the hall, our footsteps echoing off the marble floor and bare walls. My body felt weak and my wound throbbed, but I couldn't rest. I had even more to do the next day.

Not to mention a funeral and coronation to attend.

Before the sun rose the next morning, I went down the cool stone hall of the cellars, barefoot and still in my night-clothes.

I shielded the candle's flame in my hand as I passed the servant's room where Cait slept. I hadn't wanted her to be alone down here, but I didn't want my father to think she was anything other than an ordinary servant.

My father. Every time I thought of him, my stomach tightened.

The candlelight flickered against a wooden door at the end of the hall. I lifted a key to the lock and slipped into the windowless cellar.

Except we didn't use it as a cellar.

On the far wall was a wooden target. There were plenty of weapons stored in this room, but knives were what I'd grown to appreciate most in the time I'd spent down here. I picked up six of them, their steel handles and blades identical to the ones I'd lost.

I searched for one more weapon. When my hand touched the cold barrel, I shuddered, my side aching as I felt the pain of the bullet. I could never use it on anyone, but I needed it for my plans.

I left the grim room and locked the door before hurrying away.

The stairs creaked as I crept back to my bedroom. The first morning light peeked through the gaps between the heavy curtains, the rays landing on a scene of destruction. The sheets were ripped, a chair overturned, and goose down covered the floor.

I carefully set down the pistol and all the knives except one, then picked up one more pillow from the bed and slashed through it, sending feathers into the air. I stepped back and smiled before pulling open the curtain. It would've been nice if I could break the window to add to the effect, but my father was likely to notice it on our way out. Instead, I cranked it wide open.

I turned around and analyzed the scene.

There was just one thing missing.

I went to the dresser and opened my pearl clutch, taking out the glass jar. No doubt the butcher had been shocked when a grimy Cait showed a Class A rank card and selected his bloodiest cuts of meat, but it had been enough to fill the jar.

Blood splashed onto my hand when I twisted open the lid. Just then, a rhythmic knock sounded on the door.

"Mara?"

I set down the jar and wiped my hand on the bedsheets before crossing the room. A long breath later, I summoned the courage to unlock the door.

I opened it a crack and peered out. "Yes?"

"So." My father's voice sounded almost upbeat. "Today's the big day. I hope you're not too weak to enjoy it."

I tried to put excitement into my tone. "No, not at all."

He looked at me curiously. "So, your bout of, uh, depression is gone?"

"Long gone."

He smiled widely. "Good. Be ready as soon as you can. We're expected at the Brennin House in less than an hour." He turned and began to walk away.

I cleared my throat. "Just one thing."

He stopped and looked back, a hint of a frown on his face.

"I hired a lady's maid. I hope you don't mind. I just figured since I'll be queen, it was time, you know?"

His gaze drifted over my head and he took a step closer.

"I'll be ready soon!" I slammed the door and locked it before he could see the disaster inside.

Sighing with relief, I went back for the jar, ready to paint the room red.

CHAPTER
FORTY-THREE

I stood at the bathroom mirror, weaving a black ribbon through my braided strands. Cait waited in my connected bedroom.

I'd changed into a black mourning gown, which only emphasized the contrast of my pale hair. I'd even put on makeup for the first time in my life—powder to hide my tan, color on my lips, and a liner on my eyes. It didn't matter if I looked pretty. I just couldn't look like Bryn Yarrow.

I put on a gold necklace that had belonged to my mother. It felt heavy and uncomfortable on my collarbones. When I could hardly recognize the woman in the mirror, I decided I was ready.

"Wow," said Cait when I went into the bedroom. "Not bad."

"Thanks." I smiled. "Oh, and while I'm out, why don't you go see your family?"

She slumped against the wall. "Will they want to see me? I didn't exactly make them proud."

"You might be surprised. Besides, you'll regret it if you don't go."

She gave a tiny noncommittal nod.

"Whatever you choose, watch the clock."

Dozens of carriages brought the city's nobles to the gates of the Second House. My father climbed from our carriage first and helped me out. I wasn't sure if it was because of my injury or if he was putting on his noble act, but I pulled my hand away as soon as my feet touched the ground.

We crossed the fragrant grounds and followed the crowd into the grand entry hall. It was the same size as ours but decorated with ornate gold-trimmed furniture, larger-than-life portraits, and enormous crystal chandeliers. Our home was stark in comparison.

One particular portrait caught my eye. Young and serious blue eyes peered from the canvas with uncanny realism. The boy looked younger than the Graham I knew, and not a perfect match, but I still couldn't look away.

My father put his hand on my shoulder and whispered. "You're holding up the line."

I glanced at the nobles behind me, trying to smile when they greeted me with deep bows.

We went past the entry hall into the ballroom. Heavy draperies covered the windows, blocking out the daylight, and black suits and gowns filled the candlelit room. The smooth floor reflected black and gold. For a moment, I saw a lake mirroring a sky of stars. I squeezed my eyes shut as a tingle ran down my spine.

When I opened them, my eyes landed on the open gold-leafed casket in the center of the room. An empty space surrounded it as if nobody dared to get too close.

I pulled away from my father and went to it. My feet didn't stop until I reached the casket. Desmond Brennin's face was peaceful but gaunt and gray. His body would soon be sent out to sea on a pyre, and Graham wouldn't be here to see it.

I bowed and said a quiet poem for the dead, adding in a few whispered words of my own. "I'll bring him home. I swear."

I lifted my head and caught Maeve Brennin's glare from the far end of the room. Even under house arrest, her stiff back and turned-up nose were as proud and contemptuous as ever, but the redness around her eyes revealed her weakness. Despair, guilt, distrust. Regret.

She was even more alone than I was.

Whatever resentment she'd had toward Graham hadn't completely extinguished her love. She'd hidden it behind her hunger for power, but I knew enough about love now to realize it didn't look the same on everyone.

I almost walked right up to her. I almost told her I was sorry. For her husband. For Graham. For my betrayal. But I had to keep up appearances. Most of Cambria believed she'd attempted to assassinate me. She'd eventually stand trial and could even be executed for treason—unless I brought Graham back.

That was all I could do to help her now. I couldn't say a word to her without everyone in the room getting suspicious, so I held back.

"Lady Stroud." A man bowed in front of me.

I didn't know who he was until he stood from his bow. When I saw his face, I wished I could run.

Graham's haughty cousin smiled at me. "I am Patrick Donovan of the Eighth House. It is a privilege to finally meet you after all these years. It is under unfortunate circumstances, however . . ." His eyes narrowed and he tilted his head to the side.

I put on my most gracious smile, one he never would've seen on Bryn Yarrow, and curtsied. "I am so very charmed, Sir Donovan." My accent was so flowery that I tried not to wrinkle my nose. I knew I looked and sounded completely different than the day I'd met him on the library steps, but his expression unnerved me.

His smile returned. "You are most welcome. I hope you are making a quick recovery. If I may be so bold"—he leaned in a little closer—"have you made a selection for the position of First Immortal yet?"

"I certainly have."

"Oh." He raised an eyebrow. "Well, I would love to hear whom you have chosen, milady."

"Of course you would." I curtsied. "Now if you'll excuse me, sir." I walked away from him, exhaling out my fears.

"Mara?"

I flinched at my father's voice.

He came to my side and whispered. "What was that about?"

"Just giving my condolences."

"That was brave of you," he said. "Ready to get out of here? You'll have to endure a thousand congratulations after your coronation. Let's not wear you out just yet."

I put my hand on his arm and smiled. "I'm ready."

He patted me on the back and led me from the ballroom. "That's what I like to hear."

My back stiffened at his touch. I never wanted him as my enemy, but that's what he'd become.

THE SKY WAS UNUSUALLY BLUE WHEN OUR CARRIAGE arrived at the back entrance to the Academy. To the side of the gates, waiting alone with a full bundle in her arms, was Cait. Her black maid's dress was smooth, and her hair had been tamed into a thick braid, but her smile carried the same rebellious mystery.

The carriage stopped and I gestured for her to come over.

"Your maid's here?" asked my father.

"I had her bring my coronation gown. I was afraid something might happen to it if I left it in the carriage while we were inside the Brennin's house."

He laughed. "Since when have you worried about dresses?"

"Since the whole city started watching me."

He frowned. "Well, I guess that's for the best."

"You wanted me to be queen, didn't you?" I asked, my voice tinged with bitterness. "You'll have to deal with a few changes."

The footman dismounted and opened the door for Cait. She climbed in and sat next to me, avoiding my father's frown.

The carriage rolled forward again, taking us through the gates reserved for the most important people in the city.

I felt like nothing but an impostor.

We crossed the grounds and an Enforcer led us through the Academy's doors and up a grand staircase. To the right. Down a hall. Left. Another hall. The building was huge and I couldn't afford to get disoriented. Not when I'd need to take the quickest way out.

In a wide hallway, I saw Maeve Brennin dressed in black and escorted by two guards. The golden crown on her head lent a strange contrast to her shame. The Academy must've let her leave her house for the ceremony since the former ruler's surviving family traditionally passed on the crown, but she clearly couldn't have been less pleased. She was used to being revered and protected. Now she was seen as a criminal.

She looked over her shoulder as she passed, watching my every move until she turned a corner.

The Enforcer leading me stopped in front of a door and handed me a key. "Your dressing room, milady."

"Thank you. My maid will assist me with the rest."

He bowed and walked away.

"I'll wait here," said my father.

"No, no, no. I'm fine. Go take your seat." I smiled. "Please."

His forehead shone with sweat and his mouth was tight.

"Really, Father."

He turned his back to Cait and lowered his voice. "You didn't *tell* her—"

"Tell her what?"

"There's just something in her expression that looks like she . . ." He leaned toward my ear. "Like she *knows*."

"Well, she doesn't," I said, "so you can stop glaring at her."

He took a deep breath and stood tall again before walking down the hall and out of sight.

"Were you able to visit your family?" I asked Cait.

She sighed. "They weren't home."

I put the key in the lock and pushed the door open. I'd expected something small, but the dressing room was almost as big as my bedroom at home. A grand chandelier lit the windowless room. The walls were covered in a gold damask print, except the one opposite the door, which held one enormous mirror. Combs and ribbons spilled over the top of a marble vanity, along with all sorts of stuff I wouldn't know what to do with.

I wondered if they'd given Maeve a chance to take out her belongings or if she'd chosen to leave them here.

Cait unwrapped the dress in her arms. It was heavy and white with elaborate embroidery and hundreds of iridescent pearls. I picked up what I'd hidden in the center, letting the dress fall to the floor.

It was my father's pistol. Since I'd soon be staging my own murder, it could come in handy. I passed it to Cait. "Keep it hidden."

She took the gun and rolled it into her apron.

"Will you help me put this thing on?" I asked, picking up the dress from the floor. "It must weigh fifty pounds."

"Of course. That's what maids do."

I laughed. "Sorry. I'm sure you hate this. But it's only until tonight."

She unbuttoned my black mourning dress. When it was loose, I pulled it over my head and stepped into the white one.

"I'm afraid," Cait said softly.

"It's okay. Just aim the pistol toward the sky. You won't hurt anyone."

She shook her head. "Not that. Of Lachlan. What if it's . . . not the same?"

"Oh." I pulled the lacy sleeves over my arms, not sure what to say.

She began to tie the bodice. I winced as the stiff material tightened on my side.

"Do you worry about that? With Graham?"

"After what happened, I'll be lucky if he—"

Before I could finish my sentence, the door swung open.

I spun around, my heart pumping panic through my veins. Maeve Brennin's furious glare landed on me. She wasn't supposed to be left unguarded, but here she was.

"*What did you just say?*" she screamed, lunging toward me.

I backed away, tripping over my long gown until the giant mirror on the wall stopped me.

"You said his name! I heard you!"

If she went on like this, her screams would attract every

Enforcer in the Academy. If she had the power to manipulate the guards to leave her alone, then I didn't trust them to believe my word against hers.

"Shut the door, Cait," I said.

She did as I said, hopefully blocking off at least some of the noise. I remembered the pistol in Cait's apron and wished I held it instead. Maybe it could scare Maeve into shutting her mouth.

"What reason do you have to talk about my son?" asked Maeve. She pushed closer until I could see every frown line on her face. "Tell me."

I leaned into the cold mirror, but she only pushed closer.

"Everyone thinks I killed him," she said. "But I suspect *you* know the truth."

I didn't know what to say. She'd see through my lies.

"It was you. Or your father. No one else had more to gain." The tremble in her voice revealed she was on the verge of losing all composure. "I *will* find a way to expose you."

I believed her. I had to make peace with her at any cost. A desperate idea popped into my head and came out onto my tongue before I could stop it. "Your son is alive."

CHAPTER
FORTY-FOUR

MAEVE'S BLOODSHOT EYES WIDENED. "I BEG YOUR pardon?"

Cait shook her head in warning, stopping when the queen glared at her through the mirror. If this went wrong, I'd ruin her chances too.

"He's alive," I said.

"How dare you?" She backed away. "Is this another Stroud lie? I've seen how your father manipulates."

"It's not a lie." My heart fluttered in a wild beat. Why did people trust me the least when I actually told the truth?

The lines around her mouth softened, but the next moment, they hardened into anger once more. "Then the crown belongs to him!"

"I agree."

"What? Why in Irvine's name would you give up the throne for him?"

I didn't know how to answer. I felt a blush warm my cheeks.

Her mouth rounded and she nodded slowly. "Oh. And all

this time I thought the Strouds were heartless." Her voice turned deep and threatening. "Tell me what you know."

"We were both kidnapped and shot," I said.

Her mouth pinched together. "By that criminal, Bryn Yarrow. I already knew that. But you claimed he was dead."

"I said that to protect him. I might be able to help him, but *only* if you keep all of this a secret."

"But I have a reputation to save!"

I thought carefully before I spoke. "The best way to save your reputation is to bring him home. But for now, you'll have to swallow your pride and keep quiet. I made a deal with Yarrow, but I can't fulfill it unless you listen to me."

"Where is he? Where's Yarrow? And how can *you* help?"

"I'll tell you," I said, "if you do something for me first."

"I knew it." Her lip curled and her glare returned. "You *are* trying to manipulate me.

You have no proof Graham's alive, or that you've ever spoken a word to him!"

I took a deep breath and hoped my next words wouldn't betray Graham further. "He told me about Ewan and the roof."

The queen reeled back. She stumbled and gripped the back of a gilded chair, her hands whitening. All traces of pride dissolved from her figure.

"Will you help me save him?" I asked.

Maeve's face grew as pale as her hands. "How?"

"I need the city—and especially my father—to think I've been killed. If you could let them think that's true, maybe even threaten me or—"

She slowly looked up and fixed her gaze on me, her eyes burning with hatred. "You want me to take the blame."

"Just until Graham is home."

"Never."

"With all due respect," I said, "it can't make your situation much worse."

Maeve shook her head, her fists clenched. "You must swear to tell me where he is and how to find Bryn Yarrow."

My eyes flitted to the floor before landing on hers again. "I will. I swear."

Cait lowered her eyebrows. I wanted to give her a reassuring look, but I couldn't let the queen suspect that I wouldn't keep my promise. I held my breath, waiting for an answer.

"I couldn't," Maeve finally whispered.

A knock echoed through the room.

She flinched but kept her eyes on me.

"One moment," called Cait.

"Is everything okay in there?"

It was my father.

"Yes," I managed to squeak out. "I'm coming." I turned to Maeve, my voice soft. "Do we have an agreement?"

She was quiet.

Cait checked the back of my dress to make sure all the buttons were in place. I was terrified to look back at Maeve. I'd said too much.

Cait and I hurried into the hall, closing the door behind us.

My father smiled. "I never thought you could look so nervous."

I took him by the arm and led him down the hall, glancing back at the door one last time. Maeve hadn't come out yet.

I took my seat in an ornately carved high-backed chair in the center of the Academy's upper balcony. My father sat in the chair to my right, his mouth set in a constant smile.

Cait was hiding in the building with the pistol.

I shielded my eyes from the sun. The crowd filled the square to its full capacity. Beyond the gates, more citizens were gathered, pressed against the fence. My father reached over and held my hand in an uncharacteristic gesture. I didn't have the heart to push him away.

The Academy bell rang three times, marking the start of the ceremony.

Sir Pearce stood at the podium and recited a traditional speech about Irvine and the Immovables. I toyed with the pearls stitched into my heavy dress, hardly focusing on a word of it. His voice was dry and passionless. This was the last moment he'd hold his precious title.

I glanced to my left. Cael sat beside me with an insufferably proud smile. His mustache was gone, and he wore the laurel-embroidered tailcoat of an Immortal. The sides of his dirty blonde hair were cut short under his black hat.

Past him was Maeve Brennin, flanked by her guards again. I hadn't noticed when she'd taken her seat. She watched me, her disdain no milder than before, but her eyes glistened faintly under the afternoon sun.

The First Immortal ended his speech and turned toward us, his face grim. "Enforcer Ruskin, please stand."

Cael stood and stepped forward until he faced Sir Pearce near the edge of the balcony. The older man reached for the golden pin on his own high collar and paused, looking back. First at Maeve, then my father, then me. His frown twitched and his expression darkened. He sighed and unclasped the pin before bringing it to Cael's chest and securing it to his suit.

"I present—" his voice caught and he tried again, louder but still emotionless. "I present First Immortal Cael Ruskin."

The crowd applauded politely. Thankfully, I wasn't expected to clap, because I couldn't have. The demoted Immortal turned and walked away.

It was Cael's job to finish the ceremony.

"Lady Mara Stroud," Cael addressed me, his voice stronger than the older man's. "Please rise."

I got to my feet and went to the podium with my heart pounding and my hands trembling.

"Imperatrix Brennin, please join us."

The color drained from Maeve's face as she stood and walked toward me. For just a moment, I felt a strange camaraderie. Neither of us wanted to be here.

I glanced back at the building. Any moment now, Cait should fire the pistol.

Cael recited a ceremonial poem before lifting the intricate gold crown from the queen's head and placing it on mine. I gritted my teeth when he touched me.

Maeve narrowed her eyes at me before returning to her seat.

"I present Imperatrix Stroud," Cael's voice boomed.

The crowd clapped without much enthusiasm. Cael pushed a scroll into my hand, then sat down, leaving me alone at the podium. I swallowed and tried to keep my breathing slow, but my throat tightened and my heart fluttered. This was Cait's cue. But the pistol didn't fire.

Until then, I'd have to give a speech. I crumpled the scroll in my hand. Cael had written some nonsense for me to read. The crowd blurred and Graham's face filled my mind like a song I couldn't forget.

What would he say if he were here?

I had no idea.

But even if I did, I didn't want to say it. I wanted *him* to get his chance.

I smoothed out the scroll. "My loyal Cambrians." My voice was strong and clear over the quiet square. "I am immensely grateful for the opportunity to serve as your queen. Sir

Kendrick Irvine entrusted my ancestors with this profound privilege, and I solemnly promise to uphold his expectations." My mouth was too dry. I swallowed again, but it didn't get better. All I wanted was to hear that pistol. The words swam on the page and my thoughts fled, leaving me with nothing to say but the truth.

I looked up at the waiting citizens. "I know you are tired of words. So am I."

Shocked gasps erupted from the balcony and the crowd below.

I smiled. "Let my actions, not my words, reveal my character."

Before I could continue my unplanned speech, something grabbed my head, ripping the golden crown from my braids. I clutched at my scalp and spun around.

Maeve gripped the crown, her eyes wild. "This doesn't belong to you!"

I backed away, wondering if this was her answer to my request, or if she was just crazy.

"Guards, restrain her!" my father shouted.

The men dashed forward.

"You won't last one day as queen!" Maeve screamed, holding up the crown. "This should've been my son's." Her arm extended and the crown flew over the balcony and into the crowd.

Guards grabbed her and pulled her into the nearest doorway, her screams still echoing through the square.

Thank you, Maeve.

She'd be furious when I didn't tell her what I'd promised, but I hoped she'd be desperate enough to keep my secret anyway. My eyes and ears finally returned to the present, reminding me that I stood in front of a buzzing crowd.

My father touched my shoulder. "Are you okay?"

I was still catching my breath, and my scalp stung where Maeve had ripped out my hair, but I smiled. "No harm done."

I bowed deeply to the crowd before turning around and crossing the wide balcony, away from my father, past Cael, past the Immortals. My feet picked up speed until I was running.

An uproar filled my ears.

I darted through a doorway and into the halls, turning left and right until I rushed down the stairway and out the back. Cait met me at the carriage, climbing into the driver's seat behind the horses.

"The plan," I said. "What happened?"

"The queen's threat was much more exciting than a few shots in the air. And it still gave you an excuse to run."

"True, but how'd you know she'd do it?"

She shrugged. "Lonely people are the most desperate."

I smiled, climbing into the carriage. It began to roll the moment I stepped inside.

The guards opened the gate and the horses sped into a trot. I pushed the curtains aside. A tall figure emerged from the doors of the Academy, rushing after the carriage until he realized he was too late. My father.

I almost felt sorry for him.

WITH MOST OF THE CITIZENS CROWDING AROUND THE Academy, the streets were nearly deserted, allowing the horses to pull the carriage at a gallop. Sneaking into the neglected grounds of the First House hadn't been a problem either, with no guards around to see us climb the fence.

We waited for nightfall on the overgrown grass. I'd changed into trousers, my ruined gown buried in the grounds of the abandoned house. Only its pearls remained in the bag I carried.

They'd make a good bribe if I could find a fisherman willing to let me borrow a boat.

When the last light faded from the sky, Cait and I headed for the wall. I held a knife in each hand, the handles wrapped in leather, and I carried a long rope over my shoulder. Cait's curly hair was coming loose around her face and her wild eyes were alive with anticipation.

I thought of the night Graham and I climbed it, remembering the lies I'd told to reassure him.

No more.

"This will be the most dangerous thing you've ever done," I said. I'd climb up with my knives, then toss a rope down to Cait, but that wouldn't make it easy.

She lifted her head. "I know."

"Good."

I lifted a knife and anchored it between two stones. My feet left the ground and the exhilaration of hope spurred me upward. I was on my way back to Graham, fighting to fix my mistakes. And this time, I'd be powerful enough to save him, though my title had nothing to do with it. I was powerful because I was finally making the right choice.

To be continued in *My Noble Disgrace: Heir of Cambria, Book Two*.